Praise for Shannon McKenna

"A passionate, intense story about two people rekindling lost love in the middle of a dangerous, heart-pounding situation. Intricate storylines give the book depth and power, tying in the edge-of-your-seat ending with flawless ease."
—*Romantic Times* on *Edge of Midnight* (4 ½ starred review)

"Wild boy Sean McCloud takes center stage in McKenna's romantic suspense series. Full of turbocharged sex scenes, this action-packed novel is sure to be a crowd pleaser."
—*Publishers Weekly* on *Edge of Midnight*

"Highly creative . . . erotic sex and constant danger."
—*Romantic Times* on *Hot Night* (4 ½ starred review and a Top Pick!)

"Super-sexy suspense! Shannon McKenna does it again."
—Cherry Adair on *Hot Night*

"[A] scorcher. Romantic suspense at its best!"
—*Romantic Times* on *Out of Control* (4 ½ starred review)

"Well-crafted romantic suspense. McKenna builds sexual chemistry and tension between her characters to a level of intensity that explodes into sexually explicit love scenes."
—*Romantic Times* on *Return to Me* (4 ½ starred review)

"Summer just got hotter with the release of Shannon McKenna's new erotic thriller. An intensely emotional romance heightened by a dark, intricate plot makes *Standing in the Shadows* a top-notch page-turner you won't want to miss."
—*Romantic Times* (4 ½ starred review and a Top Pick!)

Also by Shannon McKenna

Fade to Midnight
Tasting Fear
Ultimate Weapon
Extreme Danger
Hot Night
Edge of Midnight
Behind Closed Doors
All About Men
Out of Control
Return to Me
Standing in the Shadows

Published by Kensington Publishing Corporation

Extreme Danger

SHANNON MCKENNA

BRAVA

KENSINGTON PUBLISHING CORP.

http://www.kensingtonbooks.com

BRAVA BOOKS are published by

Kensington Publishing Corp.
119 West 40th Street
New York, NY 10018

All Kensington titles, imprints, and distributed lines are available at special quantity discounts for bulk purchases for sales promotion, premiums, fund-raising, educational, or institutional use.

Special book excerpts or customized printings can also be created to fit specific needs. For details, write or phone the office of the Kensington Special Sales Manager: Attn. Special Sales Department. Kensington Publishing Corp., 119 West 40th Street, New York, NY 10018. Phone: 1-800-221-2647.

Brava and the B logo Reg. U.S. Pat. & TM Off.

ISBN-13: 978-0-7582-1188-0
ISBN-10: 0-7582-1188-0

First Brava Books Trade Paperback Printing: February 2008
First Brava Books Mass-Market Paperback Printing: May 2010

10 9 8 7 6 5 4 3

Printed in the United States of America

Chapter
1

Just a little engagement celebration, the e-mail had said. An intimate get-together for close friends, at the bride-to-be's family's country home out in Endicott Falls.

Hah. There had to be forty-five, fifty people circulating out there on the terrace and the party was going strong, music blasting from the sound system. A definite wedding vibe. No mistaking that taint.

Nick hated weddings. Everything about them made him tense. Even the super happy ones, when the bride and groom were deliriously in love and had cartoon birdies fluttering in circles around their head. Especially that kind, Nick thought, staying in his hiding place behind the climbing rose trellis. The higher you flew, the farther you had to fall. And Sean McCloud was flying very high tonight.

Watching the guy and his fiancée, Liv, laughing and kissing, stuffing tidbits into each other's glowing faces, slurping champagne, gave him the same tight feeling in his gut that he got from shark movies. Happy little kids frolicked in the surf, and meanwhile, *dadum . . . dadum. . . .* He'd never figured out why people voluntarily watched movies like that. He himself did everything in his power to avoid that kind of emotion. He'd felt enough already to last a lifetime.

He ground his teeth, scanning the room for Tamara. She was the only reason he'd come to this damn party, and the only reason he stayed, too. One more chance to pump her for info on Vadim Zhoglo. Before she cut Nick's balls off to make herself a necklace. That was the threat she'd made the last time he'd pestered her about it.

He was pondering that unpleasant prospect while he watched Davy McCloud, one of the groom's brothers, trying to persuade his extremely pregnant wife to dance with him. He wasn't having much luck at it, but a passionate kiss with lots of tongue seemed to appease him.

Goddamn show-offs, the whole pack of them.

There were plenty of hot young single women at the party, lots of plunging necklines and come-hither glances. Some of them had been strategically positioning themselves to be on his prowl trajectory. Bleah.

He used to enjoy this kind of situation, way back in the dawn of time, before his life went to shit. He used to have a smooth way with women, at least in the initial approach. He had enough charm to get them into bed and enough skill to show them a damn good time once they were there. But not a lot else, as the ladies soon found out. It got kind of exhausting after a while.

But he couldn't work up the energy to care about that tonight.

Two young girls jostled him in the doorway where he lurked, jolting him out of his reverie. They reeled away, giggling. Cute kids. About the same age as Sergei's little Sveti. If she was still alive.

Which got more doubtful every fucking day.

"Hey. Try to contain your joy, why don't you. Your enthusiasm is a little overwhelming."

Nick stiffened at the familiar voice. He took a swallow of his whiskey, and turned to face Connor McCloud, the groom's other brother, and Nick's former colleague in the Cave, the

FBI task force to which they both used to belong. The guy was clean-cut tonight, for him. Connor had probably been blackmailed into shaving and cutting his hair for the occasion, but he still managed to look rumpled. And very tired.

The cause of his exhaustion slept on his chest, nestled in a front carrier. Four-month-old Kevin McCloud. The carrier's star, moon and teddy bear motif looked truly weird with Con's dark tailored suit.

Nick frowned at the small, reddish-looking creature. "Kid threw up on your jacket," he observed with distaste.

Con's eyes went soft as he glanced down at the baby. "Sure did," he said proudly. "He's a regular little geyser. From both ends."

Nick was failing in his attempt to keep his lip from curling. He put his drink to his mouth for camouflage, took a swig.

"Excuse me for mentioning it, but that stuff is not doing your mood any good. Maybe you should slow down," Con suggested.

Nick fought the urge to snarl, and lost. "Con, it's great that you and your brothers are wallowing in conjugal bliss and baby shit. I'm happy for you all. That doesn't give you the right to preach. So fuck off."

Con's green eyes took on that piercing laser glow he got when he was in investigative mode. "It's getting to you." His quiet voice sounded worried. "That thing that happened in Boryspil. You've been tied in a fucking knot ever since. And this bug up your ass about Zhoglo—"

"It's not your bug. It's not your ass. Leave it alone." Nick turned his eyes away, and scowled out over the dark garden.

He knew what Con was thinking. He thought of it too, whenever he laid eyes on the guy, which was one of the reasons he tried to avoid his former good friend, who used to trust him with his life.

Nick's fucking finest moment. That mega lapse in judgment that had almost gotten Connor and his lady slaughtered by that psycho, Kurt Novak. And while he was torturing himself, there was Sergei to consider, split open from neck to groin, eyes still aware, pleading silently for the mercy blow. And Sveti. Sergei's twelve-year-old daughter, abducted six months ago. Who knew where, or to what.

That had been Sergei's primary punishment for betraying Zhoglo. The bloody torture and gruesome death part had been just for fun.

Nick had nightmares about Sveti's fate, when he managed to sleep at all. He'd been searching for months for rumors, clues, whispers about her. He'd gotten exactly nowhere.

Con wasn't the kind of guy to hold grudges, which bugged the shit out of Nick tonight. In his current mood, being hated was preferable to being forgiven. Forgiveness implied too much responsibility.

Con's son woke and began to squawk. The two men gazed at the infant, bemused. Con tried various cuddling and jiggling maneuvers, but the squawks rose into wails that drove into Nick's ears like nails.

"I better find Erin," Connor mouthed through the din to Nick's relief. "I think he's hungry."

Tension buzzed in Nick's body as the other man strode away, towards the glowing brunette who lit up with a megawatt smile when she lifted the squalling thing out of the carrier pouch. Erin McCloud, Connor's busty, luscious wife. The women those McCloud guys picked out to marry sure were easy on the eyes. All three of them.

The sharp poke to his shoulder made him whip into guard mode, grabbing for a pistol that wasn't there tonight.

It was just Tamara, the McCloud guys' mysterious outlaw friend. As beautiful as ever. Her currently dark hair was twisted up into a roll, her golden eyes were full of cool amusement, her perfect body was poured into a skintight gold silk minidress with a high Chinese collar.

"What the fuck was that? A stiletto?" he snapped.

She waggled long, gilded fingernails at him. "Lighten up, Nikolai."

"Don't call me that," he replied sourly. His birth name reminded him of his father. Thinking about Anton Warbitsky was a sure recipe for a stinking foul mood. He'd changed his last name to distance himself from that sadistic son of a bitch. Not that it worked worth a damn.

They shut up as a dancing couple swayed by, slow dancing to the old blues tune blaring on the speakers. It was the guy with the nose, the computer expert who hung out with the McClouds. Miles. He clutched Cindy, Connor's sexpot sister-in-law, and swung her down into a deep, flashy dip. She giggled, and he yanked her back up again for a smoochy kiss. They undulated away, entwined.

Too fucking much. At least he wouldn't be invited to that wedding. Sean's upcoming nuptials were going to be bad enough.

"Young love." Tam's voice had a metallic ring. "Sweet, isn't it?"

"I give them six months," he predicted darkly.

"Ding dong, you're wrong. They broke the six-month barrier a while back. They're working on eight months."

Nick shook his head. "Tick tock, tick tock."

"Come on," Tam murmured. "This is a party. These are your friends. Laugh, Nikolai. Smile. Even I manage that, in my brittle way. Fake it. Medicate yourself if you must. You're a cigarette hole burned into the fabric of the universe."

"I could leave."

"Don't go," she murmured. "I might be able to cheer you up."

Every muscle in his body went still. "With what?"

Her smile faded to an impassive mask. "Do you want to die young, Nikolai? Or do you want to linger in an old folks' home?"

Excitement blasted like a chill wind over the landscape of his consciousness. The hairs on the back of his neck stiffened, his skin prickling coldly with a mix of hope and dread. "What have you got?"

She stared at him. "An express ticket to hell." She waited for a beat. "Don't look so eager. You make me feel guilty." She nodded her head towards the side garden, filled with dark, unlit lumps of topiary. "Let's talk."

Their feet crunched on the white gravel path. She led him to the deserted gazebo. He tried to wait for her to speak first. If he showed too much eagerness, Tam would just play him like a cat with a mouse.

She waited him out. "What have you got?" he finally snapped.

"Not much," she said. "Rumors, whispers, favors. Possibilities. You know Pavel Cherchenko?"

His jaw clenched. Oh, yeah. He knew Pavel. Pavel was one of the men who had almost certainly supervised Sergei's torture and murder.

"Met him a few times in Kiev, when I was undercover," he said. "Arms deals. One of Zhoglo's lieutenants. A real shithead. What about him?"

"I know the woman who runs the agency that supplies Pavel with his biweekly blow job when he's stateside," Tam said. "She owes me a favor. A big one."

"What kind of favor?" Nick couldn't help but ask.

Tam smiled blandly. "Her life, among other things. The last time the girl serviced Pavel, he was all upset because one of his key men had shot himself. Pavel has a problem. He talks when he drinks. Anyway, looks like something big is coming down. He needs someone trustworthy, with perfect English, to take care of housing and security details."

Nick's mind raced. "Something big? Housing? For who?"

"How the fuck would I know, Nikolai? That's for you to find out. So, in the interests of getting you definitively killed and removing this damn stone from my shoe once and for all, I asked Ludmilla to recommend you, my friend."

"Me?" He frowned at her. "How . . ."

"Your alter ego, actually. Arkady Solokov," she said.

"How do you know about Arkady?" he demanded, outraged. His arms-trafficking undercover persona was a deeply buried secret.

Tam rolled her eyes. "So? Shall I give her Arkady's number?"

"Fuck, yeah." Nick was dazed. "Tam, how is it that you have all these contacts with the sex workers who service the Russian mob?"

"None of your business. Don't push your luck. I should probably go into hiding as soon as your taillights disappear, now that I've mixed myself up in your suicidal bullshit. What a fucking bore."

"Aren't you in hiding already?" he asked.

"It's a matter of degree," she grumbled. "I'll have to stay on the move, leave my comfortable house, my studio, my business. I may even find it necessary to make myself unattractive." She shuddered with distaste. "Be warned, Nikolai. Milla is doing this as a favor to me. If you fuck up, and she gets hurt, I will cut your throat."

"I understand," he said. "I just want to know if—"

"There is nothing else I can tell you," she said crisply. "This conversation is over. Do not ask me for anything else. And keep in mind, brokering arms deals undercover is one thing. Getting up close and personal with Zhoglo, as Arkady, is going to be very different. If you don't have the guts to do whatever Zhoglo might ask of you, you're dead. And if you do have the guts, you're damned. Think about it before I give Arkady's cell number to Milla."

"I'm thinking. I thought," he said promptly. "I've decided. I owe you, Tam. If you ever need anything from me—"

"You still don't get it, do you? I haven't done you any favors. I've just cut your life short by about fifty years." She glanced at the glass in his hand. "Depending on how hard you'd drink, of course."

He shrugged. "Maybe. I wouldn't know what the hell to do with those fifty years anyhow."

She sighed out a long breath, pressing her slender hand against her midriff. The look in her eyes mirrored his own.

Cold, wind-whipped wastes. Secrets in the shadows. Rocks and hard places.

"You want to do me a favor?" Her voice was low. "Do the world a favor. Kill Zhoglo. Don't just spy on him. Don't just hand him over to the law. Put a bullet through his brain stem at close range."

He thought about Sveti. "Tam, I—"

"Kill him if you can. If you can't, then God help you."

She turned, and disappeared into the gloomy shadows.

Nadvirna, The Ukraine

Vadim Zhoglo slowly sipped the fine brandy from the crystal snifter in his hand and gazed out at the snowy peaks of the Carpathian mountains. "Transport details for the first shipment are in place, Pavel?" he asked.

"Yes," the man replied stolidly. "Everything's arranged."

Zhoglo turned to look at him. "And you can vouch for each one of your people this time? No more surprises, like six months ago?"

Pavel's hand darted to the collar of his suit, tugging to make space for his large and lumpy Adam's apple to bob and twitch.

That was his answer. Again. Zhoglo closed his eyes. "What has happened this time, Pavel?" he asked with deceptive gentleness.

"Nothing serious," Pavel hastened to assure him. "But one of the men in place in Puget Sound had to be, ah, replaced."

"Killed?" Vadim frowned. "How is this possible?"

"Suicide," Pavel forced out, his voice gravelly and reluctant. "He hanged himself. Pyotr Cherchenko."

"Your nephew, no? The one you had me arrange those expensive immigration documents for? I see. Yet another wasted investment," Vadim said. "My condolences, Pavel. And his replacement?"

Sweat shone on Pavel's pale forehead. "A man named Arkady Solokov. From Donetsk. He's taking care of security on the island."

"And you can vouch for this Solokov? Without hesitation?"

Pavel's eyes slid away. "We've had dealings with him before. He was with Avia. He brokered those deals for the M93 grenade launchers and rockets to Liberia four years ago. He seems very competent. And his English skills are—"

"Seems competent," Vadim repeated, with ironic emphasis. "I invest millions in this project, and you tell me this person 'seems' competent."

"I had to get someone in place quickly, Vor, and I am sure that—"

"I am sure of nothing. Except that you're an idiot who compels me to take risks. Very well. We will proceed as planned. You may go."

But Pavel lingered, shuffling his overlarge feet.

"What is it?" Vadim barked. "You're boring me, Pavel."

"My—my sons?" Pavel faltered. "You promised that we could have Sasha and Misha back if I—"

"The agreement was that you could have your sons back if you corrected the error you made in that unfortunate business last year. But you have not, Pavel. You have compounded your mistake."

"Vor, please. My boys are just two and eleven, and—"

"I am not heartless. You may have one son back. The other goes out with the first shipment. To defray the cost of your errors."

Pavel's face drained to the color of ash. "One? But I—but Marya—" The clock ticked loudly. "Which one?" he whispered.

Vadim shrugged. "It doesn't matter. There is equal demand for vital organs from two-year-olds and eleven-year-olds." He smiled indulgently. "Take an evening to think about it, Pavel, by all means. Discuss it with your wife. Let me know your decision in the morning."

Pavel stood like a statue, eyes staring. Zhoglo pushed a button on his belt to summon two large thugs. They hustled the man away.

And enjoy them, too, goddammit. Just wa... Frakes Island...
on isolated running wil...
However, in terms millionai...
lot of choice on some invitati...
trespassing without an advance p...
his pool without... li...
It did seem...
would proba...
otic six-...
land...

12

Skinny-dipping. Sk... ...mping under the stars in... ...hrough Europe. Getting a cute ta... ...ionate love affairs with untamed guys with... ...ppling muscles. The list went on and on, all the c..zy things girls did before they calmed down and found The One. Things that Becca Cattrell had never gotten around to trying.

Aw, face it, already. She'd never had the nerve, let alone the time.

Becca stubbed her big toe in the dark on a board that stuck up out of the wooden walkway. She braced herself for the time it took for pain to flash through her nerves and assault her brain. That interval was significantly slowed by the alcohol in her bloodstream. It got there eventually, though, and oh *crap*, that hurt.

She lifted the uncorked cabernet to her lips and took another swig. The bottle felt suspiciously light. So did her head.

No matter. She had to loosen up. By brute force, if necessary. She was no longer willing to play her divinely ordained role as a dutiful, dependable, reasonable goody-two-shoes twit. She was going to work her way down that list, and do every one of those silly things.

...ch her.

...here wasn't a whole
... Getting plastered alone,
...s property, skinny-dipping in
...n, hey—it was the best she could
...anning.

...e something that Kaia would do. Kaia
...ly take it a step further, though, and have ex-
...ay sex in the millionaire's pool. But alas, Frakes Is-
...was deserted in mid-April. There was nobody around
...or Becca to have aquatic erotic adventures with.

Aw. Poor her. What else was new?

Kaia. Thinking about that girl made every muscle in her body contract. Becca shivered. She was naked beneath Marla's terry-cloth robe, wearing only flip-flops that slapped against the boards of the walkway. She should have scrounged jeans and a sweater from Marla's vacation garb. Being naked in the woods at night was unnerving. Too quiet for a city girl like her. The silence felt like a pillow, smothering her.

She didn't have a stitch of appropriate clothing for this island adventure. She hadn't had a chance to go home and pack before she dodged the tabloid reporters lying in wait for her in front of the Cardinal Creek Country Club. She'd been forced to sneak out the service entrance, and her boss, Marla, had rushed her straight from there to the ferry dock. *Bye, Becca. Don't hurry back. Don't get eaten by a bear if you can help it.*

Good ol' Marla. Becca silently thanked her again for the heartwarming support.

She must have looked ridiculous when the taxicat guy had brought her over from the mainland in that cool catamaran. Breasting the waves in a houndstooth power suit. Yo-ho-ho and a bottle of cab. She took another swig.

To say nothing of her red, puffy eyes, her paleness, her bluish lips. Just call her the Corpse Bride. Hah. Except that she couldn't get up the aisle as any sort of bride, corpse or otherwise.

She chased that thought away with a bigger swig of wine. Marla had assured her that she'd left plenty of casual clothes at her boyfriend Jerome's vacation home. Marla was more or less Becca's size. A bit less than more, actually. So she'd fast till she fit into Marla's jeans. The wine diet. She stumbled, reeled, caught herself on a tree. Great.

The walkway that went around the perimeter of Frakes Island was abruptly bisected by another path. She lurched to a stop. So. This was the path that led to the millionaire's swimming pool. The other direction should take her down to the millionaire's boat dock.

She hazarded a left turn. It was like going through a narrow, vaulted tunnel, the trees were so thick. Bats and moths swooped and fluttered, darting crazily. The beam of her flashlight seemed so feeble.

So did she. God, what a hopeless wuss she was.

After a couple hundred yards, the big, glassed-in poolhouse loomed before her, skirted by a broad wooden deck.

She tiptoed up the steps, shone the flashlight on the door. *Take a dip,* Marla had urged. *They never lock it. The owner is a nice, nerdy software mogul. He won't mind. They keep it warm year-round. I've swum there in November. You deserve it, after what you've been through.*

Becca fitted the key into the door. It sighed open, letting out the faint scent of pool chemicals. She reached into the darkness, groped and flicked the first switch she found, then gasped in silent wonder.

Wow. A circle of lights lit the water from beneath, creating a jewel pattern of overlapping shadows on the mosaic tiles of the oval pool. The walls of the poolhouse were floor-to-ceiling art deco glasswork.

She walked in, dazzled. She set the wine bottle down, kneeled, scooped up some water. Caressingly warm. Swim-

14   *Shannon McKenna*

ming in that would be like swimming inside the heart of a perfectly cut sapphire. Magic.

She let the bathrobe puddle around her feet like a Hollywood diva, took off her glasses and shook her hair loose over her shoulders, letting it tickle her back. Becca stretched luxuriously, savoring the anticipation before she dove.

Ah. The shock of the water on her skin was delicious. She swam slowly across the pool in a lazy sidestroke. The water sloshed and gurgled sensually as she moved through it.

So beautiful and so solitary. Bliss. Just what she needed, after the last few days fending off media vultures. The extremely tense interview she'd had today with the club manager hadn't helped much—the one about "taking some time away until the fuss dies down."

She was afraid that was a code phrase for "you're fired."

Damn it, she liked her job. She didn't love it, but she liked it, and more importantly, she needed it, with her younger sister and brother both in school and needing her help. Besides, she was the best events organizer the Cardinal Creek Country Club had ever had. She was an organizational freak. Busy, busy Becca. Wrestling a zillion details into a coherent whole satisfied her on a deep, emotional level. Kinky, maybe, but there it was.

But the powers that be at the club had a horror of bad publicity. Whether this sordid mess was her fault or not, the result might be the same. She might have to retool her resume. Do the old job hunt cha-cha-cha.

But who would want to hire a pathetic laughingstock like her?

At least if she was canned, she'd be spared the snickering from her ex-fiancé Justin's guy friends at the club. Smirking, stinking, oinking bastards.

The pool was beautiful, magical, but her soul could not be soothed tonight. Her thoughts harried her like a hungry dog with a bone. What the hell was wrong with her, anyhow? Where were her wires crossed? She was a good person, damn it. Smart, sensible, practical, hardworking, unselfish. Relatively pretty, if not a raving beauty. She gave all she could to her family, her job. Her fiancé. She deserved better. She tried so freaking hard. All the time.

But such qualities evidently did not give men erections. Men wanted a whole different set of attributes and gifts. Men wanted women like Kaia. The pigs.

Gah. If only she'd played it cooler, hadn't made such a big public deal of the engagement. But it had seemed too good to be true. Telling the four winds had made it feel more real. Justin was a great catch, after all. Charming, handsome. Rich, prominent family. Big plans. Justin was an up-and-coming prosecuting attorney with political ambitions. He'd told Becca once that she'd be a perfect politician's wife.

She'd taken it as a sweet compliment at the time. Her heart had gone pitty-pat as she imagined herself as the devoted political wife on the campaign trail with her handsome husband. Hah. How innocent.

She'd been so ready to move on from her rented apartment in a ramshackle old house. Ready to buy a real home, with a lawn for the kids she hoped to have. A minivan, with space for the car seats. Cargo room for strollers, travel cribs, dirt bikes, skateboards, scooters. Camping equipment for those family vacations. All-day shopping trips to Ikea and Costco.

Her daydreams seemed so silly. To think she'd been holding court at their bachelor/bachelorette bash, giggling as she opened up Kama Sutra bath salts and his-n-her bath towels. Prattling like a ninny about the merits of marble countertops versus tile for her dream kitchen. And all the while Justin was giving his college girlfriend Kaia "a ride home."

Some ride. Tall, sun-browned, sandalwood-scented Kaia, with her yellow cornrows. Sun tattoos on her shoulders. Funky Nepalese jewelry. Nose and navel piercings.

Ready, willing, and able to perform a blow job on Justin as he drove down a busy city street. In Becca's own car, no less. As it happened, Justin's driving had been no match for

Kaia's skill at fellatio. Becca's car had ended up wrapped around a telephone pole smack in the middle of a bustling shopping district. It was blind luck that he hadn't killed someone. Or many someones.

Kaia now sported a collar and head brace. And as for Justin, well. A ring of tooth marks on that bastard's dick was the least that he deserved. Becca could not find it in her heart to feel sorry for him.

It had just been a goodbye, for old times' sake, Justin had protested, as soon as he was lucid enough to talk. He'd implied that Becca should be grateful he'd gone for oral sex, not vaginal penetration. How noble of him, to sacrifice his own pleasure out of respect for his fiancée. She ought to be overcome with gratitude at his manly restraint.

Um, not.

She'd expressed her feelings forcefully. Justin had gotten angry in his turn. He'd said several ugly things, calculated to make a woman want to huddle alone on a fog-bound island, far from everyone who knew what had happened. Which was to say, the whole world.

Becca stopped at the edge of the pool, hoisted herself partly out and pressed her hot face against her folded arms. Tears welled up and spilled. More fucking tears. She could fill this pool with them.

The scandal was too lurid to keep quiet. Justin's family was too well known and it was all over the Internet. She'd googled herself and found thousands of mentions. And those reporters, baiting her, trying to get a reaction. Bottom-feeding bastards. The notoriety hurt. A storybook princess with a ring on her finger, she'd been recast in a crass burlesque. And not even a lead role. More like second banana. The reason poor, sex-starved Justin felt compelled to unzip his pants, just to get some blessed relief. The butt of a dumb dirty joke.

No one could talk about it without laughing, but it wasn't funny. Her ex-fiancé had another girl's tooth marks on his penis because Becca hadn't been able to keep him satisfied in bed. Justin said so, when he got over feeling guilty and started getting pissed.

She'd tried, that was for sure. Justin was an attractive guy and a good kisser. But she'd always been sort of awkward and stiff when it came to sex. She'd been so sure it would get better as their intimacy deepened, as their trust grew, when she finally had a chance to relax.

So she wasn't a red-hot orgasmatron. So sue her. She tried to please. She did her best. She tried to be open-minded. Uninhibited. But as Justin had taken pains to point out, trying to be uninhibited was a contradiction in terms. Either you were, or you weren't. Period.

That struck her as so unfair, that there were things that honest, earnest effort just couldn't change. Either you turned a guy on, or you didn't. Either you were sexy and fascinating, or you weren't. Either you were a wild woman who gave blow jobs in a moving car, or you were the bland, safe type who would make a good politician's wife.

Better now than after they got married, had kids. Narrow escape.

She shoved away from the poolside and launched into another angry lap, arms pinwheeling through the water.

Sparks. That was what Justin said she lacked. Seeing Kaia had made him realize this. Kaia was crackling with sparks. Becca wondered if the head brace would cramp her fiery sexual style. Poor thing. Big shame.

She touched the side, twisted to prepare for another push off—and two huge, strong hands seized her under the armpits and wrenched her up out of the pool. A thick, steely arm locked across her throat. Something hard pressed her temple. A gun. Oh God. A *gun*.

"Who the fuck are you?" The voice in her ear was a rasp of pure menace.

Chapter
3

Ambush.

First thing Nick had thought when he saw the gorgeous naked chick on the video monitor. Preening and stretching, tossing her hair, showing off her tits for the camera. Diving into the pool like she owned the fucking place. The babe had nerves of steel, he'd give her that much.

He scooted backward, dragging her with him till he hit the glass poolhouse wall. The place made him feel like he was in a fishbowl when the lights were on. All glass, all around, and no cover of any kind.

He braced himself for a volley of bullets to explode out of the darkness, turn all that art deco flash into shrapnel.

Didn't happen. Not yet. Any second, maybe. Any second.

He took the gun away from the girl's neck just long enough to hit the switch and kill the underwater lights, plunging them into darkness. Hell. The beeper had jerked him out of a doze, and sleep-addled dumbfuck that he was, he hadn't put on the infrared goggles before charging out here. It was a sure thing that the guys in the woods had them. If they were out there. The girl wiggled, trying to stand.

Uh-uh. Not in this lifetime. A deft kick that was calculated not to cause pain knocked her bare feet out from under her. He got her off balance so that she dangled helplessly in his grip.

"I—p-p-please—"

"Shut up. Not one word out of you. Got that?"

A shudder racked her body. Her head jerked in assent.

Jesus. How? Who? This op was so fucking secret and mysterious, he didn't even know a lot of the details himself. Who knew about his cover, other than Tam? Had Ludmilla turned on him?

Maybe one of Zhoglo's business rivals had an infiltrator. Maybe some foreign police agency had gotten tipped off, and was setting up a cozy welcome for Zhoglo when his boat docked. Nick didn't blame them, but he stood to get slaughtered from every side. And Zhoglo was supposed to arrive tomorrow—aw, fuck.

He had to stay alive.

He eased the door open, dragging the naked chick out. Her feet scrabbled and her whimpering made it hard to listen for the rest of the team, wherever they were. He got her down the walkway to the house while his brain churned out possible explanations.

One: Naked Chick was an assassin, a black widow fuck-n-kill type. OK, she wasn't packing anything he could see, but a body like hers was a weapon in itself. Might as well conk most guys over the head with a club as let them ogle tits like that. And of course there were weapons that were easy to hide.

He'd have to take a closer look. The idea sent a surge of interest into his groin. His one-eyed snake didn't care if the bathing beauty was an icy-hearted killer.

Sometimes he wondered how men lived to adulthood, let alone old age, with that much concentrated stupidity dangling between their legs.

Two: Naked Chick was a distraction to engage his attention while the ambush moved in on him. The come-and-get-me way she'd presented her body for him in the poolhouse was one mother of a distraction. A sexual spell. The way her skin gleamed when he'd dragged her up, the jewel-like reflections on the disturbed water. It was magic.

Yeah. Sudden death could be so magical.

He guided her through the door and into the main house. Nice and easy. He didn't need to be aggressive. She wasn't fighting him. In one swift move he cuffed her slender wrists together behind her back, hooking them to the banister of the spiral staircase. He hadn't lost his touch.

He stepped back, ran his eyes over her body. Wow. Whoever sent her must have a big budget. The girl was fucking amazing. He forced his mouth to close and went back to his situation analysis. *Concentrate.*

Three: Naked Chick was an expendable sex worker with no clue, and this was a perverse test from the big boss to see how Arkady behaved. Just the kind of game Zhoglo might play with a new guy to get a feel for his weaknesses.

Which would mean he was being watched. All the more reason not to lose his cool. And if he was careful, he might even get the upper hand. Worth trying.

"Who sent you?" he asked softly in Ukrainian.

She blinked, big-eyed. "Huh?"

She sounded American. Not likely, not for a job like this, Nick thought. "Who sent you? Tell me who sent you here," he asked, in Russian this time.

No response.

He tried again, in Chechnyan, Estonian, Moldovian, Georgian, in case she was a ticking bomb sent by one of Zhoglo's business rivals. He tried Hungarian and Romanian too, just in case. The big Z might have pissed off Daddy Novak. These psycho dudes were not known for their loyalty when billions of dollars were at stake.

Not so much as a spark of comprehension on her face. Just the appearance of shivering terror. But she was a professional, after all.

They'd picked their bait well, if bait she was. Stop-your-heart pretty, with all those pale, soft curves, huge green eyes. Just how Nick liked them. Not too skinny. Old-world, Eastern European type of gorgeous, not a stringy Malibu beach babe.

He especially loved the mouth. The plump, parted, quivering lips made him speculate briefly about what her sexual specialty must be. She must be stellar at giving head.

He felt sort of honored. If he rated a top-of-the-line call girl to lure him to his doom, he must have hit the big-time when he wasn't paying attention.

He wondered how old she was. He guessed twenty-three, twenty-five, max. Couldn't have been in her current profession for long. That radiant-innocence vibe couldn't be faked. Innocence faded real fast.

The visuals were perfect. She was still gleaming with water that trickled from her hair and ran down her body. Drops of water clinging to the dark fuzz between her thighs. Full tits, shown to advantage. Hey, cuffs were fun. Tight nipples. Helpless whimpers.

Nick dragged himself back to reality. Like hell she was helpless. She probably had a coil of wire fastened into her hair to garrotte him the second he turned his back.

"Who are you? And who sent you?" he asked in English.

"I'm, ah, Becca Cattrell," she quavered, her voice high and thin.

"Becca Cattrell," he repeated. "Who the fuck is Becca Cattrell?"

She shook her head, eyes wide. "Ah . . . me?"

"Not funny." He tipped her chin up. "This isn't a game. Who sent you?"

"M-m-marla sent me," she gasped out.

"Yeah? Did she? Who's Marla?"

"My b-boss," she stammered out. "At the club."

So Marla was a madam. OK. That was part of the puzzle, but not the part that interested him. "Why did this Marla send you to me?"

"Look, all she said was I could use the pool," the girl quavered. "She told me th-th-that you were *nice!*"

Nice? She sounded betrayed. He chewed on that for a moment, staring at her. "I don't know anyone named Marla," he said. "And guess what? I'm not nice."

"Oh." She blinked like a trapped bunny.

He squelched a foolish impulse to trust her. "Wait here."

Like she had any choice. He loped back into the security room to check out the infrared. Did a slow, steady sweep with the thermal imager, three hundred and sixty degrees. Nothing suspicious. He did it again. Nobody out there with warm blood and a beating heart except for wild animals.

He flicked another switch that showed two different camera angles on the spiral staircase and studied the girl from both sides. Her wet hair hung down, hiding her face. She was trembling. He had to get her warmed up.

No, he told himself sternly. He didn't. Chivalry could get him killed. He had to think like Zhoglo. No heart, no conscience, no compassion. Cold as a cadaver in a meat locker.

He studied her body. She didn't have the taut, nervy musculature of someone trained in hand-to-hand. She looked soft, touchable. Built for pleasure, not a sinewy, streamlined killing machine. He was tempted to rule out the possibility of her being an assassin. But he really did have to search her first.

He hesitated as he went by the linen closet, then yanked out a towel, cursing himself for the soft-headed idiot that he was. He decided to add to his stupidity by grabbing the space heater he saw under a shelf. What the fuck did it matter if the assassin and/or call girl was a little more comfortable while he interrogated her? Zhoglo wasn't watching. At least he hoped not.

The girl eyed him warily and Nick realized how strange he must look to her, carrying a goddamn space heater and towel like a cabana boy. Fuck it. He plugged it in, aimed a blast of hot air at her. She stiffened as he gathered a handful of her hair and twisted it gently to squeeze the water out, then let it fall.

Thoughts of that garrotte flashed through his mind. He ran his fingers through her wet, silky hair, trying to intuit the tricks a naked female assassin might use to conceal the tools of her trade.

Her hair was amazingly thick and soft. No garrotte wire in it.

She shivered at his touch. No earrings, rings, necklaces, anklets, bracelets, toe rings. She made a wordless protest as he ran his hands over the deep curve of her waist, up her back. Nothing taped up there. Then he moved between those soft thighs, another popular place of concealment. That provoked a squawk of outrage and a furious wriggle. He ignored both.

Nick brushed the edge of his hands up under her tits, which were more than full enough to conceal something taped or tucked up there. Nothing. They were amazingly soft, though. Wow.

He checked them again, just to be thorough. Hmm. That left bodily orifices, but that could wait. Hell, he barely knew the chick.

She flinched at his snort of laughter. "What's so funny?" she snapped. "Are you done groping me yet, you disgusting pig?"

"Not yet," he said mildly. He grabbed the towel and started briskly drying her body.

She tried to twist away, sputtering. "Do you mind?"

"Not at all," he replied. He flung the towel away, ran his eyes over her. She was mostly dry and her lips had more color. Down to business.

"Let's talk, Becca Cattrell," he said. "Tell me all about Marla."

"I-I-I work with her. At the club." She got points for consistency.

"OK," he said. "The club. That's a good place to start. Tell me all about this club, beautiful. Who runs it?"

"Ah, well, the CEO, I guess. James Blaystock the Fourth. It's the Cardinal Creek Country Club in Bothell. I'm the events coordinator. I arrange meetings, banquets, parties. Weddings."

Nick's mental processes flash-froze. He just stared at her. Country club? What in the flying *fuck* . . . ?

"Marla is my boss," she babbled. "Marla Matlock. She was the one who gave me the keys to Jerome Sloane's—he's her boyfriend—vacation home. It's the big A-frame on the hill. She told me she'd been coming here to swim for years. She said the owner was a harmless sort of guy—" She faltered. "I take it he's . . . not you, right?"

Nick cleared his throat as the possible scenarios morphed into new, even less welcome shapes. "No. He's definitely not me. This house changed owners recently. A few weeks ago."

She nodded. "I see. P-p-please," she whispered. "Let me go."

Nick crossed his arms over his chest. She could still be lying but Sloane *was* the name of the guy who owned the nearest house. Nick had a file on him. Jerome Sloane was a rich art dealer in his fifties, who divided his time between Seattle and San Francisco. He had files for the owners of all the other properties on the small island as well. Sloane had left Frakes Island the second week of August and he hadn't been back.

Plausible cover story, the voice in his head whispered. Anyone else could have done the same research that he had done.

"OK," he said. "Let's assume, for a second, that this is true—"

"It *is* true! I swear, I never meant to—"

"Shut up." He gave her a thin smile. "Assuming that it's true, explain to me what you're doing here in April. And more specifically, explain what the fuck you were doing trespassing stark naked, waking me out of a sound sleep and scaring the living shit out of me at"—he checked his watch—"12:40 A.M."

Her eyelashes fluttered. "I," she asked delicately, "scared *you?*"

"Explain," he growled. "And you'd better make it convincing."

She let out a shuddering breath. "I, um, had some p-p-personal problems lately. I wanted to, you know, to get away from it all. Marla persuaded Jerome to give me the keys to his island house. She told me about your beautiful pool. I just didn't think. She said nobody would mind. I guess she was, um, wrong."

He processed that. In point of fact, he had not yet had time to rig up the security system for the poolhouse, just the video. His beeper had gone off when she tripped the infrared set up at the perimeter.

This sucked. His chances of living through Zhoglo's impending visit were slim enough without involving clueless innocent bimbos who organized weddings and banquets. "Do you trespass naked often?" he asked, genuinely curious.

Dark, curling lashes swept down over enormous leaf-green eyes. She had a dusting of freckles on her nose. *Concentrate, damn it.*

"No," she whispered. "I've never done anything like this in my life. It was, um, an exercise. I'm trying to be—I want to be more, ah, adventurous."

Adventurous? He stared at her. His lips twitched. His cock lengthened. Hell, he'd show her adventure. A hot, sweaty adventure that she'd never forget. Left, right, sideways, upside down, inside out.

No, he wouldn't. "Adventurous?" he repeated.

She shrugged as best she could. "I know it sounds stupid. But I've always been a good girl." The rest of her explanation came faster. "I brushed my teeth, I did my homework, I took my vitamins, I worked hard, I put myself last . . . I guess that's why my fiancé thought I'd make such a good politician's wife—"

"Fiancé?" He came down on the word, like shark jaws chomping.

"*Ex*-fiancé." She added the prefix with vicious emphasis. "I've never had the nerve to misbehave, so the bastard figured there would be no dirt for the gossipmongers to dig up. He might as well marry a department-store mannequin, that condescending, manipulative son of a bitch—"

"Can we stick to the subject, please?"

Too late. The chick was on a roll. A detail came back to him—the nearly empty wine bottle he'd glimpsed by the pool. She must have carried it in. Finished most of it off.

"The snake cheated on me!" she said heatedly. "With Kaia! *She's* the adventurous type. Her nose is pierced. She's trekked in Nepal. She's gone on safari. Whoop-de-doo for her. Bitch."

Her fury made his mouth twitch. He hadn't smiled in so long, he almost didn't recognize the sensation. Sort of like a tic.

She didn't appreciate it. Her eyes narrowed. "What's so funny? Do I amuse you?"

"Sorry." He looked her slowly up and down. "I don't think you're a mannequin. You look real to me."

"Um, thank you, I think," she said stiffly. "I don't suppose that means you would consider taking off these handcuffs? They hurt."

He stared at her. If what she said was true, he'd endangered them both by making her curious about him. If what she said was a lie, then there was an evil plot afoot, which meant that the chances of him going on up to the Great Stake-Out in the Sky tonight were very good.

He took a deep breath, let it out. The more he looked at that gift-of-God gorgeous body, the less inclined he was to worry about it.

It occurred to him that if she really was just a naked

events coordinator, she wasn't likely to drug, stab, or poison him while they did the deed.

He stopped that thought dead in its tracks. The chick was scared out of her wits. Restrained with his cuffs. No matter how stunning she was, he had never forced the issue with a woman in his life, and he damn well wasn't going to start now. No matter who was watching.

He couldn't think of any safe way to deal with her, though. If only there was a way to scare her off the island until Zhoglo and his crew had come and gone. But keeping her quiet might be impossible if he was deliberately terrifying. She could go to the local cops, file a complaint, and screw up everything. Perhaps fatally.

So. What now? He couldn't expect her to laugh it off. Or just give her the cuffs to take home for a souvenir of an oh-so-wacky encounter with her nutty new neighbor. They would have to become instant friends for that to happen.

Every male instinct he had clamored to keep her right where she was. Naked and helpless and very close to him.

Grow up, dickwad. He let out a regretful sigh, and undid the cuffs.

Becca flopped heavily down onto knees that felt weaker than water, the second that she was freed. Long, bare brown feet planted on the floor tiles in front of her swam into focus. Her eyes traveled up over hairy, muscular calves. He wore raggedy cargo pants, cut off below the knees. Her gaze traveled over rock-hard thighs, lean hips, the . . . oh, my. The bulge at his groin.

It was a big bulge.

She swallowed, and continued up his belly, his hard, slabbed chest shown off to amazing advantage in the tattered black muscle shirt. She looked straight into his intense dark eyes. Beautiful eyes, heavily lashed. An exotic hooded slant to them. A hot, focused stare.

A rush of nervous female caution made her insides flutter. She had to get up, onto her feet, this instant. Being naked on her knees in front of this huge, scary man was making her feel . . . no.

Whatever it was she was feeling, she didn't want to feel it. Not for a second. It was unsettling. Whew.

But she was naked. At least crouching she could cover herself. She peeked up. Her eyes skittered away from his like a drop of water bouncing off a hot griddle. Scratch that previous assessment. Amend it to huge, scary, *sexy* man. She got her hands beneath her for leverage to get to her feet, but big, warm hands seized her, the span of his fingers spreading over her rib cage. He lifted her, and set her down. His hands slid away. A ripple reaction moved over her skin.

Her gaze darted around, but she soon gave up and let herself be dragged into the tractor beam of those eyes again. He was so big. But not thick-necked, pumped-up muscle. He looked hard and athletic, a predator poised to strike. He must be guarding this place—a regular Joe Homeowner wouldn't have whipped out cuffs, for God's sake, although lots of guys had guns.

His shoulders were ropy and thick. Tattoos swirled on both of them, but she couldn't make out the images without her glasses. Didn't matter. The man had his own gravitational field. It dragged at her.

His face was gorgeous in a rugged way. Smudgy shadows under his eyes. The hint of dimples carved deep beneath jutting cheekbones. Lines framing his hard, sealed mouth. A bumpy nose with a troubled past. Tangled mahogany hair brushed his shoulders. Dark, winged brows. An old scar slashed through one of them. His stubble was almost long enough to be called a beard. She wondered if she really had gotten him out of bed. He looked like he could use the sleep.

She wrapped an arm around her breasts, tried to cover her pubic hair with one hand. His eyes moved over her, a slow, hot lick over her flesh. Currents of invisible energy flowed between them, powerful and muscular. She licked her trembling lips. "Wha—what happened to your gun?" she blurted.

His stern mouth twitched. "Don't worry about my gun. I'm not going to shoot you with it. Unless you try to kill me."

"Oh." She swallowed, and licked her lips again before she could stop herself. "I'm, ah, not going to do anything of the kind."

"That's great news," he said. "Very comforting."

"Don't make fun of me," she snapped. A grin flashed across his face. Yup. There they were. Very nice dimples suddenly flanked his mouth. His teeth were very white.

"Wouldn't dream of it."

She bent, keeping her eyes locked on his, and reached for the towel. He snagged it with his big toe and moved it out of her reach.

"No," he said, very softly. "I like you just like you are. You said you were looking for adventure. Need a guide?"

She covered more of herself with her hands. "I can't believe I said that. And no. I don't."

He nodded. "OK." His voice was low and velvety. He stared at her for a long time.

"Step away from me, right now," she whispered. "Give me space."

He stepped back. Cold displaced the force field emanating from his body. Becca felt exposed. She wrapped her arms all the way around herself.

He reached for her wrists and made his move, slowly opening her arms wide. "You're beautiful."

Her chin lifted, her breasts tilted. "No, I'm not." She wanted to cry. She wanted to kiss him. What the hell was the matter with her?

It was obvious that he was aroused. His cargo pants hid nothing. He noticed the direction of her gaze, and gave her a you-wanna-make-something-of-it grin.

God, did she? Her thighs tingled. She wondered, out of the blue, how it would feel to have sex with a man that size.

He was picturing it, too. She saw it in his eyes. Fear and excitement jolted over her. Oh, boy. Hold on here. Just wait a goddamn minute. She wasn't ready for the big league. She wanted to start small.

But she couldn't have special-ordered a more perfect candidate for a no-holds-barred sexual adventure. She'd never been with a man like this guy. Her previous boyfriends had been harmless types. Accountants, computer consultants, academics. Great for help with taxes or home tech support when her laptop pooped out on her, but not for sparking thigh-tingling sexual curiosity.

This guy was a complete unknown. Other than the fact that he carried a gun with an air of casual familiarity. And had physically restrained her, of course. Handcuffs, for God's sake. Skillfully applied, swiftly removed.

Huh.

So this was how it felt to be totally turned on. A mild, pleasant glow was as much as she'd ever been able to work up before, either in company or solo with her vibrator. Nice, but hardly worth all the effort.

Maybe the extreme situation had jarred her sexual awareness to life, like a malfunctioning appliance that needed a kick to get it going.

The silence got thicker. Hotter. Sex with him would be the single most outrageous act of her life. It would be . . . perfect.

She took a deep breath, and wet her lips with her tongue. She would have smiled seductively and fluttered her eyelashes, but she didn't have that much control over her face. She buzzed, thrummed, with something like euphoria. The lingering effect of the cabernet? A little unexpected bondage? Him?

Him. Definitely.

She stared, goggle-eyed, wondering where to start. Then again. Flaunting her naked body at him was a very good start. He did seem to have gotten the message.

"Ah . . ." She swallowed again, hoping desperately that he'd take the lead.

He pulled her toward him. She almost fell against his body.

"Say yes," he said hoarsely. Then he kissed her.

To his amazement, she kissed him back.

Chapter
4

Her lips were so soft. Cool and silky, yielding to his marauding kiss with a startled whimper. Delicious inside, sweet. Her tongue retreated from his. He coaxed it out of hiding with all his considerable skill.

Her trembling body pressed against him. He wanted to jerk his pants down, shove her against the wall. The appetite for sex that had been numbed into mock death was roaring to life.

At the worst possible time. But, he rationalized, they had the rest of the night. They were safe. He would keep her safe. Zhoglo and crew came in tomorrow. . . .

She flung her head back, gasping for air.

Oh yeah. Foreplay. He was forgetting his manners. "Mmm," he said thickly, nuzzling her damp ear, drawing her earlobe between his teeth. "I fucking *love* foreplay. How about you?"

"Sure—"

He shut her up with another kiss. He couldn't explain anyway. She'd blundered into his stakeout. She was a deadly distraction, a massive, no-holds-barred fuck-up, but he didn't care. He had to have this. Had to have *her*.

She was going for it. And he couldn't stop. His body, his hands were dazzled by her body. She pushed all his buttons, all at once. He hugged her softness closer. Just this felt so good. He hadn't touched anyone in so long. His arms ached to grab her. His whole body was starved for contact, not just his cock. His mouth wanted to search and lick and taste that smooth, cool, damp skin, those sexy curves, succulent pointy tits, all puckered up and ready to be sucked. His hands roved, stroking and probing.

"I love foreplay," he repeated, nibbling her throat. "I want to lick you all over like candy. I want to leave no part untouched."

"Yes," she quavered as his hand slid between her ass cheeks, parting them, sliding lower to touch the damp, narrow seam. "Talk to me. Tell me what—"

"I want to lick you here, too." He ran a finger across the plump folds of her pussy lips, caressing the inner ruffly bits, slick and wet already. He couldn't wait to get her on her back, legs wide, so he could study every detail. "I'll lap up your juice and then suck your clit till the well fills back up and I have to lick it all away again—"

His voice choked off as she yanked his head back down and kissed him. Her clumsy ardor set off a bomb inside his chest. It was getting worse. He was going nuts, and he could not stop. Could. Not. Stop.

He kissed her back, ravenously, and let her gulp up air while he nuzzled her ears again. "I want to slide my tongue between your pussy lips and lap at it, top to bottom," he told her hoarsely. "Then I'll fingerfuck you while I tease your clit with my tongue."

"Ohhh . . ." she whispered.

"I'll keep at you until your ass and your thighs are all slippery, and you're gasping and moaning and shoving yourself against my mouth. Begging me to give you my cock."

She pulled away, breath jerking hard between her parted lips. Cheeks flushed bright, eyes dazzled. "Oh, my. That's it."

"That's what?" he demanded.

"What I wanted," she informed him. "What Justin wasn't

giving me." She wedged her hand down between their clamped, trembling bodies, and fastened around his cock, squeezing through his cargo pants. "Oh, boy. This is, um, extreme. I might have known. Like everything else about you."

He groaned. "You don't know jack about me, lady."

"I'm learning fast," she offered. "You're an inspiring teacher."

Her fingers tightened around his cock, and the next sound he made was a rasp of mingled pleasure and despair. "You're trouble."

"Wow," she murmured. "I always wanted to be."

He had to concentrate to keep from coming in his pants. The tender squeezing, the curious stroking, the ticklish butterfly pats, it was all driving him nuts.

He'd always liked lots of fooling around first. He was generously endowed and he'd figured out from the start of his sex life that if he wanted the girl to like it and ask for more, he had to go slow and max out on the foreplay. This necessity had never weighed upon him, however, since wallowing in the juicy intricacies of women's bodies for hours was his idea of hog heaven.

But if she kept petting, he was going to lose it and go at her like a wild boar in rut. He clamped his hand over hers and pried it off his cock for the moment. Then he slid his hand down into the silky wet fuzz on her mound.

He teased his way inside the damp seam, swirling his finger around in her hot lube, like some slick, delicious oil. His thumb glided around her clit, searching for spots that made her shiver and moan, and thrust his finger right up into the tight clutch of her pussy.

Her plush, cushiony cunt felt great, clenching and releasing with her upper thighs. Head thrown back, eyes closed, she looked even more beautiful.

Need clawed at him, but she was too tight, too small. He had to make her come first, till she was boneless, limp, flooded with lube. That took time.

And he was losing his mind, very pleasurably. Starting to forget why giving this red-hot sex kitten screaming orgasms until the sun came up was not a great idea.

Awareness of the danger only hours away lingered in the back of his mind, but she was about to come and he couldn't stop himself from going for it. He could feel it building in her body, in her trembling lips, in her pussy, jerking against his hand—

It hit, a glittering sugar rush of girl pleasure, throbbing through her and back through him by reflex. Her pussy tightened hard around his finger in ripples of warmth, licking and lapping over every nerve.

They rocked together, heads cradled on each other's shoulders. His nose nuzzled her wet hair. He felt her sharp teeth against his shoulder and a hot, wet stroke from her pink tongue. That was it. He hoped to God she was ready, because he sure as hell was.

He jerked his pants down, let his cock spring up against her belly, raring to go. He gripped her ass cheeks and hoisted her up against the wall, tilting his hips for the plunge—

"Do you, um, have any condoms?"

The reasonable question penetrated the fog of lust in his head like a fine needle. Sharp and irritating, poking him.

"Huh?" He shook his head, confused. "What the fuck . . . ?"

"Looked like you were going for it. Gotta have protection, right?" She licked a sheen of sweat from her upper lip. Her mouth was flushed, blurred from his kissing.

"I don't have one."

Her eyes fluttered. "Oh. That's, ah, bad. So I guess we can't, then. I guess I thought you'd just, ah, pull some latex out of a hat."

Frustration built up inside him. "Do I look like I'm wearing a fucking *hat*?"

She winced. "Figure of speech. Can't we do some of those other great things you suggested before?"

Two startling thoughts occurred to him. One, if he hadn't

thought she was too weirdly innocent to be a call girl, he was convinced of it now.

The second thought, barely glimpsed through the haze of lust in his mind, was that she had offered him an out.

He'd been hurtling into the tunnel of doom. She'd just saved him. He should be grateful to her. Hah. Right now all he wanted was to mess with her mind a little, for tying a knot in his cock.

His grip tightened on her hips. "Nope," he said. "No condoms here. No drugstore for miles. You take your chances."

Her eyes got big. "Oh. Um, that's not very smart—"

"No," he said. "It's not."

"I don't even know your name," she whispered.

He snorted. "Yeah? That just occurred to you now?"

He wanted to tell her his name. First, last, aliases. He wanted to be naked with her. Inside her. *Now,* damnit. He could have pounded the floor like a baby, but he did not. She had reactivated his self-control.

His cock had never been so unhappy.

She reached down, giving his stiff, empurpled boner a tentative pat-pat-pat, like it was a wild animal that might bite her. "Let's compromise," she suggested.

He didn't answer right away. *Do the right thing, Nick,* he told himself. *Say thank-you and good-bye.* But something else came out of his mouth. Something crude and stupid.

"OK," he said. "Blow me. Let's see if you're any good."

She jerked away and her tits jiggled as she came in contact with the opposite wall. She backed towards the door, clearly disgusted by his raging case of testosterone poisoning.

He felt like he'd kicked a kitten. "Oh, Christ. I'm sorry."

Her chin went up. "Forget it," she said haughtily. "This is crazy. I'm out of here."

"Thank God," he muttered. Then she was gone. He put his hand over his hot face. His hand shook. His whole damn body shook. His eyes leaked. Nick, the ice man. Melted down to fucking mud. What the hell had just happened to him?

It occurred to him that Becca was naked in the woods, at one in the morning, with no flashlight. Shit. She had the walkway for a guide, he told himself. But in that moonless dark, she was going to have a painful, unnerving time creeping back to the Sloane A-frame. She wouldn't die of exposure in the ten minutes that it would take her to get there. But still. Christ.

He went to the control room and grabbed the thermal imager.

He winced when he saw the red, rainbow-edged image moving on the boardwalk stumble. She crouched down to feel her way, walking almost on her hands and knees. He was tempted to follow her with the infrared goggles to make sure she got back safe.

But following a beautiful, naked woman through the dark woods with a raging hard-on like the one he had now didn't strike him as intelligent. He didn't trust himself. He'd probably end up carrying her over his shoulder to the Sloane house and nailing her there on the first flat surface that presented itself, if he could find a condom and get her permission in writing.

She was right. This was crazy. *He* was crazy.

He did the next best thing: climbed the spiral staircase to look out the window of one of the back bedrooms, from which the Sloane house could be seen. He stood there, and waited, like a statue, until he saw a light flick on. Home safe. Good.

Let her go and fucking forget about it. He hadn't done anything against the law and she wasn't likely to report him to the local cops for not having a goddamn condom. But the gun, the cuffs—fuck it. Too late now. They would ask her a lot of rude questions about why she was swimming naked in the neighbor's pool in the first place. No, nothing would come of it.

He sank down into the bed, humiliated. Goddamn it, he had wanted her, though. With all his heart.

Being alive again felt truly weird. To think he'd maneuvered, begged, pleaded, cheated, schemed, for a chance to get closer to that psycho vermin Zhoglo. He would have laughed, if he had the energy.

Nobody could pay a guy enough money to do shit like this. He was dickbrained enough to do it for free. Jesus, look at him. The most important solo op of his life, deadly dangerous . . . and ta-da . . . a beautiful naked girl waltzed in out of nowhere and made him forget who he was, what he was doing. Made him drunk and stupid with her clumsy kissing.

He wasn't a hugging sort of guy, but her arms had felt so damn good. And his finger tingled, as he thought of her tight, hot, clinging—

Stop. He buried his face in his hands, and let out a sound like a wolf's howl. If he lived through this, he was done. He would spend the rest of what passed for his life building birdhouses.

Becca's spell was potent. While it lasted, he felt like a man again. Interesting to know that his tackle still worked. He tried to shove his cock into his pants, but it wasn't ready to face reality. Like a raised fist at an activists' rally, it stayed up and stayed high. He wondered if he was going to have to jerk off to get some relief. It had been months since the urge to masturbate had even crossed his mind. Let alone sex.

He'd been too busy, too focused. Too depressed. The last time he'd had sex offered to him was at an icebound way station for human traffickers in the armpit of Russia, three months ago. Posing as a buyer while he looked for Sveti. Stone-cold afraid to find her there.

One of the traffickers had offered him the use of a piece of his merchandise. Ivana. From Belarus. Couldn't have been fourteen. Even terrified and traumatized, she was a pretty girl. Destined to be chained to a bed in a brothel, in some sex tourism hot spot in Thailand or the Philippines, until she got used up and sent off to the boneyard.

He'd given Ivana his bed to spare her having to turn any other tricks that night and slept with the rats on the filthy floor, wrapped in his coat. The cargo had moved on the next morning.

It had put him off sex ever since. He'd barely managed to eat afterwards, it had made him so fucking miserable. He could have saved Ivana, if he'd been willing to break cover, give up his search.

But he'd made a promise to Sveti's mother. To Sergei's ghost.

It made him crazy. Thousands of women and children, bought and sold, used and tossed like garbage so that Zhoglo and men like him could get richer. So that sleazy sex tourist assholes from all over the world had a constant supply of fresh meat. Thousands of Svetis, of Ivanas. And he couldn't do a fucking thing about it.

Except for this. He would keep it simple, focus on one individual. Just Sveti. If he thought about them all, he'd go nuts.

He knew in his gut that trying to stop Zhoglo and his kind was a useless effort. Even if he took out one kingpin, a thousand wannabes would hustle to fill his shoes. But he could try to find one single stolen girl and take her back to her mother. Just one. That wasn't too goddamn much to ask.

He patted the various pockets of his cut-off cargo pants until he found a lighter and the battered pack of Turkish cigarettes that his alter ego Arkady favored.

He took a deep, grateful drag of the harsh smoke. He'd acquired the habit when he was a freaked-out, fucked-up teenager and tried to quit several times. Now that he'd wrapped his mind around the fact that he wasn't likely to be needing his lungs in the long term anyhow, it seemed pointless to deny himself.

He struggled to remember what Sveti looked like, but

after six months, the finer details were gone. He remembered obvious things: long dark hair, hazel eyes, a big smile like Sergei's. A port-wine birthmark on her neck. But when he tried to see her face, a vision of Becca got in the way. All grown up but somehow just as innocent.

He looked at his crotch, let out a mirthless laugh. Thinking about Sveti and Ivana was a great way to wilt an inconvenient boner.

Useful discovery: if she kept the walkway boards perpendicular to her naked toes, she could stay on her feet without toppling onto sharp rocks and thorny, bug-and-snake-infested foliage. This was good.

Sobering reflection: she could miss the turn-off to the A-frame, and keep going in an endless loop around the island until she croaked of exposure, or got eaten for a midnight snack. That was bad.

Becca's imperfect solution was to hug the edge of the path and follow the edge of the boards with her toes, which compelled her to go at a slow, limping pace. She clung to her outrage, and somehow that kept her from sliding into screaming panic.

A bump on the ends of her abused toes made her howl, even while tears of gratitude popped into her eyes. The turn-off.

She groped for the handrail, and went up the stairs. Thin branches tickled and slapped, cobwebs broke across her face, winged things fluttered against her hair. She swatted them away as she felt her way across the deck and past the picture window until she found the door. She turned on every light in her dash for the closest bathroom.

Forty minutes or so under a pounding stream of hot water took off the edge of the cold, but it didn't wash away the touch of his hands, his lips. So that was a whole-body orgasm. She'd read about them in romances. The sensation had scared her, it was so intense.

How pathetic. To be taken by surprise by a real orgasm at the advanced age of thirty. And worse was the way his crude remark made her feel after. *Blow me. Let's see if you're any good.*

Trust Becca to get a massive crush on an overgrown frat boy. Whose name she didn't know and didn't want to know.

Frantic rummaging in the closets yielded up another terry-cloth bathrobe. Becca swathed herself and wandered through Sloane's house. The place was like the lobby of a ski resort. Big beams, flagstones, cedar paneling, huge fireplace, squishy couches upholstered in ugly plaid wool. A mirror hung on the wall. She stared at her pale face, her smudged mascara. She felt different. Her obsessive thoughts of Justin and Kaia weren't having their usual effect.

On the contrary. The penis-chomping debacle, nasty though it had been, was simply not as interesting as what had just happened to her. God knows, Mr. Big next door beat Justin hands down when it came to doggish lewdness. The big difference being that Mr. Big's doggish lewdness had been directed right at Becca's own self.

And there was no doubt that his interest had been real. There was no faking an erection like that.

Wow, she'd come close to doing the deed with a complete stranger. Her face flamed, as she remembered his final suggestion. She'd had an image of herself, trying so hard to please, the way she'd tried to please Justin. Failing. Having him judge her, for how clumsy and clueless she was.

She saw Justin, complaining in his hospital bed, looking pale and martyred and self-righteous. Kaia, in her collar and head brace, a pitying smirk on her pretty face.

So what are you going to do? Curl up and die? Sometimes Becca wanted to smack herself.

She pried one of the long fireplace matches out of the

box. Some helpful soul had already laid a fire, and it licked to life, newspaper and kindling catching flame. No moping allowed. Doing something useful was her trusted strategy for mood management, so she marched over to the cardboard boxes that sat on the table and started ripping them open.

The boxes were filled with catered foodstuffs that had been delivered to her office that day, as part of her wedding prep. Her boss and colleagues had urged her to take it all with her to Frakes Island in lieu of groceries. Nobody wanted perishables lying around in the office all week. She and Justin were supposed to have tasted the wines together, to choose what would accompany the various courses of their wedding feast. This was to have taken place on their romantic weekend getaway, this very weekend. She'd planned it all out to the last succulent detail.

Before the penis-chomping incident.

The catered food consisted of yummy dishes, mostly Italian, that could be eaten cold or popped into an oven and browned, for quick fortifying nibbles between erotic interludes in bed. Cured and roasted meats, sun-dried tomatoes, grilled and gratinéed vegetables, spring salads, cheeses, fruits, crackers and breads. Coffee beans, cream, a grinder. And here was the kicker—five eight-inch wedding cake candidates. Butter Lemon Cloud, Rum Caramel Pecan, Black Cherry Wickedness, Mocha Mousse, and her own personal favorite, Grand Marnier Triple Fudge Angel's Fall.

No one could accuse her of not being passionate about sweets.

She toyed with the idea of setting up a Justin effigy and lobbing cakes at its head, but the truth was, she was constitutionally incapable of throwing away a delicious cake. Bringing up her sister and brother on a cocktail waitress's pay made her loath to waste food even now, years later. She shoved the pastry boxes into the fridge with barely controlled violence.

The last box held the wedding notebook. She'd brought it along with the intention of burning it, to purge her system and make her feel better about herself. That was a lot to hope for, but a girl could try.

She leafed through the thing, marveling at her capacity for self-deception. The quilted heart cover alone, with precious cross stitching that read *Becca & Justin, April 18*, should have tipped her off that the relationship was doomed. Just looking at it put her in a sugar coma.

She ripped off the cover, flung it into the fire.

The carefully organized sections inside—gah. Check out the questions that had kept her up at night. Should she order personalized breath mints with names and the date printed on each one? Should she go with the individual toothpick boxes for each place setting? Was Vivaldi's *Four Seasons* too "done" for the string quartet in the garden?

She ripped handfuls of pages out, threw them on the fire. They made lots of puffs and sparks and insignificant mini-whooshes before scorching and curling up like pathetic dying bugs. She did not feel any great rush of liberating, cathartic power. Surprise, surprise.

She needed Mr. Big and his clever hands for that.

Perish the thought. She would not be talked to like that. Oaf. So much for adventure. That encounter had not been super therapeutic for her self-esteem.

One more thing to burn. The padded envelope of sexy lingerie that she'd ordered off the Internet. Shameful evidence of how pathetically eager to please she'd been. Trying to lure Justin by sheer effort.

She tore it open, and stared at the pieces with hot, unfriendly eyes. The virginal cream bustier with the not-so-virginal matching thong. The demure apricot chiffon babydoll chemise, the matching panties, the crotch of which was two thick satin ribbon strips that could be nudged to either side of the labia, leaving the way clear for, well, ahem, anything. At the time, it had struck her as a sophisticated secret to share with her fiancé, just for him. Now it struck her as desperate.

Which was exactly how she'd felt, writhing in that man's arms.

Maybe it wasn't so great to have shocked her dormant sexual awareness into life at this inconvenient moment. She'd always thought that being sexually free, like Kaia, would give her a sense of power.

But she'd been wrong before. In fact, she was wrong a lot.

Her fist closed around the apricot chiffon confection. She drew her arm back to hurl it into the fire—and stopped.

What would Mr. Big think of her sex kitten outfit? He might be rude, but he wouldn't be indifferent. She wondered what it would take to make that guy whimper and beg.

A lot more than I have going for myself, she told herself. *Don't even go there, bubblehead. You'll just hurt yourself.*

Too late. She'd already gone. She dropped onto the nearest couch and thought about it as the fire crackled.

After all. She didn't have to actually go near the man ever again. But all alone in the dim room in front of the fire, who could fault her for indulging in a little bit of wishful fantasy? Who would she hurt?

She slid her hand under the folds of terry cloth, and found herself—good Lord. Already wet and soft. Just squeezing her thigh muscles together sent bursts of shivering warmth into her legs, her knees, her toes. They curled up with each rush of excitement.

She was startled. Who would have thought that knees and toes would be invited to this party? Her intensely aroused body was like a brand new toy, and she couldn't help playing with it.

The fantasy that was the strongest was anything but politically correct.

Herself, bent over, thighs spread. Clutching the wrought iron banister, bracing herself as he penetrated her from behind. That thick shaft, that big blunt knob pushing between her labia. Opening her. The powerful presence of his body behind hers, those warm hands gripping her. Thrusting and pumping. Filling her completely. Taking her.

The feeling swelled up, lifted her, hurled her off the cliff.

She was sobbing when she came back to reality, her body still wrenched and racked by jolts of pleasure. Still in one piece. Still Becca.

She got up, bumping into the furniture without her glasses.

Damn. *Her glasses.* She'd forgotten all about them in her frantic hurry to get away. She'd left them by the side of the swimming pool. Along with the mostly empty bottle of wine and . . . oh, God.

The keys. The poolhouse key had been on the A-frame's key ring. The keys to Jerome's house. Oh, no, no, no.

That was terrible. She couldn't face a week on a deserted island alone in a myopic blur. Nor could she go back to Marla and tell her she'd lost the keys to Jerome's house. How could she justify it? Because the neighbor was rude? Because he had seen her naked when she skinny-dipped? Please. Marla already considered her a fluffy-tailed, persnickety little rabbit with a twitching pink nose. Little Miss Nervous Wreck.

God, she was sick of being condescended to. By Justin, Kaia, Marla, Mr. Big. Even her little brother and sister were guilty of it.

She gathered up every last scrap of that lingerie, and tossed it into the fire. It smoldered, smothered by the synthetic fabrics.

Tomorrow morning she would march over to retrieve her belongings. And, incidentally, take the opportunity to tell that guy exactly what she thought of him. While sober. And clothed.

Her pride depended on it. As wobbly and fragile as it was right now, it simply could not take another hit.

Chapter
5

Dr. Richard Mathes levered himself up from the damp, quivering body of his mistress and paused to enjoy the view. The charmingly submissive position, her double-jointed flexibility, the satin babydoll nightie shoved seductively up over her breasts—it was perfect.

His gaze turned critical as he observed the un-dynamic way that her breasts perched upon her rib cage. The colleague he'd referred Diana to for the breast enhancement surgery had overdone it. Smaller implants would have been better. Only in this position was the defect so evident, but unfortunately, this was one of his favorites. He liked to pin her ankles down on either side of her head and pound away with bruising force. It was the best way to wind down after a long stint in the operating room.

"Amazing." Diana licked her full lips, and wiggled as he slipped out of her body, contracting her vaginal muscles as if to trap him inside her. "I knew it would be like this today. You were amazing with Jimmie."

Jimmie Matlock was the sixteen-year-old boy who had gotten a new heart that day in a seven-hour surgery. Diana, in addition to being as skillful as an expensive call girl and always attuned to his sexual whims and moods, was also a competent anesthesiologist.

"You're so fearless," she crooned. "Nerves of ice. It makes me wet. Even in the operating room."

"You shouldn't think about sex while we're working," he snapped.

Her eyes widened. So did her legs, an automatic reflex that showed off her glistening vulva. "Scold me. I love it when you're stern."

"I know." He turned away with insulting indifference, and opened her armoire, searching for one of the fresh shirts she kept for him.

The next line in the script was predictable. "I'm free tonight and tomorrow," she said. "Can I see you?"

"No," he said lightly. "Tonight I have to go to a musical with Helen and the girls. And tomorrow I have that meeting. As you know."

Her face tightened. She sat up. "I don't understand why it's necessary to meet this Zhoglo in order to conduct business with him—"

"Do not say the name," he reproved her sharply.

She rolled her eyes. "This is my bedroom. Don't get paranoid."

"I wouldn't want certain information to slip in the wrong context."

Diana arched her chest, pressing taut nipples against the silk of her nightie. "When am I ever anything but discreet?" Her voice was a silky coo, but he heard the acid undertone. "Have I ever complained that you can never take me out to dinner? That you never touch me in public? Not even when we're in Tokyo or Hong Kong or Johannesburg. It's always room service. But do I complain?"

This part was so tedious. "No, Diana. You've been very good."

"It's insane, Richie. This idea to keep the stock supply here, instead of harvesting the parts overseas, or offshore."

Parts. Stock supply. Diana needed to distance herself emotionally from the realities of the plan they were embarking upon. He didn't.

"Those hours of travel time make all the difference," he said patiently. "And I prefer to conduct the harvest myself. For the amount we charge, I have to control as many variables as possible. I have no choice, Diana."

She looked down, twiddling with the silk nightie, her face sullen. He wondered briefly if she would be able to handle what lay ahead.

But he could handle Diana. The time-honored technique known as "diamond and emerald earrings" always worked.

"Bullshit," she said petulantly. "You have choices. Every day, when you choose to go home to that frigid bitch."

They were out of the danger zone. He ran his hands over his own fit, lean body, checking for traces of the fluids of coitus. Not that Helen ever got close enough to him to smell another woman on his person, but even so. He was always meticulous about hygiene. Came from being a surgeon, no doubt. He ignored Diana's complaining and went into the adjoining bathroom.

Strange, he thought, as he set the shower running, how an isolated incident could change a man's life. One turn to the right or left affected one's destiny forever. What was happening now had started at a medical convention in Paris, when he was an emerging thoracic surgeon with several brilliant successes to his name. He went out to sample Parisian nightlife, relieved to be away from Helen's moods and headaches and the constant noise and chaos of his young daughters.

His adventures on that dreamy night had been lubricated by large quantities of alcohol and cocaine, and extravagant sums of money. He'd ended up in a luxurious apartment, entertained until dawn by two beautiful and uninhibited Parisiennes. He'd awakened in the rumpled bed, sticky with sex. Head throbbing.

A tidy, graying man with a pinstriped suit and an English accent was sitting by the bed, waiting for Richard's eyes to open. He introduced himself as Nigel Dobbs.

It had taken a long, disoriented moment for the reason for the unusual stickiness to sink in.

Blood against the white sheets. He turned, looked. Gaped.

The girls' wrists had been tied to the posts of the wooden bed. Their throats had been cut. They sprawled, naked, eyes wide and staring. Blood, everywhere. The room was doused with it.

It had felt like a dream. He blinked gummy eyelids, staring from Dobbs back to the girls, as a business proposal was made to him.

He had been very startled, but he had remained cool. His brain had always been that way, functioning superbly in situations that others would consider high stress. Compartmentalized. He would have been a good commander on the battlefield, he had often mused.

On the one hand, he was angry at being manipulated. On the other, he was fascinated to observe his own reactions to this shocking tableau. Amid the constant white noise of daily life, a man seldom got a chance to peer into the depths of his own soul. And what, after all, could possibly be more fascinating than the depths of his own soul?

Nigel Dobbs laid out the situation in a cool, clipped voice, as if they were in a boardroom, not an abbatoir. A wealthy Ukrainian businessman who had to remain nameless was suffering from an acute heart condition. He wanted an immediate transplant. He wanted the surgery conducted by the celebrated young surgeon Dr. Mathes. Cost was immaterial.

Mathes told Dobbs that money was not the issue so much as the availability of a healthy and well-matched organ, thinking that he knew exactly fuck-all about how organ donation was organized in the Ukraine—

"Not a problem, Doctor. The tissue typing has already been done." The man's tight mouth twisted in a thin, smug smile. "We have a number of potential donors. You need not trouble yourself about that."

"But how . . . but that's not . . . but you can't just . . ."

A number of potential donors? Richard had floundered, until the truth sank in. And the bottom of the world fell away, to an abyss of nameless possibilities that made his soul quail.

And his pulse quicken.

Nigel Dobbs studied Richard's face with neutral gray eyes for a long moment and nodded, as if Richard had passed a test.

"Anything is possible, Doctor. For a price. And while we are on that subject, my client will make available to you the sum of five million American dollars in a numbered Swiss account, as a thank-you gift. In the event of a happy outcome, of course."

"And if something goes wrong?"

Nigel Dobbs smiled again. "An unhappy outcome is not an option my client is willing to consider," he said gently. "That's why he wants you. Your reputation is that of a miracle worker. He has studied you, Doctor. Every detail of your life. Your wife and your little girls as well. Lovely creatures. My client wishes to convey his compliments, and his best wishes for their continued health and happiness."

That veiled threat had gotten his attention. Another, deeper peek into that shadowy cavern. He had always loved a gamble.

He'd been perversely glad for the threat to Helen and the girls. It gave him a face-saving excuse for saying yes. Indeed, how could he not?

The odds were bad. The man's body was probably rotted by a lifetime of excess. It would be against his Hippocratic oath, and every sane principle.

Ultimately, that did not dissuade him in the least. Neither

did the slaughtered Parisian girls. Nor was the issue decided by money. Being chosen had stroked his vanity, but he had daily opportunities to have his ego stroked.

He'd done it for the thrill. He'd never felt one so strong. That morning, lying in that blood-soaked bed, the thought of what he was going to do had burned through his body and mind, dispelling his hangover like sun on fog.

It made him feel invincible. The high stakes, the secrecy, the risk. Unspeakable acts. Unaskable questions. It lit him up inside.

He'd felt that thrill again the day he replaced the diseased organ of his mysterious patient with a beautiful, healthy young heart of unknown provenance.

Some months later, there had been another call. A business associate of his previous patient had a newborn infant daughter with an irreparable heart defect. A rush job, as the child was dying.

Richard had cleared his schedule, leaped on a plane. He had not asked where the tiny donated heart had come from. Another rush of euphoria. Another five million dollars in the numbered account.

The money had been nice. He had been a relatively wealthy man before, but as Diana liked to point out, fondling her sapphire and diamond bracelet, there was wealthy and there was *wealthy*.

That child was now a healthy, thriving six-year-old. If Richard had needed to soothe his conscience, that would have been enough.

But oddly, he did not. At some point, that euphoria had burned away the part of him that pondered ethics. He did not miss it. Life was exquisitely simple without it. More profitable, too.

In fact, he reflected as he toweled himself off, he'd never had much of a conscience to begin with. Morals were artificial. Notions culturally superimposed upon persons at a tender age, who had no idea they were being mind-fucked into being docile doormats. At the service of other people. Tormented by guilt, self-doubt. Not him.

And this Sunday, he would meet with someone who could supply him with a constant supply of his favorite thrill. People would sell their souls to cheat death, for themselves, their spouses, their children.

Dr. Richard Mathes found souls very appetizing.

When he came out, Diana was at her vanity, brushing her hair. He could tell from the glitter in her eyes that she was angry.

"He wants to look over his investment?" she said. "Check your teeth, look over your pedigree? Put you through your paces?"

He opened her closet, took out a starched white shirt. He knew exactly where she was going with this. She wanted to lure him into having sex again. She labored under the fond misconception that she controlled him that way. It amused him to let her keep her illusions.

"He wants to do that alpha dog pissing thing, right? And you're looking forward to it, aren't you? You'd love to stare down a mob boss. I bet that gives you a hard-on, Richie. You're such a danger junkie."

He shrugged the shirt on. "Diana—"

"That's why you get off on sticking your hands in people's viscera," she said. "It's not to help them. It's just for fun. You might as well be jumping out of a plane, for all you give a shit about them."

Diana surprised him sometimes with her sharp side. When not in the OR, she played the part of the dizzy cunt so convincingly it tended to lull him into relaxed complacency. "You're boring me," he warned her softly.

"Just make sure he doesn't piss on you, Richie. Some girls get turned on by golden showers, but I'm the traditional type. I think I'd be turned off by the stench of urine. Even a mob boss's urine. You know?"

Now she really was annoying him. He moved up behind her, slid his arms around her in a tight embrace. He pinched her nipple and her clitoris simultaneously—hard enough to make her suck in a sharp, gasping breath. Her eyes went glassy. Her lips trembled.

"Don't be a dirty bitch, Diana," he whispered.

"You're hurting me."

"Of course," he agreed pleasantly. "You asked for it."

Richard straightened up and wiped his fingers upon the silk that covered her damp, trembling back. He resumed buttoning his shirt.

Diana let out a gasp, her hand going to her ear. "I'm missing an earring!" She knocked the stool back, and rushed to the rumpled bed. She climbed onto her hands and knees, and scrabbled through the bedclothes. "It must be here, in the bed. You were so rough."

Richard stared at her smooth buttocks. The scrap of lingerie hid nothing. Her back arched, taunting him, inviting. He could smell the hot scent of her sex from across the room. He groaned inwardly. He'd just bathed, for God's sake.

"I have to go," he said plaintively.

"Yes, of course, Richie. Go back home to wifey. Don't let me stop you. I'm just looking for my earring."

Richard unfastened his trousers and let his penis spring out, heavy and red and ready as he approached the bed. He gripped her hips, jerked them into position. Diana trembled with eagerness as he breached her slick opening and slammed against her, with the unchecked violence she craved.

He used his private trick to make himself come. In those rare instances that he was overly tired and could not bring himself easily to climax, he had only to close his eyes and bring to mind those blood-drenched Parisian girls tied to the bedpost. That image revived a flagging erection—and brought him to an explosive orgasm.

Yes, he reflected, with chilly detachment, as the pleasure

pumped through him, he could handle Diana. She would give no trouble at all.

The whole world was like that. Easily managed. Begging to be used, for his convenience, his advantage, his profit, his pleasure.

What could he do but oblige them all?

Sveti listened intently at the door of the private quarters of the guards. She could hear muted sounds of some sports event on their cable TV. She clenched her teeth and knocked. No answer.

She knocked louder. The door was yanked open so abruptly, she sprang back with a yelp.

It was Yuri, the one she feared the most. Yuri was tall, shambling, had stubble on his fishbelly skin, snaggled yellow teeth, blond hair hanging in lank ropes. He liked to pinch and grope, and his dirty, squared-off nails left cuts and dents along with the black bruises. All the children scrambled to keep out of range of those cruel fingers.

He stared at her, his shiny lips stretching into a wide grin. "Look who's here," he crooned. "It's the Snow Princess. Did you miss me, beautiful?" He seized her wrist, and jerked her into the dim, fetid room, lit only by the flickering TV. A soccer match blared. The sportscaster chattering, the horns tooting, it all reminded her of Papa. He'd loved soccer.

It was a match between Ukraina and a team from a country of dark-haired people. Italy, or maybe Spain. The dark team was ahead. The room stank of smoke, rank male feet, fast food grease.

Yuri lifted a hand-rolled cigarette to his lips, dragged on it till the tip crackled and glowed, then wheezed out a cloud of sweetish smoke into Sveti's face, making her cough. Tobacco and hashish. Aleksandra had taught her what that smell was. Among other things.

"You like your new room, your majesty?" Yuri taunted.

"Happy to be off that stinking boat? Want to show me how grateful you are, ey?"

"Shut up, you degenerate," Marina barked at him from where she lay stretched on one of the couches. "What do you want, girl?"

Marina was a muscular, horse-faced woman with close-set ice blue eyes. Her bleached hair was chopped off in jagged layers, and hung dry and motionless as dead straw. She was hard and cold, but Sveti vastly preferred to deal with her rather than Yuri. Marina kept Yuri in check.

"It's Rachel," Sveti said, struggling to pitch her voice loud enough to be heard over the blaring TV. "She's got an ear infection again. Do you have any more drops? She's been crying for hours."

She swayed on her feet, caught herself. She herself hadn't actually slept in the six or seven days since they'd been moved from the stuffy cabins of that boat. They had rocked and swayed in a hellish infinity of nausea, vomit, whimpering misery, for weeks, maybe. Time had no meaning on the boat. Time had no meaning here in the concrete dungeon, either. But at least it did not plunge and heave.

"That whining brat is always crying about something," Yuri sneered. "I'll come down and give her something real to cry about, ey?"

Sveti kept her eyes fixed on Marina's pale blue ones. "She's hot," she said. "It's a bad fever. She could die." She paused. "Like Aleksandra."

A blinding flash of pain as Yuri smacked her with his knuckles. She hit the cluttered table, but when she looked up, Marina was on her feet, rummaging through her stash of boxes, muttering.

Sveti sighed in relief. Bringing up Aleksandra was a risk. She'd overheard arguments. Someone had been angry about Aleksandra. Someone the guards were afraid of.

So, then. It was not in the guards' interests to let the children die. It left her baffled, but it was something.

Marina pulled out a glass bottle and sent it sailing through the air. Too high. Sveti leaped, scrambling to catch it. It bounced off the tips of her fingers and thudded and bounced on the ground, landing on a patch of gray, synthetic industrial carpet. It did not break, thank God.

Sveti dove to the floor to retrieve it, trying not to cry. If she cried, it would be worse. She forced her stinging eyes to focus on the bottle. Amoxicillin. Yes. That would help. She started scrambling to her feet, and was forced down by a heavy boot pressing against the small of her back. She twisted, looked up into Yuri's bloodshot eyes.

"Don't say that name again," he said. "We don't want to hear that name again. Or else you'll disappear too. Then you'll know exactly what happened to her. You want to know, Snow Princess? You want?"

She was too frightened to move. He stared down at her, smiling, liking it. Something ugly and horrible flexing inside him, growing big and strong. Reaching out to her, like sticky tentacles that made her dirty and ashamed. Inside, where she was most vulnerable.

She tightened her fingers around the smooth glass of the bottle, and twisted till she could see Marina again. "I have to go to Rachel," she burst out, her voice high. "I have to give her the medicine. Please."

Marina tamped out the cigarette. "Let her go, pig."

Yuri's laugh was ugly. "You like having the Snow Princess do all the work for you, ey? They picked a cunt for this job because you were supposed to be maternal. Marina, tucking the little angels into their beds, singing a lullaby. You're no good for that. You're no good for what other women are good for. So what are you good for? Worthless cunt."

"Shut up, Yuri. You're stoned." Marina coughed out a cloud of smoke. "Let her go, before I knock out all your teeth."

He did. Sveti fled down the corridor that led to the windowless, unventilated room where the children were penned. The din had abated. Rachel's shrieks had dwindled to whimpers. Stephan and Mikhail had spent their energy as well. She was grateful for the relative silence.

Sasha held up his precious pen flashlight for her. Its batteries were almost dead, but it still cast a watery yellowish light as she used the bottle cap to measure out what she hoped was the right dose for a two-year-old.

Rachel choked and coughed and spat out half of the medicine on the sheets. Sveti was sobbing with frustration, fighting the desire to hit the child by the time she finally gave up. She curled herself around the little hot lump of Rachel's shaking body, barely managing to stay on the narrow cot, to stare with wide, burning eyes into the impenetrable dark.

Mikhail was whimpering, thrashing in his sleep. He would wake up with screaming nightmares soon. He wet his cot and his clothes with such monotonous regularity, it seemed the whole world, including Sveti herself, stank of piss. Mikhail was five, as far as she could tell. So was Stephan. Dimitri was ten, and Sasha eleven.

Of the lot of them, only Sasha had been with her from the beginning, with Aleksandra, in that big, decaying apartment in Kiev. But Sasha wasn't very good company anymore. He had stopped speaking a couple of months ago. The little ones had come later, after Aleksandra had been taken away. None could talk much. Mikhail and Dimitri seemed as if they might be retarded. It was hard to tell. She felt dulled herself, after the boat, after days in a hole with no air, no windows. Day and night were artificial; either the fluorescent lights were on, buzzing like crazed insects, or the children were left in the stifling darkness.

No sleep tonight. Never, when she had to deal with Yuri. She shuddered with dread. Dealing with him made her remember everything that Aleksandra had told her before she vanished.

Everything that Sveti had been so much happier not knowing.

Aleksandra had been taken from her parents as a reprisal,

too, like Sasha and Sveti, but she had been taken months before them. She was two years older than Sveti. Worldly wise, cynical. And very ill.

She had been the one to point out what Sveti had been too inexperienced to see, after she saw how Yuri stared at the younger girl.

She'd nudged Sveti one night with her elbow before bed, flushed and shivering with the fevers she had every night. "Yuri likes you," she whispered hoarsely, between coughing fits. "You better watch out."

"You're crazy!" Sveti had whispered back. "He hates me! He always hits me!"

Aleksandra let out a wheezing laugh and shook her head. "He likes you," she repeated. "You know what that means, don't you?"

Sveti, a sheltered twelve-year-old, had not known. So Aleksandra told her, in gruesome, exacting detail. Everything Yuri was going to do to her, with his thing. Everything he would expect her to do to him.

"It's better to be prepared," Aleksandra had told her sagely. "It's just a matter of time. He'll get to you. They always get to you."

Sveti had been horrified, but Aleksandra had gone on to say that Sveti might as well get used to it, because probably all of them would be sold eventually. For that. That horrible thing that Yuri wanted.

"But we're children!" she protested.

Aleksandra just stared at her, mouth hanging open, and then she started to laugh. She had laughed until she was sobbing on the bed, curled into a ball, her hair drenched with sweat. Shuddering.

Sveti had not slept for a week after that.

Soon after, doctors had come, and given them many tests. Machines. X-rays. Blood tests. No one would tell them why. It had taken days.

The next day, Aleksandra was gone. Sveti had awakened

in the morning, and found the bed empty. The pillow still had the dent of her friend's head.

Sveti cuddled Rachel tighter, till the baby wiggled in protest. She tried to breathe. The dark pressed down on her like a pitiless hand.

Chapter
6

Nick had noticed this phenomenon before. Momentous events that had been dreaded for years and had taken on colossal importance in his head—when they finally arrived, he found himself cool to them. As if he were watching an old movie that did not particularly interest or engage him. His father's death had been like that. A series of details to attend to, a long look at the body in the coffin. The sharp-boned face so like his own, but wasted, sunken. Etched with the lines of sour disappointment that he'd worn ever since Nick's mother had died.

The look he had then turned upon his son.

Nick had looked inside himself, searching for some emotion he could put a name to. He'd found nothing.

So it was with the arrival of Vadim Zhoglo.

The boat appeared with no warning. It was chance that he'd been monitoring the camera that watched the cove at 10:42 A.M. He'd had just enough time to scramble into some decent clothes, yank his hair back, splash his face. Then the superficial adrenaline rush had drained out of him, and he'd settled into this weird, sedated calm.

Too calm. Any man greeting Zhoglo who knew what he was capable of would be justified in losing his shit. Arkady

Solokov, professional arms broker and general scumbag, should be terrified of fucking up in front of the Great Vor, and excited about advancing his criminal career.

Nothing twitched inside him as the man got out of the boat. He would have been able to pick Zhoglo out of his group of minions even if he hadn't seen the overly pixel'd long-distance photographs which were all that the combined police agencies on the planet had managed to glean.

The word for Zhoglo was blunt. Fingers like sausages, the heavy paunch of a gourmand. His silvering hair was buzzed short. His face was jowled, with heavy, pendulous lips. His iron-gray eyes were deepset in purplish, puffy bags. He exuded concentrated menace.

Nick studied him, figuring that his calm came from having nothing to lose. No wife, no kids. No unfinished business other than finding Sveti. And avenging Sergei.

Sergei was still been alive when I found him. Spread-eagled to the hotel bed, mouth duct-taped shut. Slit open, his guts pulled out and heaped onto his chest. Conscious.

Whoa. He usually managed to block that memory from slicing into him unawares. He averted his eyes as the men filed past. The only one he knew personally was Pavel. The man looked like shit, grayish and thin. He'd aged ten years since Nick had seen him.

Zhoglo went by. He didn't appear to see Nick at all.

He let out a breath he hadn't known he was holding and fell into step behind the last man, an obedient dog who knew his place.

"Welcome, Vor," he said, in Ukrainian. "I hope the voyage went well—"

"Shut up, cretin," barked the last man in the line, a big, hulking blond. "You're not here to make noise."

Nick shut up and followed them up the walkway. The buzzer at his belt vibrated.

His stomach tightened with a chill premonition.

It could be an animal, blundering past one of the sensors. The men were ahead of him, spread out widely, almost to the house.

"The Vor's hungry," the last guy said over his shoulder. "Prepare a meal for him. And don't fuck it up. Bad food makes him irritable."

Nick froze for a second, letting the distance between them lengthen. Prepare a meal? Him? Pavel hadn't said anything about cooking.

"What does he want to eat?" he asked.

The blond guy shot a contemptuous glance over his shoulder. "Ask him, asshole," he said. "Your problem, not mine."

What did he have in the kitchen, anyhow? His appetite was for shit these days. He choked down the occasional frozen dinner when the feeling of emptiness inside him became physically debilitating. He couldn't cook worth a damn. He could barely use the microwave.

Maybe this was it. The stupid detail that would get his throat slit.

There was a chorus of rough, barking exclamations. Several guns jerked up simultaneously. *Clickity-click*, rounds were chambered.

"Who the fuck is she?" one of the guys snarled.

She? Oh, fuck. No, no, no. His artificial calm evaporated in an instant. He lunged through the clot of men to see . . .

Yes. Becca. *Fuck.*

Clothed this time, but she might as well have been naked, for all the diaphanous blue peasant blouse and the skintight jeans revealed.

Dead silence. The men stared at her, hungry-eyed.

She looked even prettier than last night. Her hair, dried, was a mass of brown curls. The color of the blouse made her skin look luminous. Her full, gleaming pink lips trembled. Unlike last night, she had good reason to be scared now.

Transfixed with dismay, he didn't track the movement of the guy next to him before a hard clout to his face with the man's pistol knocked him back. "What the fuck is she doing here?" the guy hissed.

Zhoglo turned to Nick, a smile curving his mouth. "Nice touch," he said. "I appreciate initiative in an employee. A welcome gift? How kind."

The bottom fell out of his gut, and tumbled down, down. He scrolled through the possible responses he could make, calculating how quickly—or, worse, how slowly—they would get her killed.

He swabbed the blood streaming out of his nose with his hand.

"Ah, actually . . . no," he forced out, voice froggy.

Zhoglo's smile froze. "No?"

Nick swallowed. Hot blood trickled down his throat. "She's the, ah, cook."

Becca stared at the guns. Feeling faint, she stared at the blood streaming from Mr. Big's nose.

One of the men stepped forward. A short, fat man, in expensive clothes. He spoke, his voice low and cultured, in a language she didn't know. Mr. Big replied in the same tongue. The fat man's smile disappeared. He had not liked the response.

The temperature dropped. So did her stomach.

These were people from another world, a world she did not want to visit. Oh, was this ever a mistake, and oh, was she sorry. Forget keys, glasses, pride, self-esteem. All she wanted was to curl up on her couch, pig out on Oreos and watch Jane Austen movies on DVD.

Her eyes focused on Mr. Big. He looked unconcerned by the blood coursing down his chin, but he stared at her with a burning intensity.

She didn't dare look away from him, with those guns pointing at her, those men staring at her body. He was her only point of reference.

It had taken her that whole night to work up the nerve to come back, and the whole morning to get ready. She hadn't had much to choose from, just what she found in Marla's closet, and the cosmetics rattling around in her purse. Her houndstooth power suit and stale white silk blouse and heels weren't an option. Marla's clothes were snug, though, and Becca hadn't wanted to seem like she was looking for masculine attention. The jeans were tight, and she had to cover up the chubby bit of belly that hung over the waistband with something loose. The blue peasant blouse was the only thing that fit the bill. The low-cut neck was sort of provocative, but she figured he had seen everything she had last night anyway, so what the hell.

These men stared at her. As if she were stark naked all over again.

The fat man stepped closer to her. She shrank back, opened her mouth to say, *Excuse me, gentlemen, but I see that this is a very bad time, sorry to have intruded, now I'll just disappear, OK? Bye!*

Her mouth worked. A papery squeak came out. Not a word, or even part of one.

The fat man approaching her did not carry a gun. He was shorter, heavier and older than all the rest of them, but when his light gray eyes fixed on her, she shrank away. His lips curved into a nasty smile.

She stared back, a fuzzy little animal hypnotized by a snake.

His eyes were strange. Opaque, like tinted windows on a car. He laid his damp, heavy hand on her shoulder. Ran it up underneath her hair, and gripped the back of her neck. His long nails cut into her skin.

Goose bumps popped out over her body. He said something incomprehensible, in a questioning tone. Tilted up her chin. She felt horribly vulnerable, with her throat exposed, as if he were going to bite her. She sucked in air, tried to speak. Tried again. "I'm, ah, sorry?"

"You are American?"

Uh, what else? She nodded as best she could with her neck hyperextended.

Mr. Big spoke up. "I was just telling him how I hired you to cook for him."

Her eyes flicked toward his. Mr. Big's face was expressionless, but she caught the urgent flash in his eyes. She tried to nod again. "Yes," she said in a strangled voice. "Cook. Yes. Of course. I'm a very good cook."

"Really?" the fat man purred, petting the bump of her larynx with his forefinger, then pressing it. He settled his finger over her fluttering pulse point. "What is your name, my dear?"

"B-becca," she stammered.

"Becca," he repeated. "And what, exactly, do you cook?"

Her throat hurt under the pressure of his finger. She barely heard her own voice, her ears roared so loudly. Booming echoes, black spots dancing, she was going to yark, or faint—

"Crepes à l'orange," she said, seizing at random on the recipe at the top of her head. Her brunch favorite when she wasn't counting calories. "Or if you'd prefer savory instead of sweet, a soufflé laced with a creamy blend of f-four Italian cheeses. Accompanied by sourdough loaf, grilled ham, and a refreshing cocktail of fruit nectar and prosecco."

The silver-haired man's eyebrows twitched up in surprise. "Mouthwatering," he said. "I will sample both."

"If you w-wish," she quavered. "No problem at all."

"But look at you." He spun her around until she faced him, ran his finger along the loose neckline of the blouse. "Explain this. To me, this shirt, this hair, these breasts, so beautifully displayed . . ." His fingers closed around one of them, squeezing until she gasped. "You are not dressed to cook. I think that you are here . . . to fuck."

"We didn't know you were coming this morning," Mr. Big broke in. "She didn't know that—"

"Shut up." The man's hands tightened on her breasts. "I

am tired of listening to you bark like a dog. What is your name, dog?"

Mr. Big's eyes looked like a caged predator's. "Solokov."

"If you speak again out of turn, Solokov, I will have you clubbed unconscious," Silver Hair said. His breath was hot against Becca's neck, scented with licorice. She shrank from the smell as if it were poison gas. Felt the nasty lump of his erection pressing her bottom.

Her gorge rose. She'd never been so afraid.

"So. If you did not bring her here for my enjoyment, Solokov, I can only conclude that you brought her here for your own," the fat man said. "That was selfish." The last word was like a snake's hiss. He nuzzled her throat again. "Pretty," he went on, his fingers drifting lower, between her breasts, over her belly. "Very pretty."

Becca shook. The man's hand moved slowly, every eye following its path. It clamped over her crotch. Her eyes locked onto Mr. Big's.

Don't scream.

She understood his unspoken command. Screaming would escalate the situation. But she had to do something to stop this downward slide into the pits of hell.

"Aren't you hungry?" Her voice came out of her, almost brisk.

The fat man looked annoyed. "Excuse me?"

She flapped her jaw for a few seconds, failing to remember what Mr. Big had called himself right away. "I'm sorry you don't approve of my outfit. I will be happy to put on something more appropriate as soon as possible. Solokov brought me here to cook for you. May I get to it?"

The horrible pressure of his finger against her crotch eased. She almost wilted to the ground in relief.

"Cook, then," he said. "I am tired of the swill from the boat."

She scurried across the boardwalk, and made for Mr. Big

as if he were a lodestone. She grabbed his sinewy arm, nails digging deep.

She forced false assertiveness into her voice. "I need help, if you want me to do both crepes and a soufflé," she informed the fat guy. "It'll cut my prep time in half. If you're hungry."

The man let out a dry chuckle. "Go with her, by all means," he said to Mr. Big. "We will discuss the disposition of your fascinating, succulent little cook after I have been mellowed by brunch."

She bolted for the house, dragging Mr. Big along behind her.

Nick reeled in her wake, towed along by Becca's fingernails, which were sunk into the meat of his forearms. As soon as they were into the foyer, she whirled on him, winding up to demand explanations that he didn't dare give.

He clapped his bloody hand over her mouth, and dragged her along in his turn, down the corridor towards the kitchen.

She tried to tug his hand away, mumbling and squeaking. He shoved her against the wall, bumping air out of her lungs. Just to give him a second's advantage before she started jabbering again.

He leaned forward, trapping her with his body weight.

"Listen to me, and listen good," he hissed into her ear. "You are in deep shit. If you want to live through this, shut up and do exactly what I say, and I mean exactly. If you don't, you'll die. Soon. And badly."

She started to shake. Damn. He was overdoing it. He didn't want her to panic and fall apart on him.

"There are cameras and mikes everywhere in this fucking place," he went on. "This is the story. I hired you to cook for that guy. I offered you two thousand bucks for the weekend. You don't know me. You don't know who he is, and you don't care. I haven't told you any details, and you're not interested in them. You're just here to cook. I'm going to lean back. Nod and smile if we understand each other."

He stepped back, slowly lifted his hand.

Her face was daubed with his blood, her eyes glittering with tears. She dragged a jerky breath of air into her lungs, and nodded.

Smile, he mouthed.

She tried, lips quivering, tugging at the corners. She couldn't quite make it, but it was good enough for him. She tried to speak.

He covered her mouth again. Leaned in close. "Whisper."

"Can't I just run away?" she squeaked. "I'll never say anything. I never saw anyone. I'll just disappear. I promise."

He considered it. Yeah, maybe she could. And then they would rip his guts out for the security breach, like they'd done to Sergei. "Do you have your own boat?"

She shook her head. "I have to call the taxicat at Shepherd's Bay."

It would take the catamaran a minimum of forty minutes to get to Frakes Island from Shepherd's Bay, assuming it had no other jobs lined up. More like an hour, realistically. He couldn't cover her for that long.

He shook his head. "Sorry," he whispered. "Won't work."

She reached out, and gently prodded his sore nose. "Are you going to be OK?" she whispered. "Is it broken?"

He was taken aback. "No," he said, almost flustered. "No big deal."

"It looks terrible," she said. "All that blood. He hit you so hard."

God, she was innocent. He'd taken worse from his dad for letting the coffee boil over. "Nah. Guy hits like a girl." He shoved her ahead of him, herding her into the huge kitchen. "Well?" he said. "Cook, then. Impress me."

Her green eyes narrowed. "First, wash off that blood," she

said. "It's unhygienic, and unappetizing. Are you still leaking?"

He dabbed at his nose gingerly as he turned on the faucet, and glugged dish soap into his hand. "It's stopped," he said, leaning to splash and rub, splattering pink drops all over the sink. Becca joined him, scrubbing at her own blood-smeared hands and face.

"Sorry I got blood on you," he said. "You don't have to worry about it, though. I'm HIV negative, last I checked. Which was recently."

He turned away before she could snag him in those big green eyes. He grasped a roll of paper towels, ripped off a wad to sponge off.

"Me, too," she whispered.

He jerked his head around. "Huh? You're what?"

Her face was hot red. "HIV negative. Just so you, um, know. Guess we should have had this conversation last night, but we didn't."

His hand tingled with sense memory, the slick heat of her pussy tight around his finger as she came. His hands clenched.

Great. Now he could walk this tightrope over the flames of hell with a hard-on, too. Just to make things a little more interesting.

"That's great news, baby," he growled. "Can we get to work?"

She scooped her hair back, twisted it into a rope, and knotted it at the nape of her neck in a loose bun. Swirly brown bits came loose, swinging under her chin.

He dragged his eyes away. "What did you say you'd cook?"

"Soufflé, and crepes à l'orange," she said. "I need eggs. Milk. A lot of butter. A pinch of flour, for the béchamel. Some grated nutmeg, and an assortment of good cheeses. Peccorino, parmesan, asiago, gruyère, anything flavorful. Fresh fruit to purée, prosecco to mix with it, ham to grill, and some bread, to complete the menu I proposed. For the crepes, more eggs, more flour, more butter, some sugar, orange-flower water, kirsch, Cointreau and a dash of cognac. And coffee, of course."

Nick stared at her. "You really can cook."

"I can do a lot of things, Mr. Big," she said acidly. "Face down killers and whip up a tasty brunch? No problem. I do it all the time. So, what don't you have? I can fudge some ingredients . . . but only some."

Mr. Big? Right. He had never told her his name. "Ah . . ." He shrugged, lamely. "I'm not sure."

She flung the fridge open. The inventory didn't take long.

Eggs he had, because they were the type of food that he could prepare. Even scorched, they were edible. And when he was in one of his moods, he just cracked one over his open mouth and gulped down the cold, mucousy glob like a protein pill. He figured it would be a funny joke if he croaked from salmonella poisoning one day.

Butter he had, because toast was another one of those foolproof food items. Milk he had, being as how cold cereal was a third quick-n-dirty survival edible. A few more odds and ends . . . and that was it.

Becca made a disgusted noise, and flung open cabinets, rifling through the contents and plucking things out. There was flour but not much else. She whirled, eyes sharp. "Is this a sick joke? I cannot make a gourmet breakfast for that guy out of stale bagel chips, instant oatmeal and pimiento Cheez Whiz!"

"Don't play diva on me, babe," he said testily. "I didn't come up with that fancy menu, you did. Look in the other fridge or the freezer—"

"Diva, my ass! I've got some decent food over at the A-frame. I'll just, ah . . . go get it."

Yeah. And try to disappear, writing both of our death warrants in one smooth move. "You can't walk out of here," he told her. "They're covering the approach. I'll go get the stuff. You just get started."

"Here? Alone? With . . . them?" Her eyes widened.

"I'll be quick," he promised rashly. "You'll be fine."

She swallowed hard and he saw her back straighten up as she snapped into drill sergeant mode. "The small white boxes have specialty cakes in them," she said briskly. "Get as many as you can. The cheese plate, the ham roast and the fruit are all in the two big white boxes in the fridge. Get both. There's beef and vegetables. And condiments. Don't forget the prosecco. It's chilling in the door of the fridge. Get as many bottles of wine as you can carry. I think we'll need all the help we can get."

Nick pounded up the back staircase and vaulted off the deck, which curved around the huge outcropping of granite that the house had been built around. Clambering down that way put him at a thirty-yard uphill slog to the Sloane house, which he covered in seconds.

Once inside, he assembled the stuff Becca had asked for, tossing it helter-skelter into the boxes, packing wine bottles into plastic bags.

A thought occurred to him. He left the kitchen, and searched through the house until he found it. A little black purse. He dumped the contents, pawed through them. House keys, lipstick, tissue, comb.

He put the lipstick in his pocket for no very good reason.

Cell phone. Wallet. He thumbed through it, plucking out the plastic, the driver's license, everything with her name and address printed on it. The wallet he tossed into an empty drawer by the bed. The credit cards and cell phone he shoved in his pocket, to bury under a rock outside.

He loaded himself up like a donkey, and took off. Sliding and scrambling through clinging vines and thorny bushes, all to make the perfect three-cheese soufflé for the evilest scum-sucking motherfucker in the known universe. It was surreal.

A sound jerked out of his chest, so rusty, he almost didn't recognize it. Laughter.

Mr. Big? How the fuck had she come up with that?

Better not to speculate.

Chapter
7

Keeping busy was the trick. Squinting fiercely, Becca located bowls, utensils and small appliances. Whiz, bang, and there it all was, neatly assembled on the central island. God, how she loved a kitchen with counter space. Too bad she was using it to feed her potential murderers. Or rapists.

Yeah. Béchamel first. Then the crepe batter. Watching butter melt and flour sizzle soothed her rattled nerves. She counted the slow stirs until the sauce thickened, up to ten and back down to zero, over and over, so she wouldn't fall to screaming pieces.

No disasters so far. She set the white sauce aside to cool and whipped up batter for the crepes, grateful for the well-seasoned electric griddle she'd found in a bottom shelf. She'd be able to do six crepes at a time on that thing. Some day, when she'd finally landed Mr. Right and had the perfect kitchen, she'd get herself one of those. A professional-grade food processor, too.

Good girl. Keeping it together. Cool as a cucumber.

The door burst open. Startled, Becca sprang into the air and made a sound that only dogs could hear.

It was Mr. Big, laden with boxes and plastic bags. The

wine bottles clanked together. She was so relieved, she almost burst into tears. "Oh, thank God."

"This shit is heavy," he grumbled.

She tore into the boxes. Mr. Big watched, his mouth dangling open. Ingredients for the soufflé, arrayed in a row on one section of the counter, elements for the crepes on another. Her mind whirled with logistics, timing, sequence. Should she get the soufflé in the oven before starting the sauce for the crepes? If the soufflé was done too soon, they wouldn't be ready to serve it on the spot. It might fall. She couldn't serve a flat soufflé to those guys. They had guns. They would shoot her.

She decided to grate and chop the savory ingredients, then whip up the orange sauce, then assemble the soufflé and pop it in the oven, which left exactly twenty-five minutes to bake the crepes on the griddle and get the ham browned, the fruit blended and the bread toasted. Assuming she had six arms, and that somebody else would deal with linens, dishes and cutlery. And she thought she had job stress at the club.

Mr. Big proved to be worse than useless as a line cook. He was slow, sullen, clouded and uncomprehending.

"What do you mean, orange zest?" he grumbled. "What the fuck is fucking orange zest?"

"If you have to ask, never mind," she snapped. "Grate the cheese into this bowl, fast. Then wash the grater. I need it for the zest. And cut these herbs. Very fine. That should be simple enough for even you."

"Stop bitching," he muttered. "Nobody asked you to get mixed up in this."

"I just came back for my glasses and my keys," she whispered fiercely. "I had to! I'm blind as a bat without my glasses! You might have warned me about this last night! Instead of—instead of—"

"Warned you?" he shot back. "Jesus Christ, I tried to scare you away from here last night. At least until I—we, I mean—got distracted. But any female with half a brain would have run like hell. What was the matter with you?"

Her fault, huh? As fucking*if.* She wrenched the bowl of grated cheese away from him and dumped it into her warm béchamel.

Half a brain, her ass. Hah. Scare her? Sure, if scaring her included kissing her senseless and giving her a transcendental orgasm. And now the jerk was mangling her herbs, too.

"Stop that," she snapped. She yanked his cutting board away and tossed him a peeled onion. "Chop this," she ordered. "Very fine."

He whacked his knife down on the board. The two halves of the guillotined onion flew off the board and rolled to opposite corners of the room. "Christ," he said, in a savage undertone. "What a fucking mess."

"Tantrums do not help," she pointed out sweetly.

He collected the onion, chopped it with a glower that would have intimidated her if she had the time to be intimidated, which she did not. She stared at his chopping technique. "Finer," she said snippily.

"What do you mean, finer? Any finer than this, and it'll be paste!"

"Finer," she reiterated. "Then put them in the saucepan, and stir them constantly. Do not let them burn. They need to caramelize."

He muttered, dumped, stirred. She turned her back to deal with the eggs, sifting through the words he had just said as she separated the whites from yolks.

She dropped the yolks into her béchamel, stirred them gently into the mix until the mixture was tinged with bright sunny yellow. "So, what you're saying is . . . last night you were trying to scare me away? You didn't want me and I just didn't catch on?"

He grabbed a paring knife off the counter and stabbed it into her cutting board, in the midst of her heaps of chopped herbs. They scattered. She stepped back with a soft gasp.

"Wrong," he snarled. "We did what we did because we both wanted to. But I sure as hell didn't think you'd come back. I hoped you wouldn't. Now shut up, do as you're told, and do not fuck with me. Clear?"

She plucked the quivering knife out of the board, and delicately reassembled her piles of herbs, before sprinkling them into the mix.

"I think all this macho bullshit is just for the camera," she whispered. "I really think it is. You're as scared as I am."

"Fuck and double fuck. On top of it all, you're delusional. For the love of Christ, Becca. Shut up and *cook*."

Clink, clink. The utensils against the china made a delicate, musical sound. Becca bent over Zhoglo's plate to lay another slice of ham on it, at such an angle that her tits practically fell out of her blouse. Her face was pale, but composed. Eyes demurely lowered.

Mouth closed, for once. Zhoglo's poisonous vibe shut even her up.

She had class, Nick had to admit. Iron self-control, too, except when Nick needled her. Most girls he knew would be curled up in the fetal position sucking their thumbs under this kind of performance pressure.

The meal had gone well, so far. The fragrant, steaming food had been completely demolished. The platters were bare.

Becca leaned over again with the crystal pitcher of mixed fruit and fizzy wine, filling champagne flutes with a geisha's detached but sensual grace. Four sets of male eyes fastened onto her body. Five, if he counted his own. His jaw hurt from clenching so hard.

She'd make a good undercover agent, he thought. Who would guess what lay beneath that sex bunny exterior? Watching the woman put that meal together had been like watching an Olympic sporting event. Every gesture choreographed for maximum efficiency.

So far, so good. The cook ruse was holding. The meal had been consumed. They had made another shuffling step forward on the tightrope over the pit of man-eating lions. If only she weren't so fucking pretty, she might have a chance in hell of getting through this alive.

Zhoglo polished off the grilled ham, wiped his mouth, and turned his pale gaze upon Nick. "Does she understand this language?" he asked in Ukrainian.

"No," Nick replied.

"I would like for her to satisfy some other appetites, after I digest, of course. The food was delicious. I was betrayed by greed."

A fist grabbed Nick's vital organs and squeezed. "That wasn't part of our understanding when I engaged her services," he said. "My first priority was to make sure the food would be good, Vor—"

"And your second priority was to have something pretty to fuck while you waited on the lonesome, boring island, no? You simply do not want to share. You do not impress me, Solokov."

Nick opted not to reply. There was nothing he could say.

"But after such a tasty meal, I can be reasonable," Zhoglo went on. "If I am sufficiently entertained."

Nick's dread deepened, widened. "Entertained?"

Zhoglo's eyes sparkled. "We have nothing to do this afternoon but stare at this oppressive greenery. So entertain me. With your little friend." He jerked his chin at Becca. "I like spectator sports."

Nick's eyes flicked to Becca. She'd sensed the vibe, gone on alert. Her hands wound together, white-knuckled and pressed against her belly. Her mouth was tight, her eyes big. Silently beseeching him.

"Vor," he said slowly. "This woman is not a professional prostitute. She is not prepared to perform in this way. She will not be able to function as your cook if I do as you propose."

"No?" Zhoglo's lips twisted into a sneer. "Then what good is she?"

"What's on the menu for dinner, Becca?" Nick asked in English.

"An appetizer of spicy Calabrese sausage and an assortment of fine cheeses, to start. Vegetables, roasted and au gratin. Tuscan crostini, with paté, tapenade, roasted red peppers and porcini sott'olio," she said, with reassuring promptness. "Pepper-rolled beef, accompanied by a Montepulciano red. Herbed baby red potatoes, glazed carrots. Fresh sliced exotic fruits with crème Chantilly, coffee, Grand Marnier Chocolate Torte, and an assortment of digestive liqueurs."

Zhoglo blinked a few times. He let out a sigh, and gazed at his plump, steepled fingers. "Very well," he said, sounding faintly petulant. "I will compromise, for the sake of a decent meal."

Nick was about to sigh in relief, but the man kept talking.

"Take her to one of the bedrooms and fuck her there," Zhoglo went on. "We will watch on the monitor in the security room. Will that sufficiently insulate our little dove's delicate female sensibilities? She will still be functional afterwards, no?"

Zhoglo's eyes shone into his, bright and blank and impenetrable. He jerked his chin, a what-the-fuck-are-you-waiting-for gesture.

"If you doubt your ability to perform, one of my men would be happy to screw her in your place," he added softly. "They would be most enthusiastic at the prospect." He paused. "All of them would be."

"What's up?" Becca asked. "Was something not right with the meal?"

"The meal was superb, my dear," Zhoglo said in English. "I'm just waiting for the entertainment, that's all."

Becca looked from Nick to Zhoglo. "I'm afraid I don't understand."

Zhoglo snickered. "By all means, Solokov. Enlighten her."

Nick seized her by the arm, and towed her out of the room.

Becca scurried to keep up with him. His grip hurt her arm. Something was up. Something bad. When Mr. Big bitched and grumbled, she could relax and breathe. But when every trace of emotion vanished from his face, and his eyes went dead and flat, her guts knotted up, her knees started to knock, and spots danced in front of her eyes.

Entertainment? She didn't like the sound of that at all.

He dragged her up the stairs. She got even more nervous, although logically speaking, she should be happier the more distance she put between her and the scary, slobbering guys with guns.

She stumbled on the carpet runner, and he jerked her up to her feet, without even looking at her face.

He slapped the door open into a big, bright bedroom. A picture window looked out over a waving sea of endless evergreens and a heavy gray sky. The glass was beaded with raindrops.

He wrenched off his shirt. She stared at him, speechless. Terrified by the shuttered, implacable look on his face.

He pushed her up against the wall, his big hands stroking her shoulders as he leaned to whisper in her ear. "Showtime, babe. See the video camera mounted up in the corner?"

His meaning sank in. "No way," she said. "You can't be serious."

He unwound the knot of hair at the nape of her neck, and smoothed the tangled strands down around her shoulders, the gesture oddly tender. "Dead serious." He whipped the blouse over her head before she had time to react.

She whacked frantically at his hands. "No! You can't! I have absolutely no intention of letting you—mmph!"

He clapped his hand over her mouth. "I bartered him down to this," he muttered into her ear. "It's me, for the camera, for their viewing enjoyment, or all of them, on the dining room table. Get me?"

She stared at him over his hand, hitching desperately for breath.

"The only reason you're not on that table right now is because that bastard loves to eat. He doesn't want to incapacitate the cook, and compromise his fucking gourmet dinner."

"Oh, God," she whispered. "Oh, my God, this is not happening."

He unhooked her simple cotton bra and tossed it away. She shrank to cover herself. He caught her arms, pinned them wide, to give anyone who cared to a good, long look. "Sorry, beautiful, but this is part of the script," he said. "Nothing personal."

He popped open her jeans, yanked them down along with her panties. She looked wildly from him, to the camera, back at him, trying to cover her naked body. But what horrified her most was the cool, businesslike air with which he was unbuckling his belt.

She gathered her breath to scream. He covered her mouth again, leaning in close. "Don't panic," he murmured, his voice a hot tickle in her ear. "We're going to do some theater for those scum-sucking shitbirds, and you need to make it convincing." He lifted his hand slowly off her mouth, and gave her a hard kiss. "I'm going to put my hand on your crotch," he breathed against her ear. "I'll be gentle. When I signal with my hand, scream like I'm hurting you. Like I'm doing something horrible. Got it? Shake your head, now. Say no, like I'm threatening you. Go on. Do it."

She did so, frantically. "No," she gasped out. "No, d-don't do that. Please, don't do this. Please, please, please."

She listened to her own voice babbling, and observed that this was not theater. Never had words more sincere come from her mouth.

"Good girl," he murmured. He gripped her bottom, hoisted her up so she was straddling his hips, her back pressed against the wallpaper.

He slid his hand between their bodies, cupping her labia

with his fingers. Tenderly, as if he were protecting them. He patted her there.

"Now," he whispered. "Go for it. Scream. Fight me."

She did. Oh, did she ever. She struggled and writhed, slapped and scratched and bit. She couldn't hold back an explosion of anger and shame. She was a natural disaster, a shrieking catastrophe.

He held her, contained her with his unrelenting strength. He clamped her wrists together, pressing them against her chest. She felt folded up, squished and breathless against his rock-hard bulk.

She exhausted herself in the end. She could have been screaming for hours. Days. He would have held her for as long as she needed it.

She dissolved into silent sobs.

He let go of her hands, tilted her chin up so she was staring into his eyes. She panted. Blood trickled out of his nose again. There were angry scratches on his cheek, his chest, his shoulders, but he didn't look angry at her for savaging him. Just quietly intent. He fumbled with his jeans, rearranged her body against his, and slammed his hips upward, hard enough to make her cry out. But he wasn't inside her. His erection bobbed against her inner thigh with each thud of his body against hers.

Theater.

His eyes demanded that she play along. She could do nothing else. She was as shaken as if it were for real, anyway. Her fingernails dug into the thick muscles of his shoulders. She whimpered with each hard lunge. They weren't actually having sex, but this rough faking it was the most intimate act she'd ever engaged in. He was inside her mind. She could feel him. His iron will held her together—he sustained her with his fierce energy. Under impossible circumstances, he was trying to protect something intangible and precious.

Her sense of self.

She squeezed her eyes shut. It was a hopeless attempt, doomed to failure, but it made her feel absurdly cherished. She loved him for it.

Something strange was happening to her, as if she were a radio tuning into a brand new frequency. She forgot about the lust-crazed spectators downstairs. An enormous heat was building up, burning in her throat, her chest. Something twisted open inside her. It hurt. And it shone.

She couldn't tell if it was an emotion or a physical sensation that was clawing through her body. Too intense for pleasure . . . it was a shrill, piercing rapture, charged with terror. It took her, shook her. She screamed, and fainted.

When her eyes fluttered open again, he was very still. He was soaked with sweat, his big, hot body vibrating with tension.

His eyes were wide. He looked shocked. Almost afraid. He scooped her up again, carried her over to the narrow strip of carpet between the bed and the wall. He bumped down onto his knees, then gently set her down on the thick white carpet. He braced himself over her, lying between her splayed legs, jeans halfway down his thighs. His arms shook. His erection rested, feverishly hot, against the curve of her groin.

She gasped for air, smelled dust, paint, carpet. She reached up to his face, touched his bloodied nose, then the scratches on his jaw.

Sorry, she mouthed.

He shrugged. *It's OK*, he mouthed back.

She glanced up towards the video camera, and back at him, silently asking if they were still in its range. He twisted, shook his head.

Becca wiggled, positioning herself. Then she seized his cock, fitting the blunt head against herself. Sliding the tip of him between the folds of her labia. He sucked in a harsh breath, as if he were in pain.

The contact was electric. As if every individual nerve was

being kissed, loved. The slow, slick stroke of flesh against flesh was the sum of all those uncountable tiny caresses, all those little tender exchanges.

You sure? he mouthed silently.

She lifted her hips, seeking more of him in answer. Sure wasn't the word for it. She would implode if he didn't. She needed him.

He let out a heavy sigh and settled between her legs, letting his weight drive his broad shaft slowly deeper inside her.

She curled herself up, propping herself onto her elbows to watch. His thick hair dangled, tickling her breasts. A drop of sweat from his forehead fell right over her heart. Hot. She touched his cheek again, soothing those angry marks, soothing his taut grimace.

He pushed, deeper. The stretch hurt, but she had never felt so open, so yielding and hungry. She let out a low, ragged moan.

He put his hand over her mouth and shook his head.

She understood. This wasn't theater. This was real, and just for them. Stolen pleasure. She kissed the palm of his hand. Arched up to take more of him inside herself. He kept his hand over her mouth and it was a good thing, because she could not stop gasping. The pressure kept building. He rocked and she glowed, soft and liquid around his invasion. Every cautious stroke sent jolts of pleasure sparking along her nerves.

He folded her legs higher, going deeper still. He was completely inside. The glow got hotter, sweeter. Her whole body flushed with pleasure.

She'd never given herself to any man on this emotional level. Not from holding back, but simply because she'd never known that it existed. It was like waking up after being asleep all her life. Acquiring eyes, ears, with no warning, no explanation. Everything he gave to her, she wanted to transform and give back to him, tenfold. Blessing him with it.

Not much time, he mouthed. *Sorry.*

She nodded. Tears trickled from the corners of her eyes. Their hips rocked together in a seductive, swirling rhythm that brought her to constant, endless shuddering peaks and crests of pleasure.

She writhed, body and soul in explosive movement, as energy rushed out of her in ecstatic pulses. Into him, and back again to her, redoubled. And redeemed.

Chapter
8

Back off, dickhead. This is Helsinki Syndrome, or something. A temporary psychological glitch. The woman's scared, she needs to glom onto something. You're handy. Don't get intense about it.

He need not have bothered trying to reason with himself. Not while his body was trying to get as deep inside her as he could. It felt like lightning, blinding him but blazing into every dark, hidden corner of his mind. His desperation laid bare. Death on every side. Get what he could, while he could. Last chance.

So he put it to her, just like she clearly wanted it. Her small, strong body heaved and bucked against his. She clawed at his ass, wordlessly demanding. He gave her what he'd never dared to give any woman: his own hunger hammering away at her, unchecked. His rampaging, oversized prick, driven deep and hard.

She was cushy and tight, milking him with every long, licking stroke, the fantastic friction caressing him, again, again. She took all of him, every inch. Without a condom . . . God, it felt so fucking good. So hot, so wet.

The room was silent, just muted thuds, ragged breath. He kept her mewling sounds muffled behind his hand. Their time was up, but it didn't matter. The drumroll in his balls was already deafening him.

From far away in his mind, he remembered that he should yank it out before he came, but it was just a thread of thought, and it frayed into nothing when the torrent raged through him.

His orgasm was a fountain of violent, sobbing spurts that went on and on and on. As soon as he could control his body, he heaved his limp, sweaty torso up off her. She sucked in a gulp of air, eyes fluttering open.

God, she was pretty. Even with her face ravaged by tears and smeared mascara. The running black paint just accentuated how beautiful she was. How intensely bright the color of her eyes.

He levered himself away. Her soft thighs were still clasped around his. She flexed them, hung on. Didn't want to let go of him.

Her lips formed words, but they were soundless.

"Huh?"

She licked her swollen lips, leaving a glistening film of moisture. "Who are you?" Her whispery voice was ragged from screaming.

He dragged his cock out of the tight clasp of her body. She was dripping with his come. He willed his heart to slow down from that frenzied gallop. "Nobody you should be hanging out with, beautiful."

He broke eye contact before the tears welling into her eyes could overflow, and flopped onto his side, squished against the wall on that narrow strip of rug. He stared up at the ceiling fan.

He'd cracked. It was predictable, after all the bad shit that had come down. But his timing sure sucked.

He'd had good sex, great sex, even awesome sex, but he'd never had sex that made him think he was losing his grip on reality. He didn't dare to look at her. He was about to start crying, for fuck's sake.

Breathe in, breathe out, asshole. Just keep it together. Breathe in, breathe out. That's the way.

She touched his chest. He recoiled from the contact. "Don't get mushy on me, beautiful," he muttered. "It was a great fuck. Leave it."

Dead, flat silence followed his whispered words. He got that just-kicked-a-kitten feeling again. It felt bad.

She was no kitten, though. She was a bad joke, she was a knife in his back, she was the worst luck he'd ever had. Look at him. Death on every side, and he was fucking wildly on the rug and getting all emotional about it, like a thirteen-year-old who'd just lost his virginity.

Although he did not recall being this emotional when he first did the deed. Even at thirteen, he'd been a tough little bastard. He'd just smoked a cigarette and played it real cool. *Hey, babe. No biggie.*

Not an option here. He was destroyed.

She was trying to sit up. He jerked her down onto her back again, struggled up onto his knees and lunged for her discarded blouse and jeans. He shoved them into her hands.

"Show's over," he hissed. "Put these on before you get up in front of the camera."

She gave him a short, jerky nod. She tried to unroll the blouse, but it was snarled, rolled like a nylon stocking, and her hands shook.

Seconds ticked by. He couldn't stand it any longer. He yanked it out of her hands, muttering various imprecations in a muddled mix of Slavic languages until the wad of fabric resembled a blouse again.

He yanked it over her head, tugged it down over her body. She rolled and wriggled until they got it over her torso, and batted his hands away with a catlike hiss when he tried to arrange her tits under the gauzy fabric. Her nipples poked through, without the barrier of a bra.

She writhed on the floor like a lap dancer as she tried to

get her jeans over her hips. Her skin was damp and they stuck to it. She took them off to start over.

He didn't even know what he was doing until he'd shoved her knees wide open. He wanted to look at her pussy.

She struggled, but froze when she heard the low animal sound that came out of the back of his throat. A sound that said *It's my right, and I'll look if I damn well please.*

She clutched his hands where he held her knees, vibrating like a tuning fork. But she let him look.

His exhausted cock twitched and lengthened. Her cunt was as pretty as the rest of her. A miracle of nature, on the scale of sunsets, flowers, starry skies. He imprinted her on his visual memory, the way his fingers knew her, the way his cock knew her. The way his mouth wanted to know her. He was a connoisseur of women's bodies, but Becca's moved him beyond belief.

They didn't have time for this, but he couldn't stop staring at the gleaming dark curls, slick from sex, the pale glow of her thighs. The sinuous narrow slit, the pink inner folds deepening to crimson shiny and hot. Beckoning him. He whiffed her scent, mingled with his own. She was dripping wet with his come. His heart thudded. He'd never seen that before. He kept his sex life rigorously light. He didn't want problems, repercussions. By definition, that made him a firm believer in latex.

The sight had a strange effect on him. A tug in his chest, a fluttery emptiness in his insides. He wanted to lick and taste and suck and savor her, till she screamed. The woman was a live wire. He'd never had anything like this. He wanted more. Hours of it, but they didn't have hours, or even minutes.

He let go of her knees. They snapped shut, like a sprung trap. He hauled her up onto her unsteady feet and yanked up his jeans. "There's an attached bathroom," he said. "Go wash up."

She collected her jeans and underwear, and hurried into the adjoining room. He sank onto the bed, slack-jawed, and listened to water rushing through the pipes. A plan. He had to come up with a fucking plan, but his brain kept slamming against bricked-up dead ends. *Break it down, asshole. Get outside the box. Think, goddamnit.*

His chance to worm his way into Zhoglo's operation was already compromised beyond recall. He hadn't gathered any intel, hadn't planted gulper bugs or beacon locators into Zhoglo's or any of his men's belongings. He hadn't found out what they were doing, or where.

He hadn't found out anything about Sveti. And he had to swallow that down and let it go. Think purely in terms of salvage.

Becca wasn't going to last out the night in this snakepit. They would eat her alive.

If you don't have the guts to do what Zhoglo asks of you, you are dead. If you do have the guts, you are damned.

Tam's words echoed in his head. He'd thought he was dead enough inside to go all the way, get killed. A guy could get used to anything, even being doomed. But now—

He heard voices in the bathroom . . . what the *fuck*?

He was on his feet, bathroom door slapped open in a nanosecond.

Becca cowered against the wall. The bidet swirled and bubbled. Zhoglo's bulky body filled the doorway that opened onto the corridor. Soapy water streamed down her legs and puddled onto the shiny floor around her feet.

She regarded Zhoglo as if he were a gigantic scorpion.

Nick stared from one to the other, like a fucking idiot. Yeah, and what now? Come to her rescue? He wanted to wipe that vicious piece of shit off the face of the earth for the bulge in his pants. For that smile on his swollen, self-satisfied face.

But there was a vid cam in the bathroom and four big guys armed to the teeth downstairs. He could kill Zhoglo with his bare hands, but even if they did manage to jump from the upstairs deck without breaking any bones, Becca was barefoot. They'd be mowed down at twenty meters.

"Magnificent performance." Zhoglo's voice was oily. "Her orgasm, in particular, was extremely realistic. Continue washing, please. A beautiful girl with her hand between her legs, ah. I could watch forever. Go on, finish."

Becca flipped off the water. "Thanks, but I'm all done." Her voice was cool. "I just need to dry off. If you two gentlemen would excuse me?"

Nick was stupefied at her nerve and Zhoglo was startled, too. He stared at her blankly for a few seconds. Then he pulled a hand towel off the rack and held it out to her. "No, I will not excuse you."

Bright color flared in Becca's pale cheeks, but she heard the menace in his voice and kept her mouth shut. She reached out to the towel rack where she had tucked her underwear and jeans.

Zhoglo snatched them out of her reach. He examined the plain cotton panties, sniffed them, and tucked them into his pocket. "No, my dear," he said. "You look charming just as you are." He slung her jeans over his arm.

Becca stared at the man and suddenly her face changed. She gave him a bright, professional smile.

"Well, then. I was meaning to ask you, sir . . . would you prefer coffee or tea for your afternoon refreshment?" she asked. "And would you like Rum Caramel Swirl cake, or Lemon Cloud?"

Wow. Good thought, bait and switch. Nick wanted to cheer.

Zhoglo rubbed his chin. "Coffee," he replied. "With cream. Both cakes."

"Thank you," she said demurely. "I'd better run then. There's a lot of prep work for dinner. Excuse me." She shoved past Nick, into the bedroom. He listened to her soft, quick footfalls retreating out of the room. He hoped she wouldn't make a break for it. Act like prey, and predators snapped right into action.

Nick and Zhoglo stared at each other. "You are breaking her in nicely," Zhoglo said, switching back to Ukrainian.

For what, fuckhead? Nick's jaw ached from staying silent.

"Fiery, hmm?" Zhoglo's eyes narrowed as he observed the blood and scratches on Nick's face. "I marvel at your restraint. Any woman who did that to my face would not long be recognizable as human."

You never have been recognizable as human, shithead.

He swallowed the words back, and smiled thinly. "I barely noticed," he said, turning to the sink. He splashed some water on his face. "I wanted you to eat well. I can't cook."

"Your concern for my comfort moves me. But then again, a man can be generous with the world when he has just fucked a beautiful woman, no?"

"On your orders," Nick said.

"An onerous task, was it? You seemed enthusiastic."

Anything Nick said could get his guts ripped out. He kept his mouth shut.

"You are soft, Arkady," Zhoglo said.

Nick jerked his chin towards the bedroom. "That looked soft?"

The guy stared at him, as if he were a bug on a pin. "I shall ponder that question when I watch the playback," Zhoglo said. "I asked Kristoff to film it. Of course. Would you care to watch it with me?"

The back of his neck crawled. "Ah, no thanks. I can remember it."

"You know why I insist upon electronic eyes and ears in every room, no?"

He shook his head. "No, Vor."

"It takes away the element of uncertainty," he said. "I do not have to wonder whether or not I am being spied on. No lapses. It keeps my employees discreet. And there is the entertainment aspect." Nick nodded.

"It's time we had a conversation," Zhoglo said. "Join me for the coffee and cake, no? I wish to know all about you, Arkady Solokov. Every last detail."

Two hours later, Nick felt like his brain had been hammered flat. The asshole was one hell of a relentless interrogator. No surprise, that.

"Have another piece." Zhoglo shoved the plate across the table towards Nick. "Tell me again about those years with Uncle Dmitri in Debaltseve."

Nick stared down and grabbed a gooey chunk of rum caramel whatever. Maybe a shot of sugar would help.

"It's Donetsk, not Debaltseve," he corrected. "I worked for him there for six years. Then he sent me here to oversee his export operations. He got me a green card, in '93. I've been based here ever since."

Zhoglo clasped his hands over his swollen paunch. "Brokering arms deals?"

"Among other things. Heroin, hash, girls," Nick said wearily.

"And what was his wife's name, again? Margaritka?"

"Magdalena," Nick corrected him, around the mouthful of crumbs.

Zhoglo turned to Pavel, who stood behind him with the automatic rifle cradled in his arms, the barrel of which was directed more or less toward Nick's head. "Pavel, isn't your wife Marya from Donetsk? Perhaps you two are related. The world is small."

Pavel shrugged indifferently.

"It's possible," Nick said. "I wouldn't know. I haven't been there in over a decade."

"An interesting story, Arkady," Zhoglo said slowly. "Consistent, plausible in every detail. And yet, I confess, there are things which perplex me."

Nick pulled his brain into focus, with a painful wrench of mental muscle. "What things are those, Vor?"

Zhoglo steepled his fat fingers and frowned. "Subtle disparities between the man you describe and the man I see before me here."

Nick composed himself. OK. He was going to die. He'd been fine with that before Becca showed up and messed with his mind. Caring put a man in chains. He missed the floating freedom of indifference.

He calculated the angle of Pavel's gun, evaluated various suicidal strategies, seeking the one which would give him the best chance of killing that filthy bastard before Nick bought it himself.

"You strike me as self-possessed, cool, clear-headed, and highly intelligent. You ought to have risen further in life than you have by the age of . . . forgive me, but how old are you, exactly?"

"Thirty-seven on the eighth of April," Nick said.

"Thirty-seven, yes. I would think you would already be a pakhan in your own right, carving out your territory in our profitable global trade. Not just a middleman for minor arms and drug deals. Or a pimp." Zhoglo clicked his tongue, staring at Nick out of slitted gray eyes. "Which brings me to the presence of this woman on the island. She does somewhat cancel out my impression of your intelligence."

Nick manufactured a hangdog look. Goon gone wrong. Play the part, he told himself. "It was stupid, Vor," he admitted. "I ask your pardon."

"You do not wish to be in the position of asking my pardon again."

"I know. And I won't." Nick meant it.

"It does perplex me." Zhoglo went on. "That you would bring her here, knowing that she can never leave this place. I assume you have organized a pretext for her disappearance."

Nick tried to swallow, but his spit had dried up. "Ah. Um. Of course. But you have to admit that she is something special."

"Considering that she is disposable, I am surprised at your sentimental regard for her," Zhoglo mused.

Nick cleared his throat, clutching his mug to hide the fact that his hands shook. So their videotaped sex hadn't been enough. The fucking shark wanted blood.

"She's not my usual type," he said sullenly. "I reacted, that's all. She took me by surprise. And it was of prime importance to keep her in good working condition. As I told you, Vor, I wanted you to eat well—"

"Yes, yes, your care for my creature comforts has been duly noted. Even so . . ." Zhoglo dug into his jacket pocket and took out a pack of cigarettes. He shook one out, and held out the pack to Nick with a benevolent smile. "Please, Arkady. Indulge. You look tense."

Nick lit up and sucked in a lung-blistering drag.

Becca came in with a fresh pot full of fragrant steaming brew. She leaned over Zhoglo's shoulder, did her graceful geisha routine. The gurgle of liquid in that fucker's cup sounded sexual. Nick's jaw ached as she came around and gave him the same treatment. Her tits bouncing under sheer fabric, that whiff of violets—did she have to look so fucking good? Was it necessary? The eyes of every man in the room followed her until the door clicked shut.

"Mmm," Zhoglo murmured. "I love that air of haughty innocence. Attractive, if short-lived, by its very nature. It is always enjoyable to watch a woman learn her true place. I look forward to it."

The smoke left a bitter taste, like a mouthful of dirt. Nick coughed.

"You must keep your cook presentable until this evening," Zhoglo informed him. "A guest is being brought from Shepherd's Bay. I wish dinner to be served to the two of us at seven-thirty."

"Do you need someone to pick up your guest, Vor? I—"

"Yevgeni will handle that," Zhoglo said smoothly. "Becca will provide just the right touch of decadence, half-dressed as she is. And my guest might enjoy her. I'll offer her to him first, while she's fresh and dewy. It is civil to share, no?"

Nick choked on smoke, and coughed again.

"For now, your duties shall be simple," Zhoglo said. "Until I know exactly who I am dealing with, you will restrict yourself to setting tables, chopping vegetables, polishing silver. And live sex shows, of course."

He swallowed. "Ah, yes, Vor."

"Speaking of sex shows, I had regretted not organizing sexual entertainment for my new associate. And behold, my desires are neatly fulfilled. Convenient. She will do beautifully for my guest."

Nick nodded. "I'm, ah, glad."

"After he leaves, however, it will no longer be necessary to, how did you put it? Keep her in working order? We will leave tomorrow morning. She can be put to good use before she is dispatched. My men enjoyed her performance. They have been sitting on a boat with their dicks in their hands for days."

Nick forced his mouth to open. "And your breakfast, Vor?"

Zhoglo shrugged. "I was tempted to wait until after breakfast. She has such a way with eggs. But I would prefer to conclude this business tonight. Even I am capable of forgoing my luxuries now and again."

"I see," Nick said.

"You will do the final honors. Any method you like. The procedure will be taped, of course. What arrangements have you made for disposing of the body?"

Nick cleared his throat again. "Ah . . ."

"I see. You do not have a plan," Zhoglo said. "Now it is clear why you have not risen high in life. You are a man who thinks with his cock."

"No," Nick said. "I have a plan."

"You are pale," Zhoglo observed. "You are attached to the girl?"

Nick shrugged. "No. But she is an excellent cook. It seems a waste."

"You should have thought of that before you brought her

here," Zhoglo chided. "But it is better that the loss be painful for you. One cannot have something for nothing, no? Sacrifice is necessary to obtain something of value. It makes you value it all the more. My trust, my confidence—they have value, Arkady. Incalculable value."

"Yes, Vor," he muttered.

"This shall be your sacrifice," Zhoglo said briskly. "Look upon it as an initiation ceremony. After tonight, you will be one of us." Zhoglo leaned over, and slapped him heartily on the back. His hand thudded against Nick's body, jarring him as if he were made out of cement.

"You shall see," Zhoglo encouraged. "It will be worth it."

Chapter
9

If she kept her mind on a narrow wavelength and charged forward in a state of constant activity, she could function.

Drain the marinade. Roll the beef in the peppers and spices. Cut radish roses. Trim yellow bits from the parsley sprigs. Peel and shape the baby carrots into perfect, uniformly smooth bullet shapes—

Wrong turn. No bullets. She pinwheeled in her head, seeking her delicate balance again. Back onto that narrow track. The Task at Hand.

Go, go, go. Cook a fabulous meal while a cold-eyed thug held a gun on her and stared at her body like he wanted to take a bite out of it. Mr. Big was keeping them both company.

In this bizarre context, Marla's diaphanous peasant top had morphed into a slutty thing that barely covered Becca's butt cheeks. Her nipples showed right through. So did her pubic hair. She could be wearing a feather boa and tit tassels for all it hid. A clove of garlic fell from her numb fingers, and she stared down at it, unwilling to flash any bare, sensitive bits to retrieve it.

God, how she missed her underwear.

Mr. Big scooped up the garlic for her. Everything he did made a mess and cost her precious time, but she couldn't think of dismissing him. She would start to gibber and scream if he left her alone. He was the closest thing to an ally that she had in this house of horrors.

She gave him low-risk, busywork jobs to perform, just to keep him close to her. His eyes had that flat, dead look, mouth tight and sealed, the look he'd had before he'd dragged her upstairs and—

No. She wasn't thinking about that. Stop. Ignore it. All of it. Especially the other man who crouched like a fat spider in the salon, waiting for his dinner.

She was actually quite good at ignoring terrible things. She'd gone through intensive training when she was twelve, when Dad got sick.

Dwelling on that episode of her life was a big screaming no-no, in terms of mood management. But she was miles beyond mood management right now. She was hanging on to sanity by her fingernails.

Just like she had back then. She recognized that sick ache. Grief. Fear. They were hard to tease apart. Hell of a time to be thinking about the bad old days. Maybe her life was flashing before her eyes. She was going to miss her life.

OK, back to the past.

Mom had forgotten that she even had kids, she'd been so focused on taking care of Dad. Becca didn't blame her for it. She'd been the oldest child, nine years older than three-year-old Josh, ten years older than two-year-old Carrie. She'd taken over cooking, groceries, diapers. She'd kept the little kids bathed, gotten them off to sleep, heated Carrie's bottles, cut the crusts off Josh's toast, kept them occupied so they wouldn't be a bother.

She'd soon discovered that being busy helped. It left no time to think about Dad lying in the bed with the morphine drip, that hollow look in his eyes that told her the morphine wasn't enough. No time to dwell on bedsores, bedpans, the smell of disinfectant. Mom's haggard face.

Becca focused instead on getting oatmeal into Carrie's

wriggling body, peanut butter sandwiches and scrambled eggs into Josh's. Getting the laundry done, the dishes washed, the garbage taken out. Busy, busy, busy. It helped. It really did.

By the time it was over and the stash of funeral casseroles had all been eaten, Becca was too deep into the frantic busyness habit to stop. Just as well, too, because Mom fell apart definitively after Dad's death. She was used up. There was nothing left for the rest of them.

From then on, it fell to Becca to keep it together. She learned to write checks and pay bills at the age of twelve. When she was thirteen, she learned the dire consequences of forgetting to pay property taxes for two years in a row. She put off creditors, dealt with the bills herself so that the past-due notices wouldn't send Mom off on a crying jag.

Or sink her into an even darker mood, when she would sit on her bed staring at the bottle of morphine capsules. Dad had hoarded a lethal dose of them early in his illness to have a way out if it got too bad. He'd never used them, but it had comforted him that they were there.

It didn't comfort Becca. She combed the house for them when her mother was out, hoping to flush them down into the sewer, where they belonged. In the end, her efforts were in vain. Terrible things happened no matter how prepared you were.

No amount of scurrying and effort could stop them. No mercy.

Dad's stash hadn't gone to waste, depending on your point of view. By the time Mom swallowed those pills, Becca had become expert at a lot of things, and seeing things from everybody else's point of view was one of them.

She understood Mom's despair. She understood Josh's fighting, his problems in school. Carrie's clinginess, bedwetting, nightmares, anxiety attacks. She understood the bank's regretful necessity to foreclose. Mortgages had to be paid. That was how the merciless world worked.

She understood their relatives, none of whom wanted to deal with the financial and emotional can of worms that was her orphaned family.

She even understood the point of view of the life insurance people, when they'd informed her that the policy was void in the case of suicide.

Well, of course. Any reasonable person could see why. Becca was a reasonable person. She'd been reasonable about giving up going to college, in spite of the scholarship she'd been offered. It was flattering that they'd offered it, but it paid only tuition. Not for a roof over Josh and Carrie's heads. Not for food for three, pediatricians, school clothes, sneakers, and all the rest.

Yeah, she understood everybody's point of view but her own. She couldn't afford a point of view. It was a window she didn't dare peer out of. She was terrified of what she might see.

Anyway, fuck it. Remembering all that wasn't going to help her now. Her eyes caught the gun-toting guy leering at her. He licked his lips. Rearranged his testicles.

Oh, God. Her stomach flopped, turned upside down.

No choice but to face it, straight on. Stark reality. As bad as it got. Like the day she found Mom on her bedroom floor.

What had happened upstairs with Mr. Big had leveled her defenses. Neurotic though they might be, they'd been all she had. They were in ruins. Colors were overbright, noises jangly, too loud or else fading out. The faces of the men in the kitchen stood out in high contrast. Carved by shadows sharp as knives, as black as ink. She glimpsed horrible things in the depths of their eyes.

"Keep it together," Mr. Big whispered, shoving a paper towel into her hand. "Mop up your face. Stop sniveling. Get ready to serve wine and the appetizers."

Sniveling? Snotty *bastard.* She dabbed her eyes and pressed the paper towel against her mouth. The anger focused her. And he knew it.

He stuck his hand into his pocket and rummaged till he came up with . . . her pink lipstick. Of all things.

"Showtime again. Don't faint on me, for fuck's sake." He uncapped the lipstick and held it out to her. She applied it with a shaking hand. It was warm from his body heat.

He looked her over, and tugged her plunging neckline up so that her nipples no longer peeked over the edge of the blouse. She grabbed his hand. "Please, don't," she said. "If you do, it shows my—"

"Aw, fuck." He scowled at the tuft of pubic hair that he had revealed.

"It's one or the other, you see." She shook with hysterical giggles.

He muttered something vicious in that unknown language, and put the tray with the decanted wine, wineglasses and appetizers into her hands.

The glasses rattled. He put his hands over hers to steady them. His hands were so warm. Strong.

He nudged her along in the direction of the dining room. They stopped outside the door. He leaned down, gave her a swift, firm kiss on the cheek.

"Watch out," he muttered. "And *smile,* goddamnit."

He opened the door and gave her a push that made her stumble a little. Becca stretched her pink, shiny mouth, feeling like a plastic doll. Her bare toes gripped the carpet to steady herself. She felt damp with chilled sweat. Stippled with goose bumps, all over her body.

Someone had lit the candles. The tapers glimmered. Her nearsighted eyes swam with tears. She could barely see the two men seated at the table. Tears swirled the points of light into a bright blur. She squeezed her eyes shut, let them flash down her face. She couldn't wipe them away with a tray in her hands.

The men swam into focus as she approached. *Smile, goddamnit.*

She could do that. Smiling, acting cheerful while she was actually dying inside was a skill at which she excelled, although she secretly wasn't sure whether it was a skill she should be proud of. But it was coming in handy now.

The two men stopped talking as she approached the table. She had a brief moment of total vertigo, and a switch was thrown inside her.

She couldn't call it courage. It felt more like an automatic default mechanism kicking into action. An emergency generator that came on during a power outage. Just enough juice for basic function. No frills.

She set the tray on the sideboard, flashed a brilliant smile at the men seated at the table. She set out their glasses, poured their wine with practiced grace. Automatic gestures, programmed into her from years of waitressing jobs and catering gigs. She caught a glimpse of the Spider's guest when she poured his wine. He didn't really notice, being busy checking out her boobs.

He looked like he belonged at her country club. Late forties, handsome, distinguished. Graying temples, white teeth, perfect tan, reeking of privilege.

"And what have you prepared for us, my dear?" the Spider asked.

She smiled, smiled, smiled, as she set out the antipasti. "You'll start with four different types of bruschetta, and an assortment of fine Italian cheeses and sausages. Then we'll move on to roasted zucchini dressed with mint and lemon, eggplant gratinée, grilled portobello mushrooms, and roasted stuffed red peppers. Wafer-thin slices of Piedmontese capicollo, dressed with flakes of grana, arugula, and the very best Pugliese olive oil, followed by slices of spicy Calabrese sopressata . . ."

And so on and so forth. Hyped-up foodie blather was second nature to her. Thank God for her years of restaurant work. She had been able to put a feast like this together and buy a little time.

Or maybe not. She noticed the lustful greed smoldering in the Spider's eyes.

When she retreated to the door, she was uncomfortably aware of the men's gaze fixed on her bottom, the undercurve of which hung right out of the loose peasant blouse. It took all her self-control to walk slowly.

The door closed. She sagged against it, gulping in air.

Time wore on, and as dinner progressed it seemed, at least on a superficial level, to get easier. It even took on an air of apparent normality—if she ignored her lack of underwear, the scowling armed guard, and everything else that had happened that day.

Snippets of the conversation floated through the barriers of fear and tension in her brain. The two men didn't talk of murder, drug trafficking or anything obviously evil or illegal. She tried to remember the headlines she'd glanced at online a day or so ago. *Homicidal Sex Fiends Invade Pacific Northwest*? Nah. Nothing like that.

The Spider and his guest chatted about world politics, global economics, natural gas, the stock market. But as they consumed more wine, they began looking at her in that unmistakable way that made her body cringe with dread.

She almost dropped a filet of beef right into the Spider's wineglass when he grabbed her buttock. His hand was moist and hot, his pudgy fingers pulling up the blouse until her bottom was completely exposed.

"Beautiful, hmm?" he commented to his guest. "Look at this. Perfection. So round. Smooth as a rose petal."

She was motionless, her gorge rising as those humid fingers traced the cleft of her bottom. Poking, prodding.

"Very." The Spider's guest let out a manly chuckle. The smug sound of a guy who was not unused to situations like this.

She made the colossal mistake of meeting his eyes, her pink smile plastered across her face like a rictus of pain.

He didn't really see her, even when he looked straight into her face. His eyes glittered with speculative interest. He lifted his glass to the Spider. "To beauty," he said, and drank deeply.

"To desires fulfilled," the Spider added. They drank again, their throats working.

The Spider's hand tightened. "Turned into a statue, my dear? Put that meat upon my plate and refill my guest's glass."

She poured wine into the proffered glass, noticing the burnished gleam of a wedding band on the man's hand. Cheating slimebucket. As before, her anger focused her. She drizzled the meat with sauce, imagining herself spitting on it instead. The Spider grabbed her blouse, tugged it. One of her nipples popped out. Her control snapped, and she jerked away. "Excuse me. I'll just go and get the . . . the f-f-fruit."

As soon as the door closed behind her, she ran, hand over her mouth, and barreled into something as unyielding as a brick wall.

It proved to be Mr. Big. He grabbed her shoulders.

"Please," she gasped out, from behind her hand, before he could start scolding her. "I'm going to throw up. Right now. *Please.*"

He swung his arm around her shoulders and scooped her along in his wake, hustling her out onto a side deck.

Just in time. She hung over the railing, vomiting up her very soul, along with the half sandwich and coffee Mr. Big had insisted that she choke down earlier.

She dangled there, slung over the railing like a forgotten rag doll, spitting out the bitter strings of snot and bile. Eyes streaming, nose bubbling, bare ass hanging out for anyone to see. Not that she cared.

A big, warm hand on her shoulder made her jump. It was just Mr. Big again, shoving a wet linen napkin into her hand. She cleaned her face. "I c-c-can't go back in there," she stammered. "I'm too scared."

"You have to." His face was resolute, hard as stone.

She pressed the wet rag against her shaking mouth and

tried to suck enough air into her lungs to speak, to make him get it. "You don't understand," she gasped out. "He keeps putting his hand between my legs. I think they want—that they're going to—"

"Becca." He gripped her shoulders. "I am trying to help you." He enunciated each word so that they punched into her head. "But the timing's not right yet. You have to go back. I need . . . more . . . time."

Vibrating with fear, she didn't fight back.

"Do you want to live?" he hissed.

She stared into his eyes. She mouthed one soundless word. *Yes.*

"Then buy me more time. Serve the fruit, the coffee, the dessert. Stay sharp. Keep your eyes open. Be ready for anything. And whatever you see me do, don't scream. Got that?"

He waited a few seconds, and gave her shoulders a tooth-rattling shake. "Got that?" he hissed.

"Got it." The words came out in a halting whisper.

He snatched the wet napkin out of her hand, and swiped it roughly over her face, beneath her eyes. She felt like a bewildered kitten being groomed, knocked and battered around by its mother's tongue.

He pushed back the hair that clung to her damp face, spun her around and gave her a push towards the door. "Get on with it."

She shuffled like a robot to the kitchen to collect the fruit and crème. Her mind looped and spun around like a carnival ride, struggling to derive hope from what he'd said. Trying to help her? That was good, as far as it went. Buy him time? Did he mean by letting those men have sex with her? She stumbled down the corridor, tried to picture it.

Could she . . . ? To save her own life?

No.

She pushed open the door, let the emergency generator kick into action. Smile, smile, smile. Her heartbeat was deafening in her head.

Becca began serving the fruit plate with practiced grace, the fan of pineapple here, gleaming strawberries there, the fleshy strips of mango, the pyramid of raspberries. She drizzled crème over the berries, letting some puddle to the side. A subtle turn of her serving spoon mixed berry syrup into the puddle, creating a delicate butterfly-shaped swirl.

Voices booming, fading, swelling in volume again. ". . . structure is completely outfitted with state-of-the-art equipment, and the waiting list is already growing. I'll conduct one last round of testing before we—"

"We can talk business onboard," the Spider cut him off.

His guest's eyebrows rose. "I beg your pardon?"

The Spider slanted his eyes meaningfully toward Becca and back to his guest. "I wish to avoid electronic eavesdropping. My boat is under constant guard. We'll go out a hundred meters from the shore, and discuss the practical details there."

"Ah. As you wish," the man replied doubtfully.

"Focus upon pleasure, rather than business," the Spider invited, as his hand slid up Becca's thigh, his fingers digging into her groin.

Becca's hands jerked. A strawberry fell, bounced off the Spider's powdered-sugar-dusted plate and onto the table, leaving an unsightly streak that stained the linen with a smear that looked horribly like—

Blood. She fished the berry up, murmuring an apology. His fingers slid into her pubic hair, groping.

"Before we take the boat out, would you like to have her?" the Spider offered, as casually as if he were offering his guest a drink.

"But I—but—" Her protest choked into a squeak as his hand turned to a claw, and his long fingernail dug into her clitoris.

The pain was awful. Faintness rolled over her. If only she could just let go, fall back into the dark. Forever. She stared at the obscenely red, wet, gleaming fruit on the plate. Hung on to consciousness.

"You could have her right here, or there are bedrooms upstairs, if you require privacy," the Spider said. "Whatever you prefer."

The other man cleared his throat. "My. I am tempted."

She looked into the man's eyes. It was true. He was considering it. She could tell from his flush, the slackness in his mouth, the emptiness in his eyes, that he was imagining it. That he was aroused. He looked right at her, but he still didn't know she was there. All he saw was himself, using her.

The hatred she felt was so intense, she wanted to spit into his eyes, grab a knife, stab it right into his throat.

She could never endure that smug, self-satisfied face, reddened with wine and lust, hanging over her as he humped away. Her stomach lurched. Good thing she'd emptied it. Or maybe not. Projectile vomiting was one sure way to kill a man's sexual buzz.

On the other hand, the Spider would be unamused.

Buy me time, Mr. Big had said. But what would she have to pay for it?

She focused on the Spider's pudgy face. "What about dessert?" The voice that came out of her was pure restaurant robot, breathlessly feminine. "I'm flattered at the attention, gentlemen, but you don't want to miss my Grand Marnier Angel's Fall cake. It's a flourless but tender chocolate torte that melts in your mouth, flavored with orange liqueur, layered with mousse, and enveloped by a thick layer of dark Belgian chocolate."

At the mention of dessert, the Spider released her clit. Her knees almost buckled in relief. He gave her buttocks an approving squeeze. "Perhaps we'll wait then, my dear. Just long enough to sample your masterpiece."

The other man blinked. "Certainly," he muttered. "Whatever you wish. A very small piece for me, please."

Smile, smile, smile. "I'll go prepare the dessert tray."

She made it out the door, but that was it. No more buying time for anybody, for any reason. Her sanity was shattering.

She would use what time she had left to search the utility closet for something toxic to drink, or else run out screaming into the night and let them shoot her in the back. She would do any crazy, desperate thing before going into that room again.

That resolve firm in her mind, she hurtled towards the kitchen—and tripped over something big and dark sprawled across the corridor. Splat, she landed facedown and hard, in a puddle of—

Blood. Lots of blood. Her head lifted, slowly. She squinted into the kitchen, tried to focus her nearsighted eyes.

She abruptly wished that she hadn't.

Chapter
10

Becca's timing sucked. Why was he not surprised?
Nick lowered Yevgeni's twitching body to the ground and
wedged as much of it as he could into the vid cam's blind
spot. Damn. Five more seconds, and he'd have been able to
intercept her in the corridor.

Still, he was cool—back in the ice cave. The more blood
he spilled, the deeper he went. It was always that way.

Don't scream, he told her with his eyes. He'd left Anatoli
in one of the vid cam's other calibrated blind spots, but anyone watching the monitor would have noticed her tripping
over an unseen obstacle. Luckily, the arterial gout had aimed
itself down. Walls spray-painted with blood tended to catch
the eye. He wiped his knife hastily on the guy's shirt.

Becca looked, appalled, at the blood she'd slalomed in on,
at her crimson hands, at the wet red knife in his fist. Her pupils
dilated. Her mouth sagged. Time to beat hell out of there,
Nick thought, before she sucked enough air into her lungs to
start the screaming meltdown he could sense coming.

He yanked her to her feet, staying low, and dragged her
over the pile of dead meat formerly known as Anatoli. She
was slippery, but blood got tacky soon enough. Like glue.

Back through the corridor, onto the side deck where she'd

lost her lunch. She made a high-pitched noise when he dragged her over the third corpse, shoved into the shadow of a conveniently overgrown tree.

Three down out of seven. Pavel was bodyguarding Zhoglo in the dining room, Mikhail was guarding the boat, Kristoff manned the vid monitors. One more was unaccounted for, probably on his way back from the dock. In a very few seconds, Kristoff would notice that he had lost visual contact. He would try to raise the other guys on the comm gear. He would fail. And Nick and Becca would be toast.

To her credit, Becca was quick and light on her feet. She made a lot of noise gasping for breath, but she wasn't screaming.

He came to a stop at the blind curve on the wooden walkway, steadied Becca and strained with every sensory organ for information about what was around that bend in the dusk-shrouded forest. The vibration that had alerted him resolved into actual noise. The frantic speed of the guy's thudding bootsteps told him they'd been made. No point in not using his piece then.

The tall blond guy came barreling round the corner, talking softly into his comm. There was just time for his eyes to widen before *thhhtp*, the bullet from Nick's silenced SIG 229 drilled him in the forehead. The guy's head snapped back and he ran on out from under himself, thudded heavily down and slid, half-on, half-off the boardwalk.

Easy. He dragged her past the corpse. Four down in less than five minutes. Not bad, for toast. Becca was starting to stumble, legs shaking beneath her. Going into shock, probably. The joke would be on him.

It was a miracle they'd gotten this far. He'd worked out the formula for this opportunity in his head. Several separate windows of opportunity had to line up perfectly long enough for him to jump through them and bring Becca with him.

He couldn't take out seven armed guards at once. It had to be when Zhoglo and his new associate were distracted by their dinner and Becca's tits. Guarding them would occupy Pavel. It had to be at the change of the boat guard, so that one man would be patrolling the front approach, not two. It had to be in careful sequence—front deck, corridor, kitchen—and done in dead silence, no gasps, shrieks, grunts or gunshots. It had to happen in quick succession. And finally, Becca had to appear at the right moment, keep her mouth shut and her shit together. Which she had. So far.

At this point, it broke down to running fast and hoping hard. Hoping the Vor's manpower was reduced enough so that he would cut his losses and let them go for now. Hoping that he wouldn't want his men to race after them with the boat, leaving him stranded and vulnerable on the island. Lots of hopes. Hope was a bitch. Nick mistrusted it bitterly. It set a guy up for disappointment every time.

He jerked her to a stop. She stumbled onto her knees. He leaped off the walkway, and plunged into the foliage, dragging her behind him. She made noise as the thorns and rocks tore up her bare feet.

Tough shit. Feet healed. Dead didn't.

He pushed on, shoving through branches, abandoning stealth. It was all about speed now. And he had speed hidden down there in the water, if they could get to it before they got drilled.

He'd thought long and hard about providing himself with this bolthole, as if the implied lack of total commitment could jinx him. It had. He should have managed himself like the commanders of armies in ancient times had managed their soldiers. Lighting fires behind the troops. No retreat possible.

His last chance to find out Sveti's fate was gone. He'd have given up everything he had, every last drop of his own heart's blood, for that.

But he hadn't been able to give up Becca's.

The horizon opened up before them at the water's edge, with the last of the sunset staining the sky, the fishy, weedy smell and gurgling of water all around them. There was no beach, no dock, just white roots sticking out over the dark water like bones, the water heaving and sucking and lapping beneath them.

He let himself noiselessly down into it, and grabbed Becca's waist, expecting her to shift her weight for him. She went rigid, clinging to a tree, shaking. Seconds ticked away, lost forever.

He lifted his hands, rage pricking at his calm. "You've got two seconds to decide," he said. "Come with me, right now, or go back to him. Try apologizing. Smile pretty. See where it gets you."

She laid her shaking hands on his shoulders. He lifted her down.

She sucked in a sharp breath at the water's icy bite and slogged clumsily after him, stumbling over boulders in the dark water.

She tripped, would have gone under if he hadn't grabbed her. As it was, she was soaked up to her armpits now, teeth chattering.

Great. If she hadn't been going into shock already, this would do the trick. He ducked under the low cave formed by a couple of dead trees that had fallen into the water, unmoored the camouflaged Zodiac Futura inflatable that he'd borrowed from Seth Mackey. He dragged it out.

An excellent toy. He had to get one of these for himself, if he survived. Powerful outboard motor. Speed tubes with hydrodynamic lift to zoom over the surface of the water. He heaved Becca into it. She rolled in like a sack of potatoes. He clambered in after her, braced for the slice of lights through the trees, gunshots.

Nothing yet. Too good to be true.

The motor hummed smoothly to life. He moved out to deeper water, trying to hug the shore until they rounded the curve, and then he let out the throttle.

*   *   *

Becca had never been so cold. She'd never imagined such cold. Every muscle of her body convulsed individually as they tried to heat her up. She dragged herself slowly up from her huddled position.

The wind slapped her, whipped at her wet hair, dragging tears from her eyes. She noticed in an emotionless way that her blouse had been torn from her shoulder on that rampage through the forest. It dangled in a sodden swag, completely exposing one goose-pimpled boob.

She barely noticed.

He was saying something. She leaned forward, struggled to hear over the roar of the wind in her ears. "Huh?"

"Thermal blanket," he said, pitching his voice just loud enough to reach her ears and pointing. "There. Get it before you freeze."

Her numb fingers were about as responsive as a bunch of stiff dead fish, but she finally found the thing, and clawed open the waterproof plastic packing. She wrapped it gratefully around herself.

She peered at Mr. Big as he gazed ahead. Hair flying back off his face, eyes narrowed against the wind, the image of stony concentration.

His sleeve was stained with blood up to the elbow.

Visions of what she'd just seen assailed her. Pools of blood, gaping slashes in thick throats. The stupid surprise on the face of the guy with the hole between his eyes.

She'd been pushed over so many unthinkable barriers today, she was in an altered state. The menacing bulk of the islands rose out of the vast expanse of silvery water, towering over them like huge beasts about to pounce. The sky was cobbled with lumpy clouds and night was coming on fast. The lurid stripe of pink on the horizon faded before her eyes.

She was in limbo. Her grim, silent escort was terrifying as the hooded ferryman on the river Styx. Skilled at killing. As if it were something he did on a regular basis. She gulped. It made her throat hurt.

She stared at her toes, so cold they no longer even felt like they were hers, and tried to speak. She couldn't suck enough air into her lungs to make a sound. Islands flew by, plumes of spray arced behind them. Finally, she made herself heard over the roar of the motor, asking a question she didn't think he'd answer. "Who *are* you?"

His gaze didn't even flick down. "Not now!" he yelled.

Not now? She'd been scared out of her wits, abused, insulted, threatened. "I want some goddamn answers!" she shrieked.

He slowed the boat, killed the motor. They slid forward in the sudden silence on leftover momentum, rocking side to side on the inky black heaves.

"OK, then. Listen hard. Hear anybody coming after us?"

She listened. She heard wind, water, her own chattering teeth.

"No," she said.

"The correct answer to that question is 'not yet.' Followed by, 'but pretty fucking soon.' Do you have any idea how lucky you are to be alive?"

"Oh, I'm supposed to be grateful?" Her voice shook, splintered. "Gee, thanks! I want to know why I was in danger of getting killed in the first place! Who were those psychos? And who the hell are you?"

"Your timing blows. Shut up and—"

"Stop it!" She grabbed his arm. "You've been saying that all day! Shut up and do as you're told, or die! Guess what. I no longer give a shit!"

"Fuck." He shook her off and she thudded heavily down to the bottom of the boat on her butt. "Do you want us both to drown? Stay still."

She rose up onto her knees. The boat rocked violently. "What, am I *bothering* you?" she hissed.

"Hey." He grabbed a handful of the thermal blanket and jerked her closer to him. "You may find this hard to believe, but slitting throats is not one of my top five favorite activities. Truth is, it puts me in a foul mood—"

"You're insane!"

"Right. I started out that way and went straight down from there. Now listen. Arguing is a waste of time that could cost us both our lives. Do you understand that?"

The force behind his words knocked her backward. Everything she had just witnessed him do came back to her again in a sickening rush. He operated, if that was the right word, with the lethal precision of a specialist.

The bubble of manic courage was popped. She was cowed again. She gave him a small nod, and huddled into the blanket.

He turned away. The motor roared back to life. The boat picked up speed until it was skimming over the choppy, wind-whipped waves.

Maybe it was enough to get through the day with her life intact. She could worry about her pride later.

Becca kept her mouth shut for the time it took to get to Crane Cove. Nick was grateful for that small favor. The ice cave in his mind was great for certain complex mental activities, like calculating bullet trajectories and wind vectors, but it was not the mental place to be when dealing with a stressed-out, hysterical woman.

They rounded a bend, and the lights of Crane Cove spread out before him. So there was to be no high-speed boat chase, no bullets flying. Almost home free. It was uncanny how lucky they'd been.

First, he had to get Becca squared away, returned to wherever she belonged, and then he would have to face up to his own personal failure.

He pulled into the marina. It seemed quiet enough. He'd considered renting a slip at Shepherd's Bay, which was closer, but the marina was small, and people were more likely to comment on his boat or notice his truck. Crane Cove was no bustling metropolis, but it was several times larger than Shepherd's Bay.

And they were conspicuous. He was soaked, spattered with blood, and he had a near-naked woman in tow. Anybody who saw him would have lots to tell the private investigator whom Zhoglo would send. He'd used a false ID to rent the slip. Looked like that ID was a goner, if the place had a security camera. He hated compromising alternate ID's. They were expensive.

He moored in his slip. Dim lights, no sound. A nothing evening in Nowheresville. Good. He climbed out of the boat, hauled on a line to draw it closer to the dock, and beckoned to her. Spent a teeth-grinding eternity waiting for her to collect herself to her feet and get out.

True to form, her blanket slipped seductively down to show off the outfit. Classic Penthouse Pet material: naked tits, transparent fabric clinging to tight nipples, dark muff. Her hand was like ice when she grasped his. Her legs shook under her like a newborn foal's.

"What now?" she asked. Her voice was husky and raw from the wind.

He yanked the blanket away from her and wrapped her up like a burrito, then scooped her into his arms. She protested and wiggled, but she was effectively neutralized, swaddled in the blanket.

"We'll talk in my truck," he muttered.

"Your truck?" She stiffened in his arms. "Wait! Aren't we going to the police? We have to tell them what happened, don't we?"

He nuzzled her fragrant hair, noticing at random that she still smelled faintly like violets, though she tasted like salt. "In my truck," he reiterated. "Where we won't be seen or heard."

"But I—but we—"

"And after we talk, if you still want to, I swear I'll leave you at the local cop shop," he lied. "Cross my heart."

That calmed her down, and he made good time through the walkways of the deserted marina. The darkened shopping district was quiet too. The empty street outside the gate was dotted with pools of orange light at regular intervals. Nobody in them. He hurried to the long, graveled strip along the water that functioned as marina parking.

There was a bar up the street. Nick saw the flicker of a large-screen TV, heard a guttural roar of male voices crying out in unison. Some big sports event—that explained the deserted streets. He had no clue what the sport might be. He'd been out in orbit for too long.

There was his truck, waiting where he'd left it some days before. Not stolen or vandalized. One advantage of living in Nowheresville. Except that he'd grown up in a place like this, and he'd been the kind of no-good punk who'd have made sure that any abandoned truck was properly fucked up before its owner came back to claim it. At the very least he would have slashed the tires. They must sedate the teenagers in this town. But he'd take any luck he could get, however undeserved.

He bundled Becca into the passenger seat without ceremony and got that sucker fired up with a roar of the motor, spattering gravel. Becca braced herself on the dash and gave him her owl-eyed look. She fumbled for the seat belt.

He dragged his cell out of his pocket, and punched in a number.

An irritated female voice answered in Ukrainian. "Who is this?"

"Milla. It's Arkady," he said rapidly in the same language. "It's all gone to shit. My cover's blown. So watch your back."

"What? What? He will kill me now! You asshole! You fool! How can you do this to me?"

"Just thought I'd warn you," he said evenly. "Good luck." He hung up over the woman's shrill protests. There was nothing else he could say.

Becca gazed at him. "And the police?" she asked.

He chose his words carefully as he stepped on the gas. "This is the deal with the police," he said. "If you tell them what you saw, they're obliged to investigate. A lot of things might happen, all of them bad. Most likely some locals will be killed before they get wise to exactly what they're dealing with. As in cold-blooded murder. Film at eleven. And no, I'm not being sarcastic."

"But isn't that just what we're going to tell them?" Becca forced the words out from between her chattering teeth. "Exactly what they're dealing with, I mean."

"We can tell them anything we want," he said. "Men and women with families will still get killed. It's a statistical certainty."

"Ah." Her throat worked. She put her hand up to it, massaged it.

"And there's another thing, too," he went doggedly on. "Right now, he doesn't know anything about you. Not your name, your address, your work, nothing. You have no idea how fucking fortunate that is."

"Oh, but I do," she snapped. "Since you never miss an opportunity to remind me of my great good fortune."

He was relieved to hear that snippety tone. A woman in shock would not be giving him hell. She was so much tougher than her sex bunny looks would suggest.

He found his train of thought. "What I'm saying is that if you blow the whistle on Zhoglo here, that gives him a place to start when he comes looking for you. And he will come looking for you. Count on it."

"Is that his name?"

Nick slammed a hand into the steering wheel. "Yeah."

"But the police would never give him my—"

"You have no idea how powerful this guy is," he said. "He's got a reach you cannot imagine. Info can be accessed on shared databases, Becca. It can be hacked, stolen, bought. Everything is for sale. He's already corrupted the feds. He'd get around the local law."

The bitterness in his voice silenced her, but only for a minute. "Why would he bother looking for me? I was just the cook, right?"

He made a derisive sound. "Where do I start? He didn't get a chance to fuck you, for one thing. That's reason enough right there."

"Never mind," she whispered. "Sorry I asked."

"And you saw him," he went on relentlessly. "You saw his new business partner, too. You were scheduled to get snuffed the minute you got a good look at Zhoglo's face, Becca. Let alone all the rest of it."

She kneaded the silvery blanket with desperate, nervous strength. "Who is he?" she whispered.

"You don't want to know. The other reason he'll want you is because he'll want me. He's capable of chopping my dick off and feeding it to me piece by piece. Not exaggerating."

She winced.

"Given what happened tonight, he'll assume that you're the path to me. And he'll be coming for me. Like a freight train."

She was quiet for a long time. He was almost lulled into thinking that she'd conked out into a swoon of exhaustion and would leave him in blessed peace. Then she cleared her throat. No such luck.

"Um, this is kind of a hard thing to say, so please don't get mad at me, OK?"

He braced himself. "Have at it."

"Ah . . . you did what you did to those men to save me. To get me away from the island before that guy . . . before he could . . ."

"Yeah," he broke in, impatient. "And?"

"Well, first off, thank you," she said, in a breathless rush. "I don't know why you did that for me, but thank you."

The pause after those words begged the question, so he thought about it for a second. "I don't know why I did it either."

He got the sense that what he'd said was not the answer she had hoped for. This did not surprise him. The reality of Nick Ward always shocked the ladies, once they got a clue what they were dealing with. Usually, he fled the scene before that development.

"Well. Hmph," she said, with a disapproving cough. "What I'm trying to say is that, ah, considering your work, and, um, the people you associate with, I understand why you don't want to have anything to do with the police. But I'm very grateful to you for saving me, and therefore, when I make my statement, I won't mention you. If you just take me to the station and let me go, I won't say one word about you. If they have me look at pictures, and I see yours, I won't ID you. It's not like I know . . . hey, stop that! What's so funny?"

So Becca thought he was one of Zhoglo's goons. It was inevitable, but for some reason it struck him as funny. Dry laughter snorted out of him, racking his chest, making his throat hurt, his eyes sting.

"Oh, that's good," he said, wiping his eyes. "That's great, Becca. Tell them you took out four armed mobsters and fled the island all by yourself. The naked girl commando. Sounds like a video game. They'll be coming in their pants when they take your statement."

"Do not make fun of me." Her voice had gone chilly. "There's nothing amusing about this. At all."

"Oh, no," he agreed. Laughter jolted his ribs. "Not at all."

She waited, radiating disapproval, until he got himself under control. "Are you finished?" she asked. "Can we discuss this like adults?"

Becca had nerve, talking like that to a guy she took for a badass criminal. "I was infiltrating that organization," he said. "I'm not one of his thugs. I was undercover."

She gazed at him, agape. The silence was sweet. He savored it, for as long as it lasted. Which wasn't long.

"Oh. So by getting me out of there, you, ah—"

"Blew my cover? Wasted years of preparation? Trashed a once-in-a-lifetime opportunity to bring that motherfucker down? Yes, yes, and yes. Lives were at stake, sweetheart. I traded them. For yours."

Her eyes were huge, her mouth pursed into a shocked *O*.

"This evening, I was supposed to kill you," he went on, his voice hard. "After the big festive gang bang, of course. That would have been my entry fee to Zhoglo's exclusive club. I had to get you out. So here we are, babe."

She sucked in a shuddering breath, pressed a hand to her mouth. "Oh, God. So you're from the police—or some agency—?"

The flinch was involuntary. He could only hope she didn't notice. "Not anymore," he said. "I used to be."

"Used to be?" She looked bewildered. "Then why are you doing this?"

"A lot of things went wrong." The last thing he wanted to think about was that rotten, convoluted story of betrayal and torture and murder. "I'm working on my own."

"Meaning?" She looked puzzled.

"I had my own personal reasons to investigate this prick. I've been waiting for years for a chance to get close to that bastard. I found one, it was cranking along, and ta-da . . . you showed up, to take a dip in the pool."

"Oh, my God," she whispered. "I am so sorry."

"Me, too," he muttered sourly. "What a fuck-up."

"A fuck-up?" She sounded offended. "You saved my life!"

"I didn't go to Frakes Island to save your life," he pointed out. "Believe it or not."

She chewed on that. "I'm sorry that I made difficulties for you."

Difficulties? The woman had a talent for understatement.

A relatively tranquil twenty minutes passed before she piped up again. "Tell me the truth about something," she said.

He hesitated. That sounded like a trap. "If I can," he hedged.

"You were lying when you told me you'd take me to the police station, weren't you? No way in hell would you do that. Because what you are doing is illegal, right? A rogue operation. And the powers that be would not be happy with you for doing it."

He let out a short, explosive sigh. "That's correct."

She twisted her hands together. The blanket had fallen open, displaying her tits in all their lush, pear-shaped glory.

He jerked his gaze back to the road, focused on the yellow line. Like he had time for this juvenile shit.

"Don't lie to me," she said. "That's something that I really hate."

It's not all about you, sweet cheeks. He stopped the caustic words just in time, and was congratulating himself for his uncharacteristic self-control when a stupid answer burst out of him. "I won't," he said.

That startled him. He didn't even know if the words were true. What the hell. He would make them true. By keeping his big mouth shut.

He had to unload this chick, pronto. Before he did something really stupid. He could feel the momentum gathering in his balls.

"So . . . so what are you going to do with me, then?"

The quiver in her voice annoyed him. "Don't know. Chain you to a radiator?" he snapped. "It may be the only way to keep you safe."

She shot him a look as if he were Godzilla and shrank to half her size against the door. Fuck. "I was kidding, Becca," he growled.

"I cannot believe you would kid about that right now."

"So dock me a sensitivity point. I'm an asshole. By the way, I'll take you wherever you want to go. Run to the cops if you want. The only way to stop you would be to lock you in my basement, but I'm tired and that sounds too fucking stressful right now."

"What a lovely sentiment," she muttered.

"But be aware," he went on grimly. "If you do go to the cops, that bastard will come for you. He will find you. And you will die. And so will I."

"Thanks for the warning. That's just great to know. Just great." Her voice was burbling, hands over her face. Aw, shit. He hated tears.

He drove, trying not to listen to the pathetic sniffles and snorts from her hunched form. "Stop it," he exploded. "I'm sorry!"

"Oh, piss off, you condescending bastard."

He was comforted by the smackdown. He liked her feisty.

Chapter
11

Zhoglo stared down at the four blood-soaked corpses, his face expressionless. Anatoli had been with him for twenty years, faithful as a hound, and about as intelligent. But he had valued the man's loyalty. Anatoli's throat gaped open from ear to ear. Yevgeni's too. Ivan had a bullet hole drilled between wide, startled blue eyes. A promising young man, intelligent and ferocious. And Yuri. Three hundred pounds of pure muscle, but his bulldog neck had been snapped like a baby chicken's.

Arkady Solokov had gotten away clean, with the girl. While Zhoglo's armed, highly trained, ruthless guards tripped over their feet and died. The man was a professional killer—but who had hired him? And why?

The list of candidates was endless. It baffled him.

He was furious with himself. He should have known. In fact, he had known on some level. Solokov had been too calm, too sealed, too difficult to read. High-risk. He should have shot the man where he sat.

But no, Zhoglo had decided to wait, to observe Solokov's behavior during the orgy he'd planned and the subsequent execution, before drawing his final conclusions. He had miscalculated. Nothing infuriated him more.

It did not track. Killing the girl would have pulled Solokov still deeper into the Vor's confidence. In fact, he'd suspected that Solokov had brought the girl here just for that purpose. Aside from the other man's wish to have something to fuck on long, boring nights, she would have been a gift of blood for the Vor.

So. The girl's continued existence was important to the man for some reason, but if this were the case, why in God's name bring her here, to certain death? It made no sense.

It had been decades since he had gotten his own hands red. He had long ago delegated such duties to the eager young thugs on the bottom rung of the power ladder, hungry to show how ruthless they could be. But he was so furious, he wanted to slash and cut again. Watch hot blood spatter and fly. Feel muscles and nerves twist in agony against the slick blade of his knife. Hear the screams ring in his ears.

If he got his hands on the throat of that treacherous whore, he would kill her himself. No, both of them, taking turns, making it last for days. Until their throats were too ruined to scream.

The murder in his eyes had silenced even Zhoglo's tedious dinner guest. The Heckler & Koch that Pavel had pointed in his face, and the presence of four bloody bodies had done their part to subdue him.

He cowered in the wingback chair, eyes wide.

Zhoglo had no reason to think that the doctor was responsible for this debacle, but he still wanted to kill the man. His air of entitlement was acutely annoying to a man who had grown up fighting the dogs on the streets of Kiev for scraps.

It would be enjoyable to watch Mathes grovel and beg for mercy. But as always, thrift prevailed. He had invested a fortune in this project. The profit potential was vast.

And the man did have a useful skill. Zhoglo himself was alive because of it. He rubbed the surgical scar, thinking of the young, muscular heart inside that pumped his blood so vigorously. It had belonged to the eighteen-year-old son of a man who had tried to defraud him with a seventy-million-dollar bank scam.

The man had been very contrite. He had, after all, other children.

The doctor's eyes glittered with excitement. A thrill junkie, Zhoglo realized, with a twinge of disgust. Another addict. The world seemed overrun with them sometimes. That annoyed him too. It grated upon his nerves that this fool dared to associate with Vadim Zhoglo for the amusement value. No doubt he wanted to alleviate his boredom with his respectable, privileged life. The urge to kill the man swelled.

He took a calming breath, let the impulse subside. There would be killing enough later on to satisfy him. All in good time.

He turned to Pavel. Pavel seemed steady, but there was a subtle tremor to the gun that only Zhoglo's trained eyes could see.

"You were the one who arranged for this man to handle security, were you not, Pavel?" Zhoglo asked. "You were the one who put this poisonous snake into my pocket."

He made a quick gesture at Kristoff. The man stepped forward promptly, jerking his gun up to train it on Pavel. Best to be careful.

Beads of sweat hung on Pavel's gray forehead. The man forced himself to speak, through stiff looking, whitened lips. "I knew the man, Vor. He was with Avia. He worked as a middleman for the—"

"He almost destroyed us," Zhoglo echoed softly, nudging Yevgeni's limp corpse with the shining toe of his dress shoe.

"When Pyotr—Pyotr was supposed to take care of security, and when he—" Pavel stopped, swallowed a few times.

"When he shot himself in the head, you mean? Your worthless nephew? Clearly, incompetence is an inherited family weakness."

"After Pyotr . . . died, I had to find someone quickly."

"You chose the wrong man," Zhoglo said. "Whose idea

was it, Pavel, to use Solokov? Who put it into your empty head?"

Pavel's mouth worked. "I think, ah, Ludmilla mentioned to me that Solokov was in the area. I thought—having a man already in place . . . and his English is excellent, so—"

"Ludmilla? Who is Ludmilla?"

Pavel's eyes squeezed shut, as if he were bracing for a blow. "She runs an escort service," he said. "In Seattle."

Zhoglo stared at him for a moment. "An escort service? Poor Marya. How disappointed she would be. But then again, fucking whores is nothing compared to what you have already done to disappoint her. I doubt she would notice, or care, at this point."

Pavel dropped heavily to his knees. The gun sagged in his limp grip. "Please, Vor," he said raggedly. "Take me instead."

Zhoglo scowled at him. "Take you? What are you talking about?"

"Send Sasha back to his mother. Take my heart, liver, eyes, kidneys, all of it. Barter them, sell them, whatever."

"You?" Zhoglo began to laugh. "Pavel. Be serious. Who would want your rotten organs after the vodka you have guzzled, the junk you have shot into your veins, the diseased prostitutes you have fucked? The whites of your eyes are yellow. Your skin is pitted. You look like a walking corpse. I would not be surprised if you were HIV positive and riddled with ten different strains of hepatitis."

"Vor, Sasha is only—"

"I am sorry to say it, my friend, but your body is useless as a bargaining chip. But Sasha, ah." Zhoglo was smiling in earnest now, starting to feel much better. "Lovely, sweet, virgin Sasha. His various parts are as clean and fresh as newly plucked flowers."

Pavel covered his mouth with a veined, shaking hand.

"But don't despair," Zhoglo went on. "Your good behavior may still be worth something if it saves Marya and your other little son, no? I must do some calculations and assess my financial losses in this disaster. Your mistakes are expensive, Pavel. I fear it will bump poor little Sasha to the head of the line. Such a shame."

Pavel made a hoarse sound. Zhoglo reached down, and took the Heckler & Koch from the man's nerveless fingers. He used the barrel to tip up Pavel's face. Pavel's eyes were wide, staring. Swimming with tears.

"Now, my friend," he said softly. "Tell me everything there is to know about this Ludmilla."

"I have known her for years," Pavel said. "From back when she lived in Ukraina. She was married to Aleksei Dubov in the nineties. They operated brothels in Kiev. She and Aleksei moved girls in the pipeline to western Europe, the Middle East, America. Then Dubov was killed."

Yes, yes. He had ordered the man's death himself. He had not known, or else he had forgotten, that Dubov had a wife. Zhoglo made an impatient gesture for the man to continue.

"Ludmilla married a Hungarian, who died shortly afterwards, and set up business in Budapest. Then she married an American—"

"Don't tell me, let me guess. He died shortly afterwards? Clutching his throat after a glass of wine?"

Pavel coughed. "Heart attack. After she was widowed, she set up business in Seattle. We have supplied her with girls off and on. I don't understand. She is not stupid, and she is a good businesswoman. She has everything to lose by crossing you, and she knows it. So I think that—"

"Don't think, Pavel." Zhoglo dug the gun barrel into the hollow under Pavel's cheekbone. "The results of you trying to think are damaging to me."

Pavel closed his eyes. "Shall I kill her, Vor?" he asked, hoarsely. "Or bring her to you, for questioning?"

Zhoglo considered it, tapping the gun barrel idly against Pavel's temple. He concluded after a moment that it would be unwise to kill this Ludmilla before his imagination had exhausted every possibility of using her. She was his only tenuous link to that stinking turd Solokov and his lying, green-eyed whore. His only tool to feed false information back to whoever had really hired Solokov.

In the end, of course, Ludmilla would die, screaming. He would see to the matter personally.

"Not yet, Pavel." He patted the man's cheek with the gun. "Not yet. But you will be paying a visit to your favorite madam very soon. Take him"—he gestured with the gun toward the surgeon—"and get him back to the mainland. Out of my sight."

"Do you want me to kill—"

"No, Pavel. Deliver him to wherever Yevgeni picked him up. Do not kill anyone. Idiot. And hurry back. It will be your task to dispose of all these bodies. It is the least you can do."

Zhoglo watched Pavel herd the surgeon out the door. The man's gabbling, excited questions receded into the distance. He lit a cigarette and turned his gaze away from the spectacle of soon-to-be-rotting meat sprawled on the floor. All that money wasted in recruiting, training. His cadre of bodyguards cut by more than half.

He hated waste. It was an obsessive tic, for a man who was filthy rich, but he was convinced that his thrift was one of the reasons for his prodigious success. It came from growing up on the streets of Kiev, he supposed. Thieving and whoring to eat. Nothing taught a man the value of money like near starvation.

In fact, the idea for this project had sprung directly from his loathing of waste. It had come to him while overseeing the punishment of one of his business rivals, mere months after his own heart transplant. Seeing human organs tossed about with abandon had gotten him thinking.

He'd tallied the resale value of the gory offal that had been scooped out of the fellow's abdominal cavity. It was a considerable sum.

He'd mulled over this, as he gazed at the moaning, mutilated creature. One could not strictly call it a man any longer, since that which defined manhood had been separated from him.

It was by no means a new idea, but he was sure that no one as well financed and well organized as himself had ever attempted it.

And on the eve of the debut of his project, it had been infiltrated. The audacity of the culprit infuriated him.

Like any intense emotion, it unleashed a desire to eat, despite the large meal he had just consumed. Powerful stress always induced a violent, cramping hunger in his belly, like the hunger he remembered from his boyhood, foraging for survival in maggoty garbage heaps.

The lying whore with bouncing breasts had spoken of a Grand Marnier chocolate torte. God forbid that, too, should go to waste.

He stubbed out his cigarette on the floor and made his way to the kitchen. There it was, on a dessert tray by the door. A tempting confection covered with a coating of dark chocolate, drizzled with syrup.

Unfortunately, Solokov had chosen just that spot to open the jugular of one of his men. The dessert tray had been liberally sprayed with blood. Zhoglo shrugged inwardly. Gouged out a piece with his fingers.

His men would not begrudge him a few drops of their heart's blood, he thought, stuffing it into his face, gulping without chewing.

And he was anything but squeamish.

The long drive back to the city was as surreal as the boat ride. Heat was blasting over Becca, but she couldn't stop shaking. She drifted from one waking dream to another, nightmares where she was always helpless, always naked, always cold, legs sunk in icy muck. Men with sliced throats that gaped like wet red mouths screamed their rage at her in some harsh, alien language. The Spider's pink, smiling face, eyes sparkling with unholy glee as he reached to fondle her breasts. In her dream he didn't stop there. His fingers slid right through her skin as if she were made of butter, and closed around her heart, squeezing with cruel iron fingers until she thought it would explode—

After that one, she forced her eyes to stay open. She hurt all over. She shook with adrenaline, vibrating at a screamingly high frequency, despite her exhaustion. She felt so exposed, as if lights were glaring down on her in a sports stadium. No cover. All the painful, shameful, embarrassing truths about her, right there for all to see. How small and stupid she was. She had made enormous mistakes.

This guy had risked his neck, done something incredibly brave and difficult and dangerous to save her.

Lives were at stake. I traded them. For yours.

She owed him for that and it was a debt she could never repay. There was no point in trying to find out his name. He would never tell her the real one anyway, if he was running true to form.

She wrapped her arms around herself, clutching the thermal blanket, trying to endure her own existence, second by second. Time ground by. Her feet hurt, her joints hurt, her wrists hurt from breaking her fall into that puddle of blood, her shoulders hurt from being handcuffed to the banister the night before—it was hard to find a place that didn't hurt.

The one small redeeming thing was that Mr. Big was not a ruthless criminal.

Wonderful news.

Not that it mattered. He was a ruthless something else that was probably just as bad. That he'd saved her life against unbelievable odds and that he made her wild with sexual excitement when he took a break from being a hero was beside the point. Irrelevant.

Besides, he had to despise her, for screwing up his operation. He'd only had sex with her—all-the-way sex—because he'd been coerced. The night before didn't count. It would be silly to take it personally.

All things considered, the experience they'd shared was not a good foundation for a relationship. Hell, it wasn't even a foundation for a one-night stand.

She buried her face in her hands, tried to burrow into a hole in her mind and just hide there.

She jumped when she felt his hand on her shoulder. "Huh?" she said. "What?"

"We're there."

She looked around. The world was a blur without her glasses, particularly at night. She wrenched her brain into line and squinted until she could make out the big, ramshackle house where she lived in the top-floor apartment. Dawn was far away. The cold orange glow of streetlights reflected off the thick cloud cover.

"How did you know where I lived?" she asked.

"Went through your purse at the A-frame," he said. "So I could ditch your license and your plastic. Didn't want him to find it."

"So that's why you had my lipstick."

"Yeah. Don't know why I stuck that in my pocket."

She blinked. He'd thought of everything. Her purse and stuff were gone, but only because he'd been trying to save her from the start. Becca struggled for something meaningful to say that would not come across as idiotic. Before he disappeared forever.

So sorry for screwing up your life. Thanks for saving me from a fate worse than death. The sex was great too. See ya.

She wondered if she would ever see him again and fought a jolt of odd, irrational panic at the idea of him just fading into black. Leaving her alone, unmoored. Her inner world smashed to junk.

He drummed his fingers on the steering wheel. Probably trying to think of a way to get her out of his truck. Her tongue felt thick.

"I'll walk you up," he said abruptly.

Yikes. She didn't want him to leave, but neither did she want him in her apartment. He was so big and bloodstained and unfathomable. He could contaminate her nest. Infect it with danger, uncertainty.

Aw, hell, the damage was done. And she couldn't refuse him.

"OK," she whispered, but he was already out the door and circling the truck, bundling her out onto her shaky legs.

She wouldn't have made it up the staircase, anyway. His arm clamped around her waist and took most of her weight off her feet.

She had a blank moment as she stood there, staring at the locked door. Keys. Her purse. He'd just explained that they were light years away, in another universe.

"I take it you don't have a spare under a plant?" Mr. Big said.

She shook her head. "My landlady lives downstairs," she said. "But I can't . . ." She looked down at her disreputable self.

"No," he agreed. "You can't." He bent down, peered at the lock, then fished for a pocketknife and pried a narrow hooked thing out of it.

In a couple of minutes, the door swung open. The familiar scent of vanilla and rose potpourri wafted out. She stumbled forward.

Mr. Big grabbed her arm, pulled her back. "Me first. Just in case."

His gun appeared in her hand. Her eyes skittered away from it as he slunk into the dimness inside. It didn't take him long. Her place was small. He came back, waved her in. She fumbled for the light switch.

He clashed with her place. He looked so dense and vivid,

prowling around among the light colors, the sheer curtains. Her place looked even smaller with a huge, shaggy, slit-eyed, bloodstained guy stalking through it clutching a gun.

Twitching curtains aside, squinting out windows, he stared at everything as if he expected something to jump out and bite him. He ran his fingers over a fuzzy afghan that was draped over the sofa. Poked a squishy pillow, prodded the floppy silk flowers that dangled off a shelf. He peered at her bookshelf, her CD rack. Carrie's prints. Josh's weird, abstract art photography. And the family photo gallery over the couch.

"That the guy?"

He'd found the one of Justin that she hadn't gotten around to ditching yet. "Yes. How did you know?"

He shrugged. "He looks like an asshole. You should take it down." He removed it from the shelf and handed it to her. Becca tossed it into a wastebasket, frame and all. Nothing to do but agree with him.

Her life before Nick seemed like something that had happened a long, long time ago. She was embarrassed when he stared up at the stuffed animals on the shelf, the battered ones Carrie and Josh had played with when they were tiny. He probably thought she collected them. Babyish, but people did it.

He made no move to go. She pondered the options. There were no social rules for what had happened. Should she offer him a drink, as if he'd just brought her home from a date? Should she, what, make him coffee?

This was her last chance, though, to ask the question that would haunt her forever if she didn't. Even though she was afraid of the answer.

She clutched the edge of the table for support, and swallowed several times. "You said, um, that lives depended on this operation. That you'd traded them for mine."

His eyes narrowed. "Yeah," he said, warily.

She took a deep breath. "Whose?"

He was silent for so long, she'd concluded that he wasn't going to answer at all. She was about to pass out from holding her breath.

"I was overstating it," he said. "She's probably already dead."

Her eyes popped open. Something twisted, knife-sharp, in her chest. "She?" she whispered.

His jaw tightened. A muscle twitched. "A little girl," he said. "Abducted last year. From Boryspil, in the Ukraine. Her father was an undercover cop. He was helping me. Someone ratted him out. He was killed. I don't know where the security leak was. But I know it was my fault."

Her throat tightened, started burning. She waited for more.

His shoulders lifted. "There's no reason to think she's still alive," he said. "But I promised her mother . . . I was hoping I could tell Sonia something. Put an end to the wondering. I won't be able to do that now. But fuck it. I probably wouldn't have been able to anyway."

She pressed her lips together, hard.

"It was a long shot," he said. "But since you asked, that's why I gave a shit."

The knot in her throat reached critical mass. Tears spilled out.

He looked dismayed. "Oh, shit. Please. I shouldn't have told you."

She tried to choke it back. "I'm so sorry. Was she—"

"I don't want to talk about it. I think about it as little as possible, or else it drives me bugfuck. Forget I said anything."

His words knocked her back. "OK," she whispered. "I just meant . . . I wish I could fix it. I wish there was something I could do. To help."

His unreadable gaze slid over her bedraggled, torn-up,

something-the-cat-dragged-in self. "There is something," he said.

She brightened, mopping away tears with her forearms. "Really? What can I . . ." Her voice faltered as her body translated what lurked in the hooded depths of his eyes.

Something tightened in answer, low and hot in her body.

How could she even think about sex, after what had happened?

But she was. Oh, she would. In a heartbeat. She ached to grab onto him. He was so strong and solid, seething with energy. So hot.

Of course, she wanted to grab onto anything strong. She felt so vulnerable and scared. She was desperate for comfort, but this man wouldn't give her any comfort. He was anything but comforting.

He would take, and take, until she was all used up. She could feel his hunger from across the room. And she felt so fragile.

She inched back with instinctive female caution. His eyes narrowed. "For fuck's sake, cut the scared kitten routine. I won't force you. I may be an asshole, but I'm not that kind of asshole."

Her back straightened up. "I'm not a scared kitten." She tried to sound dignified, and ended up sounding stiff. "I just thought you were referring to something I could do that was, well, important. Not just . . ." She cleared her throat, with some difficulty. ". . . ah, opening my legs."

"Believe me. You opening your legs feels pretty goddamn important right now."

She crossed her arms over her chest, a flush of anger heating her from the inside. "Sure it does. Until your hard-on's taken care of. Then you'll brush me off like the useless, inconvenient piece of fluff that you think I am, and off you'll go, to do whatever dangerous crap you do all day, and forget that I even exist."

He looked cautiously amazed. "Whoa. What, do you feel left out of the action? You mean you actually want to participate in more of this suicidal bullshit? Haven't you had enough?"

"That's not the point!" she raged. "I'm just sick of feeling like a . . . a thing! A toy to be used and passed around!"

He moved so fast, it felt like a split instant. She was across the room from him, and suddenly, her shoulders were clamped in his tight grip. He was lifting her up off her feet and onto her tiptoes.

Her eyes were inches from his searing gaze.

"I never passed you to anyone," he said, his voice deliberate. "I never treated you like a thing. I killed four men tonight trying to get you out of that hellhole. So you can just back off."

Her mouth worked, but no words came out. She just stared at his face, immobilized by the anger burning in his eyes.

"Do not blame me for what he did to you," he said.

"I—I d-don't blame you," she stammered.

"Yeah? You don't? Good. What's your fucking problem, then?"

She stiffened in his grip, bracing herself by grabbing his broad wrists. "My problem is that look you've got on your face, you jerk!" she shouted. "I messed you up, so now I owe you? You saved my life, so I have to give you sex? Is that your macho reasoning?"

A smile touched the edges of his mouth. He set her onto her feet.

"It's simpler than that," he said. "My macho reasoning is, every time I touch you, you can't stop coming."

The rest of her furious diatribe dissolved in her muddled mind, utterly forgotten.

"It's some kind of magic." His voice was ragged velvet. He touched her cheek with a callused fingertip. "The way you go off for me. Like a bomb. It makes me crazy."

"I—I—"

"But now that you put it that way, it's true. I have had one bitch of a night because of you," he said, in a tone of mock discovery. "And yes, babe. You do owe me. Big-time."

She focused on his wet, bloodstained sleeve. "It's not that simple," she whispered.

He rolled his eyes. "You've got a genius for making simple things complicated. It was one of the first things I noticed about you." He glanced at her body. "Actually, more like the sixth or seventh thing."

She started to shake, fighting hysteria. "I'm not the complicated one. I don't even know your name! After all this drama, and blood and sex, you've never even told me your real—"

"Nick," he broke in.

She floundered, cut off in mid-rant. "Huh?"

"Nick Ward. That's my name. Nikolai Warbitsky is the name on my birth certificate. I prefer Nick Ward. Happy now?"

She flapped her jaw, rattled. And moved. *Nick.*

Oh, please. She felt moved? To have his goddamn *name?* One of the most common, basic, cheap units of information that human beings could exchange? It was a pathetic crumb he'd offered her, not a precious gift.

Anger at her own deluded self sharpened her voice. "Happy now? Oh, yes. I'm thrilled. That's the magic word, huh? Tell me your name, and voilà, my legs open, like the Red Sea parting!"

He let out a startled bark of laughter. "Don't get biblical on me, sweetheart. Make a decision. You going to give me what you owe me, or are you just going to dick me around?"

She squeezed her eyes shut, shuddering with sensation as his hands stroked her bare shoulders. His fingers moved over her skin with a seductive gentleness that belied his words. He pressed his mouth against the top of her head. She felt his lips move against her scalp, felt the warm cloud of each exhalation. His tangled locks tickled her shoulders. Waiting patiently. So sure that he'd win in the end.

"Why do you have to be such a jerk?" she whispered.

He shook his head. "I don't know," he muttered.

His honesty made her bolder. "You make it so hard for me."

He trapped her easily as she tried to twist away from his grasp. "Yeah, well, tough. Life's hard for everyone, babe."

"Shut up. Don't be flip. If you could just be gentle . . ." she trailed off in a whisper.

He tried to pull her closer again.

She fought against him. "I want you to stay," she said. "I want to say yes to you. But when you act like this, it's almost impossible to do."

He caught her chin, turned her face to his so she could see the hot gleam in his eye. "Almost?"

"Oh, damn you. Stop it." Her face went hot, and her chest tightened up. Her heart tripped and galloped. Her throat squeezed shut.

He nuzzled her hair and spoke against her neck, his deep voice vibrating through her whole body. "You want me to go? Say the word."

She didn't answer, couldn't move.

"OK," he murmured. "I'm not getting a straight answer out of you, so I'm going to interpret that cryptic silence to my own advantage. If I'm wrong, tell me quick."

She bit her lip. Two tears flashed out of the outside corners of her eyes and coursed down her face.

His lips moved against her cheekbone. The hot, wet cat rasp of his tongue as he licked them greedily away made a wrenching shiver of pleasure shake her whole body. She felt a tug, a ripping sound, and the soggy peasant blouse was pulled off and flung away. She stood before him, bare naked.

A state of being that was starting to feel alarmingly normal.

She touched his face. "Wait. You've got, um, blood on you. I don't want to look at it anymore. Could we, ah . . ."

He wrenched his sweatshirt off. His boots followed. He took off socks, jeans, and in no time, a naked man was dragging her into her own bathroom and setting the shower running like he owned the place.

"We could both use a wash," he said. "It'll relax you."

Hah. Not freaking likely. She almost laughed as he muscled her into the hot spray. Relax, her ass. Like she could, with a demanding sexually charged guy crowding her into a steamy corner in her own tiny shower stall. He was all around her, a solid wall of wet, gleaming man flesh, his hairy chest brushing against her nipples, his erection prodding her everywhere she turned. His hands slid all over her body. The shower was ridiculously small for even one normal-sized person, let alone two. She bumped her elbows in it when she was by herself.

And Mr. Big—Nick—was huge.

Chapter
12

Bad idea. Worst one he'd had in a long time. He should leave, run far and fast, forget this chick ever existed. He'd blown the op to keep her safe, and here he was compromising her again.

But he didn't want to go to his empty condo and sit there on his couch, staring openmouthed into the dark. Deafened by the silence, the flatness, of having failed again. He didn't want to crawl into the oblivion of a bottle, either. His father's time-honored solution to all problems.

He wanted to stay right here. With her. This place smelled good. Like her. Fragrant, soft, female. Problematic and complicated, too.

He was going to flood her dinky bathroom, but he couldn't be bothered worrying about it while resisting the impulse to lift her up, brace her against the wet wall and thrust his prong deep and hard. If they emptied the tank and the shower went cold, he would never notice.

Back off. Go slow. He shouldn't be making moves on her at all, after what she'd been through. He knew that, but it was just a thought that rattled around his brain, with no executive power, no influence on his behavior, no moral clout. Just a random, free-floating observation.

His, his, his, was the primeval refrain from the deepest part of his brain. He wanted to lose himself in her body, warm himself with her heat. It made him feel alive. And he actually wanted to feel alive.

It startled him. He hadn't wanted that for longer than he could remember. It was so much safer to be numb.

He knew exactly how a guy sweet-talked women into sex, how to be suave and seductive, blah blah, but he was a slavering wolf thing tonight, lunging at the chain. No games, no charm.

She was motionless, eyes shut, head flung back as he washed her, but he felt her body respond with shivers and sighs, subtle vibrations, a soft yielding to the stroke of his soapy hands. He sudsed up the scented shampoo, working it through her long hair. Frothy clots of foam slid seductively over her curves. The hot water had brought a blush of pink to her translucent white skin. About time. He ran his hands over curves and hollows, soaping and rinsing.

He kneeled to wash her bruised, scratched feet. She hissed with pain, though he was as gentle as he could be. Then legs, knees, thighs. He saved her pussy for last, and treated it like a freshly opened flower, barely touching it. He just caressed it with his fingertips and then rinsed the soap away with the spray from the detachable shower head.

There wasn't any way to keep his erection from poking and prodding her, so he didn't try. He put the shower head back, pulled her closer and hoisted up his dick so that it poked upright, sandwiched between their bellies, the heart-shaped head nestled hopefully below her tits. He pressed against her, wondering how to break the passive statue spell. He cupped her ass in his hands.

He nuzzled her earlobe, and took a chance. "Your turn," he said.

Her eyes fluttered open, as if she'd been in a trance. He put the shampoo in her hand. She gazed at it like she'd never seen shampoo before. He had to prompt her, opening the bottle, pouring it out.

He was mesmerized by the way her tits bounced and swayed as she reached up to soap up his hair. "You're too tall," she complained.

He sank to his knees, which put his mouth right at the level of the mound of her soft belly. He nuzzled her, eyes shut as her gentle fingers scraped and scrubbed at his scalp, stroking in fragrant foam.

Oh, God. Huge turn-on. Hot suds sliding voluptuously down his face, stinging his eyes, gliding over his shoulders, plopping around his knees. The view from below of the underside of her tits, the skin of her wet belly against his lips. When the last shampoo was rinsed away, he got to his feet, offered her the shower gel. She looked at him blankly.

"Do exactly what you do when you wash yourself," he suggested. "The same principles apply. You know, lather, rinse, repeat?"

"Smart-ass," she muttered, but she was smiling.

He was gasping with pleasure. Her slender hands slipped and slid all over his chest. She lathered up his pit hair, his chest hair, let her fingers trail down over his abs . . . and stopped. Chickening out.

He waited as long as he could stand it. "Missed a spot," he prompted.

She let out a nervous sigh, squirted more gel into her hands, rubbed it into foam, and gripped his cock.

Pleasure licked up his nerve endings like teasing tongues of flame. The drumbeat of his heart deepened to a heavy, pounding throb.

He gripped her hand with his fist and squeezed, dragging her hand up and down the shaft to show her the pressure he liked, the speed. Then he let go, let her have at him with those slippery fingers, any way she wanted. Didn't matter what she did. It was all good.

Every stroke, even the nervous, tentative ones, turned him on. When she cupped his balls in her hand, he realized that he was in trouble. He was going to blow his wad, right here in the shower.

Unacceptable. He hadn't had that problem even as a teenager.

He met her questioning glance when he clamped his hands over hers, stopping the tender strokes. "I don't want to come yet," he explained brusquely. He grabbed the first towel he saw, muscled her out of the shower and started rubbing her down.

She stood there, vaguely bewildered, as he dragged terry cloth over her body. That hot perfumed smell of her rosy, curvy body made his mouth water. Literally. He dropped down to his knees on the soggy bathroom rug and combed his fingers through her muff, parting the dark, wet ringlets to get down to the tender stuff—

She stiffened, stumbled back against the sink. Put her hand to his face to hold him away. "No."

He froze. "What? You don't like it?"

She looked distressed. "I'm sure that I'd like it fine if you did it," she said, her voice small.

"What happened?" he rapped out. "Say it."

She flinched. "Zhoglo hurt me. There. With his fingernail. While I was serving the fruit. It's no big deal, but—"

She squeaked as he rose up and hoisted her up onto the sink. "Let me see," he growled. A haze of fury made him almost dizzy.

"Oh, no." She tried to wiggle down. "Forget it."

"Shut up and let me see." He shoved her legs apart.

The makeup light over the mirror wasn't enough, so he flipped on the switch by the door. Becca winced and covered her eyes as the steamy little room was flooded with harsh fluorescent light.

He parted her labia, pulled the hood back to look at her clit. Sure enough, an angry red line sliced right across that button of flesh. The bastard hadn't broken the skin, but still.

Fucking ouch. His balls clenched in sympathy as he looked at it.

It made him so angry, he wanted to put his fist through a wall. Not Becca's wall, though. That was all she needed tonight. A little property damage, to finish off her very special weekend.

He cupped his hand over her pussy and dropped a kiss on the baby-smooth skin of her groin. "That goes right to the top of the list of reasons why I need to kill that sadistic piece of shit," he said.

"Really, it's OK," she hastened to soothe him. "It's not any—"

"Shut up with the 'it's OK' bullshit," he snarled. "It's not OK. It sucks. Face up to it."

She shoved his hand away from her crotch. "Don't tell me to shut up." Her tone was crystal sharp. "I'm tired of it. Don't do it. Ever again."

He stepped back, chastened. Suddenly aware of the water dripping down from his hair, puddling around his feet. His dick bobbed and swung. Ever hopeful, no matter the circumstances.

"I'm sorry," he said. "I'm just angry. At him. Not you."

She gazed at him, eyes narrowed, chin tilted up. Slowly, some of the haughty starch eased out of her graceful posture. Her tits jiggled tenderly as she slid down off the sink and onto her feet.

"Well," she murmured. "Thanks for the sentiment. I suppose."

He took hold of his self-control with both fists, and forced the words out, hoping desperately that she wouldn't take him up on it.

"You don't have to do this," he said heavily.

"Do what? You mean . . ."

"Me. You don't have to do me." The words hurt his throat. "It's a bad time. I know that. I don't want to hurt you. I'll leave. If you want."

She didn't speak. He didn't dare look at her. He held his breath. Forty or so agonizing seconds went by. He ventured a cautious glance.

Her expression was soft. Hope soared. His cock twitched and throbbed, hoisting itself impossibly higher. Ready to rock and roll. Maybe trying to be halfway decent had actually paid off for once.

That was so seldom the case. In his experience.

"I don't want you to leave," she whispered. "Please stay."

Relief made him dizzy. "If I stay, we're having sex," he warned.

Her face was hot, eyes averted, but she nodded.

He was getting on with it. Quick, before she changed her mind.

Dawn hadn't lightened the windows in the bedroom. Nick followed her in, padding like a big, silent panther behind her.

He went from window to window, jerking the curtains closed. He peered at the window fastenings, the warped wood, the peeling paint, the thin, uneven glass. "This place is a security nightmare," he growled.

She had nothing to say to that. She'd never given it a thought before. Now she would probably obsess about it all the time.

Nick scowled at her antique bed: the carved bedposts, the fluffy comforter, the puffy bolsters, a heap of larger pillows, smaller pillows on top, lace and satin and embroidered pillows for accents. "Sweet Jesus, what's with the pillows? There must be twenty of them!"

"Don't ask," she said primly. "It's a girl thing."

He swept his arm across the bed, tumbling them all to the floor with one ruthless swipe. He peeled back the comforter and top sheet, tossed them over the wooden footboard, leaving a snowy field of unbroken white. A blank canvas, waiting to be filled.

He nodded toward the bed.

She clambered on, feeling foolish and shy. There was something so businesslike and deliberate about how he just got right down to it. She couldn't see his face all that well. She hoped desperately that the semidarkness would help her ease her well-documented sexual hangups. Though with her luck, they would probably come crowding back into her bed, now that she was back in the real world.

The bed creaked under his unaccustomed weight. He pressed her down onto her back. She shivered against the chilly sheet, but then he climbed on top of her—and oh, he was so big, so heavy, and all over her. Steely hard and so hot, smelling of soap, and beneath it, the tang of male musk. His feverish heat, his concentrated intensity, left her breathless. Water dripped from his hair. He pinned her down as if he were afraid she would wiggle away.

Like she had a chance in hell.

Then he started kissing her. Doubts, fears, sexual hangups, it all melted away into a creamy swirl of excitement. A clutch of hunger.

His lips were warm and coaxing at first, but the kiss changed, became demanding, compelling, using a silent, wordless language she hadn't known she understood until she found herself obeying every unspoken command. She opened to his seeking mouth. She touched his tongue with hers, and the contact set off a sweet shimmer of heat, making her nipples tingle and ache, her back arch, bringing forth a liquid rush between her legs. Her thighs fell open. Her breasts felt taut, swollen and sensitive where they rubbed his chest.

He lifted his face from hers, smoothing her hair back. It took her a minute to recognize the dry, jerky sound coming from him as laughter.

"I'm nervous," he admitted.

That racked her overstimulated, jittery body with a burst of giggles. "You? Oh, come on! Give me a break."

"Really. I swear. I can't touch your clit, so I'm out of my

comfort zone. I like to start with a girl's clit. It's like the key to the castle."

It was a needle jab of annoyance, to hear about his sexual routines with other women. Mr. Sensitivity.

She shoved at his chest. "Great," she snapped. "I'm glad that you have to do something different from your usual sexual routine. Maybe it'll set me apart from the teeming masses just enough so you won't be shouting other women's names. One can only hope."

His body vibrated with laughter. "No worries, babe," he said, settling his weight between her legs. "You're in a class all your own."

She struggled for breath. "Key to the castle, my foot," she scoffed. "It's not like you have to convince me. The castle door is unlocked. In fact, it's wide open. And the drawbridge is down."

He went very still, staring intently down into her face, as if he could see right into her. He cupped her face. "Maybe you don't understand what I'm getting at," he said. "I don't just want to fuck you. I want to make you come until you scream and fly to pieces. White-hot, high-decibel, end-of-the-world orgasms. You get me?"

She stared up into the shadows that hid his eyes, open-mouthed.

"Like this afternoon," he went on. "On the island. Remember?"

Like she was ever going to forget it, in this lifetime or the next. She forced out a nervous cough, as the heated memory played in her head. Of how helpless, how terrified she had been. How unspeakably vulnerable. "Ah, yes," she whispered. "I, um, do remember that."

"I liked that," he said lazily. "That was special."

"Oh," she said inanely. "Uh . . . yes. It was."

He kissed her till she was gasping for air, and lifted his head again. "I've never felt anything like that," he went on, nuzzling her temple, his hot breath tickling and caressing.

"Didn't even know that kind of thing was possible, to tell you the truth. But now I'm hooked on it. It raised the bar for me. I won't ever be satisfied with less."

Oh, man. She was so in for it. Tension gripped her. "Well, you should know. That was kind of an aberration for me," she confessed.

"Yeah?" He sounded like he was smiling. "We'll see about that."

"That was not a challenge," she added. "Just a statement of fact."

"We'll see," he repeated stubbornly.

She felt obscurely alarmed, as if she'd presented herself to him under false pretenses. God forbid he find out how sexually blocked she really was. "I mean, the circumstances were extreme," she hurried on.

He was laughing at her now. "That's cool. I can do extreme."

She swatted at him. "Stop it! You're playing dumb on purpose!"

He caught her hand in his, turned it, pressed a lingering kiss to the damp palm. "Calm down, babe," he said softly. "I don't think it's your job to worry about it. I think you should leave that all to me."

He just didn't get it, the arrogant . . . argh. "But I—"

"I'll do whatever it takes to get you off. Got a problem with that?"

She opened her mouth, trying to think of some response that didn't sound hysterical or crazy. Problem? Hah. Problem was putting it mildly. Her problem was how fragile she felt, and how charismatic he was, the way he tore down her barriers as if they were tissue paper.

But what was she supposed to say? *Gee, do you think you could just, you know, turn me on just a little bit less?* Right. Sure.

She swallowed over the bumpy quiver in her throat, and

shook her head. Officially, for the record, she had no problem with that.

"I can't scream, though," she informed him primly. "So put it out of your head. My landlady's bedroom is right below this one. She'd probably call the police. She's elderly. And very religious."

"Great. That gives me a benchmark. When the cops are hauling me away in cuffs, that's when I know I did good."

He scooped her up, lifting and tugging until she was on her knees facing him, straddling his crossed legs. He propped his cock up so it stuck straight up between them. He gripped her waist and lifted her higher, nuzzling her breasts. "Tits are a nice way to start," he observed. "I've barely had a chance to look at these properly, what with one thing and another." He cupped one in his hand, drew the sensitive tip into his mouth and lashed his tongue around it. "Your tits are amazing."

The blunt compliment made her tingle and go gooey and soft. So did the delicious swirl of wet warmth from his hot mouth. "Ah, thanks," she murmured. "So's, ah, that. Whatever you're doing to them."

The low vibration of laughter reverberated through his body, and then he buried his face between them. Wallowing, licking, lapping. Worshipping them.

Her breasts had never been particularly sensitive before, at least not that she'd noticed. She'd figured they weren't one of her erogenous zones. Wrong. They were the center of her universe, glowing points of light, of heat. His passionate caresses made her whole chest melt from the inside, shivering and soft, intensely alive. Shining.

His slightest touch sent sparkles up her nerves. She twisted, started, with electric jerks and shudders as he slowly unraveled her, begging with his mouth for something she could not grasp.

Surrender. Trust. That was what he wanted, what he silently demanded. Her resistance made her shudder, brought a gush of tears to her eyes. She dug her fingers into his hair and reminded herself exactly why his technique was so slick, his sensuality so fiercely focused. It was to prepare her to be physically capable of taking that ridiculously large thing of his into her body. There was nothing particularly personal about it. He was just being practical.

The thought made her angry. Which wasn't really fair. After all, it was to his credit that he took his time, tried to please.

But damn it, she was going to start biting and clawing if he didn't give her some relief. She lifted her head. "Nick," she whispered. "Please."

He wiped his mouth. "Please, what?"

"Just do it," she pleaded. "Please, get on with it. Now."

He shook his head slowly, a lazy smile on his lips, a gleam in his heavy lidded eyes. Pleased at the power he wielded over her. Proud of her desperation. She wanted to scream, pound on him, but she could barely speak. She was afraid to move.

"Come first," he said. "Then I'll give it to you."

She dug her nails into his shoulders. "Don't be a tease," she snapped. "I swear. I will. In about two seconds, if you would just—"

"No. I want one of those mega-galactic, call the cops orgasms before I put my cock in you. I want lights flashing, sirens screaming, people yelling into megaphones, the whole deal. Got me?"

She tugged his hair, hard. "Is that some stupid macho rule?"

"It's *my* stupid macho rule." His teeth grazed her throat. "That's how I know for sure that you're ready."

Her nervous energy was breaking up into helpless, shuddering laughter. "Sounds risky," she coughed out. "They might haul you away in cuffs before you get any satisfaction for yourself."

He snorted. "I don't think their response time is that good."

"But really. No jokes. I swear, Nick," she assured him. "I'm so ready. I've never been so ready in my life."

"Then give me what I want." His velvety voice stroked and soothed, but behind it was unyielding steel. "Show me you're ready. Don't waste time telling me."

She writhed in speechless frustration. So close . . . and yet she had no clue how to get from where she was to where she needed to go.

His arms slid around her waist, and down, cupping her bottom. "You want some more help?"

She hid her face against the tangle of dark hair that covered his neck, and nodded violently. She didn't know what he meant by that, nor did she care. Anything was good, anything at all. Just more. Just *now*.

He reached down between her legs, his fingers brushing delicately over the sensitive seam of her labia, and parted her, insinuating one long finger slowly inside. The contact jolted her closer. She swayed over him, undulating like an exotic dancer over his delving hand, hips jerking, squeezing around him. Panting. Embarrassment forgotten.

"Yeah. That's good," he muttered. "Such a tight, perfect, gorgeous pussy. I think my finger is about to come all by itself." He thrust two fingers in, curved them into a gentle hook, stroking and pressing a tender spot near the entrance of her snug channel. She jolted over his moving hand, as his rough voice urged her on. "Take me deeper. Pump it, harder . . . faster . . . there. There you go. Almost there . . . oh, yeah. Yes, yes, *yes*. Oh, Christ, that's so sweet."

It was. Just like before, it was heavenly and wonderful, the wave lifting her, pitching her over.

She was infinite, boundless. Lost in the pulsing, surging bliss.

When she got her leaden eyelids open again, she was flat on her back, panting in sobbing gasps. Legs splayed wide and limp. She felt like a flower beaten down to muddy earth by a rainstorm. Nick was poised over her, braced on his arms. She sensed rather than saw his triumphant grin. She was destroyed and he had only just begun.

She licked dry lips, tried to speak, but her voice was gone. Her throat was dry from panting. Sore and rough from screaming.

"Your landlady must be shocked to the depths of her puritanical soul." He sounded pleased with himself.

Her chest jerked with breathy laughter. "Did I, ah, make noise?"

"I thought the windows would shatter."

"Don't be silly," she said tartly. "Well, then. I guess the cops will be here any time. You'd better hurry and get on with it, hmm?"

He grasped her hand, put it on his cock, covered it with his own as he swirled her fingers around his glans, rubbing up and down the broad shaft. She could barely close her fingers around it.

"I never hurry," he said. "I take my time. Come what may. Let them lay siege. I'll go out in a blaze of glory. But I'll die happy."

The image made her wince. "Don't even say that word," she whispered. "Please. Don't even joke about it."

He ran his fingertip tenderly over her trembling lower lip. "Sure thing, babe," he said gently. "Got any condoms?"

The question jolted her abruptly back to mundane reality. She tried to remember if she did. She had hardly ever entertained Justin in her dinky apartment. He had found it cramped and irritating, and had much preferred his own sleek bachelor condo, all done up in cool matte metal and black leather. "No, I don't think that I do," she said.

He nodded, unsurprised. "I won't come inside you."

It was a risk, but her idea of risk had been radically redefined today, and she was in no condition to argue. He fitted her hands around the base of his shaft, against the springy thatch of dark hair, and swirled the blunt tip of himself against her, nudging and prodding until he was firmly lodged. He forged slowly inside.

She gasped. She was hypersensitive after that violent orgasm, and the deep penetration was overwhelming, slick and soft though she was. He pushed deeper, each short, hard shove jerking a whimpering gasp from her throat. The room was getting lighter, and she could see the grim line of his mouth, the tautness of his jaw. His eyes burned into hers, as if he were trying to make her admit something.

She braced her hands against his chest, holding him at arm's length, but he made a low sound and yanked her hands out between them, trapping her wrists with one big fist.

"Take me," he said. She heard the pleading behind the harsh command. He jerked her legs up over his big shoulders and leaned, squeezing her legs high, swirling that throbbing club of flesh inside her.

Filling her with himself. So deep.

She didn't know how she would survive if he started to move, but he did, slow, heavy lunges that ground her hard against the mattress. His shaft stroked and pressed and slid over a bright glow of awareness, creating a delicious, aching friction that got more and more intense until it was too much. She had to retreat from it. She turned her face away, squeezed her eyes shut. Panted, in short, sharp breaths.

He jerked her chin around. "Look at me!" His voice slashed across her ragged nerves, and her eyes popped open, swimming with startled tears. "Don't hide away inside your head."

"But I—"

"I need you. Right here. With me," he said more softly. His hips came down heavily with each stroke. "Look at me. I need you."

She stared back, and the intensity amplified, like a feedback loop. The bed squeaked and rattled, unused to such hard use. His thrusts got deeper, faster, their gasps, moans and whimpers sharpening as they struggled in a desperate, heaving knot. She crested again and again, wailing as her body drew him impossibly deeper, bathing him with slick juice, clutching and milking his phallus with each ramming stroke.

Suddenly he wrenched out, and hunched over her, face contracted in a grimace that looked like pain. Hot, jerky spurts hit her belly, in a climax that seemed that it would never end.

Nick lay on his back afterwards, eyes burning.

He knew the script. He was supposed to cuddle her, sweet talk, make her laugh, if possible. Another silly crack about her landlady and the cops would be good. She'd given all she had to give. She was amazing. She'd held nothing back.

Neither had he. That was the problem. He couldn't do the nice-guy postcoital routine in this condition. Not if his life depended on it.

He was scared out of his fucking wits.

And exactly what had made him think he'd be able to nail this girl, blow off some steam and walk away, relaxed, refreshed? Jesus. He'd fallen to pieces when he'd fucked her that afternoon in front of the vid cams and that monster, Zhoglo. Of all places to get emotional. Needy. He hadn't felt that since he was a little kid. Look at him, begging her to look at him. Inches away from sobbing in her arms.

He still wanted to. She was so sweet and generous, underneath her shield of sarcasm. He could feel how it would be, how she would wrap herself around him, twine those slender arms around his neck, press those jiggly, petal-soft tits against his face, let him nuzzle and kiss and lick her. She would cradle his head, croon comforting things, and he would melt into her. Dissolve into her tender warmth until he no longer existed, until it was all comfort, all bliss. All safe.

Nope. It wasn't right. She was too nice a girl to be mess-

ing around with him. He was too cold, too cynical, too rude.
A depressed, egotistic bastard, just like his daddy. His sharp
edges would bruise her.

They were bruising her now. She lay there, breath still
hitching. Waiting, while he lay there like a bump on a log,
throat frozen, muscles locked, staring at the fucking cracks
in the ceiling.

He could sense how badly she wanted him to reach for
her. They all wanted it. This part was always awkward and
sad and flat. His least favorite moment in the sex act. When
he disappointed them.

But what skidded him into a heart-thudding panic was
that he wanted to reach for her, too. He wanted it bad. That
woke up feelings he'd forgotten about, an abandoned place
inside him with barbed wire, chain link, Keep Out signs.
Goddamnit, he could not afford this frivolous bullshit. He
was marked for death, as would be any woman Zhoglo could
connect to him. Especially Becca.

Hell, she was marked for death on her own merits.

Zhoglo would find him eventually. The bastard was filthy
rich, wily, persistent. It was just a matter of time.

He pictured it. The best he had to offer the chick. *Hey,
wanna get a new face and go into hiding with me in Outer
Mongolia? C'mon, didn't you say you wanted more adventure in your life?*

No. One searing lay and he was out of there. It was the
only way.

He dragged himself up, and sat slumped on the bed with
his back to her, just like the stony, indifferent bastard that he
was. The colder he was, the easier it would be for her to dismiss this night as a big mistake with a heinous asshole. So
she could forget and move on.

He felt weird about spurting his come all over her, too.
There was a sleazy vibe associated with coming on a woman's
body, like he was marking his territory or some crap like

that. He'd probably watched too much porn. Not that he watched a whole lot, since the stuff bored the shit out of him, but when he channel surfed on sleepless nights, it was hard to look away sometimes, when it had been awhile.

Speaking of marking his territory. He could have gotten her pregnant this afternoon. That zinged through his body. Froze up his chest muscles until he couldn't breathe at all.

"Um, Nick?" Her voice was timid, nervous. "Are you . . . OK?"

"Nope," he said, his voice muffled. "Not particularly."

"Did I—was it something that I—"

"No," he cut her off. "You're the best lay I've ever had. You're white-hot. You are not the problem."

"Then, ah . . . what is the problem?" she faltered.

He made a rude sound. "You met my problems today, babe. My problems almost got you raped and killed. Any more questions?"

He got up, thigh muscles weak and wobbly, and waded around in the pillows, kicking them aside to get to the door. His filthy, sodden clothing was strewn in the corridor outside. He yanked the clammy fabric of his jeans up over his legs. A crumpled pack of cigarettes fell out.

He picked it up, shook it. One last smoke rattled around, bent but not broken and, amazingly, not soaked. He fished in his pocket and found a lighter. Might as well smoke that sucker up. Celebrate saying goodbye to Arkady.

And Sveti.

Pain stabbed through him. He went back into the bedroom and grabbed the SIG he'd laid next to the bed. He shoved it into his jeans, carefully not looking at Becca. On the plus side, it was good to be done impersonating a scumbag drug dealer and arms trafficker. That had been a big flesh-creeping bummer.

He looked around Becca's bedroom, and quickly concluded that no woman who piled twenty lace-trimmed pil-

lows on her bed was going to let him stink up her apartment
with smoke. The way he was acting, she'd probably tell him
to take his cigarette and shove it up his ass.

It would be exactly what he deserved.

Oh, boy. That stung. Becca squinted at the door that had
swung shut, after Nick had retreated into the blur of the corridor.

That was about as bad as it could get. Her worst-case scenario. It made her realize just how many silly, hopeful fantasies had been bubbling in the back of her head, when they
were dashed to pieces.

She had no one but herself to blame if she felt slapped
down, used, sad. She had to dig her dignity out from under
the rock where she'd hid it and act like a grown-up. She
dashed her tears away, sniffed. Enough wishing for something she just couldn't have.

No, worse. Wishing for something that didn't even exist.

Maybe she'd been subconsciously hoping that sex with
Nick would make everything magically better. It hadn't. It
couldn't. The sex itself had been beyond her wildest dreams,
but if anything, that made it worse. It made the contrast between her stupid fantasies and cold, flat reality that much
more hurtful.

She stumbled into the bathroom, groped for a washrag with
trembling fingers. She soaked it, and wiped the semen off her
body as she stared at her face, barely recognizing herself. She
looked different. Those big, bruised-looking shadows around
her eyes, the feverish color in her face, the glassy brightness
of her eyes, the puffy redness of her lips. The wild snarl of
hair. She looked like a woman on the verge of . . . she was
almost afraid to imagine.

She'd seen four dead men, seen one of them actually die.
She'd been subject to adrenaline dumps that would have

felled a bull elephant. She'd been terrorized, shamed, slimed; she'd risked rape and torture and murder.

And then she'd risked Nick. Whew. What a night.

She felt small, battered and scared. Like prey. Something shivering and helpless and fuzzy, waiting for the talons and the beak. Great sex had no power to change that, no matter how violently she came.

It was just the current state of her soul. Very roughed up. A little tenderness or understanding might have helped, but it was quite clear that Nick was absolutely not capable of that.

And? So? Get over it, she lectured herself. The man had risked his life to get her out of there. Being alive and more or less in one piece was something to be grateful for. Even if she felt like a pile of total shit.

She should suck it up. Keep her priorities straight. Be tolerant of his bad attitude and his supremely crappy post-sex etiquette.

After all, hey. He'd had a tough night, too. She almost giggled. Her goofy rationalizations sounded ludicrous sometimes, even to herself.

She pulled her vintage silk dressing gown printed with the red cabbage roses off the hook in the bathroom, and wrapped it around her shivering body as she slogged through the pillows.

She tripped over something in the corridor and almost pitched forward onto her face. She squinted, trying to bring it into focus. Nick's boot. A soggy man's sock was draped across it. Her breath snagged in her chest.

Oh. Wow. So he hadn't left without a word or a glance, after all. He wouldn't have walked out of her apartment barefoot.

She made her way unsteadily out into the kitchen of her tiny apartment. No Nick. He would be a big, blurry dark silhouette, taking up all the space, breathing up all the oxygen. He made the apartment feel so small.

Nick. She still hadn't gotten used to having a name for him. *Nikolai.* She found herself repeating it, over and over. Rolling around the word in her mouth. Liking the tight, hot feeling it gave her in her chest.

Already obsessed. Oh, dear. That was scary stuff. Very bad.

She caught a whiff of cigarette smoke as she approached the door. She cracked it open, and peered out. Nick sat on the steps leading down from her porch, wearing only jeans. Tattoos swirled over his broad, muscular shoulders and back. Smoke wreathed his head. He glanced back. She resisted the urge to shrink back inside like a child caught peeking at the grown-ups. This was her own apartment, damn it.

He turned his back without acknowledging her. Went back to his cigarette and his silent contemplation. Dismissing her.

She closed the door, leaned her forehead against it, and repeated the grown-up/dignity/self-control lecture, from start to finish. Then she got busy. Her time-honored coping mechanism. Coffee. Yes.

She measured it out, with trembling hands. Poured in the water. Stood there, hugging her shaking self as she waited for it to drip out into the pot. Wondering if she was glad he was still there . . . or not. Why hadn't he just left? He clearly didn't want anything to do with her.

And what was she shaking with, anyhow? Fear? Excitement? She didn't recognize it. It had no name. But it couldn't possibly be healthy.

She didn't even have the nerve to ask how he took his coffee. In the normal universe, she would holler, "Cream or sugar?" In this one, her throat was locked in her chest. She poured two cups, doctored her own. Stared at the other mug of strong, bitter black brew, breathing in fragrant steam. She hated it black. So harsh.

Aw, the hell with it. She kicked the door open and carried

the two mugs out just as they were. He was as mean as a snake. It was the cup of coffee that he deserved. It suited his rotten character just that way.

She picked her way on her bruised feet out over the warped, peeling porch, and ogled the bulky breadth of his back and shoulders, the way his torso tapered sexily down to lean hips. Finally, she was close enough to check out the tattoos. Hypnotic designs that looked somehow martial and menacing, despite their sensual grace.

His gun was stuck in the back of his jeans, a chilling reminder of what they'd just gone through together.

She averted her eyes from it with a shudder of distaste.

The pearly dawn was cool and damp. Too cool for the silk robe. His dour silence damped down the normal sounds of morning. No traffic, voices, airplanes taking off—even the birds were afraid to twitter and cheep when Nick was moping.

She set the coffee down beside him with a thud that made the liquid slosh over the rim and sat down a couple of stairs behind him.

He reached for the cup and took a swallow without acknowledging her. She waited. Nothing.

"You're, uh, welcome," she prompted.

He didn't speak. He didn't nod. Wow. Breathtaking. It took balls to be that rude. But balls he had, in abundance. No doubts there.

She cast around for another starting place, wrapping the robe more tightly around her quaking body. "Aren't you cold like that?"

He shook his head, took a last drag on the cigarette, and ground it out. "My body temperature is a couple notches higher than normal," he said, his voice distant. "Like I'm always running a mild fever."

Then why are you so cold? She wanted to scream the words.

She didn't. Dignity was all she had to cling to, but anger

bubbled beneath the surface of her rationalizations and justifications.

"Did you hear anything those guys said to each other when you were serving dinner?" he asked abruptly.

She winced. "Do I have to think about it now?"

He turned, stared at her. "Yeah," he said. "Right now."

She closed her eyes, trying to remember. "Lots of general chitchat, about economics. And then the country club guy said—"

"Country club guy?"

"That was how I thought of him. Rich, handsome, privileged, Ivy League type. He said something about the structure being outfitted and the waiting list growing. That he wanted to conduct more testing. Then the Spider interrupted him, and told him they'd talk business later."

He nodded, and turned away.

She was sick of being dismissed. She grabbed a handful of his hair. "You look like a caveman, with your hair snarled up," she said.

He took a gulp of coffee. "I am a caveman," he said.

She rolled the matted lock between her fingers. "You might want to rub some conditioner into that before you try to comb it."

"I'm not going to bother combing it," he said. "I'll just buzz it off. I'm sick of looking like a St. Bernard anyhow."

She was startled. "I can't imagine you with short hair."

He shrugged. "Got to change how I look. The more change, the better." He looked back over his shoulder at her, eyes narrowing. "So do you. Go blonde, maybe. Go short for sure. Get colored contacts. Today. Better yet, leave town for good. That's the best idea of all."

She was startled. "I can't do that! I work! I have responsibilities!"

"Who cares? Re-order your goddamn priorities. If you want to stay alive, anyway. You can't fulfil your responsibilities when you're dead."

"Oh, great. So we're back to the inspiring theme of how I'm destined to die a horrible death? Early in the day for that."

He glared back through the tangled caveman hair. "I'm not trying to bum you out," he said. "I'm trying to make you face reality."

Face reality, her ass. She snorted, thinking suddenly of Justin and Kaia in the hospital. "What is it about men wanting to make me face reality these days? Justin told me a bunch of stuff about myself that I didn't want to hear, either, but I think you take the prize, Nick."

"Justin?" He made the connection. "Oh, yeah. The asshole. The one who was banging the other girl. The one whose photo you just tossed. So I'm worse than him."

She choked on a sip of coffee. "Ah, not exactly," she said, coughing. "I take it back. He was worse."

He looked perplexed. "Worse how? He was banging two chicks at one time?"

"No!" she snapped. "He—"

"Was doing a guy? Switched sides on you, huh?"

"Would you shut up and let me talk?"

He made a silent zipping motion over his mouth.

"You have to promise not to laugh," she told him.

"I don't laugh much," he said. "I wouldn't worry about it. Besides, you told me some of this already."

She pressed her hands over her cheeks, which were heating up, despite the goose bumps on the rest of her body. "Not in detail. The night of our engagement party," she began, "there was this girl there. Kaia. I didn't know her. One of Justin's college friends. Tan legs that reached up to her chin, cornrowed blond braids, pierced nose, tie-dye, Barbie goes to Woodstock. The daring adventuress. She wowed the crowd with her tales of trekking in Nepal and crewing on a yacht on the South Seas. Justin told me he'd never been involved with her—"

"He lied," Nick interjected.

She glared at him. "I figured that much out all by myself.

So anyway, I was mixing up a round of daiquiries, and Justin asks me, can he use my car to give Kaia a ride to the train station. And I thought nothing of it. Until the hours started going by." Her voice trailed off. They listened to the wind swishing the tree boughs below the porch.

"Fucking cheating weasel," Nick said, meditatively.

"Yup," she agreed, her voice demure. "Well, anyway. Turns out Kaia was giving him oral entertainment in the car. As he drove."

He twisted against the railing, his face full of wary fascination. "How did you find out? Don't tell me he was dumb enough to confess."

She gave him a lofty, disapproving sniff. "No, he did not. I found out when I got the call. From the hospital."

"Hospital?" His eyes widened. "What the hell happened?"

She breathed out the tension in her chest. Amazingly, after all that had happened, the story still made her miserable. "Evidently, Kaia was so amazing at the art of fellatio, Justin forgot that he was driving a car. My car, to be precise. On a busy street. In a shopping district."

Nick let out a low whistle, and his mouth started to twitch. "Oh, man," he said, with evident relish. "What an asshole."

"Yes, that he is. My car was totaled, of course. Kaia had a neck injury and a bad concussion from the steering wheel. And Justin, well." She shrugged. "That weasely cheat is lucky he still has a dick at all."

He sucked in a breath. "You mean she . . . oh, sweet Jesus." His face contracted in a spasm of involuntary masculine sympathy.

"Chomp," Becca said stonily. "He deserved it. The snake."

Nick sagged, put his face in his hands. His back began to shake.

He was laughing at her after all. She jabbed him with her forefinger. "That's not fair," she protested. "You promised!"

He waved his hand in the air, racked by another convulsion. "You are amazing, babe. How you do this to me, I do not fucking know."

"You said you never laugh, but you're always laughing your head off at me," she grumbled. "Why is that, I wonder. Am I so comical?"

That set him off again. He hid his face and vibrated.

Becca resigned herself, and waited for his laughter to die down. She slowly realized that he couldn't stop. He kept trying, but it was like watching a swimmer caught in the surf. The waves kept sucking him down again. Was he . . . God, no. He would probably rather die than let himself cry.

She laid her hand tentatively on his hot back. "Are you, um, OK?"

"Don't. Please. You'll make it worse." His muffled voice shook.

She petted him as if she were gentling a skittish animal. "I'm glad that my humiliation is so entertaining for you," she said. "Go ahead. Hyuck it up at my expense, Nick. I'm used to it."

"Aw, fuck." The shaking of his back redoubled. "Please. Shut up."

"I guess it is funny in a way," she went on, philosophically. "Gives the term 'man-eating slut' a whole new meaning, doesn't it?"

He made an explosive sneezing sound, and off he went again.

Watching him in the grip of a laughing fit gave her a curious feeling of power. It would probably do him good, since a macho caveman like him would never have the sense to give in to tears. This worked just as well. She stroked the thick, trembling contours of his back and waited.

It took a while, but he finally lifted his face from his hands, wiped his eyes, muttering under his breath in whatever the hell that twisty, thick-sounding language he'd spoken all weekend was. Grinning.

Her breath caught, her jaw dropped. He was so gorgeous

when he smiled like that. Radiant. She loved the crinkles around his eyes, the grooves around his mouth. Wow. She had to remember to breathe.

He gave her a wary glance. His grin faded. "What's that look?"

Her mouth went dry. "I . . . I was just thinking how beautiful you are when you smile," she whispered.

Not a muscle moved in the mask of his face, but she felt the light go on inside him. And the answering one flare up inside her chest.

Chapter
13

A voice was yammering on about how he would trash it, yada yada, how much more it was going to hurt her if he kept on down this road, how bitterly she would hate his guts, blah blah, so on and so on.

Didn't help. This mindless wanting was inexorable and huge. He swung around to face her, sank to his knees in front of her. Kneeling like the desperate supplicant that he was.

He stared at her face. Jesus. Becca was dangerous, she was so fucking pretty. She had to tone it down. Wear a bag over her head. People would remember her face even if they had no particular reason to do so.

She made his eyes ache. That hot pink blush, the delicate line of her cheekbone, her jaw. And that mouth just did it to him, especially that pouty lower lip with the seam down the middle. So sexy, so soft. One look at that mouth would have made him stone hard, if he had not already been so. His dick strained in his jeans, like he hadn't just had the most amazing volcanic lay of his whole life. And the cockteasing robe gaping over her cleavage did not help matters.

Her knees poked out of the crumpled robe. He put his hands over them. Her tongue flashed out to moisten her lips.

He stared into that dim triangle between the draped panels of silk over her clamped thighs, where the hot stuff hid.

Her pale white knees were covered with scratches and scabs. He leaned down, kissed them. The callused spots on his hands snagged at fragile fabric, until his hands found skin, and greedily sought more, pushing the silk up over her legs. The robe gaped at her navel right under the knotted sash. Showing her dark muff.

Her legs shook too much to keep them clamped against the relentless pressure of his fingers. He pressed them open, and stared down into her shadowy mysteries, the holiest of holies. Her beautiful cunt was ready for him.

His fingers tightened. His balls, too.

The unmistakable purpose on his face made her scramble back. She lurched to her feet, batting his hands, and swathed herself with a swirling flutter of rose-print fabric. "Cool it, right now! My landlady is downstairs and the neighbors can see us from their window!"

"I don't care," he said.

"Of course you don't," she said crisply. "You're a caveman. We've already established that."

"So can I throw you over my shoulder? Drag you into my cave?"

"No, you may not!" she snapped. "This is *my* cave! You can carry in the coffee mugs, and put them in the sink. That's what you can do."

"Shouldn't have asked," he said. "Asking was a big tactical error."

She folded her arms under her tits. Her nipples poked through the threadbare fabric. "Too bad you didn't think of that before."

Laughter threatened, but he had plans for the next half hour that did not include another sobbing fit, so he breathed it carefully down. He scooped up coffee cups with one hand, Becca with the other, and pushed her, stumbling ahead of him into the kitchen. He deadbolted the door, rinsed the cups, and set them carefully in the drainer.

He turned to her. "So?"

She gave him a narrow look. "So what?"

"I didn't just put them in the sink," he said. "I rinsed them out."

She rolled her eyes. "Oh, boy, Nick. I'm overwhelmed."

"Good." He pried her arms away from her chest and jerked the robe down over her shoulders so that it bared her breasts, and trapped her arms in the folds of silk. He caught her arms, trapped them behind her back. "You like being overwhelmed. It gets you off."

"You overdo it," she whispered, and moaned into his mouth as he claimed her lips in a ravenous kiss. The puckered buds of her nipples tickled his chest, and he explored the sweet, silken, coffee-flavored depths of her mouth as he pressed her closer.

"Maybe," he said. "But it works for you."

"This part, yes. Just not what happens after," she said.

He stared down into her wide, somber eyes, ringed with long wet black lashes. She wasn't fooling herself this time.

Her statement hung between them like a lingering chord. She waited for him to deny it. For him to reassure her that it wasn't true.

But he couldn't. The rules weren't going to change just because he wanted them to. Being locked into this cage made him furious. Sick of the fucked-up situation, sick of eating poison, constrained at every step, by danger, duty, guilt and fear, sick regret.

He wanted this. The universe could chuckle at the cosmic joke at his expense all it wanted, but he would have this one thing. For him. Not for always, but for now, for right now, he would have it. Have *her*.

He spun Becca around till she faced the wall and buried his face in her neck as he wrenched open his jeans, dragging up handfuls of her dressing gown. He filled his hands with the warm silky curves of her ass, the hot cleft, the slick folds between. He fit himself to her, pulling her hips back to get the angle right, and they cried out together as he shoved his cock into the tight, wet clutch of her.

The sweet friction, the fluttering resistance of her pussy around his cock head almost did it. He forced himself deeper, thrusting inside until the whole length of his cock was kissed with her dew, clasped in that tight, throbbing sheath.

She cried out, her slender arms trembling where she was braced against the wall, her cunt muscles fluttering and clenching around the intrusion. "No," she said. "Don't. It's not . . . I don't like it."

He stopped cold. His instincts rarely led him wrong in sex. At least not in this phase of it. He touched her ass cheeks, with slow, soothing strokes, trembling with his own desperate eagerness to let go and have at her. "This way I won't rub your sore clit." His voice was raw with effort. "I can make you come this way. I promise. You'll love it."

"It's not that." Her voice shook. "I just . . . it makes me feel the way I felt with . . . with *them*." Her voice cracked.

He knew instantly who she was talking about. His arm tightened around her waist. His body shook with the strain of staying still. He gritted his teeth, cursed silently. Women and their goddamn complicated notions. It was like blundering through a fucking maze.

"It's not your fault. The way they looked at me, but they didn't see me. At all. When I can't see your face, it makes me feel . . ." Her voice trailed off, and he heard her swallow. "Alone. Worse than alone. I'm sorry. I'm not blaming you."

"Don't apologize. You're the last one who should be apologizing right now." He ground out the words as he eased his cock out of her.

They stared at each other for a moment, and he picked her up and carried her into her bedroom. She stiffened, grabbed his shoulders like she was afraid he was going to drop her.

He deposited her on the bed. There was a cheval mirror by the dresser. The answer to his prayers. He dragged it over, situated it in front of her so she was staring at herself. She tried to smooth her hair. Curled into a knot, wrapped her arms around herself.

"I'll look right at you. Eyes locked. The whole time," he told her.

She looked uncertain, that rosy, blurred lower lip caught between her teeth. Her eyes big and haunted.

"I can't see anything but you," he urged her. "I swear it."

She wiped away tears, shook her head. "I just feel so messed up," she whispered. "I told you, I'm not the adventurous type, and this whole thing was awful. It wiped me out."

"What's adventurous?" He circled the bed and stared into her eyes from behind, stroking his hands over her hips, cupping her ass. "You say this Kaia was the adventurous type? Trekking in Nepal, crewing on a yacht, rave parties in Thailand? Sucking some engaged guy's dick while he drove his fiancée's car? Bet that made her feel like a real wild thing. I know the type. Spoiled kids, living out their fantasies in controlled conditions. Daddy's credit card in the fanny pack, right along with the passport and the satellite phone and the hash pipe."

"I do not see how that is relevant. Oh, God . . ." Her eyes closed, and she sucked in a sharp breath as he parted her hair on the back of her neck with his lips, and pressed hot kisses against her nape.

"Bet the silly bitch never cooked a kick-ass gourmet meal for the kingpin of a global criminal syndicate," he murmured. "Bet she never served it to him practically naked without missing a beat. And then escaped to tell the tale. With the likes of me, hot on her tail. Check you out."

She started to shake. "Don't make me laugh. It's not funny."

He slid his hands up the silky insides of her thighs, and stroked her pussy. "I just want to make you understand," he said. "That Kaia cow doesn't know shit about adventure, babe. I'm talking the real kind, where you risk your skin, where you wish to God you'd stayed home. That you'd never even gotten out of bed."

"Oh," she breathed.

"But you do," he coaxed her. "You got through it. And you're OK, because you're tough. And strong. And so gorgeous, it's killing me. I won't look away from you for a second. I can't. Give me this. Please."

It took a long time for her to overcome her inner resistance. The waiting almost killed him. He stared at her, hypnotized by the contrast of his darker hands against her luminous skin. Her tits overflowed his hands, so full and soft. He nibbled her neck, smooching at that sweet spot on her nape that never failed to send a melting shudder down her back. His fingers traced patterns on the luscious underswell of her tits. He sucked in hungry gasps of her scent. His cock bobbed between her thighs, purple and bursting with readiness.

A vague realization was coming to him as he waited, teeth gritted. He had to grasp for it, since most of his brain was occupied with the desperate desire to fuck her. No space left for complex reasoning.

He'd always hidden the dark stuff from the women he'd been with. Deadly violence and its inevitable aftermath. Things he'd been forced to see, things he'd been forced to do. No woman had ever been stuck in that place with him. No woman he'd ever been with could have understood what it meant. What that level of stress did to a person. How it could wear you down, cave you in. Make you empty inside.

He'd have done anything to keep her from knowing it, but she did know it. And that changed things. It erased a barrier between them.

He couldn't tell if that was good or bad. He was guessing bad.

But God, she felt so good. His hands moved over that

smooth skin, and slowly, she leaned forward, caught herself with her hands. Arched her slender, graceful back, parting her thighs.

Presenting her perfect ass, her gorgeous pussy to him, with perfect trust. Her eyes blinked into his, wet and dazzled. Her lips were parted with excitement.

It shocked a sting of tears into his eyes, which horrified him. He had to break eye contact and press his face against her slender back. Amazed that she would give him so much.

She deserved so much more than he ever could give her in return.

It made him angry. Frustrated as hell. *Control*. He nudged his cock into her. It was never an easy glide, even as wet and slick as she was. She was as tight and snug as a leather glove. He had to work it in slow and steady, nudging and coaxing, but she shoved back, accepting him.

He raised his head, forced his eyes open. He'd promised to look at her. His face in the mirror was a grimace of self-control, but his eyes held raw emotion.

So did hers. Once they'd locked, a mechanism engaged that he had no control over. He couldn't have looked away if his life depended on it. He tried to listen with his body as he stirred her around with his cock, feeling for the angles, the strokes that made her shiver and moan, but he lost control, he was sucked into the vortex. He had to give in to his body's demands and hope to God that it worked for her, too, because he couldn't stop, couldn't . . . stop. Not at all.

She gasped with each hard lunge, jerked her hips back eagerly for more, and then he felt the energy inside her, gathering for a leap—

And she went off, with that wonderful pulsing clutch at his cock, and he thundered down to join her, when some dim part of his brain remembered—

He jerked his cock out of her just in time and spurted hot jets of pearly white come all over her ass, her back.

Her arms sagged. She collapsed onto her belly. He followed her down, braced on his elbows so she could still breathe. Glued to her with come. Pressing his face against the delicate bumps of her spine. Let his own tangled hair absorb his tears. Struggling to breathe into lungs that hitched and caught.

She wound her fingers around his wrists, and hung on, a fine tremor in her fingers. She knew what was coming. She was no fool.

He was the foolish one. For giving in to it. Not once, but twice.

He felt desolate, hollowed out. Washed up on the barren beach of reality again, like he hadn't gotten a clue the first time. He never learned. He had to get out of here, once and for all. Before he tried to comfort himself again, with her body, and made the same goddamn mistake. Over and over. Worse each time.

He was as much of an addict as his daddy, with the juice. He just hadn't found his drug of choice till now.

And fuck, was he humbled.

He pried his fingers away from hers and dragged himself up. Back turned, jeans half-fastened. Into the bathroom, to splash come off his belly. He couldn't risk another shower. Getting naked and wet only led one place with Becca.

He was careful not to look at her as he rummaged on the floor in search of the rest of his clothes.

"So this is routine for you, after sex?" she said, her low voice drifting in from the bedroom. "Acting like an ice cube, not looking at me, not speaking to me?"

He opened his mouth to reply. Stopped himself, closed it tight. Anything he said could be used against him in a female court of law.

"What did I do to deserve this?" she asked quietly.

He found his shirt, yanked it on, and grabbed his boots as he went back into her bedroom to put them on. He owed her that much. "Sweetheart, whatever you think you want from me, you're better off without it."

"Would you just look at me, goddamnit?"

Her whip-crack tone startled him into doing just that. He focused on the swirly fall of her dark hair rather than her big, hurt eyes. "The hair has got to go," he said, distractedly. "Cut it off today, Becca. Get some colored contacts, too. Dark brown. Definitely."

"Don't change the subject!" she snapped. "Why do I always get the feeling that you're punishing me for something that I didn't do?"

He shook his head. "That's way too deep for me."

"Bullshit." Her voice held an edge. "There're no video cameras in here, Nick. No bad guys watching to see if you're evil enough to suit them. You could ease off. Just, you know, a suggestion."

He plunked his ass down on the carpet amidst all the pillows to yank on his clammy, disgusting socks. "It's all real," he said. "What you see is what you get."

She pondered that as she knelt there on the bed. In her fury, she'd forgotten all about cringing and hiding. Her chin was up, her color high, eyes shining. She was crazy gorgeous. Power shining out of her.

"Well, then," she said. "I guess I see something you don't."

"You see what you want to see," he said. "Most girls do."

He could feel her hurt in the thick silence that followed. She persisted a minute later, tough as nails. "I don't believe it," she said.

"Believe what?" He yanked a boot on, tried lacing it. The damn thing was waterlogged, the leather laces swollen and stubborn.

"Your mean and horrible act," she said. "I just don't buy it. You did an amazing thing for me last night, and I just can't believe—"

"No." He struggled with the fucking bootlace until it

snapped in his hand. "What I did last night was *fail*. Get it through your head."

She dragged in a hurt breath. "It was not your fault that I came over to that house. And rescuing me from death does not equal failure!"

"That's not what I meant," he growled. "It was my job to come up with a solution to that problem that didn't involve fucking my cover. I failed to do that. Years of my life, down the drain." He shrugged, and rose to his feet, letting the unlaced boots flap. "This is salvage, babe. I'm trying to look on the bright side. Insofar as I can. At least I got some spectacular sex out of it. You burned me alive. I will never forget it."

She swung her legs around and perched on the other side of the bed, her back to him. "OK," she said. "I give in. You are mean and horrible and awful, Nick. You can stop trying to convince me. It must take a whole lot of your energy, and I know you must be tired. Just go."

Her words made his stomach sink to unplumbed depths he'd never imagined. "It's better you know that right off," he said heavily. "That's better than being disillusioned later. Trust me."

She made a sharp gesture with her hand. "I tried to trust you," she snapped. "You keep throwing it back in my face. Just leave, OK? I've had enough."

Those were the words he needed to break the spell, get him moving. He reached out to touch the glossy hair waving down her back, and gathered it all into his palm. It felt warm. Slick and vibrant and alive. It made him sorry to do what he was about to do, but hey.

"You're a sweet girl, Becca," he said.

She shook with bitter laughter. "Is that a good thing or a bad thing? With you, I don't dare guess." She jerked her head, trying to shake off his hand.

He tightened his grip, slid it farther down the length of hair. "It's an observation, not a compliment," he said.

"Let go of my hair. And thanks so much for the distinction. God forbid I should think you capable of doing or saying anything nice."

"God forbid," he agreed. "A girl like you should stay away from assholes like me."

"Thanks for the tip." Her head jerked round as she heard the *snick* of his knife, but he was too quick. Two back-and-forth slashes with the razor-sharp blade, and a thick hank dangled from his hand.

She shrieked with outrage, launching herself at him. "My hair! What the hell? How *dare* you. *Why did you do that?*"

He tossed the shorn hair onto the bed, where it swirled around itself. It looked much reduced, separated from her.

Becca's remaining hair dangled between her ears and her shoulders, a raggedy, irregular inch shorter on one side than the other.

"You weren't taking me seriously," he said. "I didn't want to have to wonder whether or not you'd do as I say. This way, I know."

"You overbearing, controlling son of a *bitch!*" She punctuated every word with a violent shove.

"I see you're finally getting a clue."

"Get out!" she yelled at him. "Just get out of my place, you . . . you *asshole!* Get out!"

He stumbled backward before her onslaught, hastily scooping up his SIG from where he'd left it on her dresser. Leaving a fully loaded piece lying around within reach while lopping off a chick's hair with his pocketknife was not one of the brighter moves of his spotty career.

He allowed himself to be herded out the door. It slammed in his face. The sound reverberated in his ears.

Well, hell. He'd burned his bridges. Spectacularly. But then again, burning bridges came naturally to him.

He moved down the stairs, like he'd been preprogrammed by someone else. Someone who did not wish him well. Out with the keys, into the truck. Put it in gear. Conflicting

thoughts jostled in his head. He should have left her a number. If the worst happened, and Zhoglo—

No.

A) Chances of something happening diminished expo-
nentially if she had no contact with him. B) If Zhoglo found
her, she wouldn't have a chance to call for help. She would
never see it coming.

And he'd be better off not knowing.

He drove, mechanically, to his condo. Parked in his slot.
Sat there, for a long, timeless interval, mind blank. He finally
dug into his pocket and pulled out the coiled-up hank of
satiny brown hair that he'd swiped.

Fondling it. It was the only word that fit. It was so amazingly soft. What the hell was this, something sick, like a tro-
phy? He didn't know.

He'd better jump-start his brain, start thinking again, if he
wanted to survive. He tried, but it was like flogging a dead
horse.

The only sure thing was that he should stay on the move.
And the hell away from Becca. A brief stop here to get his shit
together, and he was gone. If Zhoglo took him down, the first
thing the guy would go for when he started to hurt him
would be Becca's whereabouts. Nick had no illusions about
how long he'd be able to hold out under a highly skilled tor-
turer. It didn't matter how tough you were. Eventually, they
got to you.

He wished he'd scared her bad enough to make her run
someplace far and unknown even to him, but the stubborn
broad was impossible to intimidate. Though it was also true
that he could not un-know her name or former address. The
biggest threat to Becca's safety right now was the information inside his own brain. He wasn't going to sleep at night
knowing Zhoglo was out there, nosing around for her.

Not that he slept much anyhow. Not since Sveti and
Sergei.

He wandered around his condo, at a loss. The apartment

seemed unfamiliar. Empty, cold. A parking place for his stuff and, occasionally, his body. Never a home. He hadn't spent any real time there for years.

It didn't take long. There wasn't much. A couple of guns, some favorite knives. His hard drive, his laptop. Some photos of his mother. He had none of his father and wanted none. Besides, if he wanted to remember what Dad looked like, all he had to do was go to the mirror and give himself a snake-eyed, sealed-mouth, pinched-nostril glare. He was a dead ringer for the man. All that was missing was the smell of alcohol that had exuded from Dad's every pore.

He took down the photo of Sergei and Sveti that hung on the blank wall. It was grainy, poor quality, snapped on a cell phone. He wasn't sure why he'd framed it. He was never in this house to look at it.

He snapped open the cheap frame, and tucked the photo into a padded envelope. Looking at Sveti's sweet smile made his stomach cramp. He stared at it. Tried to swallow it down. The truth, like a nasty pill.

The best he could do for Sveti at this point would be to simply eliminate Zhoglo. That was starting to look impossible, aside from suicidal. But hey. What the fuck else did he have to do with himself?

One more thing. He pulled his fly-fishing tackle box out of the closet, and rummaged till he found a plastic ziplock baggie, the kind drug dealers used to portion out their wares. He pulled the feathery fishing fly out of it, tossed it into the guts of the box and rooted around till he found a length of thread. Then he sat down under the light at his dining room table, and took Becca's hair out of his pocket.

It took him a while, to soothe and stroke and restore the handful of hair back to its original glossy perfection, but once it was done, he coiled it into a circle and threaded the red filament carefully around to hold it in place. His fingers were deft from years of tying fishing flies. The one thing Dad taught him that had been of any use.

Then he tucked the ring of hair into the padded envelope with the photos. A moment later, he plucked it out, put it back into his pocket.

Christ, he was so tired. Down to his bones. Sometimes he caught himself wishing that Zhoglo would just get a move on and kill him already, so he could get some fucking rest. But the joke would be on him. He'd probably go straight to the hot place. Pitchforks and flames.

Life sucked. Why should death be any different?

He was pondering that heartening thought when the phone rang. He read the display. Aw, fuck. It was Tamara.

He might as well get the red-hot-poker reaming session over with sooner rather than later. He picked up the phone. "Yeah," he muttered.

"You idiot." Her voice burned through the telephone line like acid. "You can't even get yourself killed like a real man."

He rolled his eyes as he stalked into the bathroom, and tucked the phone between shoulder and chin as he rooted through the cabinet for the clippers. The blades on the thing were dull for sure. He hadn't cut his hair in over three years. "Thanks for your touching concern." His lame attempt at irony reminded him of Becca's prickly sarcasm.

Bravado, covering up that cream-puff interior.

"Concern. Pah. Stupid goat's dick excuse for a man," Tam hissed in Ukrainian. "I just got a hysterical phone call from Ludmilla. She thinks she's going to get her tits cut off, and she has good reason to think so. Smooth move, Nikolai. Whatever the fuck you did, it is going to cost me. I should never have tried to help you. You were supposed to kill him, you asshole! I thought you were on a suicide mission!"

Man, that bitch could be cold when she was inconvenienced. "I was," he said. "Then it morphed into murder suicide. And I choked."

"Morphed . . . what the hell are you talking about? Use short sentences, yes? Small words. What happened?"

He yanked the scissors out of the bathroom drawer, pushed

the speakerphone button and laid the phone down onto the sink. He stared at his reflection as he held a thick, snarled clump of hair away from his head, and brutally scissored it off. It fell into the sink with a soft thud. "A girl," he said.

"A girl? What girl?" Her voice was getting shrill.

"A girl happened," he said, through clenched teeth.

"Wait a minute." Tam hesitated for a moment. He could almost hear the gears crunching in her head. "You don't mean to say you brought a girl to the—"

"Fuck, no," Nick snapped, hacking off another clump. "She just appeared. She was staying on the island in another house. That house was supposed to be empty. I checked. Repeatedly. She showed up, out of nowhere in the middle of the night to use the fucking pool. The night before the big Z showed up."

"Oh, God," Tam moaned. "Men and their fucking hero complexes."

"I tried scaring her," he snapped, defensive. Best to skip the details. Tamara really would cut his balls off for a necklace. "She was tougher than I thought. She'd left her glasses at the poolhouse before I chased her off. She came back to get them the next day."

"Don't tell me. Let me guess. At the worst possible moment?"

"Ran smack into the Vor and his boys as they were coming up from the boat," Nick said wearily. "Unfortunately, she was pretty. Zhoglo licked his chops and decided to have her for lunch."

Tam made a disapproving sound. "So you fucked yourself, me and Ludmilla, to bail out this clueless honey's ass, hmm?"

Nick's silence was her answer. Her laughter had a bitter edge. "Didn't have the guts to watch them cut her to pieces, did you?"

His throat bobbed as he tried to moisten his dry, ragged

throat. "Didn't have the guts to do the cutting," he said. "Hate to say it, but I have my limits."

"Hmph. You're soft, Nikolai. Soft in the head, limp in the spine. But I bet there's one part of you that's as hard as a diamond, hmm?"

"Tam, it's not—"

"I hope her sweet tail is worth it, jerk-off. I hope she fucked your brains out. Not that she had far to go. I don't think there was much rattling around in there to begin with. What am I supposed to do about Ludmilla? Any bright ideas on how I can keep her from getting her tits cut off, Nikolai? I've called in all my favors. Now I have to deliver some."

He stared down at the scissors in his hand, pondering. Ludmilla was one possible point of future contact with Zhoglo that he might be able to exploit. Zhoglo was going to want to have a talk with Ludmilla. That was a big drag for the madam, but any woman who made her living taking advantage of helpless and destitute young women knew how to look after her own interests.

In this case, though, her interests and his were right in line.

"I'll talk to Seth and Davy," he said. "I'll arrange twenty-four-hour-a-day surveillance of her agency. Two guys constantly nearby, and ready for quick intervention, if he sends anyone to take her out."

"Oh? Really? Do you have any idea how expensive that will be, my friend? Who's going to pay for it?"

"I will," he said rashly.

"You?" She cackled. "You're an unemployed ex-fed. You will pay with exactly what winning lottery ticket? Exactly which rich dying uncle? You're an orphan, Nikolai. I've seen your bank account, your tax returns. You've cashed in your last CD, you've borrowed against your pension. Unless you have an offshore account I haven't noticed yet, your resources are all tapped out."

"You invasive bitch," he said mildly, sawing off more hair. "Get your nose out of my wallet."

"Just looking out for my own interests, darling," she purred.

"Front me the money," he suggested. "I'll sell my condo and pay you back."

"I will hold you to it," she warned. "Kind of amusing to think of you huddled under a bridge in your cardboard home. As I dine by candlelight. On fine china."

"Whatever blows your skirt up, Tam."

She made an irritated sound. "This is in the interests of killing him now, no? You are finished with whatever other foolish heroic notions you had before? And don't expect me to believe that you care about Ludmilla's safety. Your hero complex doesn't go that far."

He thought about the flinty-eyed, bleached-blond Ludmilla, and shrugged inwardly. "I don't actively wish her any ill," he hedged. "And yes. It is in the interests of killing him. Now, anyway."

Tamara made a disgusted sound. "Get it right this time. I should have hired a sniper to take him out from a distance."

"You didn't hire me," he said evenly. "You weren't paying me, last time I checked. And I never said this was going to be a straight hit. I had my own agenda. But it's fucked."

"What agenda, Nikolai?" Her voice was flat.

He flung the scissors into the sink, cursing his own careless words. He was so fucking tired now, he was babbling. It was dangerous to let Tam know too much of your business. He yanked out his pocketknife. What worked for Becca's hair would work for him. He sawed off chunks until the sink was full of dull, snarled hair.

So different from the satiny coil of hair he'd cut off Becca. So soft. His hand closed into a fist, remembering the silken feel of it in his palm.

"I'm waiting, Nikolai," Tam prompted.

He grabbed another hank and attacked it viciously. "So keep waiting," he growled. "Wait all you want."

The silence after his words made him twitch. Tam was ruthless, supernaturally smart, and her hidden agendas were incomprehensible. Dealing with her was like dealing with a space alien. You just had to suck in a deep breath, roll the dice, and hope she didn't kill you.

"This is about that mess in Ukraina five months ago, isn't it?" she said softly. "When Sergei got killed? And his daughter abducted?"

Shock rippled through him. He let the knife drop on to the heap of hair. "How the fuck do you know about that? That's classified!"

"I have my sources," she said, cool as a cucumber.

"Con," he grated. "That stupid flapjawed son of a bitch—"

"You're still hoping to find the girl, aren't you? How old was she? Eleven, twelve?"

He stared down at the black plastic thing that kept talking to him, torturing him, not letting him be.

"Oh, Nikolai." Her voice had softened. She sounded sad. "You act so tough, but it's all bullshit. You know she's dead, don't you?"

He couldn't breathe, or speak. *No,* the voice in his head said. *Maybe she's not.*

"Dead, or worse than dead," she went on, matter-of-factly.

That made his tissues all contract. "Shut up, Tam," he snarled.

"Can't bear to think of it? Get it through your head, big boy. The truth will make you free. One way or another, she's past saving now."

Nick made a noncommittal sound, and took one final slash at the last long hank that dangled down over his eyes. His hair stuck out every which way now, like it had been chewed off by rats on crack. He turned on the clippers. The low, pervasive buzz of the machine filled his ears.

"Can't hear you, Tam," he said loudly. "I'm cutting my hair."

He took his time, running the clippers over his head, and

his beard. He'd chosen the longest setting, since he didn't want to look like a plucked chicken. He'd done this himself every couple of weeks back in his clean-cut days, but it was trickier when the hair was longer.

When he finished, he stared at the results, grim and unsatisfied. He did not look forgettable. He looked like a short-haired, stressed-out, evil-eyed thug who'd gotten a well-deserved pounding. He turned off the clippers. The sudden silence vibrated strangely in his ears.

"I know what you're trying to do, Nikolai," Tam said quietly.

He grunted. "That's great, Tam. That makes one of us."

"You're trying to save your soul," she said. "Watch out, my friend."

The hair clipper fell into the sink, bouncing on the thick pad of hair. He swayed forward, gripped the sink for support. His insides empty. No ground beneath him. Just an endless, sickening fall.

"It's dangerous to pin your soul on a lost cause," Tam whispered into the phone. "The girl's gone. Zhoglo ate her. Face it, deal with it. Pin your soul on something else. Believe me. I know what I'm talking about."

He breathed down a sudden urge to throw up, sucking in harsh, audible breaths as rage built up inside him.

"I see why you'd feel that way," he said. "Nobody saved you, did they? They left you in the dark, right? Were you past saving, too, Tam?"

It was a blind lashing out, a shot in the dark. He didn't know shit about Tam's mysterious past. No one did. But he knew from the sudden change in the quality of the silence that he'd hit the mark. Dead on.

He already felt like shit about it.

"Fuck you," Tam whispered. She hung up.

He picked up the phone, wound up and slammed it into the mirror. Right between the reflected image of his own glaring eyes.

Crash. The mirror shattered, making a depressed well in the center surrounded by radiating cracks. Sharp shards of mirror glass hung askew and pattered into the sink.

Seven years of bad luck. He stared at the mirror. Like any kind of luck could top what he'd been having lately.

Chapter
14

Kristoff was bored in the new house. There was nothing to do yet. No one wanted him to help, after his failure in the control room on the island. The Vor was in a foul mood and caution dictated staying as far out of his way as possible. So Kristoff huddled in the back suite, his nerves still badly rattled by what had happened the night before.

In fact, he was surprised the Vor hadn't killed him by now, for not reacting fast enough. Perhaps it just hadn't occurred to him yet.

He felt guilty. He'd been staring off into space, imagining how it was going to be to fuck that girl when his turn came. Watching Arkady with her on the vid screen had gotten them all worked up.

And then, out of nowhere. Poof, boom. He was gone, with the girl. Leaving four corpses behind, like a blood-sucking demon from hell.

He pulled out his laptop and logged on, surfing the porn sites. He sifted through the trash that interested him less, perversions and fetishes, gay, S&M. He was a traditional man, with traditional tastes.

Oral. Yes, he liked oral. He typed his brand new American word, "blow job," into the search engine.

Millions of hits. He sorted, clicking on the pictures. He opened his pants as he admired the girls, their gleaming, painted lips distended around various outsized phalluses, and stimulated himself idly as he perused their wonderful variety. All colors, shapes and sizes, but none as pretty as the girl on the island. Her tits had been without equal.

He clicked on another jpeg, enlarged it, and stared at it, jaw sagging. Not possible. It was like magic. He had been thinking of her, and there she was. The girl from the island.

But it was a normal photograph, not porn. She was looking back over her shoulder, her long dark hair swirling in the breeze. She looked harried, distressed, her mouth open in some reproof as she flapped her hand at whoever was snapping the picture. She wore glasses.

He read bits of the text with some difficulty.

Rebecca Cattrell, long-suffering fiancée of our naughty Don Juan, was unwilling to comment about her man's mangled member . . . everyone wants to know about the famous blow job that ended in scandal, heartbreak, and a million-dollar lawsuit, to say nothing of the emergency room . . . has already been permanently entered in the annals of urban myth . . .

Kristoff's erection wilted from the sudden lack of attention while excitement of another kind burgeoned in his belly. He tucked himself briskly back into his pants, picked up the laptop and carried it down to the dining room. This might help offset last night's disaster.

Pavel was serving a huge cut of thick steak to the Vor. Seared on the outside, red on the inside, bleeding all over the plate. The Vor was attacking it with his usual ferocity.

What he had on the screen gave him just enough courage to approach the table and endure the flinty look the Vor gave him.

His boss sawed off a pink chunk, and stuffed it into his mouth. "What could be important enough to interrupt my meal?" he hissed.

Kristoff placed the laptop on the table, and angled the screen towards his boss.

Zhoglo stared at it. The chewing action in his plump, distended cheeks slowed, and then stopped. He gulped down the lump of steak unchewed, and began to laugh.

"You worthless, stinking turd," Ludmilla hissed at him in Ukrainian. Her heavily made-up dark eyes looked daggers at him through the oversized vid screen in Davy and Seth's big underground workshop, and her crimson cupid's-bow mouth worked furiously. "I want nothing to do with you and your stupid schemes, your suicidal urges. Tell your stupid men to go away and leave me be. Tell them to fuck off. I do not want to die."

After Tam's scolding, and Becca's parting shot, Nick was inured to females spitting insults at him. Good thing, too, because Milla was without equal in that department. She was the Olympic athlete of the filthy epithet in Ukrainian, and not too damn shabby in English, either.

"Your best chances are with us now, Milla," Nick repeated patiently for at least the tenth time. "As soon as I get a fix on him, I'll go after him and take him out. And you'll be free and clear."

"Hah! You said you'd kill him before, you fool, and you did not manage it. And you leave me out there swinging in the wind, and you tell me you want more from me now? Pah!"

"You'll be free and clear," Nick repeated obstinately. "And Aleksei will be avenged."

That had been a risk. He knew that Aleksei, Milla's first husband, had been slaughtered by command of Vadim Zhoglo over twenty years before, but he didn't know if she had been genuinely fond of him or not. Aleksei had been a pimp too, and Ludmilla had been one of the girls in his stable before he married her and began showing his young wife the ropes of the trade.

Judging from the downturned, suddenly old-looking sag of her mouth, she had genuinely liked him.

"What do you care for Aleksei?" she snarled.

"Nothing," Nick said, with perfect honesty. "Never knew the guy. But you did. That's what matters. Wouldn't you like to see that bloated flyblown sack of shit die for what he did to you?"

Ludmilla's mouth shook with something like suppressed disgust. "You are an incompetent bastard. Using me, like a piece of toilet tissue, to clean up your shitty messes," she hissed.

Ooh. Ouch. And this from a woman who raked huge profits off selling women's bodies to anyone who cared to buy a piece.

"Won't you sleep better at night once he's finally dead?" he coaxed. "Come on, Milla. Swallow the pill. Follow through. Let them plant the bugs. They're quick, they're professional, the equipment will be invisible and the signals will be weak, since the receivers are right on the other side of the wall. It won't set off any detector alarms. And the guys will be right there to protect you if Zhoglo—"

"Pah! Don't lie to me again. I am not a fool. Your men give not a shit for me," she spat. "They will not care if Zhoglo cuts me into chunks for the cookpot. They will watch and laugh."

"They will be right next door. Their orders are to protect you," he repeated. "That's what they're paid to do. You have my word."

"Your word. Hah. I spit upon your word." Ludmilla made a catlike snarling sound, and flounced angrily away from the vid cam.

A couple of quiet minutes went by, and he decided to take that for an assent. He'd gotten no more frustrated phone calls from Marcus and Riley, the guys Davy and Seth had sent over to bug the luxury penthouse apartment from which Ludmilla ran her business.

He lowered his pounding head into his hands. He wished he could be the one, but his face was too well known by now to get anywhere near Ludmilla. He could never pass himself off as a building repairman or a telephone tech. All he could do was watch the vid feed from afar.

He was making an effort, such as it was. He was doing everything he could think of. He just wished to God he could think better, clearer. Faster. He wished he could sleep. And stop thinking about Becca.

Stop seeing that look on her face when she shoved him out her door. And that classic parting phrase. *Get out. You asshole.*

God knows, it hadn't been the first time he'd heard those particular words from a woman. He didn't know why it was bugging him so damn much this time. He realized that he had his hand in his pocket. He was clutching the ziplock baggie that held her hair.

Shit. He jerked his hand out, cursing under his breath.

"So? Did you persuade her? That is one hard broad."

Nick turned at the dry voice, and faced Seth Mackey, the guy who was more or less unwillingly helping him. "I think so," he said dully. "I think we're in."

"And now?" Seth crossed his arms over his chest and scowled.

Nick blew out a weary breath. "Now we wait. And I watch."

"In real time? Twenty-four hours a day? Nobody else can identify those guys, and none of us speak Ukrainian. We can't spell you, man."

"I know that," Nick growled back. "I've been told. More than once."

"It'll be tedious. You'll go nuts," Seth warned. "You have to sleep."

"No, I don't. And I already am nuts." In truth, the idea of

staring at vid screens of empty rooms sounded kind of relaxing, after all the blood and guts, and women scolding him. "It'll have to be me," he said. "Unless you come up with a better idea."

"Yeah," Seth said, with alacrity. "Passive gulper bugs. We remote retrieve the info every couple of hours and analyze it on the spot."

"That won't help Milla if they come to take her away," Nick argued wearily. "And it'll be too late to follow whoever might come. Forget it."

"So that's why we're providing bodyguards for this woman? At your expense?" Seth's lip curled. He had no use for pimps of either sex. "Didn't know you were so freaking fond of the greedy bitch."

"I'm not," Nick said, through gritted teeth. "I think she's an icy-hearted hag. But I still don't want her to die because I fucked up."

Seth shook his head, a wondering expression on his dark face. "Shit. You're worse than the McClouds. I had no idea you were so principled. I figured you for . . ."

"What?" Nick snarled. "The kind of asshole who would fuck over a friend and leave him to die? Is that what you figured?"

Seth's eyes narrowed to dark slits, mouth tightening.

"Sleep deprivation," Davy McCloud intoned from the doorway. "It's ugly. Turns a normal man into a raving pig dog shithead. I've been observing its effects in my brother ever since his kid was born."

"Yeah, and you're next, dude," Seth said, with a quick grin. "What have you got left? Five weeks? Less? Get ready."

Nick swiveled his head on his sore, aching neck and stared at the huge blond guy, built more or less like a refrigerator, who filled the doorframe. "Are you saying that I'm a raving pig dog shithead?"

"No. You need to get some rest. And lighten up," Davy said calmly. "Nobody blames you for Novak."

"You did," Nick pointed out. "You hated my guts for years."

"So? What if I did? I got the fuck over it." Davy strode into the room. The chair creaked under his weight as he sat down. "And so should you. No harm done. So chill. It's getting old, already."

The men fell silent. Nick felt like a hysterical idiot for bringing it up at all. Thinking about it made him want to fall into a crack in the ground. Talking about it, particularly with a McCloud, was worse.

But Con and his lady had gotten through that adventure. They were alive, happy, even reproducing. That event had been superseded by brand new nightmares: Sergei, with his entrails piled on his chest. Sveti, in an unmarked grave. Or huddling some place worse than death.

Hell, it was a wealth of guilt, betrayals, mistakes, fuckups. An embarrassment of fuel for his nightmares.

"This isn't going to work unless we can find somebody else who speaks Ukrainian," Seth fretted.

"How about me?" asked a soft, feminine voice.

All three men's heads whipped around. It was Raine, Seth's wife, who had accompanied him to the SafeGuard headquarters today. She was a slender, ethereal chick with silvery gray eyes and a cloud of blond hair that hung to her ass. The woman was mouthwatering, but any intelligent guy who took one look at Seth Mackey looming possessively over his wife quickly averted his eyes from her. And didn't look back.

"You speak Ukrainian?" Nick said, amazed.

Her slender shoulders lifted. "Pretty much. My father and uncle emigrated from there in the sixties. I spoke it with them until I was twelve. They came from Kiev, and the language I remember will be years out of date. But I speak Russian, too. I'll understand quite a bit. I could spell you at night, at least, when there's not likely to be a lot of action."

"No way, babe. You've got better things to do with your nights than sit around watching that nasty bitch selling her wares. And you need your sleep," Seth said testily, patting her belly. "Especially now."

She laid her hand on his shoulders with a tender smile that was so private, Nick looked away, embarrassed. "Just until you find someone else you can trust who speaks Ukrainian, OK?" she wheedled. "Don't worry. You don't have to lose any sleep yourself."

"Yeah, right," Seth grunted. "Like I could sleep, alone, if you were here, manning vid screens. Tiring yourself out." He shot Nick an unfriendly look. "I think it's a shitty idea."

"I think it's great," Raine said brightly.

Nick rubbed his burning eyes, and blinked at her. "Thank you," he said simply, in Ukrainian. "That would be a great help."

"It's nothing," she replied in the same language. "My pleasure."

Seth gave her a mock-evil squint. "Don't talk to other guys in a language I don't know," he growled.

Nick looked around on the shelves until he found a pile of telephone books while the others were snickering at the guy, and forced his stinging eyes to focus until he found the Seattle yellow pages. He yanked it down off the shelf, flipped through until he got to *R*.

"What are you looking for in there?" Seth demanded.

"A Realtor," he said.

Davy scowled. "What for?"

"Gotta sell my condo." He stared down, daunted by the sheer number of possibilities. Pages of Realtors, for fuck's sake. How could he tell who to call? "I have to pay for this crazy shit somehow."

Davy snatched the phone book from him, and flung it. It thunked heavily back onto the shelf, slid, and fell facedown onto the floor.

"Stop being an asshole," he snapped. "Before I lose my patience."

Chapter 15

Click. Beep. "Becca, this is Marla. I know you're not up at the island, because Jerome went there today to check on the place when he heard that the house next door burned to the ground. Were you aware that he found the place wide open? Front door swinging, alarm deactivated, lights on? There was a raccoon in the kitchen going through the cupboards! The place was a disaster. I'm sure I don't have to tell you how unhappy Jerome is about this, and how badly this reflects on me. I'm baffled, Becca. It's not like you at all. And since you're not at the island, why aren't you back at work? We have that banquet tomorrow night, and two weddings this weekend! We are swamped, and I mean swamped. Give me a call, if you value your job. And do let me know at least that you're all right."

Click. Beeeeeeeeep.

Becca stared at the phone from her position sprawled on the couch. It was on the table in front of her, within arm's reach, but for the fact that her arm was too heavy to lift.

Value her job? Huh. Did she? It was far too weighty a question for her brain to contemplate.

She was too miserable to care. Nothing seemed to have

any value. Everything she'd ever accomplished, all her fretting and saving and striving, seemed like so much frantic scurrying on a hamster's wheel. Who cared about it? Who thanked her for it? Who did it really benefit?

No one. It was busywork. Meaningless, empty busywork. Her life was made up of the trivial details no one else had time to care about.

No wonder Nick hadn't been interested in sticking around. Or coming back. Or giving her his phone number. Or even asking for hers. Just a couple of bouts of hot, sweaty sex to work off his adrenaline jag, and he was done with her. She could hardly blame him. She had nothing to offer him.

And oh, man, the pity party was getting ugly, but she couldn't seem to snap out of it. She'd already tried her usual tricks. The Oreos lay on the table, packaging ripped and ravaged. Music annoyed her, movies bored her or filled her with a vague sense of dread. She'd tried a scented bath, with bath pearls and bubbles and perfumed goop. She'd even broken out her emergency stash of Godiva. Nothing worked.

So get busy. Get off your lazy bum, her helpless, hijacked, practical self lectured her miserable, depressed, useless self. *It's the only way.*

So very busy, her depressed self scoffed. Like always. Busy, busy Becca. Too busy to notice that what she did had no meaning. None at all. Zip.

The phone rang again. Becca groaned, flung her head back and her hands over her ears, bracing herself through the interminable shrill six rings, and her own tooth-grindingly cheerful outgoing message. God, had she ever really been that perky? She wanted to smack herself.

Click. Beep. "Hi, Becca? Are you there? It's Carrie. I've been calling you for three days now and you're never—"

"Carrie?" Becca pushed the stop button on the machine. "I'm here." For her baby sister, she'd break the paralysis.

"Oh, thank God. What the hell is going on? Are you OK?

I talked to Josh, and he said he hadn't been able to reach you either! And I tried you at work, too! They told me you were out! Have you been sick?"

"No," she mumbled. "I just . . . didn't feel like going."

"Didn't feel like going?" Carrie echoed her words in a disbelieving voice. "Wait. Don't you work Thursday nights at your catering job?"

Becca felt a zing of alarm, swiftly smothered by another wave of weariness. "Oh, shit," she said heavily. "Yes, I guess I do. I, uh, forgot."

Carrie was eloquently silent for a moment. "This is just too weird," she said. "You've never forgotten an appointment in your entire life."

"Oh, stop it," she said crabbily. "I'm not that much of a robot."

"What's the matter with you? Is it about that scum-sucking man slut, Justin? Would you like me and Josh to flatten him for you?"

Becca hesitated. She'd fretted over how much she should tell her younger brother and sister about what had happened on the island. She'd decided that for the time being, she would go with a highly edited but literally true version.

"It's not about Justin," she said. "I, um, had an encounter this weekend."

"Encounter?" Carrie made an impatient sound. "What do you mean? A close encounter of the third kind? A romantic encounter?"

"I think romantic would be overstating it," Becca said cautiously. "Intense would probably be the better word."

"Oh! You mean sex? Yowza! You bad girl! I didn't know you had it in you! Did you get Justin out of your system?"

She blinked, startled by the question, and realized that, for all her misery, none of it was caused by her ex. Her feelings about Nick were oh, so much more compelling. Not that it made the situation any better.

Misery was still misery, after all. No matter what caused it.

"I suppose I did, though I wasn't thinking about it in those terms at the time," she said.

"So? What's he like?" Curiosity sharpened Carrie's voice.

"Not my usual type," Becca said. "Big. Tough. Lots of muscles. Long hair, beard stubble, tattoos. A foul mouth. Sort of . . . dangerous."

"Woo-hoo! He sounds virile. So? Was he, you know, good?"

"I tell no tales," Becca said primly.

Carrie made a disgusted noise. "Hello? Becca, this is me, Carrie. Your sister. We're alone. I'm legally an adult. Was he good?"

She took a deep breath, and it rushed out. "He was amazing," she confessed. "Absolutely unbelievable."

Carrie crowed with delight. "Oh, thank God you've finally gotten properly laid! I was wondering if it would ever happen! It wouldn't have ever if you'd married the dickwad. So when do we meet Mr. Muscles?"

She winced. "You won't. It ended. Very badly."

"One of those one-night stands where the guy never calls again?"

Becca let out a long, measured sigh. "I guess so. More or less."

"Those suck," Carrie said sagely. "But it's probably just as well. He's just a rebound boy. Slam, bam, thank you, Sam. Those Neanderthal types are great when the lights are out, but you can't take them to the opera. You can't let yourself get depressed about that."

She was obscurely irritated by her sister's superior, lecturing tone. "Actually, it would appear that I can," she snapped.

It always needled her when Carrie played the role of the more sexually experienced sister. At nineteen, she was just too damn young, but Becca had always been too frantically busy keeping her orphaned family afloat to do the role justice herself. Carrie had picked up the slack with great enthusiasm. It worried Becca sometimes.

Carrie was still nattering on. Becca jerked her attention back to her sister's voice. ". . . up to Seattle, just to check on you," she was saying. "It's definitely time for a visit."

Panic exploded through her. She sat bolt upright. "No! Carrie, no. Don't come up. Please."

"Good God, Becky. Why the hell not?"

Becca floundered for a credible explanation, but she found herself mired in unspeakable memories instead. Gunshots, pools of blood, slashed throats, the Spider's wet smile and glittering eyes, it was all far too close to her, too real. The toxic vibe infected the very air she breathed. She didn't want Carrie and Josh anywhere near it.

And she couldn't do anything crazy, like disrupting their lives by taking out a loan and sending them both to Argentina without telling them everything. Telling them struck her as even more dangerous.

"But I'm worried about you," Carrie said plaintively. "It's not like you, Becca. Not answering your phone, forgetting to go to work, picking up dangerous strangers and having wild sex with them . . . it's weird. I think you need some serious, heavy-duty, industrial strength cuddling."

Her heart squeezed, and tears rushed into her eyes. "You're a sweetie, honey, and I appreciate the concern, but I don't want to interrupt your studies. You can't lose your scholarship. I can't—"

"Yes, yes. I know. You can't help me with rent and tuition both. I know, we've been through it."

"Please," Becca pleaded. "I can't handle a visit now. I'm just not presentable. I need to lick my wounds alone for a while, OK? And oh, before I forget. I lost my cell phone. Here's my new number. Got a pen?"

"Go ahead," Carrie said.

Becca recited the new number to her. "Could you give it to Josh? And as soon as things calm down, I'll come down to see you. I promise."

"Hmm. We'll see," Carrie hedged. "I'll talk to Josh."

"Carrie, I'm serious," she said, edging on desperation. "Please—"

"Talk to you soon, Becky. Big, smoochy kisses, OK? Bye."

The connection broke. Becca stared at the phone in her hand, silently cursing her stubborn little sister. She flung the phone in the direction of the table and missed. It tumbled to the floor and began to beep forlornly.

Just as well. She didn't want to get an angry phone call from Gilda, the manager of DeLillo's Fine Gourmet Catering, Becca's off-and-on night job. She didn't want to grope for lies, excuses, justifications, for feeling so bad. She just wanted to stare at the sky through the window as it turned from cobalt blue to black.

It got so terribly quiet. She pushed the button of the TV remote, did a desultory surf, and settled on a channel with *Friends* reruns. That was the only thing that felt safe and bland enough to watch.

The doorbell rang, and the illusory sense of safety dissolved like smoke. In an instant, she went from feeling limp to feeling every muscle go rigid, with terror.

Who . . . ? The Spider had found her already?

She got up, stumbling down onto one wobbly knee and kept herself bent over in the dark so no one looking in the windows would see any moving shadows as she crept towards the door. Kicking herself for not thinking to turn on the porch light before. Turning it on now would announce her presence behind the door like a trumpet fanfare.

Oh, hell, her security was useless anyway, so Nick said. And the Spider's guys could shoot her right through the freaking walls, if they felt like it. They probably had thermal imaging devices on their damn guns. She should get over herself. She forced herself to stand up.

She put her eye to the peephole. There was enough light from the streetlamps to see the tall, broad silhouette. Those night-dark eyes.

Nick. Oh, God. It was Nick.

A wobbly rush of fresh feelings went through her. A thrill of excitement, mixed with shame and fury, and a sharp tang of fear.

And a hot, sweet twist of awareness between her legs.

No way. Not in a million years would she let that bastard get that close to her again. No matter what pulsed and throbbed inside her.

She put her hand up to the mass of curly hair that swung a couple inches below her chin. She still couldn't get used to all that volume the shorter length created around her face, but she was past the worst of the shock, at this point, and the hairdresser had done a nice job in shaping it, so she was coping with the hair trauma. No thanks to him, though. She shoved her glasses up the bridge of her nose, and squinted through the peephole.

Wow. He'd cut his hair too, just as he'd threatened. He looked very different. The spiky brush of hair stuck out every which way. The bruise under his eye had faded to a purplish line slashing downwards diagonally, from the inside corner of his eye to under his cheekbone.

He wore black leather. She was not one bit surprised.

His dark eyes stared into hers, unwavering. It was like the door didn't exist at all. He knew perfectly well she was there. Staring at him. Cowering behind the door like a goddamn mouse. Whiskers trembling.

She undid the old lock, the new lock, the deadbolt, the chain, and pried out the kitchen chair she'd wedged under the knob. She yanked the door open, and gave him her coldest frigid-bitch look.

"You," she said. "What do you want?"

He didn't answer. Seconds crept by, stretched into minutes.

She realized, at length, that being cold and mean would have no effect on this guy. He wouldn't get the subliminal message. Nor would he get embarrassed or flustered, or feel in any way at a disadvantage. Why should he? Mean and cold was his normal default setting. It probably made him feel right at home. Comfortably familiar. God only knew, tenderness and intimacy had scared him half to death.

This was silly. They couldn't stand there having a staring contest all night, and having the door open to the night made her twitch. She stepped back, and gestured him ungraciously into the apartment.

He closed the door behind himself. The room was so dark. She stood there, rigid with uncertainty. Nick flipped the light on. She flinched, putting her hands up to her eyes. Since that weekend, turning lights on when it was dark outside made her feel scarily exposed, like being in a fishbowl, even with the blinds closed. She'd been creeping around in the dark and she had the bruises on her shins to prove it.

He stared at her fixedly, his thick, straight dark brows knitted into a scowl. "I told you to go blonde," he said.

Her chin went up. "What are you going to do about it? Highlight me by brute force? Tie me down and do foil tips?"

His eyes flashed. "If I had you tied, it's not your hair I'd go for."

She was struck dumb for a moment. She took a step back, raised a shaking finger, waggled it back and forth. "Uh-uh. Don't start with me, Nick. Don't even think about it."

He lifted his shoulders in a casual shrug, but the intensity of his gaze was unwavering. "Your hair looks pretty," he said. "I like it."

Her hand flew up to touch the short ends before she could stop herself. "Don't flatter yourself," she said. "What you're looking at is a miracle rescue."

That appeared to roll right off his back. "You should change the color, though," he said blandly.

"I doubt those guys would recognize me," she said. "I wasn't wearing glasses, I had lipstick all over my mouth, and I was bare-assed under that slutty blouse. Probably all they ever saw was my chest and butt."

She instantly regretted the thoughtless words when Nick's

gaze fell directly to her chest and butt. She was so not up to intense male scrutiny right now, and particularly not his. It would be difficult for her to feel any less schlumpy than she did right now, clad in her billowing flannel buttoned-up-to-the-neck granny nightie. And those hideous, squinchy black rectangular eyeglasses perched on her nose, the ones her girl-friends had persuaded her to buy because they gave her face "structure." Her nice, normal ones had been forever lost on Frakes Island. Her hair was a mad, staticky cloud of dark curls, her face was wan and pale, completely bare of any help cosmetics might have given.

In short, she looked as plain as a mud fence. And she hated it.

"I recognize you just fine." His voice vibrated with inten-sity. "And if I do, he would."

She shivered. "Well, whoop-de-doo," she said, with fake bravado. "I recognize you too, in spite of your new hairdo. So there. Go blond yourself, why don't you. I dare you. In fact, I'll make a deal with you. Bleach your hair, and I'll bleach mine. Sound good?"

He looked away, and his mouth betrayed him for a brief instant, twitching before he could flatten it into a tense, hard line again.

"Nick, what are you doing here?" she demanded. "This is a bad idea. You should go."

He frowned, and his jacket creaked as he folded his arms over his chest. "I just thought I'd check on you."

"Ah." She let out a long sigh, waited. "I see."

"And so? How are you, then?" he prompted.

She swallowed. "I'm awful," she whispered.

He reached out to smooth a lock of her hair back, his eyes deep and somber. She flinched away from his touch.

He let his hand drop.

"That's what I figured," he said.

She winced. "That bad, huh?"

He shook his head. "No. You're gorgeous, Becca."

"Oh, please." She twitched aside the kitchen curtains to peek out the window, a gesture that had become compulsive. "Get real."

"No, really," he persisted. "You look like a beautiful woman who's hiding. But you can't hide from me. Not now." He moved up behind her and kissed the back of her neck. "I've watched you burn like a house on fire. You can't cancel that out of my head. Don't even try."

She shuddered at the tender touch. "Look, Nick." The words burst out of her violently. "Don't bother to come on to me, OK?"

He kissed her nape again. "Why not?"

"Because I know that story. I know how it ends. I am not going to do that to myself again. So go. Just piss off. Good-bye."

His snort of laughter exploded against her sensitive neck, hot and ticklish. "Tough chick," he murmured. "I'm devastated."

"You are not. Do not condescend to me, you bastard."

He stroked her shoulders and the heat of his palms burned right through the flannel. Gripping her, with gentle, implacable strength. "Heartless Becca," he murmured. "You mean, all my heroics count for nothing? I've got no points racked up with you at all?"

She wrenched away so violently she almost lost her balance, and wrapped her arms tightly around her shaky, uncertain self. "Let me get this straight—this owing you sex in exchange for my life thing. How long is the statute of limitations on that?"

He circled around in front of her, eyes gleaming. "It's indefinite."

She blinked at him, outmaneuvered. "You manipulative jerk."

"Uh-oh. You've figured me out," he said. "I am so fucked."

"Ah, no, in fact. You're not. Or rather. You won't be." Her back hit the wall, bumping against the rack where all her utensils hung. A ladle and the cheese grater slid off and clattered to the floor. "Got that?"

He looked wistful. "I've got that."

His meekness made her suspicious. She waited for him to go. He started shrugging off his jacket.

"What are you doing?" she demanded, panic edging her voice.

He flung his jacket over the back of a chair, revealing a plain black polo shirt that did nothing to hide his unbelievable physique. "You got a problem with me sitting down in your kitchen?"

"Why?" Her voice was getting shrill. "What are you going to do?"

He looked elaborately helpless. "You tell me. What do a man and a woman do together when they're not having crazy monkey sex? The imagination boggles. I don't think I've ever gotten this far in a relationship with a girl. Not past the monkey sex, I mean."

"Don't you dare make fun of me, Nikolai—"

"We could argue about money," he suggested. "I think that's a big classic. Or maybe we could just, I don't know. Have some dinner?"

"Dinner?" She squinted at him. "Are you being facetious?"

"I wouldn't mind dinner," he said innocently. "Got any food?"

She started shaking, with jittery laughter. It was too weird. A feral, mythical being from that dangerous otherworld she'd accidentally visited was smashing through the barriers of her bland little life. Sitting down at her kitchen table, and demanding to be fed.

"What do you want to eat?" she asked, at a loss.

"Anything's fine," he said. "I'm not fussy. As long as it's not cheese soufflé, or crepes à l'orange."

She burst into tears, so abruptly she shocked even herself,

and stood there sobbing in the middle of the kitchen, embarrassed beyond belief.

"Becca! Oh, Jesus. I'm sorry. I was just joking. Bad joke. I didn't mean to—aw, shit!"

Suddenly, he was hugging her. Which was wonderful. Her body drank in the sudden, delicious contact with his big, solid body, loving it.

She jerked away before she could disgrace herself further. "No. No, I'm sorry. I'm OK," she babbled, wiping her eyes with the sleeve of her nightgown. "Really. Fine. Just kind of shaky."

"I didn't mean to—"

"Of course not. Don't worry about it." She tried to smile, and skittered backwards until she hit the fridge when he reached for her again. "Don't worry. How about an, um, omelette? And some toast? I think I even have some orange juice. Would that do it?"

He sank slowly, reluctantly into the chair again, looking worried. "Fine," he said. "Are you sure you're—"

"Fine. Great. Really." She scurried around, yanking out bowls and utensils. As always, being busy helped. She pulled eggs out of the fridge, cracked the two she would cook normally for herself, and glanced over to where he hunched in his chair, black-clad, elbows on his knees, eyes gleaming like a panther poised to leap.

Four more eggs. She cracked them into the bowl. Stuck six pieces of bread into the toaster oven. Butter into the skillet, herbs, cheeses, a slice of ham to brown, that last handful of cherry tomatoes. Slice and dice, grate and toss, and by the time the toast was on the table and the omelette sizzling in the pan, she was feeling much more herself.

He'd already devoured all the toast before she even slid the omelette onto the big serving platter she'd chosen for his plate. She tossed in another six slices of bread without comment.

He dug in, sighing with appreciation at the first bite, and stopped with the fork halfway to his mouth, frowning. "Aren't you eating?"

She shook her head, thinking of all the Oreos she'd devoured in her last desperate attempt at mood management. "Not hungry."

He looked uncomfortable with that. "You have to eat," he protested. "Here. Eat half of this."

She suppressed the rush of tenderness. Tenderness with this guy could only end in disaster. She was already pushing her luck by feeding him. It was like giving food to a wild animal. It upset the balance of nature. To say nothing of the balance of her own shaky sanity.

"Go ahead," she said. "Bon appetit."

He gave her a long, slitted look, and gave in, going at the food before him with focused enthusiasm. In a couple minutes, he was wiping his highly polished plate with the last triangle of toast.

"You're still hungry, aren't you?" she asked.

He shrugged. "I'll live," he told her. "It's lots better now."

She got up and peered into her fridge. She didn't have much food that was fit for a creature like him. He wasn't the type to appreciate a no-fat lemon parfait yogurt, or a handful of sliced cucumbers. There was cream cheese and there were bagels. Good chew toys for wild beasts.

She hit pay dirt in the freezer when she found some of her frozen homemade lasagna. One of them was good for two meals for herself when she was alone. That should do it for him. She set one to nuke.

In the meantime, he finished off her bagels and the cream cheese, polished off the ham and drank every last drop of her orange juice. She set the lasagna before him. He practically inhaled it.

She regarded him with something approaching awe. "You are a bottomless pit," she said. "Have you been starving yourself?"

He scraped out the last bit of pasta and chewed it, looking blissful. "Haven't eaten in a while, I guess. And nothing tasted good. Everything tastes great here, though."

"What's 'a while'?" she demanded.

He pondered that for a second. "Couple days, maybe? Can't remember."

She sucked in a breath. "Days? Why? Have you been sick?"

He frowned. "I just forgot, that's all. I had a lot on my mind. Don't you ever forget to eat?"

"Um, no," she said baldly. "Not a chance in hell."

"I've been busy," he said, sounding vaguely defensive.

"With what?"

He swiped the butt end of a bagel chunk all around the inside of the cream cheese container to wipe up the last smear, stuck it into his mouth, chewed. Deliberately not answering her.

She busied herself by rummaging through the freezer. There it was, the very last lasagna. An offering to lay upon the altar of idiocy. She peeled off the foil, flung it into the microwave, and turned to him.

"You're trying to find that guy, aren't you?" she accused him.

His gaze flickered, and slid away from hers.

"Why?" she demanded. "Why not cut your losses and let him be?"

"And if you run into him or one of his goons at a rest stop on the interstate?" he asked. "How do you think that's going to play? You want to stare over your shoulder for the rest of your life?"

"Oh, please. Don't even try. This is not about me," she snapped. "I'm a bit player in this drama, and you know it."

"Let it go, Becca," he said. "We're not discussing it."

A lump rose in her throat. It ached and burned. She couldn't justify this emotion, couldn't explain it or reason with this tangle of pain and fear and confusion. She just felt lost, scared. In the dark, in the fog.

She turned her back to him, to hide the hot liquid sting in her eyes. "Then why the hell are you even here?" she forced the words out around the choking lump. "Did you just come to torture me?"

She let out a sharp gasp as he grabbed her from behind, yanking her down onto his lap, with her back to him. Omigod. Her chest locked.

She tried to twist, get off, look him in the face—she wasn't even sure what her intentions were, but she couldn't move in any direction. He held her fast, arms clamped around her waist, pinning her elbows to her sides. He pressed his face between her shoulder blades.

His body vibrated with tension. His grip was almost painful. His breath bloomed, rhythmic against her spine. A moist, pulsing beat that came into focus as if he were kissing her. Or licking her.

He didn't speak, just held her, hiding his face against her back. She felt awkward, perched on his lap, her nightgown draped over his knees. Unable to take anything more than the shallowest breath.

Another emotion unfolded slowly in her. An aching desire to give him the tenderness he so clearly needed. But he wouldn't let her turn, or embrace him, or kiss him. He wouldn't talk to her. This tight, shaking, silent embrace was the only way he could ask for it and all he would accept from her.

He reached out to her, and hid from her. In the same moment.

She was afraid to speak or stir, unwilling to end the fragile intimacy. They were finally together, even if they were balanced on the head of a pin. She finally pried one of his hands loose and pulled it up to her face. She kissed his scabbed knuckles. They sat there, in that silent, magic bubble, until the microwave started to ding.

He sighed, and his arms loosened. She slid off his lap and stumbled across the kitchen to stab the button to make that sound stop. She slid the steaming dish out of the microwave, laid it on the counter. "Nick," she began gently. "Can you tell me—"

"No," he said. "So don't ask."

She flinched, then took a deep breath and tried again. "But I—"

"I'm not talking about it." The harshness of his voice was like a blow, and of course, she was wide open to it, now that he'd coaxed her into feeling like this. Fragile and unshielded.

She pressed her hands to her face. How many times would she have to go through this same torture before she got a clue?

"I'm sorry," he said in a halting voice, after a moment of dead silence. "It's not that I don't want to. It's that I just can't. It's not safe."

Nothing's safe anyway, you idiot. Nothing will ever be safe again.

She wanted to scream the words at him, but she just dragged in a shuddering breath, and opened her mouth. "Tell me the bastard's full name," she said, her voice savage. "I deserve to know something about the guy who wants to rape, torture and murder me. He must have a record. Or something."

He was silent for so long, she was sure he would blow her off again. Then he cleared his throat. "You won't find it. Anyway, it's Vadim Zhoglo," he said. "Ukrainian mafiya kingpin. Very bad, evil motherfucker. But you know that."

"Yes," she whispered. She knew that.

Now that she had that scrap of information, she was at a loss. It wasn't as if she had anywhere to put it, anything to do with it.

She thought of another random detail. Maybe he was on a roll, maybe he'd tell her more. "How is it that you speak Ukrainian?"

"My mother came from there," he said. "And my father's family. He was second generation. My great-grandparents came over in the teens, before the first world war. My dad was bumming around the world in the seventies, after he was discharged from Vietnam. He made it all the way to Kiev to see where his grandparents had come from. He met my mother, married her, brought her back here. I learned Ukrainian from her. Russian, too."

"Oh." The sudden influx of personal information was dizzying.

The lasagna was steaming on the counter. She placed it on the table in front of him. "That's it for my larder," she said. "Eat."

He looked alarmed, but he dug right in. "I cleaned you out? Damn. I'll take you to the supermarket. Buy you some groceries."

The idea of doing something so mundane as grocery shopping with him struck her as both surreal and wonderful. Her heart twisted.

Anger soon followed. She stared at him, polishing off her food. Just look at her. Fatuous fool. Cooking for him, getting all soft and teary over pathetic crumbs of attention from him. Shame on her.

"Stop it, Nick," she said crisply. "We're not shopping for groceries, any more than we're going to have sex. Stop jerking me around. Is that why you came here? For entertainment? To get me wound up, watch me bounce off the walls? Is that a stress reliever for you?"

He rubbed his eyes, shaking his head slowly, and she noticed how red-rimmed and shadowed his eyes were. His face was drawn.

"I'm not here for entertainment," he said. "I don't understand it myself. I've been trying to stay away from you—"

"Trying?" She was utterly baffled. "Away from me? But I thought . . . it seemed like you never wanted to see me again."

"Yeah. I tried. It was convincing, huh? I shouldn't be anywhere near you." The volume of his voice was low, but its raw intensity slashed across her nerves. "Zhoglo'll get a line on me soon. Not many guys answer my description who can do what I do. I'm more findable than you. Harder to kill, maybe, but easier to find."

"Thanks for that heartening observation," she muttered.

He ignored that. "When he finds me, he'll want you. You're not a bit player in this drama, no matter how much you want to be. Not anymore." He grabbed a handful of her nightgown in his fist and pulled it until she stumbled closer. She grabbed his shoulder to steady herself. "So I should stay the fuck away from you. Simple, huh?"

She stared down into his eyes. Her fingers dug into the muscles of his shoulder. "Evidently not," she whispered.

He grabbed her other hand, and laid it on his other shoulder, shaking his head. "I just wanted to be with you," he said, sounding almost bewildered. "Just for a little while, to make sure you were OK. I drove around for an hour, trying to make sure I wasn't followed. I'm reasonably sure I wasn't. But even so. It was stupid. I'm sorry."

"Oh, Nick," she whispered. She could hardly breathe.

"Do us both a favor, Becca. Throw me out. Tell me to fuck off. I can't seem to do it on my own steam. I need help. So help me. Please."

The contradictory double level of his plea was exquisitely painful. Tears slid out of her eyes. "You're asking the wrong girl."

He let out a rough sound and jerked her closer, between his knees. He pressed his face against her breasts.

Her arms slid around his neck of their own volition. Her hands cradled his head and her fingers slid through the silken brush of buzzed-off hair. She dragged in a breath, inhaling his scent.

"I will not have sex with you." She whispered the words, slowly and deliberately. "You hear me, Nick?"

There. The gauntlet was flung down. Even though the melting heat between her legs made her almost certain that she was lying.

Damn it. She had to at least try to resist him. On principle.

She felt the change in his face against her breasts as he smiled. "I hear you," he said. "So? What do we do now? We've done the food thing, so what's left? Arguing about money? I'll give you shit about your credit card bills and you can bitch me out about my speeding tickets."

"No, thanks." As if she were going to play-act at being a real couple with him, even as a joke. The very suggestion seemed freaky.

"How about we bleach your hair?" he suggested. "I'll go get you a box of the stuff at the Rite Aid."

She recoiled. "You are never laying hands on my hair again!"

"OK," he said meekly. "So? Dominoes? Got a Monopoly board?"

She didn't have the heart to throw him out, after that halting heartfelt confession. She was such a fool for the fluttering combination of anticipation and doom. The glow of hot excitement between her legs.

"You can watch some TV with me," she conceded. "If you want. Something bland and undemanding. But don't try any funny stuff."

"OK. No funny stuff. Roger that. I love TV."

His suddenly cheerful tone told her that he'd reached the same conclusion she had. He was over the hard part. It was just a matter of waiting for the right moment now.

He was home free, the arrogant, manipulative jerk.

Chapter
16

He followed her into the living room, where her TV glowed and chattered in the dimness, and sat down smack in the middle of her couch, slouching his long body with lazy grace. Leaving her no place to sit but beside him. She tried to leave a minimal safety margin between them when she set her butt onto the cushion, but the laws of couch physics changed in Nick's proximity. The weight and mass of his big body bowed the springs, and she slid straight into the magnetic pull of his body. Wedged against him. Thigh to thigh.

He was so hot. The gravitational pull of his body so powerful.

His muscular arm had been draped lazily over the back of the couch, but now it was draped over her shoulders. The side of her face was pressed against the fresh-smelling cotton of his black polo shirt. She identified aftershave, detergent, a tang of salty male sweat, and oh, dear, oh gosh. She was in big fat trouble. The whole side of her thigh had gone nuts and was having a shivery little mini-orgasm. Pleasure rippled down her leg, up her side, just from the hot contact.

His hand, too, curled around to cup her shoulder, stroking

her. Trying to calm her down, lull her into docile complacency. Hah.

She jerked forward, struggling out of his octopus grip, grabbed the phone from where it lay on the floor and put it back into its charger stand. Then she groped for the remote and stuck it in his hand, just to give him something to do other than pet her and hypnotize her with the force field of his seductive, restless male heat.

"Pick something," she ordered him. "As long as it's not sports."

He clicked around with a swiftness that made her dizzy, and found something on the science channel about volcanos.

Volcanos, for the love of God. She wanted to make a snide comment about it, but the words muddled in her mouth as he began to stroke her shoulder again. "Hah. Very slick," she said, breathlessly.

"Is it?" His teeth flashed in the gloom. "I haven't used tricks like this to get my arm around a girl's shoulders since junior high school."

"Oh, no?" She tried to laugh. "I suppose you no longer needed to, after, hmm? At that point, they all started flinging themselves at you?"

"Pretty much," he said blandly.

"Spoiled rotten," she muttered.

He slid deeper into his careless slouch, pulling her tighter against the sinuous length of his body. Drawing attention to the very long, thick bulge in the front of his jeans. Not trying to hide it in the least.

She tried to ignore it, but it was so blatantly evident, lit up by the TV screen images of Hawaiian volcanos spurting magma. Rivers of lava. The scientist narrator droned on. She was motionless, unable to breathe. Hypersensitive to every breath he took, every shift of his weight.

She pretended to watch TV until she was an electric, shivering mess. A morass of emotion. His other hand was now resting on her thigh, and was caressing it, in a slow, sensual rhythm that made the fabric creep and bunch up above his hand, moving by tiny, steady increments.

"You think you're so sneaky," she whispered. "I see exactly what you're doing. It won't work."

"It won't?" He reached the hem and placed his hand below it, on the bare skin of her thigh. Her muscles jerked in response. "My reasoning was, if you don't notice, then it's working. And if you do notice and you don't stop me, then it's also working."

"Oh, please. You are such a—"

Her words choked off as he kissed her.

She stiffened, but he held her face and insisted, his warm lips exploring hers with slow, pleading gentleness. Not opening or invading, just offering her a reverent intimacy that she could not resist.

Her eyelids fluttered, her body was racked with a shudder of surrender, and she arched, relaxing into his grip. Her head dropped back into his waiting hand as the kiss changed, became hot and hungry and clinging, making her gasp for breath, gasp for more. It might be smoke and mirrors, might be just a cheap illusion of the tenderness she needed, but it didn't matter. She would take it. She ached for it.

He slid off the couch, swinging around so that he kneeled in front of her, pulling her face forward so he could keep kissing her with all the sweet intensity she longed for. He shoved the coffee table away to make room for himself, and pressed her knees open so he could scoot closer.

She was seduced utterly by his sensual gentleness, his generosity. He had won, but she didn't care, because the kiss had its own wonderful momentum, its own agenda. There was no way to tease apart who gave, who took, and the sheer beauty of it was so keen, it made her shiver and ache, with the longing to surrender everything to him.

He lifted his head slowly, eyes hooded and dilated, and

dragged his hand roughly over his mouth. His breath was hard and ragged.

"How's your clit?" he asked.

The question jolted her out of her sensual haze with a painful bump. "Good God, Nick, that was blunt!"

He grinned. "Hey, why beat around the bush?"

She actually laughed at the lame pun before she could stop herself. "Oh, please. What a comedian. Don't quit your day job. Oh, wait. I take that back. Do quit your day job. Please. I hate your day job."

He ignored that, stroking her knees, his eyes intent. "Well? Last time it was too sore to touch. Is it better?"

A flush of anticipation turned her cherry red, flustered and dizzy. Her thigh muscles clenched and released beneath his warm, stroking hands. "I told you we weren't going to . . . ah . . ."

"For fuck's sake, what does a guy have to do to get a straight answer out of you?"

She winced. "Um, a guy has to ease off a little," she whispered.

He rolled his eyes. "What did I say this time?"

"It wasn't so much what you said. It was your tone. So matter of fact. How's your clit? The same way you would say, how's your sciatica? How's your bunion? How's your Great Aunt Edna?"

He leaned forward and pressed his face against her bared thighs, shoulders vibrating from startled laughter. "Oh, babe. You kill me."

"I certainly hope not. Please don't laugh," she said, in a small, stiff voice. "I'm not trying to be funny. I'm just nervous, that's all."

He lifted his face. "Nervous?" His voice was incredulous. "With me? After all we've been through? Why, for Christ's sake?"

As if she should have to spell out why a gorgeous, mysterious, insatiable sex god who had saved her from an unspeakable fate might make her, well, nervous. Hah.

He lifted up a wad of the billowing skirt of the nightgown. "I love this thing," he said. "It smells like . . . mmm. Like . . ."

"Fabric softener?" she suggested.

His teeth flashed in that seductive grin. "It's sexy."

She looked down at the thing, her mouth twitching. "Oh, shut up," she said. "You are lying. Like a rug."

"Speaking of rugs." He hoisted her nightgown up over her waist, then her breasts. "You never answered my question. About your clit. Oh, man. Look at you. I'm not lying now. So fucking sexy."

She was naked beneath the nightgown. Faint with gratitude that her most recent comfort ritual had involved shaving her legs and slathering herself with lotion.

"It's better," she confessed breathlessly "Almost, um, normal."

Right. As if normal was a word that could describe how her crotch felt right now when he smiled like that. That hot, tingly glow was about as far from normal as it was possible to get.

He gripped her hips and pulled until her butt slid forward on the couch, and she sprawled there, helpless and tangled, her head propped up against the sofa back, her nightgown rucked up to her neck in big, billowy folds. A big, gorgeous male silhouetted against the backdrop of the chattering TV screen, staring at her intimate bits. Stroking her, opening her, dragging slow, lazy, wet kisses over her trembling thighs, against her mound, teasing and tantalizing—

He lifted his head. "So how is your Great Aunt Edna, anyhow?"

She melted into laughter just as he put his mouth to her and the shock of it set her off, then and there. A long climax wrenched through her, jerking breathless little sobs of pleasure from her throat.

After the spasms had eased down to a delicious glow, he gazed at her for a moment. "Thank you," he said.

She giggled shakily. "Huh? Me? Aren't I the one who should be thanking you?"

"No," he said, still caressing her clitoris with his slowly circling thumb. "You're so sweet to me. In spite of everything. I don't get it."

Tears rushed into her eyes. "Believe me," she said with total honesty, "neither do I."

He bent down and went at her again, lapping her, suckling her, sliding his tongue with delicate skill along the involuted folds of her sex, as if hungry for some sustenance he could obtain only by pleasing her.

And he did. He melted her down completely. Moved her, the way he had with that embrace in the kitchen. He knew how to deliver unspeakably sensual pleasure with his licking, lashing tongue, his delving fingers, his clever lips. His tender ferocity unraveled her, but she felt the pleading behind it. Like he was desperate for something, and this was the only way he knew how to ask for it. Or to earn it.

And she couldn't withhold anything from him. He had her under a spell. She had no choice but to offer him everything, the chaotic glow of her emotions and the desperate eagerness of her response, shining brighter, rising to a crest—

And it broke, and the wave pulsed through her, washed over her, leaving her naked, and brand new. As tender as the dawn.

Time had warped and expanded, into an infinite, dreamlike interval with no beginning, no end. It moved, but like a slow river and they were afloat in it, sometimes dozing, sometimes tossed in the rapids or churned in a pulsing mass of chaotic foam, then floating on in a pool of delicious sloth again. Finally, when she was boneless and spent, he lifted his face, wiped his grinning mouth and grabbed both her hands. He tugged until she was forced to sit, her naked thighs flanking him where he knelt before her, holding both her hands tightly.

His burning eyes asked a question. No need to put it into words. He pulled a condom out of his pocket, and tucked it into her hand.

"You do the honors," he said simply.

She stared at him, wondering at his skill, maneuvering her into needing desperately what she'd tried so hard to withhold. Chump that she was. No way could she live without it now. She needed everything he had to give her. A little part of her felt scared and weak and foolish to let herself be used again, but there seemed to be another person rising up inside her who wanted to do the using. Ravenous for Nick's raw male sexuality. His power and vigor, his life-giving heat.

She leaned forward, slid her hands beneath his shirt, stroking his hard belly, gripping his lean waist. Feeling the smooth, powerful play of the layers of muscle moving and shifting beneath her hands as she shoved his jeans down over his hips and let his cock spring free.

Whoa. It never ceased to amaze her. The sheer size of him, so broad and blunt. She caressed him, admiring every detail, the luxurious suedelike softness of the skin, the distended veins pulsing along the length of the broad shaft. Oh, wow. Perfection.

She loved the heat of him, all that thundering urgency and power held rigidly in check, waiting for the moment to serve her pleasure. She gripped him with both hands and squeezed, stroked, felt him gasp and arch and shudder, groaning at the tight, twisting stroke of her hands.

She ripped open the condom. The phone rang. They froze.

"Let the machine get it," she told him. "It's probably just my boss, calling to fire my lazy ass."

Six rings was too damn long to wait. She had to reprogram the thing for three, now that she was avoiding the whole world. Click, beep, and the outgoing message played. She was changing that, too.

"Becca? Pick up if you're there. I just talked to Carrie, and she—"

"Oh, God. It's my brother," she said, lunging for the phone. "Josh? I'm here."

"Good!" Josh harrumphed. "It's about time. Carrie told me you were a wreck. Not going to work? What the hell is that about?"

That was irritating. "I'm hardly a wreck," she snapped. "Can't I be depressed sometimes, too? Can't I have a bad day now and then?"

Josh was silent for a moment. "No," he said. "You can't."

Chills of guilt shuddered up her spine at her own thoughtless self-absorption. Josh had been only eight when their mom had given in to her despair and eaten that lethal handful of pain pills.

No wonder he couldn't handle her being depressed.

That was one of the reasons she'd always tried so desperately hard to keep her spirits up, or at least the appearance of them. She wanted to give her siblings at least that much security. An illusion they could count on.

And they still counted on it. For all their vaunted independence, for all their irritating juvenile attitudes, when she wavered, they freaked.

"What the hell is this I hear about you picking up a guy?" Josh's voice was as huffy as a disapproving grandpa. "Some tattooed thug, Carrie said? Gross, Becca. I mean, I understand about you being pissed off at that prick Justin, but for God's sake, you could get, like, a disease! You have to be more careful!"

Becca stifled her laughter with her hands, to hear her own desperate, bleating, sisterly lectures playing back to her out of her little brother's mouth. "I don't want to discuss that right now, OK?"

Josh was instantly suspicious. "Why not? And are you laughing? What's so funny? You don't sound depressed at all! What's up?"

"I'm not laughing, you idiot. I just—"

"Is that guy with you? Right now?" His voice rose to a squeak.

"Damn it, Josh, I—"

"You were having sex with him! Right? That's why you didn't answer your phone. Holy shit, Becca. Are you, like, nuts?"

"Calm down," she snapped. "Can't I have a private life?"

"Put him on," Josh said ominously.

"Oh, don't be ridiculous. I will do nothing of the kind."

"Put him on!" Josh's voice was obstinate. "I want to talk to him."

Becca put her hand over the receiver, and gave Nick a pained look. "I'm really sorry," she said. "I don't know how this happened. It's my little brother. He wants to talk to you."

"How much does he know?" Nick asked.

"Nothing about the rest of it," she whispered. "Just about you."

Nick hesitated for a moment, and took the proffered phone as if it were a live bomb. "Yeah?"

The kid lit into him like a fighting pit bull. "Who the hell are you? And what do you think you're doing with my sister?" His youthful voice cracked with the force of his emotions.

Nick coughed. "Who wants to know?"

"I'm Becca's brother, Josh Cattrell. And if you mess with my sister, I'm going to kick your ass."

"Oh-kay. I'll keep that in mind," he said. "But just for the record, what exactly constitutes 'messing with her'?"

"You know exactly what I mean," the younger guy hissed. "So you're this foul-mouthed, tattooed lowlife we've been hearing about?"

An involuntary grin wrapped around his face. He slanted a look at Becca and put his hand over the mouthpiece. "Foul-mouthed, tattooed lowlife?" he repeated softly.

"Oh, no," Becca moaned, clapping her hands over her cheeks. "This isn't happening. I did not say that!"

Nick shifted back onto his knees, still grinning like a fool, and realized, startled, that he was enjoying himself. It had been so long, he'd forgotten the sensation. "As you can see, your sister and I have this really great mutual respect thing happening," he said, eyeing her.

"Are you seducing my sister?" the kid bellowed.

He wished. "None of your damn business," he said mildly. "Butt out."

"Fuck, no! No way am I butting out! If I don't butt in, who will?"

Nick had nothing to say to that, having never had siblings, or any family at all who gave a fuck about him after Mom died. The concept of family butting into his business was foreign to him. Still, he liked the feisty kid, even if he was getting reamed out. Josh was protective of his sister. He put his heart into it. He got points for that.

"Bad enough what that slimy buttface of an ex-fiancé did to her," Josh fumed on. "Now she's picking up punks off the street? Jesus!"

Punk? Nick stomped on the laughter before it escaped. It wouldn't endear him to the guy. "She didn't exactly find me on the street."

"I don't care what gutter she scraped you out of. Like, what the fuck are your intentions?" the kid bellowed.

"Intentions?" he repeated, at a loss. Christ, he lived from second to second, just trying not to get killed. He never intended anything.

"Are you just going to dip your wick and then fuck off?"

He had the odd sensation of something or someone speaking through him. "No," he said slowly. "That is definitely not my intention."

"Uh, good." Josh sounded nonplussed. "Because if it was, I'd, like, have to kick your ass."

"Gotcha," Nick soothed. "I get the ass-kicking part. Loud and clear."

"Do not hurt her." Josh's voice wobbled with intensity. "She's taken enough shit from worthless bastards. She deserves better."

"Yeah, she does," he said. "And, uh, I won't."

He felt like a lying prick. Christ, with his track record? He'd never gotten close to a woman without eventually hurting her.

Josh hung up. Nick let the receiver drop from his ear, dazed. Another surreal vignette. Fending off the furious brother while his dick waved wild and free outside his jeans, like a flag in the wind. Wow.

"Your brother's very protective of you," he observed.

Her hands were still clamped over her cheeks. "I'm so sorry," she said. "He's really excitable. I shouldn't have given you the phone."

"It's OK," Nick said. "I kind of liked him, actually."

She dropped her hands into her lap, incredulous. "You *what?*"

"He gives a shit," Nick said. "I like that quality in a person. My only problem is, I'm not sure whether I promised to marry you, or keep my hands off you. And if I get it wrong, he'll kick my ass."

She dissolved into giggles, tears squinching out of her eyes. "Don't worry," she said breathlessly. "I won't hold you to either one."

"Have you got any more family that I should be looking over my shoulder for?" he asked. "Dad with a shotgun? Mom with an Uzi?"

"Just a sister. Carrie's nineteen. Josh is twenty," she confessed. "Our parents died a long time ago. I raised the two of them myself."

He blew out a long breath. "Wow. That's heavy."

"Yeah, it was, pretty much." She gave him a tremulous smile. "Well. I guess that kind of killed the moment, huh?"

Shit, shit, shit. Mayday. Going down. "Depends," he said, trying to maintain a deadpan expression in the face of his own lust. He grabbed her small hand, pulled it down and wrapped those soft, smooth fingers around his turgid cock. "Personally, I think the moment's alive and well. In fact, this part of me never even noticed the interruption."

She stared down at him, stroking and exploring with those light, feathery fingers till he thought he would scream. "I see," she whispered.

"If I'm going to get my ass kicked, I might as well make it count, right?" He retrieved the condom from where it had fallen on the rug, and put it into her other hand. Crossing his fingers. Please. *Please.*

She shook with a burst of silent giggles, and finished ripping the condom open and pulling it out one-handed. It took her forfuckingever to pry the thing out and fumble it over his dick. He was just about to end the ticklish torture, yank it out of her hands and get it on himself when she finally rolled the lubricated latex slowly down the length of his shaft, with one long, tight, fantastic squeezing stroke.

"It looks awfully snug," she commented, sounding worried.

"It's great," he said, his voice strangled. "Please. Do that again."

She made that soft little laughing sound, and obliged him, petting and pulling and milking his cock until he was gasping for air and clutching her, his arms shaking.

God, he loved that sound, that breathy happy gurgle. He wanted to hear more of it. It made him feel . . . he didn't even have a word for it. He didn't even have a place for the feeling, but it spurred him to grab her and kiss her again.

That awkward hand job was the most erotic sensation he'd ever felt. He'd got lucky, damn lucky. A soft, fragrant, laughing woman filling his arms, her soft lips opening, her shy tongue retreating before his, and then slowly responding. Becca was sweet beyond belief.

He cupped her head and deepened the kiss till he was practically drowning in her—and knocked those weird black glasses askew. Oops.

She straightened them, giggling helplessly. "I can't believe I forgot I still had these on."

"Leave them," he suggested, starting on the buttons at her neck.

"But they're hideous," she protested.

He stopped her hand as she was about to pry them off. "It's a look," he explained. "It's a classic porn motif. The formerly frigid sex bomb secretary, right after her sexual awakening, but before she thinks to ditch the specs and lose the tight bun. Add virginal lingerie and you have yourself a fantasy."

"Oh, please. Spare me." She yanked the glasses off and flung them onto the coffee table. "Men are such pigs."

"Oh, absolutely," he agreed, lifting the huge, tentlike flannel thing off her. Finally naked. As stunning as ever. No. More, even.

He held out the nightgown. "Get up," he said hoarsely. "Let me put this on the couch, under you."

She blinked at him, looking dazed and confused. "Huh?"

"For the wet spot." He tugged her to her feet and spread the thing out deftly beneath her. He tossed her back down on top of it so that she bounced, her beautiful, pink-tipped tits jiggling seductively.

He gripped her hips and slid her ass back down to the edge of the couch. "You're dripping pussy juice like a ripe peach," he muttered. "I can't get enough of it. Except that if I don't fuck you now, I think I'm going to die."

She smiled at him, biting her lip with that uncertain look, but she opened for him like a flower as he folded her legs high and wide, that wet pink pussy open to him. Offered to him.

It hit him like a blow to the chest, as he positioned himself, jeans half-down. He breached her tight opening and started pushing inside her. How sensual she was, how generous. The look in her eyes. She clutched his upper arms as he forged his way deep inside. When he started to thrust, she made husky, surprised sounds with each slow, deliberate stroke.

They found their rhythm together, him listening, her gripping his ass and wiggling, and settled into a deep, wonderful plunge-twist, swivel-glide that made her gasp with pleasure, lifting herself to him.

Oh, God. So good. He'd lived without anything so good for so long, he'd forgotten feelings like this existed, or else he'd put the memory aside, persuaded himself that they were a luxury. Something you could do without and probably should, like sugar or booze.

But no. This feeling wasn't like that at all. It was more like water, oxygen. A flat-out necessity. You went without it for a while, and you choked, and then you croaked, and you blew away like a dried leaf.

He'd been drying up and dying inside for years. And hadn't known it. Hey, dying felt so damn normal after a while.

The pace quickened without him noticing, because Becca was grinding herself against him, gasping and whimpering as she worked up to one of her awesome, call-the-cops orgasms. He concentrated on bringing her off, massaging her clit with his thumb as he stirred her around with his cock, finding where those sweet spots hid, and ah . . . there she went. Arching and jerking, her strong cunt muscles squeezing his cock, milking, begging him to join her. Fill her.

Not yet. Not fucking yet. No way. He wanted this to last forever.

As soon as she had more or less settled down, panting and gleaming with sweat, he resumed thrusting. It went easier now, slicker and smoother. A deep plunge in, a tight, aching slide out. First the quivering resistance of her plushy pussy on the driving instroke, and her jealous hug-and-grab on the outstroke. Outrageous.

Thank God for the latex. It kept him honest, or he'd have lost it in an instant. It damped the sensations down just enough for self-control. He managed to bring her off a couple more times, but every time she came, it got hotter, harder, wilder. Just a small part of his brain watched from a distance as he went at her, moving her, spreading her. Pumping and ramming against her. The slap of his balls against her wet, slick ass, the sawing of breath, those pleading moans, his, hers, hoarse and dry and desperate. The thundering rumble in his head, of a gathering orgasm that drove him along before it like an oncoming storm.

Sobs, shouts, as something inside him shattered and gave way.

Layer after layer in his mind was smashed through like a wrecking ball, crashing through brick and mortar and concrete, dust and rubble. Each rhythmic explosive charge knocked him deeper into nowhere.

When he came round, he was horrified to find that they were on the floor. Holy fuck, how did that happen? The coffee table was overturned, books scattered everywhere, her glasses on the rug, the phone beeping, fallen out of its charger. Becca lay beneath him, gasping for breath beneath his weight. Arms clutching his neck. One leg wrapped around his waist, the other twined around his ankle.

He started to lift himself off, his muscles weak and trembling with the aftermath, and felt her pussy clench around him, echoing the cling of his arms. Unwilling to let him go. It was nice. He liked it.

Which was weird, for him. That kind of move from a woman after sex usually made him feel suffocated.

He had no idea what he'd done in those last few moments during that . . . was it a blackout, for Christ's sake? He was almost twice her size. He hoped he hadn't hurt her. That she didn't hate his guts.

"Sorry," he whispered, studying her face.

She smiled, with her eyes closed. "You're weird, Nick."

"I know," he said, in heartfelt agreement. "You OK?"

She stretched luxuriously beneath his weight. "First, you make me come like never before, and you thank me. Then, you make me come again and again and again . . . and what do you do? You apologize."

"I lost control," he growled. "I could have hurt you."

"News flash," she said. "You didn't. And I doubt that you even could." She opened her eyes, suddenly somber. "Not during sex, anyway."

He slowly withdrew himself from her clinging sheath, but she twined both arms around his neck and squeezed. "Nick? I have to tell you something."

He braced himself, gut clenched against the ache of nameless fear in his gut. "Yeah? What?"

"If you do your standard post-sex routine and get all mean and grumpy and sour, and run out on me, you aren't ever going to have to worry about Vadim Zhoglo again."

He started to grin, warily. "I won't?"

"No, you won't," she said. "Because I'll kill you myself."

He almost collapsed right on top of her as the shudder of laughter cut him off right at the elbows. He got to his feet, with some difficulty, peeled off the extremely full condom. Then he pried off his shoes, and shoved down his jeans, stepping out of them. "I'm not running off," he assured her. "See? I can't. I'm naked. Just ditching the latex. OK?"

"Hurry back. I mean it." Her voice was steely.

He did, still shaking with silent hysteria. But when he came back into the room and stared down at her gorgeous body lying on the ground, his laughter suddenly faded away. It bothered him, to see her lying naked on the floor. She looked too helpless there. Too vulnerable.

He'd rather see her naked bouncing through a field of flowers, or naked in a bathtub, or naked in a forest cascade.

Better yet, naked tucked snugly into a soft bed. And him on top of her.

His cock started to stir, and grow heavy and long between his legs. He crouched down and pulled her to her feet. "I didn't run away. But I'm warning you right now. I'm a chronic insomniac."

"Yes? And so? What of it?" she asked crisply.

"Since I can't sleep, I'll let you take a wild guess as to my top favorite alternative bed activity," he offered.

Her eyes dropped to his cock, which had stretched out to full length and was now starting to do the super duper hydraulic lift trick.

"Good God," she said faintly. "You're kidding."

"Does that look insincere?"

"But don't you need to rest? Don't you ever relax?"

"Nope," he said. "I hope you don't, either."

She let out an explosive breath. "If you can't relax after sex like that, then you're in a world of hurt, buddy."

The laughter that wrenched through him threatened almost to turn into sobs. He wrestled it down as he kneeled to pull the rest of the condoms out of his jeans pocket, and then waved the long, dangling strip of silvery foil packages in her face before he scooped her up, cupping her ass so that she straddled him. "Tell me about it."

"Hey." She wiggled halfheartedly, and then clamped her thighs around his waist. "Is this another of your sleazy, manipulative games?"

He kicked her bedroom door open. "Of course. That's a given."

He couldn't be bothered to get rid of the mountain of pillows, so he tossed her into the midst of them, and jumped on her. She giggled and shrieked and struggled as he wrestled her into position, ripped open a condom with his teeth, expertly smoothed that sucker into place.

He'd meant for this one to be playful. Lah di dah, frolick-

ing around in the piles of fluffy lace pillows like a couple of
horny bunnies. As always, though, things took a turn.
Straight into a place he'd never been, had no procedure for,
no rules, no training. No clue.

First, it was that searing, electric moment of connection,
staring into her beautiful eyes as he started pushing his cock
into her. Then that shivering, aching swell of emotion, as the
pleasure intensified into something almost unbearable. The
laughter petered out, the smiles faded. They just stared into
each other's eyes, awestruck.

All he could do was hang onto her and fuck desperately.

Something was happening to him, something huge and un-
stoppable. As natural as the sun rising, and just as miracu-
lous. He had to close his eyes against it, bury his face against
the pillow to muffle the sounds he was making, soak up the
hot damp from his eyes.

They clung to each other as his body hammered against
hers. She clawed at him, raising herself, inciting his frenzied
thrusts with her clutching fingers, her wild cries, and he was
blasting off, oh God.

She found her way over the brink with him, and they were
flung out together by the force of it, across infinite inner
space inside their minds but, amazingly, together. He didn't
lose her, in that lonely place.

They were fused. One glowing, perfect entity.

That perfect bliss dissolved into consciousness again. He
forced his heavy eyelids to open and stared into the darkness.

His chest felt hot, so soft. He marveled at it. Speechless,
limp. Terrified, that it might desert him again, as mysteri-
ously as it had come. Leave him cold and constricted as a
clenched fist once again.

Part of him pleaded: *Let me feel it. Please. Let me feel it.*

And the other part: *You're going to pay for this in blood,
dickwad.*

He grabbed her damp, limp body almost defiantly. She

murmured in her sleep, but didn't wake. Thank God. He was in too much of a state to feel all of this crap, and deal with her feelings too.

This stuff was tricky. A guy had to walk before he tried to run.

He still had the condom on, but his dick was hard enough to keep the thing in place, and would probably remain in that state for as long as he was anywhere in Becca's proximity. So he stayed put, staring down at her face as she slept. Admiring how beautiful she was. The touseled mop of curls against the white pillow, the sensual weight of her sweet, sexy body, snuggled up to his. Heavy and warm and limp with perfect trust.

He got worried that she'd get chilled, after all that heaving and bucking and sweating, but it was a complicated business, getting the blankets and sheets tugged down beneath her sleeping body without waking her up. She finally stretched and yawned, and gave him a radiant smile that made his heart hurt like someone was squeezing it.

"You'll get cold," he said gruffly. "Let me get the covers over you."

"Not a chance," she said lazily. "You're like a bonfire."

Since she was definitely awake, he decided to get rid of the latex and its liquid load. By the time he came back to the bedroom, he'd come to a decision, as final as it was outrageous.

And he was prepared to enforce it. By any means necessary.

"Get up and get dressed," he said. "You're coming with me now."

She sat up, looking bewildered. "Nick? What on earth?"

He crossed his arms over his chest. "If I can't persuade you to get out of town and go into hiding, the safest thing for you is to come with me now," he explained grimly. "I know of a safe place you could stay."

She shook her head, in helpless confusion. "And all that carrying on you did about how Zhoglo's gunning for you, and therefore I'm safer far away from you? Blah blah blah?"

He widened his stance, clenched his fists. "I can't stay away from you," he admitted. "Particularly not now. So I'm not going to try. The next best thing is to stick to you like glue. Any butthead mobster comes within fifty yards of you, I'll blow his ass off."

"Ah, thank you, I think," she said faintly. "Is this some sort of courtship ritual on the planet that you're from, Nick? How very romantic. I appreciate the depth of feeling behind it."

"Cut the sarcasm," he said harshly. "I'm dead serious."

She hesitated, doubt plain on her face. He sensed that she was trying to choose her words carefully, so as not to push his wacko paranoid buttons. Which bugged the shit out of him still more.

"Nick, I don't think that Zhoglo will have any way of finding me—"

"I know some people," he went on, his voice roughening from pure desperation, "who can keep you safe. Even if I get wasted. And they could help you get a new identity, too. If it came to that."

Becca recoiled at his words and wrapped her arms around her chest, as if she were suddenly cold. "Nick," she whispered. "It's not so simple. I've got family. They count on me. I can't just disappear."

He said something filthy in Ukrainian in a savage undertone.

"I cannot come with you now," she said, her voice quietly stubborn. "I have to go to work. I have responsibilities. I'm in real danger of losing my main job already, and I can't afford to. I'm helping my brother and sister out with college costs."

Nick scowled. "Mind if I point out the obvious? They can get their own fucking jobs."

"Excuse me?"

"They can't count on you if you're dead. You're coming with me," he repeated, but he could tell from the look on her face that he'd lost this round. She wasn't going to play along. Damn the stubborn woman. He fought the impulse to put his fist through her wall. He did not do shit like that. Ever. That was the kind of thing his father had done.

She cleared her throat. "Nick, try to be reasonable," she coaxed. "I'm going to be at the Cardinal Creek Country Club all day long. Do you really think I'm likely to run into the Ukrainian mob there? It is, let us say, not a multicultural institution. They would do a background check on the Queen of England before they served her a cup of tea. It's actually embarrassing, how snooty and exclusive the place is."

But I want you with me, I want you safe, I want iron and steel and concrete and electronic walls around you, layers of them. He wanted to scream it, but his own knee-jerk macho pride was reasserting itself.

He'd be damned if he'd grovel and beg.

"Who are these friends of yours, anyhow?" she asked.

He shrugged. "Never mind," he said sourly. "If you're not going to take me up on my offer, then why the fuck do you care?"

She made an irritated sound. "Don't get all pissy and offended on me, Nick. I don't deserve that."

"Think about it," he said roughly. "Just think about taking a vacation from your life and disappearing for a while. Please, Becca."

After a moment, she inclined her head. "I'll think about it," she said quietly. "But I'm going to work today. We'll see how things go. OK?"

He rubbed his eyes, and squinted at the clock. He'd been here for about three hours. No calls from Raine in the vid room so far, but he should get back there soon to spell her, or Seth would rip both his legs off. He looked at Becca's naked body curled in the bed.

Well, hell. Maybe Raine could cope for a little while longer.

"I want to see you again," he told her. "Tonight."

A naughty smile curved her lips. "I would like that."

"When do you get off work?" he demanded.

She thought about it for a moment. "Tomorrow—that is, today, I guess—I'll probably get off some time after midnight. Not before."

He was appalled. "Midnight? What the fuck do you do there until fucking midnight?"

"Calm down," she soothed. "It's a farewell banquet. I organized the event weeks ago. Some big-shot cardiologist is retiring. Midnight is a hopeful estimate, with all the stuff I have to take care of afterwards."

He thought about it, and realized that maybe it was better that way. He couldn't get away from those vid monitors before midnight anyway. Maybe later. This way, he knew where the hell she was. The burr beacon he was planning to insert in her cell phone would help too.

"Will you meet me after?" he asked.

She looked puzzled. "Sure. Here, you mean?"

He shook his head. "No, not here. At a hotel. My neck is prickling. I don't like being in one place for too long. He'll get a fix on me."

She nodded, clearly humoring him. He tried not to be annoyed.

"I'll find a place, get checked into it. I'll text you the hotel and the name I'm checked in under. When you get off work, go straight there. Don't go home. You'll have to wait for me for a while."

"Good Lord," she murmured. "So cloak and dagger."

"Tell them you're my wife," he said.

Her eyes widened. "Is that necessary?" Her voice rose to a squeak.

"Yeah," he said grumpily, but he couldn't explain to her why.

It was hard to put into words. Calling her his wife created a barrier of privacy, illusion though it was. If the desk clerks were judgmental, suspicious women, or horny, dirty-minded men, or any combination thereof, calling her his wife would quell their inevitable speculation as to why a woman might meet a man at midnight at a hotel.

The fact that their speculation would be balls-on accurate was entirely beside the point. It was still none of their fucking business.

He didn't want to thrash through all that jealous bullshit with her, though, so he retreated into a growling sulk. "What, do you not want to claim me as a husband?" he snarled. "Foul-mouthed, tattooed lowlife that I am?"

Her lips pursed in an attempt not to smile. "Not at all," she said. "I'm just surprised. You actually said the W-word and the H-word."

He acknowledged that with a shrug. "I've got too much else to be scared of right now," he said dryly. "Later for that, OK? When I finally manage to kill the filthy son of a bitch, we can celebrate by having a big, screaming argument about my commitment issues. Sound good?"

She snorted. "I'll hold you to that."

"But for now . . ." He fished around on the floor next to the bed for the string of condoms, and stood up, tearing one loose. She sucked in a breath as he rolled it over his cock one-handed, grinning at her.

"Just what do you think you're going to do with that thing?" she demanded. "Nick, you have got to be kidding."

He lifted up the covers and slid between the sheets, gathering her hot warmth into his arms. "I'm not doing anything," he said innocently. "It's just, you know. A precaution. In case of . . . accidents."

"Accidents? Hah," she quavered, and cried out as he rolled on top of her and entered her, in one long, hard, relentless shove.

"Oops," he murmured. "Sorry. I was afraid this might happen."

She exploded into giggles, and the little shudders vibrated through his body, particularly the part he'd just slid inside her.

Hugging him, squeezing him. God, he loved to make her laugh.

Chapter
17

Zhoglo flipped through the printouts of the information that Mikhail had downloaded on Rebecca Cattrell. It was enough for his purposes. Address, place of work, employment history, driving record, banking and credit card information, tax data, medical records—a wealth of detail that bordered upon the tedious. The age of the Internet and the services of a competent hacker had rendered this cat-and-mouse game almost too easy to be entertaining.

Almost. He was sure he would manage to glean some enjoyment from the proceedings. He had been delighted to discover the existence of a brother and sister. The parents were long gone, but younger siblings would do nicely for the eventual mental torture part of his game. Almost as well as children of her own would have done.

He studied the color-printed photographs of the siblings. Attractive young people, both of them. The resemblance was striking. The girl, Caroline, studied art at Evergreen State College, and worked as an artist's model for the drawing classes. Posing naked in front of crowds of degenerate artists, the wanton little slut. He wondered if she would be as appetizing naked as her voluptuous older sister. He was looking forward to making the comparison. Caroline seemed more delicate and waiflike than her older sister, but had the same big, startled green eyes. As did the brother, Joshua, who studied mechanical engineering at University of Washington, and worked at an electronics store at a nearby mall. Both of them within easy reach. Good. Very good.

He chided himself inwardly. He really did not have the leisure to indulge in dangerous games like this. He had important business to conduct during his stay here. Vast sums of money to be made. If the Cattrells had come from a large, connected family who would have raised a fuss at their disappearance, he would have found an alternate way of unloading his vindictive impulses.

But they were a gaggle of wretched orphans with no money, no status, no powerful friends. They answered only to each other. Perfect.

Ah, how he enjoyed staging elaborate games of emotional torture. It took art to make the punishment fit the crime so perfectly, and he was a consummate artist. And speaking of punishment. He turned to Pavel, who was skulking by the door as if poised for escape. He gestured the man closer with an imperious wave of his hand.

"I have a job for you, Pavel," he said.

"To collect the brother and sister?" Pavel guessed hastily. "I'll leave immediately. I'll need to take at least two men—"

"No, not yet. Not quite yet," Zhoglo cut in, impatiently.

Pavel's eyes dilated in alarm. "What then, Vor?"

"I think it is now time for you to visit your dear friend. Ludmilla," Zhoglo said, slowly and deliberately. "You will be offering her a very lucrative contract. To provide sexual entertainment for myself and, incidentally, for my employees, during our sojourn here in Seattle."

"Vor, I do not believe that Ludmilla had any connection with—"

"Then you are a fool. Fools should stay silent, and listen."

Pavel flinched and subsided, like a whipped dog. Zhoglo resumed his light, musing tone. "You will go to Ludmilla.

By now, our enemy will have arranged to be watching and listening. This is good. You will speak to Ludmilla privately, at great length. You will speak of very large sums of money. Of ongoing contracts. Greedy, self-interested whore that she is, she will put her fear aside in hope of profit. She will offer you liquor, and you will indulge—to the point of inebriation or at least the appearance of it. You will confide in her what happened. How the Vor is so angry with you, so cruel to you. She will be horrified. She will try to comfort you. Perhaps, out of fear, or guilt, she will even fuck you."

Pavel's eyes were squeezed tightly shut. "Vor, I do not wish to—"

"What you wish, Pavel, is of less than no interest to me," he said. "The woman must be, what, in her fifties? Is she attractive?"

"Late forties," Pavel said tonelessly. "And yes. She is attractive enough."

"Ah, good." Zhoglo gave him an encouraging slap on the back. "Fuck her, then. It will relax you. You are too tense, my friend. Keep in mind, you must stay with her as long as possible, to give our enemies time to organize themselves. So they can follow you back here."

"Here?" Pavel's eyes goggled. "But Vor, no one knows that you are here. Is that safe? If I—"

"Safe? No. Nothing that I do is safe," Zhoglo scoffed. "I did not earn ten billion dollars being safe, my dear Pavel. Safe bores me. Boredom makes me testy."

"But . . . but the police—"

"The federal police will give me no trouble. I have an understanding with them. They are not the ones who stabbed me in the back, Pavel. I wish to know who did. I wish to eliminate my enemy."

"Yes, of course, but—"

"And I want Solokov," Zhoglo went on, almost dreamily. "I want him to watch what I do to the pretty Rebecca. Just as she will watch what I do to her precious little brother and sister. It is all about watching, you see, Pavel. They watch Ludmilla and you. They watch us. We, in turn, watch them watching us. And we push them around the game board as we see fit. You see, eh? How this game is played?"

Pavel looked miserable. "Yes, Vor," he muttered.

But Zhoglo wasn't finished with his flight of fancy. "This is the part of the fight where the two opponents circle each other, study each other, looking for weaknesses. It's stimulating. And ah, yes, Pavel—on the subject of stimulation, you being the expert whoregoer among us, do you have any other source of beautiful call girls in this city besides that traitorous bitch Ludmilla?"

Pavel looked perplexed. "Yes, Vor. Several. But I thought— I thought you wanted your enemies to follow—"

"I do. That has nothing to do with this," the Vor sighed. "This is a separate matter. Not for their ears. Find me a girl. Extremely beautiful. Blonde, if possible. Fresh and innocent looking. Under twenty. Intelligent enough to play an amusing charade for us."

Pavel cleared his throat, nodded. "Yes, Vor. I know just the girl."

Zhoglo gave him an approving smile. "I thought you might. Get her for me immediately." His face took on an expression of mock sadness. "Poor Marya. Does she know of her worthless husband's weakness?"

Pavel swallowed. "Ah, no, Vor."

"Not that I have anything against whores, of course. My own mother was a whore, or so I was told. And oh, yes. That reminds me. Speaking of mothers and whores, Mikhail, would you open that video conferencing connection again? There was something I wanted to show you. Were you aware that your wife was trying to desert you, Pavel? With Misha? She had gotten almost as far as Cracow when my men caught up with her and brought her back."

Pavel's face, already pale, turned a sickly gray. Zhoglo smiled inwardly. The fool, after all the expensive mistakes he had made, the money he had cost. Thinking he could wiggle out of his punishment. Thinking he could whisk his wife and his remaining son out of danger.

No place in the world was beyond Vadim Zhoglo's reach.

"I had them bring Marya and Misha to my home so that my men could keep them safe for you," Zhoglo soothed. "Rest easy. They are my pampered guests. I had Mikhail establish a video conference, as I was sure you would want to reprove the cowardly bitch. Abandoning you in your time of need. The perfidy of women. Mikhail? Is the line open?"

"Yes, Vor. One moment, while Aleksei calls the woman to come to the computer," the man said.

The digital image disintegrated into a muddled soup of pixels, and then slowly resolved into the image of Marya Cherchenko, holding her little son on her lap. Her eyes were hollowed, her mouth flat and pale in her thin face.

How odd the way perceptions changed, Zhoglo mused. He had remembered considering Marya a beautiful woman, but now she looked drained, almost old. Skin stretched over her bony face, her hair dull and lank. The way of all flesh, he thought, with a flash of melancholy.

The little boy was likewise miserable. His eyes were enormous in his pinched face.

Pavel stared at them. They stared back.

"Papa?" the little boy whispered.

Zhoglo looked on, well pleased, and wiggled his fingers in the pockets of his finely tailored linen pants. The other men in the room all had the studied blankness one might expect, as they watched their colleague's punishment. But he could feel the general level of tension in the room. It was very high. The same thought, in all the men's heads—he could see it as if it were stamped in neon on their foreheads. *This could be me.*

He made sure that these moments were public. His men needed to know what would happen if they failed him. If they did not give their best, and more than their best, in his service. Each of those men were desperately grateful to be in his good graces right now. Eager to please, to ingratiate himself. Each would bring any hint of betrayal to him, and lay it at his feet, like a cat bringing a dead rodent to its master.

Just as it should be. Everything in its proper place. The boundaries that he established kept these men safe, supported their families, gave their world structure.

He was, after all, responsible for sustaining his slice of a vast shadow economy. Without him, tens of thousands would starve and die.

Fear was a useful tool. He had learned that as a child on the streets of Kiev. A leader had to be cruel and ruthless. To use fear like a surgical instrument to remove rot before it spread and killed. It was his responsibility to wield that tool. Indeed, it was his sacred duty.

And if he also enjoyed it, well . . . who would begrudge a burdened, hardworking man of business an occasional small pleasure?

"Are you having an affair, Becca?"

Marla's sharp voice made Becca jump. The cell phone in her hand thudded down on to the computer keyboard with a rattling clatter. "Excuse me?" she asked, flushing hotly. "What makes you say that?"

Marla rolled her eyes, her lips curving into a tight, mirthless smile. "Oh, I don't know," she said. "Could it be the fact that you've just checked your cell phone for text messages for the tenth time in the past eight minutes? Or maybe the fact that you got to work today at 10:25 A.M.—"

"I told you, Marla, I had to rent a car! I called you this morning to let you know! The place opened at nine, and it took forever to fill out all the paperwork!"

"Or could it be the ninety-minute lunch hour?" Marla continued, as if Becca had not spoken. "The one that involved a trip to the mall, and a stop at . . ." She leaned over and neatly snagged the shopping bag out from under the desk, where Becca had tried to discreetly stow it. "Ah. I might have known. Victoria's Secret. And what have we here?" She pulled out a handful of intimate items, labels still dangling from them. A flesh-toned, ribbon-trimmed bustier, an insubstantial matching garter belt, long stockings with embroidered back seams. "Good God, Becca."

"That is private!" Becca yanked her lingerie back and stuffed it into the bag. "It's none of your business!"

"Well, when you start taking advantage of office time to run your own extremely personal errands, I'm afraid that it is."

Becca started to fume. "Marla, I can count on the fingers of one hand the times that I've taken an actual lunch break since I started this job three years ago!"

"Yes. I know." Marla wrapped her leathery, salon-tanned arms over her chest and pursed her lips, looking angry and worried. "You're usually so precise. I would even say perfectionist. Which is why this erratic behavior jumps out at me. Like leaving Jerome's vacation home wide open to the elements? And losing his keys . . . where was it again? In the woods, for God's sake? Not bothering to call when you got back to town? Not bothering to come to work? For days!"

"I told you," Becca said tightly. "I am terribly sorry about what happened at Jerome's house. I had . . . I had a momentary lapse of reason."

That was the best she could do as an explanation, but it didn't satisfy Marla. Becca racked her brains trying to think of a way to justify what had happened, but everything would sound lame and forced. And false. The truth was untellable.

Hey, Marla. She hadn't locked Jerome's door or brought back his keys because she'd been running for her life from a bloodthirsty villain. Accompanied by a sex god commando who was meeting her this very night to ravish her in a hotel room. Who had begged her not to notify the police, or else she'd die a grisly death. *Uh-huh. Yes. Of course.*

She had a sneaky premonition that juicy, colorful tale wouldn't be quite the thing to guarantee her continued job security at the club.

"Hmph," Marla huffed. "I certainly hope that the lapse is momentary. And that it won't happen again. I would be justified in firing you for what happened this past week. The reason I haven't done so yet is because you've always been reliable before, and you've been through a great deal, what with that awful situation with that scum ex-fiancé of yours. But I don't give third chances. Do I make myself clear?"

"Yes," Becca said tightly. "Quite."

"Good. I want you at your best for that banquet tonight. Shay will have her hands full with the birthday party this afternoon in the Blue Salon, so don't expect backup from her. The florist has arrived with the table centerpieces, or haven't you noticed? And have you checked the PA system? How about the sound setup for the jazz trio? And what about the signage?"

"Ah . . . I haven't had a chance yet to—"

"Please do so. Now. And put your cell phone in your purse. This constant checking for messages is annoying the hell out of me."

Becca stuck her tongue out at the woman's retreating back before she could stop herself, and held her phone down below the edge of the desk, surreptitiously rereading the text of the last message she'd sent to Nick. She suppressed the urge to giggle at her own silliness.

got virginal lingerie 2 go with glasses. hair 2 short for bun, but that's ur fault. love, the formerly frigid sex bomb secretary.

The phone chimed. Omigod. He'd already gotten back to her. She made sure Marla's back was still turned before she clicked to open.

cannot fucking wait

Oh, God. She could actually see his gorgeous, sexy grin, creasing up the grooves around his mouth, the gleam in his seductive dark eyes.

She practically choked on the giggles backing up inside her. She was having so much subversive fun today, more than she'd ever had in her life. And Nick was playing along. Egging her on, even. Of all the things she'd expected from him, goofy playfulness wasn't one of them.

She'd never had a wild secret affair before. It just wasn't the kind of thing that ever happened to her. And with a guy who made her feel . . . oh, wow. Her posterior ached from being spread so wide, ridden so long and hard. And as for her private parts, well. They were definitely feeling the effects of vigorous, prolonged use.

And even so, every time she thought about him, she instinctively squeezed her saddlesore thighs together around the tingle of heat. It was making her giddy, distracted. Working her into a lather of unprofessional titillation. A naughty nymphomaniac who could think of nothing but Nick's fierce dark eyes, his clever tongue, his dazzling smile. His volcanic sexual heat. His big, thick . . . oh dear, oh dear.

She needed a fan in the worst way. Whew. She was sweating.

For heaven's sake. She would fire her too, if she were Marla.

But oh, it was lovely. She hadn't had anything to feel euphoric about since . . . well, she had been dazzled for a while after Justin's proposal, and full of hopeful dreams of domestic bliss, but that was nothing on this. No fiery sexual component, no life-or-death drama.

It had taken her over a half hour to find the cell number that he had programmed into her cell, because he hadn't put it under *N* for Nick, or even *W* for Ward. After combing through her whole address file, she finally found it under *M*. For Mr. Big. That clown.

Time to check with the caterers, take delivery for table

decorations, and triple-check the settings and the gift presentation table. She forced herself to make a mental to-do list. Very difficult to do while her brain ran amok, jumping and squeaking. What a morning. Up before four A.M., dragged into the shower with Nick, with yet another explosive erotic outcome. To say nothing of the flood that had stretched down the bathroom corridor to soak the living room rug.

Then, after he'd left, the frantic destruction of her entire closet system while she tried to figure out what to wear for a sexy midnight tryst. A suitcase was stowed in the back of the rental car out in the back lot, with a few changes of clothing, makeup, toiletries, her prettiest dress, her only pair of fuck-me shoes. She'd even dug around in her bathroom until she found the diaphragm she'd gotten a couple years before. Like the shoes, it had never gotten much use. Hardly any, actually. The affair she'd gotten it for had petered out embarrassingly quickly.

For some reason, she'd never thought to propose its use to Justin, even after they got engaged, and a damn good thing, too. Maybe she'd known, on some level, that he was going to fool around on her.

The thought of using it with Nick, of having that electric, bare-skin-to-bare-skin contact with his gorgeous, um, member, aroused her almost to the point of fainting. Yeah, and Marla would really love it if she did.

She glanced down at the glossy, striped-pink shopping bag that held her lingerie, and on impulse, she rummaged in her drawer for a different bag, something plastic and anonymous. She shoved the frilly nothings into the bag and slipped out of the office, heading straight for the ladies' room. She was going to put that stuff on. Right now.

Hey, might as well wear the evidence of her mad folly on her body. At least that way, she wouldn't have to make excuses to anyone for it.

* * *

"Would you sit your manic ass down for five seconds and at least pretend to give a fuck about what you're doing?" Seth Mackey said testily. "Weren't you supposed to lie in wait for that sicko asshole?"

Nick looked over at the door where Seth was lounging, taken aback. "Huh? Yeah, sure. I was. I am. So what's your problem?"

"You," Seth said shortly. "You are my problem. That shit-eating grin on your face. You're pacing, dude. Jiggling your car keys, fucking around with your cell phone, bouncing off the walls. Yesterday you were the Zombie King. Now you're humming, for Christ's sake! What gives?"

Nick felt his face grow hot. "So don't watch." Abashed, he sank down into one of the ergonomic swivel chairs the room was furnished with and peeked one last time at his cell.

"And stop fondling that damn thing," Seth snapped. "An army of mafiya thugs could be trooping through that woman's door, and there you are out in la-la land, sex-texting your girlfriend."

Nick's head jerked around, but the crafty gleam in Seth's eyes cut off his grumpy rebuttal.

"So it's true," Seth said triumphantly. "Listen, chump. I could resign myself to having my wife stare at your fucking vid screens in the dead of night—when she should be resting—if you were lying on the staff couch, catching some z's. I figure, the pathetic slob looks like he hasn't slept in six months, give him a break. But you weren't on that couch. You went out last night. To get laid!" Seth sounded outraged.

"Aw, fuck off," Nick muttered without much conviction.

But Seth was far from finished. "Having Raine work a graveyard shift on your fucked-up project to save your sorry ass from getting shot up is one thing. But having her do it so you can waltz out of here and get your rocks off with your girlfriend is entirely another."

"Girlfriend?" Margot, Davy's wife, sailed into the workroom, her hugely pregnant belly preceding her. "What's this I hear about a girlfriend?"

"Nothing," Nick muttered. "Nobody's goddamn business."

"Nonsense," Margot teased, clasping her hands beneath the heavy undercurve of her belly. The bulge was covered by eye-grabbing purple paisley knit, which clashed cheerfully with her shaggy mop of curly red hair. "It's going to break the hearts of all our single girlfriends at the wedding tomorrow, but it does solve our seating dilemma. Erin couldn't figure out who to seat next to you. A stacked blonde, a hottie redhead, a sultry brunette? It was driving her nuts. So what's your girlfriend's name?"

"Wedding?" Nick went tense, eyes widening. "What wedding?"

Margot rolled her eyes, and put her hands behind the small of her back. "Sean and Liv. Tomorrow at four P.M. Wake up, Nick. You were invited months ago. I already reserved a room for you at Three Creeks Lodge. It has a private deck with a hot tub. You'll love it, particularly if you've got a girlfriend with you. Don't even think about squirming out of this one, buddy boy."

Nick gestured at the video screen. "Get real! I can't walk away from this to put on a goddamn suit and eat canapés! Forget it, Margot."

Margot snorted. "Oh, please. A psycho scumbag criminal hungry for your blood is no excuse to miss a great party. This is a McCloud wedding, after all. Having a dangerous villain at large is a tradition. It makes it all the more poignant, know what I mean?"

Nick grunted. "Poignant, my ass—"

"The food will be fabulous, the champagne will flow freely, and the Vicious Rumors are actually going to do the music as a special favor to Sean. They don't even do weddings anymore, since they're getting so big for their britches these days. Plus, we all get to meet your girlfriend and vet her for you," Margot concluded brightly. "Cool! I can't wait."

Nick shook his head. "Raine's going to the wedding too, right?"

"Hell, yeah. She's in the ceremony. So's Tam, for that matter. Tam's the maid of honor, as always. I'm sure she'll be pleased to see you."

"Yeah, right." Pleased to shoot him on sight was more like it. "I can't leave, Margot. Somebody who speaks Ukrainian has got to—"

"I solved that." Davy poked his head around the door, looking hugely pleased with himself. "That's what we came over to tell you. I found a guy through an army buddy of mine. An ex-Ranger who grew up in Brighton Beach, Brooklyn. For you non–New Yorkers, that's a neighborhood otherwise known as Little Odessa, a hotbed of Russian—"

"Thanks, Guidebook Boy," Nick snarled. "What's his name?"

"Alex Aaro. He'll mind the vids for you while we guzzle champagne and dance all night. He's driving up from Pendleton."

"But I—"

"We'll bring the laptops too," Davy soothed. "There's broadband connection at Three Creeks. You can get a direct video feed, and check on the madam in between each course. If you want to."

"But this guy doesn't know their faces," Nick protested.

"Establish a code word with Ludmilla. If she says it, the guys jump into action," Davy said patiently. "Simple. Stop being such a wet blanket. Here, I'll download the guy's resume. I brought the disc—"

"No!" Nick lunged to stop him from inserting the disc into the computer's drive, feeling like an idiot. "I'm, uh, using that monitor."

Davy peered at it, and started to grin when he saw the blue-toned map of Seattle glowing on the screen, and the single icon blinking on it. "I see," he murmured. "That's her, huh? In Bothell? Sweet."

"What?" Seth loped over and lunged across the table to squint at the screen. "Do my eyes deceive me? This controlling bastard is monitoring his girlfriend with X-Ray Specs? Where'd you put the beacon burr, Romeo? Her bra?"

"Her cell," Nick admitted reluctantly.

Seth crowed with delight. "Classic. Bet she doesn't know, right?" He studied Nick's stiff, frozen face, and laughed harder. "Of course not."

"He's got it bad," Davy commented. "This is how it always starts."

"What's her name, damn it?" Margot fussed. "We need to know what to write on the seating tag!"

"Becca," Nick said shortly.

Margot waited. "Just Becca?" she prompted. "No last name?"

"Just Becca," he muttered.

Margot frowned. "What, is she in hiding? On the run from the law?" She chewed on her lip, her multicolored eyes getting very big in her freckled face. "Oh, my God. Is this the girl you saved from that mafiya guy? The girl you found naked in the swimming pool? No way!"

Seth whooped gleefully. "Oh, man. This is awesome. True love, at gunpoint. It never fails."

"Oh, God. I have got to go call Raine and Liv and Erin, right away," Margot said. "This is so juicy. I love it. I just *love* it."

"Would you guys all just leave me the fuck alone?" Nick's voice was plaintive.

Davy gave him a swat on the back that just about broke three of his ribs. "No way, dude," he said cheerfully. "Get used to it."

Chapter
18

Becca circled the Crystal Ballroom slowly. The banquet was a black tie affair, and the women in evening gowns glittered and shone.

So far, so good. No job-threatening disasters loomed on her horizon yet. The Meet-And-Greet in the Sunburst Room had gone smoothly, the jazz trio was playing a sentimental tune, the sommeliers and wait staff were doing their appointed jobs, the trays of lime sorbet to follow the fish were starting to circle, the big band was set up and ready to go for the dancing, everyone was in place, everyone knew what time it was.

Fifteen more minutes, and it would be time to start mobilizing the coffee and dessert, and get ready for the speechifying. The sheer volume of details to keep track of made it almost possible for her not to think about Nick. But oh, wow. She was going to see him tonight. The consciousness of her secret date gave her a constant toe-curling pleasure, like a wild coffee high.

She was so absorbed in trying to quantify the feeling, she almost ran right into the guy as he strode through the room. She reeled to the side, turning her head away with a gasp. Oh, God. The Spider's guest. Zhoglo's mysterious business partner. The country club guy.

She turned, slowly, and ventured another peek, just to be sure.

He was in profile, looking trim and good in his tux, sliding into his seat with what looked like a murmured apology at one of the big VIP tables, next to a handsome blonde woman with a tight smile. He lifted his glass of red wine in response to something that she said.

She remembered him lifting his glass, on the island. Those glittering eyes fixed on her. The clink of glasses. Wine the color of blood.

To beauty. And desires fulfilled.

A sinkhole opened in the bottom of her mind. Beneath it yawned a hellish abyss.

Becca stumbled across the room, putting distance between them. She grabbed the edge of a table, fighting nausea. A wave of nasty faintness jangled through her body. Her ears roared, her eyes went dark. Cold sweat. Icy hands. She wanted to double over. Staying conscious was a struggle.

The reality of what had happened on the island just a few short days ago came smashing back. It had been lurking there all along, ready to pounce, destroying her fragile new equilibrium.

She could not faint. Could not. She had to get a grip. Had. To.

"Becca?" Marla's voice was sharp. "What on earth is the matter with you? Are you ill?"

Becca wiped her clammy forehead, and peeked again. His glance swept over her without snagging on her. Thank God for the shorter, fluffier hair and the face-concealing, black-framed glasses.

Becca put her back to him. "Marla?" she whispered. "The guy behind me who just sat down at the VIP table? Six-two, black tux, late forties, gray temples? Next to the old lady with the dowager's hump and the diamonds? Who is he?"

Marla's eyes narrowed, and her finely shaped brows snapped together. "Becca. This is hardly the time for—ouch! Hey!"

Becca had seized her wrist, and was gripping it with furious strength, heedless of her fingernails. *"Who is he?"*

Marla jerked her arm away, scowling. "That's Dr. Richard Mathes. He's a famous thoracic surgeon. He's giving the farewell speech for Harrison tonight! You knew that, Becca! He was late, because of some medical emergency."

Becca pressed on her mouth with her hands. "Oh, God," she whispered. She was going to heave her guts out. "Gotta run. Going to be sick," she squeaked, through the hand clamped over her mouth.

She bolted towards the ladies' room, caroming into tables, elbowing one of the catering staff who was carrying a tray of full sorbet dishes, all of which toppled, dumping themselves right onto the unfortunate woman's crisp white blouse.

Becca fled, leaving shouts of outrage in her wake. She couldn't stop and apologize, anyway. If she opened her mouth, "I'm so sorry" was not what was going to be coming out of it. Barfing on club members in evening wear would not help her cause. Praise God, there was no line in the ladies' room. She made it to the stall just in time.

The bathroom stalls in the club's ladies' rooms were little private rooms in their own right, made of peach-colored marble quarried in Italy. Each stall contained its own private sink with antique gold-toned fixtures and an enormous gilt-framed mirror. Hers reflected her own pitiful image when she finally dared to lift her head up from where it dangled over the toilet bowl. Oh, God. Very bad.

She was as white as a hospital lab coat. Eyes and nose streaming with tears, eyelids swollen and pink, mascara running copiously.

And sheer terror in her eyes. She shook all over.

Here? Why here, at one of her own events? What were the odds? Fate was having evil fun at her expense.

She lingered in the little room for as long as she dared,

wiping off the toilet, cleaning up her face, adjusting hair, clothes and facial expression. She braced herself, and tried on a cheerful, professional smile. Oh, boy. Nix the smile.

She couldn't fake or finesse this one. She didn't even have her cell phone on her, to call Nick and bleat desperately for rescue. It was in her office, in her purse, way down the corridor at the end of this wing.

She tried to talk herself down. The man wasn't going to stop chowing down on his poached salmon and take time out to murder her. Nor did he seem the type who would do his own murdering. He was, however, certainly capable of making a few discreet inquiries and then stepping around a corner to make a phone call. And that would be that for Becca Cattrell.

She would be, as Nick so expressively put it, so fucked.

She was not at all surprised to find Marla waiting outside, her taut rear end perched half-on, half-off the long marble vanity counter. Her arms were crossed, her brows knit. She looked furiously angry.

There were other women primping and washing, and Marla waited in stony silence for them to leave. Becca braced herself as the door closed behind the last woman, leaving them alone.

Marla lost no time. "You slept with him, didn't you?"

Becca stared at the other woman blankly. That took her utterly by surprise, so beset was she by images of grisly death wounds and bullet holes. "Ah . . . huh? With who?" she floundered. "I—but I—"

"Don't play dumb with me," the older woman hissed. "I'm talking about Mathes. So that's where you were all those days you didn't come to work, hmm? The phone messaging, the slut lingerie? Did he give you a fake name, Becca? Did he not tell you he was married? Christ, what an innocent you are."

Fuck a duck. Becca struggled to organize a coherent response. She just kept opening and closing her mouth as it sank in that the conclusion Marla had leaped to was a screamingly obvious one. Far more probable and believable than the awful truth.

Marla raged quietly on, her voice laced with suppressed anger. "That was his wife, Helen Mathes, beside him. Remember the tall blonde with all the bling? Big philanthropist, on all the charitable boards in the city? She attended the Mother/Daughter Tea you organized last year. With her nine- and twelve-year-old girls. Mouthy little blond brats, both of them. You don't remember her?"

Becca shook her head. "I don't remember her," she whispered.

"I very much hope that you're not thinking anything stupid, Becca. Like, for instance, that he's going to leave his wife for you." Marla's eyes swept critically over her. "Please be realistic. You're a very pretty girl and very sweet, but you're hardly a femme fatale."

"Marla, I'm not—"

"And now, damage control." Marla dragged a handful of perfumed facial tissues out of the pink marble dispenser and shoved them into Becca's hand. "I am very sorry that you've had not one, but two romantic disappointments in a single week. But this is an opportunity to show your true colors. I want to see how professional you can be."

"But Marla, I—"

"Get out there and work, just like nothing ever happened. It's the only dignified thing you can do," Marla announced. "What's he going to do? What *can* he do? Nothing, Becca. If he sees you, be classy. Smile. Pretend you've never seen him before. Smile big at his wife, too. Let him wonder what you're capable of. Let him squirm and worry. He deserves it, the lying, cheating prick. But do not let him control you!"

Marla's lecture was delivered in ringing tones that should have been accompanied by inspiring theme music. Becca stared at her boss's stern expression, and found herself wishing desperately that she could do exactly as she was told. Just go with the flow.

After all. It seemed so lurid, so improbable. Maybe the whole episode had all been some sort of crazy hallucination. A bad dream she wanted so badly to forget. Or at least ignore. Maybe if she pretended . . . and hoped he didn't notice her, or recognize her . . . ?

No. Not an option. She'd seen what she had seen. She'd surfed on rivers of blood. She had to face it, own up to it, and deal.

"I cannot go back out there," she said quietly. "I'm so sorry."

Marla's face tightened. "You're running out on me in the middle of one of the most important events of the year because you slept with the wrong guy? For God's sake, Becca! Everyone's done that a time or two! Get over it! Grow up!"

I didn't sleep with that slimy son of a bitch. I would rather die.

She wanted to scream it at the top of her lungs. She swallowed the impulse down, and it bumped like a big rock in her throat.

She both liked and respected Marla. Despite her sharp tongue and her bitchiness, she was protective and supportive, even maternal to her younger employee. Becca genuinely valued Marla's good opinion.

But at this point, she had two options. Marla could think that Becca was a weak-willed, scared slut, or else she could think that Becca was a deluded paranoid nutcase. Both options were painful.

"I'm sorry to disappoint you," she said, meaning it with every cell of her body. "I have my reasons. I just can't do it."

Marla's eyes narrowed, and she opened her mouth. At that moment, another woman came into the bathroom and headed for one of the stalls. Marla waited until the stall door clicked shut, and then leaned forward and whispered savagely into Becca's ear.

"I will give you five minutes to rethink that decision. If I don't see you out in the Crystal Ballroom after that amount of time, I'll consider that your letter of resignation, effective immediately. Good-bye, Becca. Best of luck in all your future endeavors."

She left, heels clicking angrily on the gleaming marble tiles.

Becca clutched the marble sink, white-knuckled, as the shape of her world shifted. Hope, daydreams, expectations suddenly, brutally readjusted.

Fired. So. On top of rape, torture and murder, she got to worry about how she was going to pay her rent, too. And Carrie's. And Josh's.

She tried to comfort herself. It wasn't as if she had anything to lose. There was unemployment. She'd stood on that slow-moving line before. If she didn't go out and work the banquet, she lost her job, yes. But if she did go out, she'd get dead. Dead girls held down no jobs.

She shook with ironic laughter, doubling over with her hand on her still fluttering belly. Gee. Some comfort. A real winner, that.

OK. Getting fired was definitely her clue to scram. She squelched her fear and shock, and looked out the bathroom door, looking to the right and the left. No one. She sprinted on tiptoe down the corridor towards the administrative offices at the end of the wing.

A quickie trip to her office to collect her purse, cell and keys. She tossed her coat on. Put up the hood. God, how she wished she'd bleached her hair, as Nick had begged her. Why had she been so stubborn? Why was she such a fluff-headed dork? Why?

She lingered for one wistful moment in the office she had shared with Shay, Marla's administrative assistant. Where she'd worked so hard for three years. All that effort, up in smoke. Marla wasn't going to give her a reference after tonight. She was back to square one, professionally. Waitressing, catering gigs, temping. No benefits, no health coverage, no future.

Concentrate on staying alive, birdbrain. She pried the keys to the office off her chain, and left them on Shay's desk with a note of explanation and farewell. She flipped off the lights, pushed the door open and peeked out into the hall.

She ducked immediately back inside, her heart thudding madly against her rib cage. *He* was there. Right there, less than ten yards from her office door. In the second it had taken to register who he was, he'd been too busy arguing with a woman to see the door crack open.

A dark-haired woman in a long raincoat. Not Helen Mathes.

She closed the door, very gently, and locked the knob. Trying to breathe, to think, over the deafening thumps of her heartbeat. Her insides were icy-cold mush, getting mushier with each successive adrenaline surge. She cringed against the door, tears squeezing out of tight-shut eyes. Wishing she carried a gun like Nick. That she could snap necks, slice throats, blast off asses, if anyone messed with her.

Basically, she hoped they would just go away, and give her an opening to flee. Like the cowering crybaby that she was.

Click. A door opening. *Click.* Light suddenly flooded in from the adjoining office. Marla's office. Her boss had left it unlocked. The connecting door between the offices was yawning wide open.

Oh, Jesus. She was right in their line of sight as they burst in the door, already arguing.

". . . the hell you think you're doing here, anyway! Have you gone completely insane?" Mathes hissed.

"But they sent us all the data on the blood and tissue typing!" The woman's voice quavered, verging on tears. "You've seen it! The girl is a perfect match for—"

"And you trust their doctors? Their paperwork? Their lab equipment? For the fees we're charging, I cannot have the slightest doubt about any of the details. We test, we check, we double check, and then we triple-check. Is that clear?"

Becca couldn't breathe. Her mouth shook. She was afraid that if she unlocked her lungs, and tried to suck in air, they would convulse, make a sound like a barking sob. She couldn't risk it. Air could wait.

She slid, very slowly, her back against the door. Trying not to rustle, not to squeak. Until she was down, behind the water cooler, curled up, trying to be as small as possible.

The woman gulped back tears, audibly. "But Richie, I can't—"

"What do you mean, can't? We have Edeline Metgers scheduled for two days from now!" The violence in his voice punched against Becca's jangled nerves like the blows of a fist. "Along with four other recipients. You made the arrangements yourself!"

"You don't understand," the woman whispered brokenly. "Y-you have to come with me to do this, Richie. It's too hard to do alone. You're the one who makes me strong. I can't—"

"Bullshit. We're miles deep in this, you stupid bitch. We can't go back now," Mathes snarled. "God knows, I would prefer to do it myself, but I'm stuck here and you know it. I'm giving a fawning speech for that pompous old dickwad in exactly . . . ah, great. Yes. Exactly nine minutes and counting. Great timing, Diana. You show up here, uninvited, in a trench coat and diva sunglasses at nine o'clock at night, and make a fucking spectacle of yourself at Harrison's party— Jesus Christ, did you think my wife wouldn't notice? Everyone noticed!"

"But I—"

"Go, and do as we agreed." The steely note of menace in the man's voice sent a shudder up Becca's spine. "It has to be you and it has to be now. Tonight. No other options. Do we understand each other?"

"But Richie, I'm telling you—"

Crack, the sound of a vicious slap to the face. Followed

by the sound a dog made when its tail was stepped on. Then muffled sniveling. "You are such a prick, Richie," the woman whimpered.

"I know. That's why we get along so well. Now get out, and do your job. The time to have a breakdown has passed. Understood?"

There was a muffled sob, then a whimper and a guttural moan. Becca leaned forward just long enough to see that the man was kissing her. His hand gripped her crotch, working it. The woman writhed, clutching him around the neck as if she were drowning.

Becca jerked back, feeling slimed and fouled for having witnessed it.

The woman stumbled back with a sob and bumped into Marla's desk. Mathes had evidently shoved her away from himself.

"Be good, Diana," he warned. The door snapped shut behind him.

Diana blubbered noisily for so long, Becca actually started to get bored. Her legs went to sleep from being folded up so tightly. She was intensely grateful when the woman pulled herself together and stumbled out the door, still sniffling.

Becca fell forward onto her face and struggled up onto numb legs. Stomping and staggering until the pins and needles subsided enough so that she could actually walk, she flung her purse over her shoulder, and peered out the door in time to catch the flash of Diana's beige raincoat, disappearing down the staircase that led to the back parking lot. Where Becca's own rental car was parked.

She didn't dare to examine the impulse, or she'd lose her nerve. *It has to be you, and it has to be now. Tonight,* the man had said.

Funny. Go figure. The exact same thing held true for her, too.

She took a deep breath and followed.

* * *

"Um, excuse me? May I ask you a technical question?" the soft, faintly accented female voice asked.

Josh Cattrell readjusted the fan inside the computer's hard case, and groaned inwardly at this hundred and fifty thousandth interruption. He would never get this damn computer assembled before closing time unless he could get people to leave him the hell alone. "Miss, why don't you talk to one of the other guys out on the floor?" He looked up. "One of them can answer your . . . uh . . ."

The distracted words disintegrated in his mind, like a smoke ring coming softly apart in the air until it vanished completely. Leaving the slate of his mind wiped clean. And his mouth dangling wide open.

This girl was beautiful. So outlandishly beautiful, it was like she was from another planet. Long, swinging white-blond hair, huge, dark blue eyes, bee-stung lips, flower-petal-smooth skin.

And it only got more outrageous from there. He rose to his feet so that he could send his peripheral vision downward and catalog the rest of her supernatural perfection. Double D's that defied gravity beneath a tight white tee, tiny waist with a bare midriff, pierced navel. Super lowrise jeans, clinging for dear life to the curve of a world-class ass.

He forced himself to look at her face again. He had no idea how long he'd been gawking. She was smiling at him. That mouth was amazing, full and perfect and sexily shaped. Angelina-eat-your-heart-out lips. She glowed. She shone. She was a miracle of nature, right here in Eric's Electronics Barn.

"I am so very sorry," she said, those long dark lashes sweeping down, casting fan-shaped shadows over her cheeks. "I disturbed you, from your work. Please excuse me, I will simply go and ask that other man, no? The red-haired man standing by the counter? Perhaps he can—"

"Oh, no! It's no trouble at all!" Josh said. "Ask away. Anything you like. Anything." Aw, *shit*. He was babbling, like an idiot. He hated himself when he did that.

But she was still smiling, amazingly. A tender, radiant smile, like he'd just offered her the moon.

It took all his brainpower to actually listen and understand her computer problem, with the combined difficulty of her accent and her unbelievable, insane gorgeousness, but eventually he started to get a vague clue: a desktop publishing program which went into conflict with other stuff on her computer and froze her system.

"Bring it in for me and I'll take a look," he suggested. "Did you buy it here?"

She looked suddenly worried. "No, it was a used computer."

"Aw," he said, crestfallen. "So it, uh, won't be covered by the warranty, then." Damn. He totally wanted to solve her problem, save her money, be her hero. "Um, I guess you could still bring it in to me," he suggested. "I could still take a look. Completely free of charge, of course. I'll do it after hours."

She looked radiantly hopeful. "Oh. You are so very kind. But if I may ask . . . I hope you do not think I am asking too much . . ."

"Ask! Anything," he said rashly.

"Could you perhaps consider, ah, coming to my house, to see it?" Her words came out in an anxious, embarrassed little rush. "Like a consultant? I have no car, you see, and the computer is very big and heavy for me, and I have no one who will help me here—"

"Sure! Yes, absolutely!" He was practically dizzy. Her house? This was too much. Holy crapola. He was going to blow a gasket.

"I will pay you for your time, of course," she said earnestly.

"Oh, God, no. Don't worry about it," he assured her. "It's my pleasure. It's just . . . uh . . . when?"

Her fathomless blue eyes blinked. "As soon as convenient for you?"

He swallowed, hard. "Um, how about now, then?"

Dimples suddenly appeared, and a laughing sparkle in her eyes. "Do you not have to work?" she asked gently. "I do not want you to have trouble with boss because of me."

"Oh, not at all. My hours are sort of flex, anyhow," he lied. "And I was already planning to leave early, so my boss will be OK with it."

That was kinda true. Joe had given him leave to go early so he could get a good start driving down to Olympia to pick up Carrie.

Abrupt change of plan. His little sister was just going to have to understand. A chance like this rolled around about once a millennium.

"May I ask you a personal question?" he asked.

Her lips tilted at the corners. "They are the only interesting kind."

His fingers and toes practically buzzed at the caressing tone of her voice. "Your, uh, accent," he mumbled, blushing. "Where is it from?"

"Moldova," she said. "I am here on a student visa."

"Oh, I see," he said. "I'm, uh, Josh." He stuck out his hand.

She took it, and held it. "Nadia," she offered him the name as if it were a jewel lying on a little velvet pillow.

Nadia. Wow. It dazzled him. He mouthed the name. Shivers of delight went up his spine at the feel of it in his mouth.

Her hand was so soft. And her slender, cool fingers were curled around his, holding on. Gently, trustingly. For so long, he didn't know quite what to do. Take his hand back? He didn't want to risk hurting her feelings by pulling it away. Maybe it was one of those culture clash things. Maybe Moldovans gave really long, intimate handshakes.

The effects of which went straight to his dick. Whoa. Woody alert.

"I better tell my boss I'm leaving," he said, flustered. "And, uh, if you don't mind, could you wait outside? My excuse for leaving looks really bogus if he sees me taking off with a gorgeous blonde."

She gave him a secretive smile, an under-the-lashes upward peep. "Sweet," she murmured. "I shall see you outside then. Josh."

Josh watched her go out, wondering when he was going to wake up. Holy moly. He yanked the tail of his crumpled orange uniform shirt out of his jeans to cover up this boner and any possible future ones that might pop up in that unbelievable girl's vicinity. He loped over to his boss Joe's office like he had springs in his shoes.

"Yo, Joe," he said. "I'm cutting out."

Joe frowned, glanced at the clock. "Already?"

"I told you, remember? I'm leaving early. Gotta drive down to pick up my sister. It's only an hour. I'll make it up next week."

"You better," Joe grumbled, waving him away.

He pulled up Carrie's number as he headed into the employee room to pick up his jacket and keys. The original plan was to drive down to Evergreen to pick up his sister, and then they would all-night it back up to Seattle, blasting rap on the iPod dock in the dash and plotting their intervention in the life of their dizzy older sister, who was showing serious need of sibling supervision.

They were arriving unannounced. With luck, they might even catch her with her thug so that he and Carrie could scare the guy away, if he was unworthy. Which seemed likely.

But it would have to wait. For Nadia, the whole freakin' universe would have to just cool its heels, and wait. Becca got one more day to misbehave with her thuggish boy toy before he and Carrie came down on her like a ton of bricks. He pulled up Carrie's number on his cell.

The phone rang, and rang, and rang. That was weird. He tried the wall phone number in Carrie's dorm.

"Who's this?" asked a husky female voice.

Josh recognized Elyse, who lived one room down from Carrie. "Hey, Elyse. It's Josh, Carrie's brother," he said. "Is she there?"

"Oh, hi, Josh. I don't think so. I thought she was with you. Wasn't she supposed to meet up with you tonight to drive up to Seattle? Some big hairy emergency about the sister's new boyfriend?"

"Yeah. That was the plan," he said. "It's just that I can't make it tonight, and I can't reach her cell. Have her call me if you see her, OK?"

"Will do. Bye, Josh."

That was weird. He stared down at the phone, startled out of his horny daze. Carrie was hypervigilant about being reachable, and making sure her brother and sister were too. Being out of touch, even for a short time, really freaked her out. Abandonment issues, because of how they'd lost Mom, he and Becca believed. They both made a big point of keeping phones charged up, providing contact numbers, yada yada.

Damn. That worried him. But when he stepped out of the store, Nadia was waiting for him, and the blinding force of her beauty hit him again, canceling every other thought in his head. *Wow.*

She walked towards him, a slow, seductive, hip-swaying walk. She wore high-heeled boots over her jeans. Those legs just went on and on.

In fact, there was nothing about her that was not perfect.

She slid her arm through his. "Shall we go? Where is your car?"

Her accent was gorgeous. The skin on the inside of her elbow was so soft where it touched his arm. The softest thing he'd ever felt.

"Aren't you, uh, scared?" he blurted. He was abruptly horrified at himself for saying it. Screwing his own chances. Dickbrain chump.

But her eyes just opened wider, limpid and glowing. "Scared? Why? Of who?"

He gestured, helplessly. "Oh, I don't know. Of, uh, me, I guess. Of letting a strange guy come to your house. I mean, I could be anyone."

Her smile widened, shone, dazzled him. "But you are not anyone, Josh," she said, her voice low and caressing. "You are you."

A helium balloon in his chest expanded, puffing out his chest and stretching his spine to its utmost length. It lifted him up. He floated down the mall, suspended a couple inches from the ground.

Anchored to the earth only by the tender contact with Nadia's baby-soft arm, as she towed him smoothly along to an unknown fate.

Chapter
19

Pavel Cherchenko took one freaking long time to get off. Maybe it was all the vodka Ludmilla had poured down his throat, although you would think a madam wouldn't serve up dick-killer on the rocks. She'd had a few herself.

He forced himself to watch the screen, jaw clenched. He was as uncomfortable as hell about this, and he had no doubt that Ludmilla was too. But it was Nick's luckless job to monitor them, just to make sure things didn't take an ugly turn.

Though watching Pavel's naked, hairy ass rise and fall, he couldn't help but reflect upon the fact that *ugly* was a relative term.

None of them had anticipated when they installed the hidden vid cams that they were going to have to watch her fuck anyone, least of all one of Zhoglo's men. But there they were, in Milla's big, lavish bed, grimly going at it. Yikes. Who knew.

They'd gone on screaming red alert as soon as Nick had spotted Pavel getting out of the black Beemer in the parking garage. But so far, Pavel hadn't made any move to hurt Milla. In fact, he'd made no threats at all. That alone made Nick itchy and nervous.

It seemed more like the guy was in need of a confidante. He'd started out talking about a business deal, a damn lucrative one, from what Nick could tell. Beautiful girls to service the Vor. Lots of them. He liked youth, freshness, variety. He had an unlimited budget. Ludmilla had gotten much more relaxed when they started talking big money.

But as the guy drank, he'd gotten sloppy and sad. Whining about how angry his boss was over the Solokov debacle. Ludmilla crooned her sympathy, plied him with still more vodka, and soon Pavel was weeping boozily in her arms, grabbing at her surgically enhanced tits. One thing led to another and forty minutes later, the guy was still jerking and straining on top of her, a look of pain on his haggard face. Ludmilla murmured encouragement, massaging his ass, trying to help him along. Nick cringed, prayed for the guy to come already. Jesus. Nobody was having any fun, least of all Pavel.

Finally, Pavel threw his head back, jerking and grimacing as if he were being electrocuted. Thank God. His face sagged down over Milla's shoulder. Milla turned her face squarely towards the vid cam that was hidden in a piece of hideous modern art.

She gave Nick a blood-chilling look.

Pavel rolled off and sat up on the side of the bed with his back to her, shoulders slumped.

Then, slowly, he got up and dressed with the stiff movements of a very old man. Milla rose and pulled on a frilly robe. She followed him into her spacious dining room.

Pavel popped open the briefcase he had carried in, and pulled out two thick wads of cash. He tossed them on the table and shuffled toward the door, like a guy zonked out on anti-psychotic drugs.

Ludmilla waited about a minute after he left before she opened her own apartment door and peered out to make sure he was gone. She swept to the mosaic framed mirror on her dining room wall, behind which another vid cam was hidden, and glared into the lens. She yanked open her robe. Gestured at her large, extremely round bare breasts.

"You liked this?" she demanded, in Ukrainian. "Did you enjoy the show? Did you have a good time? How about your men? Voyeur pigs."

Nick sighed and dialed the scrambled line they had established for this purpose.

She snatched the cell up from the table. "What?" she spat. "Pig."

"You didn't use the code word, Milla," he said patiently. "I was listening for it, and you never said it. The guys were ready to storm in, if you'd needed them, but he wasn't attacking you. If we'd intervened, Zhoglo would know for sure that you'd double-crossed him, which would mean going into hiding right now. Taking a new identity. Starting a new life. You didn't want that, right?"

Milla responded with a foul explosion of profanity, which Nick listened to with half an ear as he watched Pavel, making sure the guy pulled no funny stuff. But he did not. He left the way he came, getting into the gleaming black Beemer, which was now equipped with a discreetly hidden SafeGuard GPS locating device. The car weaved around in the parking garage, narrowly missing some of the other parked cars. Maybe the guy was still drunk, or sick.

Marcus was ready in another car, and moved to tail Pavel with a handheld. He pulled out smoothly after him, staying a couple of cars back.

So damn easy. Too damn easy. His neck prickled, itched. He was glad that Milla hadn't gotten hurt, but it seemed strange that Pavel hadn't thought to blame her at all.

When he looked back at Milla, she was holding the phone between her ear and shoulder, rifling through the wads of cash. She stuffed them into an oversized white purse that lay on the table.

"How much did he give you?" he asked.

"None of your damn business."

"Everything about Zhoglo is my business," he said harshly. "Keep the fucking money, Milla, I don't give a shit about it. I just want to know how much it was."

"Thirty thousand," she said sullenly. "An advance. More later."

He whistled softly as he watched the icon that symbolized Pavel's car move across the city map glowing on the computer monitor. "It's a trap," he said quietly.

She snorted. "Pah. Life is a trap," she said shortly. "All a woman can hope for is to make some decent money before the trap springs."

"Don't send him any girls, Milla," he said. "Don't do it."

"He just gave me thirty thousand dollars, fool," she snapped. "And don't you want to know where those girls go? Tomorrow he sends me an address for them, hmm? You interested in that address?"

"Of course I am," he said. "But you know how he operates. You send him a girl, he's liable to send you back her head in a box, via bike messenger. I suggest you take that money and run like hell. Today."

Milla's painted face sagged, looking oddly haggard in contrast to her surprisingly youthful, voluptuous body.

"Take that new identity," he urged her. "Take it now. Get the fuck out of town. It's weird that Pavel didn't even ask you any questions about having proposed me for the job. And now this contract, and all this money—it stinks."

She let out an explosive breath. "Stinks? Yes. It all stinks. You stink, Nikolai. New identity, pah! As what? Housecleaner? Hotel maid? Home health aide? You think I want to empty bedpans, wipe dribbling mouths for the rest of my life? That is what stinks!"

"Milla. Goddamn it," he said, through gritted teeth. "I'm doing my best. I cannot protect your life and your lifestyle at the same time."

"Fuck your best," she hissed. "I would rather eat poison."

She hung up and flounced away, robe fluttering behind her.

Nick dropped his throbbing head into his hands, and rubbed his temples. Dealing with women was way too fucking complicated for him.

Except for Becca. A deep thrill of constant anticipation had hummed in the back of his consciousness all day long. Something inside him bounced madly around like a ball in a pinball machine every time he thought about her. Which was pretty much all the time.

God, he wished he could get away from this to go play with Becca for a couple hours, but he had a feeling that fantasy wasn't going to play out. Not since Pavel made his move.

The frustration made him grind his teeth. Davy was right. He had it bad. Zhoglo was rolling out the red carpet for him, and he was feeling sorry for himself because he couldn't keep a hot date.

At any rate, he was glad he'd gotten the hotel room. She was safer there, checked in under his false name, than she was in her apartment. Even if she had to sleep there alone. Fucking waste. Big bummer.

"Uh, Nick? I don't want to flip you out, buddy, but didn't you say your girlfriend was working till midnight?"

Nick jerked around at Davy's voice. "Yeah. Why?"

Davy gestured towards the monitor of the computer where he'd loaded Becca's beacon code. "Uh, looks to me like she's leaving town. Heading north on the interstate." His voice was delicately cautious.

"What the *fuck*—?" The chair Nick had been sitting in shot backwards and crashed into the table behind him when he sprang up to lunge at that monitor.

Holy shit. She was north of Lynwood, moving at a brisk clip. At 9:40 P.M. He grabbed his cell, pulled up her number.

Davy slunk promptly towards the door. "I'll just, uh, excuse myself," he muttered. "This kind of conversation makes me tense."

But Davy needn't have bothered. The cell service informed him that the party he was trying to reach was out of area.

Wild-eyed, he stared at the icon moving on the screen. What the hell? Why would she lie to him? For what goddamn purpose? *Why?*

She could have panicked and skipped town, no one could blame her, but why then all those flirty, sexy text messages? A build-up? To throw him off the scent? Jesus, could she be running away from *him?*

An unwelcome memory started playing in his head, making him abruptly sick to his stomach. His mother. Her many attempts to run away from Dad. At first she had run away with Nick. Later on, as things got worse and worse, she'd tried to run away without him.

She never got far. Dad had kept her isolated, way out there on the endless Wyoming grasslands, so she had no friends. She did not drive. Her English had been close to nonexistent. She'd had no money. She'd always looked so defeated when Dad brought her back. It made Nick feel guilty for being so pathetically grateful that Dad had caught her.

Until the cancer had put her permanently out of Dad's reach when Nick was twelve.

He still remembered holding her hand, the look of dumb relief on her face as she finally slipped away from the relentless pain of her illness. And the stress of enduring Anton Warbitsky. A state which could be classified as a chronic illness in and of itself. He should know.

She had died whispering Nick's pet names. *Kolya. Kolyuchka.*

His stomach hurt, a hollow, awful ache. He'd spent his life trying to run away from this feeling, and here it was, large as life, bad as ever.

Aw, fuck this. Now was not the time to rake up old, harrowing memories. He had enough to feel like hell about here and now.

He programmed his phone to alert him the second Becca turned her phone back on. She had to pull this shit while he was chained to a goddamn chair, watching Milla and Pavel? He couldn't even follow her.

He was rattled, scared. And sad. Feeling sad made him angry. He was going to be interested to know exactly why Becca had lied to him.

In fact, he could not fucking wait for that explanation.

Becca speeded after Diana's receding taillights on the northbound interstate, wondering nervously just how dangerous this wacky impulse to tail Mathes's mistress actually was.

She was comforted by the sense that Diana was at least as inexperienced at this sort of thing as Becca herself, judging from all the whining and sniveling in Marla's office. Chances were, she wouldn't be on the alert for someone following her. At least, so Becca hoped.

Asphalt rushed beneath her wheels. Her eyes watered with the strain of keeping Diana's taillights constantly in sight. Every time they disappeared around a curve, she panicked until she found them again. Sped up to check the make, color, plates of the car, so she could drop back again and breathe, more or less. And drive.

She must be nuts. She should give this information to Nick. He was trained to deal with it. She herself, on the other hand, was trained to plan memorable menus. She knew six great recipes for stuffed mushrooms. She was the queen of artichoke dip. She could serve wine without dripping a single drop. She knew where to find great deals on table linens. What was she doing on the road, following a criminal?

Maybe it was because she'd been fired. Her full-time job now was to do everything possible to get out of this nightmare trap she was in, because until she did, she had no hope of anything even resembling a normal life. And besides, she believed in fate. The opportunity to follow the woman had presented itself like a flashing neon arrow. It wasn't like she could freeze frame, call Nick, pass the job off to someone else who was more qualified for it. It was her or nobody, now or never. She would have to have been a gutless wimp not to jump on it.

Problem was, she felt alarmingly like a gutless wimp. Was that a true instinct she'd followed when she ran down the hall after Diana? Or just a random electrical impulse from the depths of her frazzled brain? Crossed wires, blown circuits—how could she tell?

She tried to talk herself down. After all, she was following a woman who didn't have a whole lot of backbone, judging from the way Mathes had bullied her. Becca wouldn't have had the nerve to follow one of Zhoglo's gun-toting goons, but Diana was another matter. From the sound of that conversation, Diana was some sort of health professional, not a career criminal. Not armed. As clueless about this kind of thing as herself, Becca hoped.

Hell, if it came down to a physical confrontation, God forbid, Becca might even be able to hold her own in a catfight, if the weapons were swung purses, fake nails, insults, bitch-slaps.

However, the chances were good that Diana was heading off to meet people associated with Zhoglo. And while Diana might be incompetent as a criminal, Zhoglo's people were most definitely not.

And whatever unknown thing Diana was driving off to do both frightened and horrified her. *Blood. Tissue typing.*

Becca shuddered with a renewed thrill of fear. God, she wished Nick were with her. She wanted to call him, to tell him what she now knew: Mathes's name, Diana's license plate number, the cryptic conversation she had overheard in Marla's office. But by the time it had occurred to her to call him, she was out of area.

She squirmed, uncomfortably. He needed that information, but she couldn't stop at a pay phone to give it to him without losing Diana. Besides. She was dead sure, to the marrow of her bones, that Nick would not approve of what she was doing right now.

Hah. Talk about an understatement. His head would explode.

At least he had no clue where she was. For all Nick knew, she was still racing around at the club, working the banquet. She had until midnight before he started to worry and stew. Two and a half hours. She'd go a bit farther, and with luck, Diana would do whatever dreadful thing Mathes had ordered her to do quickly enough so that Becca could witness it and get back to Seattle in time for her date with Nick. Yeah. Right. That sounded real probable.

They were almost to a nothing special, could-be-anywhere rural area called Kimble when Diana's black PT Cruiser started to signal. She pulled off onto a long strip mall, went a couple of miles, and signaled again right before a Days Inn.

Her first big dilemma. Becca circled around a big block, her mind racing. Jesus, now what? She could hardly follow the woman in.

She reasoned it out. The front was short-term parking. Guests parked in the bigger lot out back. Therefore, Diana would have to drive her car around to the back, no matter where her room was.

Once parked in the back, Becca fretted some more, chewing her nails. So now she could watch Diana walk from car to hotel. Big freaking deal. Becca got out, on impulse, and walked in the back door. The janitor had propped it open with a mop. Thanks, dude. No key card required.

Once inside, there were two wings that led to the guest rooms, one to the right and one to the left. She could see through the lobby corridor, past food and beverage machines, ice machines, bathrooms, all the way to the front desk. Diana was still at the desk, checking in. Her clerk was a woman with very big red hair.

Diana took her key card and went out to pull her car around. Becca got busy with her cell phone, making a big show of staring down into the display and texting a bogus message.

Diana came in the back door, and turned to the right.

Becca waited until she was sure the other woman was using the stairwell rather than the elevator, and sprinted after her. Best not to ask herself if this exercise was as stupid and pointless as it was dangerous.

Don't ask. Don't wonder. Don't stop. Just do it, damnit.

She bounded up the stairs two at a time, peered out onto the second floor corridor. No one. Back to the stairs, two at a time, heart thudding. This time when she poked her head out of the stairwell, she saw a flash of beige, and a door closing. She exhaled. Her eyes locked onto it. Third from the end. She sneaked down the corridor. Room 317.

OK, great. She knew the room number. What she could do with that information was a complete blank. Her mind stalled out.

The next dilemma was what the hell to do with herself. She'd never before in her life lurked or loitered in a space where she had no right to be. Of course, she could simply check into the hotel, but then what? Hang around in the corridor till the woman came out?

Deflated, she headed downstairs and back out to the parking lot and sat in her car, staring at the hotel. Staring at her useless phone.

She was about to get out and go call Nick from the pay phone in the lobby when something blocked the light from the streetlamp. A gleaming black SUV with tinted windows swept past, pulling up in front of the back door.

Diana burst out, kicking over the propped mop, and got in. The SUV sped up towards the parking lot exit. Becca jolted into action, put her car in gear, and followed, but a Jeep Cherokee pulled into the exit and proceeded to sit there like a goddamn mountain while its driver decided what to do.

The black SUV with Diana in it accelerated on the main strip, went around the corner, and was lost to sight.

Becca screamed, honked, gestured madly. The driver, a soccer mom type, frowned at her as if to say, what's your damn hurry, lady, and punished her by oh-so-sloooooowly driving into the parking lot.

Her tires squealed as she zoomed onto the empty street, turned right, looked for taillights. Nothing. There was a cross street up ahead, at the light. She peered to the right, the left, straight ahead.

Fuck. She chose a direction at random. She came back, tried all the others, already knowing it was futile. She'd lost them.

After over a half hour of aimless driving around, staring at parking lots and cars parked on residential streets, she finally gave up and went back to the Days Inn. She slumped down in the seat and stared out at the blank, prefab building, feeling foolish and glum. Thwarted by a soccer mom from hell. How dumb.

So should she wait? Diana could be gone all night. For that matter, she could be gone for days, or for good. This involved Zhoglo, after all. She glanced at her watch. 10:40. She would wait another half hour before calling Nick, just in case Diana's errand was a quick one. Not that Becca had any clue what to do if the other woman did come back.

Oh, well. One thing at a time. She shouldn't expect this to be easy or obvious. Diana's car was her only point of reference. She had to come back to it sometime. Becca would chew her nails, wait, and watch.

God, how she'd love to have something concrete to offer Nick when she finally saw him to offset the craziness of this stunt. Maybe he'd be too astonished to yell at her. Maybe he'd be impressed with her nerve and her initiative. Maybe he'd even be happy for the help.

Uh-huh. And maybe pigs in pink tutus ice-skated in hell.

Chapter 20

Sveti and little Rachel were the last ones to go into the examining room to see the American lady doctor. The oldest, and the youngest. The others had gone in, one after the other, clutching their containers of pee. Marina had passed out the containers that morning, and it had been Sveti's stinky job to supervise the spraying and splashing of the little ones. Her one pair of pants had gotten soaked with everyone's piss. Not that they could get much dirtier or smellier.

All but Rachel. Marina had given her plastic bags with stickum to put over Rachel's privates inside her diaper to collect the baby's urine, but Rachel had tugged at them all day. None of the bags were more than slightly damp, but her diapers were soaked.

They'd tried to send Sveti in first, but Rachel clutched and screamed so hard, Yuri shoved her back and grabbed Sasha instead. Rachel got clingier every day. Sveti couldn't even go into the toilet without her anymore. Her back ached from carrying the baby around.

Sasha had been back a quarter of an hour later, and slanted her an eyes-rolling grimace, making a syringe gesture at his elbow.

Blood taking. Again. Sveti wanted to cry. The little ones

would be screaming, and she was the one they all turned to for comfort. It scared her to death and it made her feel guilty. Couldn't they understand that she was as helpless, as desperate and powerless as they were?

But they didn't. They clung, as if she could protect them somehow. And she couldn't bring herself to be cold and push them away.

She wished she could think of a way to rescue them all. Find parents for everyone. Parents like hers. Wonderful parents.

God, how she wanted her mother.

Yuri came out, holding Mikhail under his arm. The boy dangled, head down, unconscious. "Smelly little shithead. He fainted." Yuri grunted and tossed the child on the nearest cot. Mikhail shivered and moaned.

"She's next," he said, gesturing at Rachel, who was sucking her thumb, eyes huge in her little face.

He grabbed Rachel and tried to pull her off Sveti's lap, but Rachel clutched Sveti's T-shirt and a handful of her hair, mouth opening to emit a sound so shrill and loud, Yuri jerked back, and tried to slap her. Sveti flinched to cover Rachel's body with her own and took the blow on the side of her head. For a moment, she could hardly even hear Rachel's ear-splitting shrieks.

When her vision and hearing cleared, Yuri was shouting at her.

". . . brat calmed down, and bring her in with you! The doctor bitch can do the two of you together. What the fuck do I care?"

It took frantic minutes of soothing and crooning and jiggling and cuddling until Rachel's shrieks damped down to hiccuping sobs. Her hot, thin little body shook in Sveti's arms. Both of them were shaking. Rachel's screaming jarred her badly. Sveti had grown numb to many things, but the toddler's desperation sliced through her numbness and got to her. Probably because it was so much like her own.

The American lady doctor didn't look like a doctor at all. Sveti was momentarily dazzled. The woman was the first beautiful thing she'd seen in months. She looked like a magazine model or a Hollywood actress, with perfect white skin and made-up eyes. Glossy dark hair that bobbed and swung like hair on TV ads.

She wasn't smiling like a TV ad, though. She looked scared and tense. Sveti was skilled at gauging the emotional states of the people around her. Advance warning could save a pinch, or slap, or kick in the leg that left a bruise as big as a saucer.

But the American lady doctor didn't look like she would be violent or cruel. She was sweating, and it was fear sweat. Sveti could smell her as she examined Rachel. Heart, lungs, throat, temperature. She murmured in a low, musical voice into a shiny rod, recording numbers.

She pawed through Rachel's urine bags, and frowned at Sveti as if it were her fault Rachel had not peed. She wore a silver-gray silk shirt that had iridescent highlights. It looked so soft Sveti longed to touch it. There were dark, crumpled sweat crescents under the doctor's arms. Her forehead was shiny. And her red painted lips shook with tension.

Then she began preparing the needle and vials for the blood drawing. Rachel, unfortunately, knew exactly what was coming, and began to flop and shriek. Rachel was incredibly strong for such a tiny person. It took all Sveti had to hold the baby still. By the time the doctor finally got some blood out of her, Sveti was sobbing too.

The doctor looked shaken. She had to lean over, put her head down. She looked pale, sick. Maybe she was a nicer person than the guards, Sveti thought. Maybe this was a chance. For help.

Sveti struggled to remember the English she had learned from Arkady, her father's handsome friend. Arkady had lived so many years in America, he was practically American himself. She'd learned many words from him, but a lot of what she knew had slipped away.

She thought to ask the doctor for help with Rachel's rashes, her ear infections. The blood that Sveti sometimes found in her diaper when she changed her. And there was more that she was forgetting. Always more. She thrashed her tired, foggy brain, trying to remember it all.

"Baby, ear. Hurt," she tried.

The woman looked at her blankly and her gaze slid quickly away.

Sveti tried again, tapping Rachel's ear. "Baby, ear," she repeated. She tapped Rachel's forehead. "Hot. Night. Cries, cries, cries."

The woman still would not meet her eyes. She was pretending she didn't understand. She resumed muttering into her recorder.

Sveti lifted Rachel's grubby little shirt to show her the angry rash on the child's belly and chest, and spoke more loudly. "Hurts," she said. "Medicine? Baby, medicine?" Her voice was starting to quiver.

The lady doctor shook her head, made an irritated gesture. She said something that sounded final into the shiny rod, and made an impatient come-here gesture to Sveti, patting the examining table.

Her turn. Sveti sighed and swallowed back her frustration, and placed the whimpering Rachel gently on the floor. She climbed up onto the examining table and stared straight into the doctor's face, waiting for a chance to catch her eye again, but the lady was careful to keep her gaze averted. She tugged gingerly at the stained, grayish T-shirt Sveti wore and Sveti reluctantly pulled it off, revealing the grubby strip of ragged T-shirt wrapped around her chest.

The doctor went around the table, brushed aside Sveti's long, tangled dark hair, and started picking at the knots.

Back before she was taken, she hadn't had breasts at all,

Sveti thought. Months ago, she could hardly wait to get them. Breasts would mean that she was finally starting to grow up, and if she could do that fast enough, she might be able to catch up with Arkady, and he could marry her. Take her to America to live with him, where she would be happy forever. What a stupid little girl she'd been. Stupid little girl daydreams. Hah.

Now she had breasts, and she wished they would go away. They were big enough to jiggle under her shirt. She had begged Sasha for a strip of his T-shirt, which was so large it hung halfway down his legs.

Sasha had understood perfectly, even though he would not speak. He'd torn off a strip from the bottom, and helped her tie it around her ribs as tight as they could pull it, even though it itched and chafed.

And still, Yuri's eyes followed her everywhere.

The doctor had noticed the port-wine birthmark on her neck. She lifted Sveti's hair to examine it, mouth pursed, eyes squinted, and murmured again into the recorder, speaking louder over Rachel's incessant whimpering. Sveti tried one of the words Arkady had taught her.

"Birthmark," she said. "Just birthmark. No hurt."

The lady blinked, as if a plastic doll had just come to life and spoken to her, and continued on with her examination. Listening, poking, prodding, palpating. The lungs, the heart, the throat, her belly. Then the blood taking. The hot, dark blood snaking through the plastic tube. So hot, it felt like it burned the bluish white, goosepimpled skin of her arm. Sveti wished she could put her shirt back on. She felt so exposed, with her hair twisted back and those hateful breasts sticking out.

The doctor lady would not meet her eyes. Would not acknowledge that she was there. It made Sveti want to scream with frustration to see the woman talking away into the stupid shiny rod, ignoring her. While evil gathered around her like a wave, rising. When it broke they would all be crushed, all of them. She stared at Rachel on the floor, playing listlessly with her tiny toes, gray with dirt.

Her desperation swelled up until she couldn't contain it. She grabbed the woman's silk-clad arm. "Help me," she pleaded. "Help us. They do something bad to us. You got to help us. Please."

The doctor jerked her arm back, but Sveti wouldn't let go. Her blackened nails dug into the fine fabric as she pleaded incoherently in her broken English. The doctor lady said something sharp and tried to shake her off. She clung harder. She remembered no more English, it was coming out in Ukrainian now, pouring out in a garbled rush that she had no power to stop. How afraid she was, how alone, how the little children needed her too much. She was breaking inside, something horrible waited, something evil—

The lady was screaming now, mouth distorted, eyes wild, clawing and slapping to get free. Rachel was screaming, Sveti was screaming, everyone was screaming. Sveti flung herself off the table at the woman as she tried to get away, clasping her around the waist, and the doctor slapped at her face, and they were both crying, yelling—

The door burst open. "What the fuck is this?"

Marina and Yuri dragged them apart. Marina helped the sobbing, babbling lady doctor out of the room and cast a slit-eyed, malevolent glance back at Sveti as she slammed the door shut behind her.

Leaving her with Yuri. Fear exploded inside her.

He smacked her in the face. She hit the wall. The world spun, tipped and settled itself sideways. Then the tip of his boot smashed into her thigh. The pain made her shriek. He undid his belt, yanked it out, doubled it. "Idiot girl," he raged. "The doctor came here to help you. And how do you thank her? You attack her! You are an animal! Filthy . . . dumb . . . animal!" The blows rained down. He shouted hoarse insults that she couldn't understand. She cringed in the corner, making herself as small as possible. Rachel shrieked her shrill, teakettle wail.

Slowly, Sveti became aware that the blows had stopped. She tasted blood in her mouth. Yuri was no longer bellowing.

She peered up from behind the hands she'd clasped over her face to protect it. He was staring down at her body, panting. Face red. His thick mouth slack and wet. He had that look on his face. That look that froze her blood, made her belly turn over with a greasy flop of dread.

At the same time, she realized she still had on no T-shirt. Not even Sasha's strip tied around her ribs. Just those dirty cotton pants that hung down low over her bony hip bones.

Oh, no, no, no. Rachel's tiny, tear-streaked face was scarlet, mouth huge, the sound huge, the sound of terror and utter despair—

The door sprang open again. "Yuri. Come," Marina snapped.

"Later," he rasped, his eyes still fixed on Sveti. "Close that fucking door. Later."

"Now." Marina's voice had the iron ring of command. "You have to take this stupid American bitch back to the hotel. The worthless cunt is falling apart. I don't want to watch. Get away from that girl."

"She can wait," Yuri snarled. "Close that door."

"No! Do not touch her. Go buy it outside if you want it, pig. Go to that truck stop on the interstate."

"Why not?" Yuri sounded petulant. "What difference does it make? They won't know. What do they care?"

"You could give her a disease," Marina hissed. "Remember? What happened with the other one?"

Yuri wiped his scummy wet lips with the back of his hand. Sveti could smell the foulness of his breath even from where she lay on the floor. "I don't have any diseases," he said, his voice sullen.

"I will not bet my life on that, you dog," Marina snapped. "They would kill us both. Idiot. Step away from the girl. Now."

Yuri muttered something filthy and sullen, and backed away, staring fixedly at Sveti. Marina shoved him out the door, and glared down at the girl, who had dragged herself into a crouch, wrapping her arms tightly around her knees. Marina grabbed the limp T-shirt from the examining table and snapped it smartly into Sveti's face.

The unexpected blow made her whip her head back, bonking it hard against the painted white cinder-block wall. Her eyes welled full again.

"Stop whining." Marina knelt down and stuck her face into Sveti's. "And stop trying to lure him with your scrawny little tits, you stupid tart. Or there'll be trouble. Do you understand?"

"But I don't want—I wasn't—"

Crack, a hard backhand slap connected. Sveti's head hit the wall again. "Do you understand?"

Yes. Sveti's mouth formed the word, but made no sound.

Marina tossed the shirt in Sveti's face, and heaved her big, solid block of a body to her feet. "See that you do. Now get that whining brat out of my sight. I'm sick of looking at her."

She stumped out, slammed the connecting door. Locked it.

Sveti pulled the tattered T-shirt over her shivering self, wondering how it was possible to hate someone so much and still be so grateful to her. She tried to get to her feet, but the thigh Yuri had kicked buckled under her. She finally just crawled over to Rachel, and pulled the little girl onto her lap.

They huddled there for a long time, clutching each other, until it was impossible to tell who was comforting whom.

The batwing flutter of a shadow across her face jolted Becca out of the doze that had overcome her. It was that big black SUV. Adrenaline jolted through her. A Mercedes, she noticed now. Too late to catch the plate number, damn. The vehicle had already turned perpendicular to hers, and pulled to a stop in front of the hotel's back entrance.

It pulled away again, leaving Diana behind, clutching a white box to her chest. The SUV accelerated away, as if it were glad to be rid of her. Diana stared after it, looking dazed and lost. Her eyes looked huge. The raccoon effect of tear-smudged makeup. Becca was very familiar with that particular fashion statement these days.

She firmly squashed a niggling feeling of sympathy for the woman. Save it for someone who deserves it, she lectured herself. If Diana was in cahoots with that poisonous snake Mathes, who was involved with that monster Zhoglo, then she was up to no good, and that was that.

Diana stumbled over her feet on her way to the rear entrance. She seemed baffled by the fact that it was now locked, and stared blankly at the door for several seconds before fishing out her key card.

Becca chewed her knuckles and thought it over. At this point, it was unlikely that Diana would leave the hotel again. Whatever she'd been planning to do, she had done. There was little else that Becca could usefully do here—other than call Nick, come clean, and hand the whole thing over to him. Which meant she needed a phone.

But she was unwilling to leave and lose track of Diana again, after all this chasing around, losing her and pinning her down again. The pay phone in the corridor of the hotel had a clear view of both entrances. She would hang around the door and wait for an opportunity to slip in after the next legitimate hotel guest.

God, this skulking and loitering made her nervous. She sauntered towards the hotel, fishing out her dead cell phone for cover, and wishing, for the first and only time in her life, that she smoked. Just to have a believable excuse for lounging around in doorways.

Before she got halfway across the parking lot, Diana exploded out the back door and hurried to her car. No white box. She did not appear to see Becca at all—even when Becca abruptly changed course and headed back to her car. Diana was swept up in her own inner drama, thank God.

Becca pulled out after her, her heart thudding, and forced herself to keep a discreet distance. She didn't have far to go. Diana pulled over at the nearest roadhouse bar, a seedy windowless cement building with a neon sign that read Starlight Lounge.

Becca parked as near as she dared, and slumped in her seat. She held the phone to her ear and watched as Diana took off her glasses, covered her face with her hands, and wept for ten minutes. Then she sprang out of the car, lurched over to the curb, and vomited.

Becca flinched in involuntary fellowship. Ooh. Nasty. So Diana belonged to the Mighty Sisterhood of Stress Urpers. Bummer for her, that she'd chosen a life of despicable crime. If she kept this crap up, she was going to be hurling her hash left and right.

Diana dabbed her face with a tissue and stumbled into the bar. Becca got out of her car, feeling like a puppet being manipulated by an unfamiliar entity. She strode over to Diana's car and peered in.

The passenger seat was cluttered: paper coffee cups, sunglasses, a comb, used tissues smeared with mascara, a ripped-open package for a digital voice recorder. The plastic bubble that had held the small rod was empty.

A crazy, half-baked idea began to form as she stared down at the sunglasses. She gazed at her own reflection in Diana's car window. Her own hair was slightly shorter and not quite as floofy, but—hmmm.

Half of her screamed, *No, stop, back it up, call it off*. The rest of her shrieked, *Go for it before you chicken out, you pansy ass airhead, go!*

She looked for a big rock, found one a safe distance from

Urping Ground Zero, and screwed up her courage. This was going to be the hardest part. Going against all her social conditioning. If anyone saw her smashing in another woman's car window, she would just start shrieking, *That bitch is screwing my husband!*

She lifted the rock, fingers white, arm trembling . . . and hesitated. She reached out with her other hand. Tried the door.

Unlocked. For God's sake, any stress urper should know that a woman who had just puked her guts out probably did not have the presence of mind to lock her car. Unless she was a superwoman. And superwomen did not urp. No siree, no superwomen in the Sisterhood.

Becca felt like a total idiot, jittery from having worked herself into such a state. No time for dithering, though. She grabbed the sunglasses and the lipstick. She was now officially a thief. It felt odd.

She raced back to her car. Tore out of the parking lot, zoomed back to the hotel, tires squealing. No time for cogitating or knuckle chewing. She had to be quick, decisive. And as cool and smooth as soft-serve vanilla ice cream. She switched on her dome light, yanked her comb out of her purse and tried to tease her hair out into Dianaesque proportions. She slicked on some of Diana's crimson lipstick, and was startled by the harsh effect. She needed dramatic eye makeup to balance it out. Fortunately, she had Diana's Zsa Zsa Gabor sunglasses. She stuck her black-framed specs in her pocket, and donned the sunglasses. She would be virtually blind, but hey. Vision, schmision.

She glanced in the mirror and winced. She looked like a celebrity battered wife, but whatever. Becca shrugged off her coat and marched around the building, then flounced in as if she owned the place, squinting to get her bearings.

There were two desk clerks. One was the redhead who had checked Diana in. She sailed past them, down the hall, into the stairwell, knees wobbling. Estimating the time it would take a guest to get to her room and discover she'd left her key card inside.

She swept out again, grateful to find the big-haired red-head busy on the phone. She smiled at the other, an older woman with gray hair.

"Hi. I'm Diana, in room 317," she said. "I'm so embarrassed, but it looks like I've locked myself out. Could you do up a new card for me?"

The woman smiled, tapped into the computer, and nodded. "Sure thing, Ms. Evans. I'd be happy to do that for ya."

Please don't ask for picture ID. *Please*.

Fate was kind. Moments later, card clutched in her sweating hand, Becca floated down the corridor, disbelieving, over her own sprinting feet. Terrified that it had worked. She was getting ever more expert at digging her own grave. Look at those shovelfuls of dirt, flying wildly this way and that.

She let herself into Diana's room. The door slammed shut behind her. She felt a moment of letdown. No immediate revelations. It looked and smelled exactly like a million other economy hotel rooms. Two beds, quilted synthetic spreads, bathroom near the entrance, TV, wall unit air conditioner, ugly art. Empty. No suitcase, no purse. The box, the box. She had to find that white box.

She found it in the bathroom, perched on the fake marble countertop. She approached it with a feeling of dread in her belly.

Becca took a deep breath, and lifted off the top. OK. Not a human head, or an embalmed space alien. Just a rack, with seven neatly labeled vials of dark liquid suspended in it. She lifted one out, and realized that the liquid inside was blood.

Beneath the rack were several small containers containing clear yellow liquid. Urine, for sure. Then there was a handful of sealed plastic bags with big cotton swabs inside them. The blood, urine and bags were neatly hand-labeled. *F*-121396-88991. The numbers followed a pattern. Two *F*s, the rest *M*s, which she assumed referred to male or female. Then a six-digit number that she assumed was a birthdate. Then a five-digit number. No names. If they were birthdates, 96 was the earliest year. Then a 98. The others were all in the aughts: 01, 02, two 04s. One 06.

Children. Small children.

Another shudder went up her spine. Shadows, monsters, slithering in the dark, out of plain sight. She was afraid to know the answer to this riddle, afraid it would be something very bad.

She wished, piercingly, that Nick were there. Then she dragged a pen and scrap of paper out of her purse and hastily copied down all the numbers on the vials. Why, she had no idea. But it couldn't hurt.

Rattle, fumble, click. Someone was trying to open the door.

Becca's heart practically leaped out of her mouth, she was so startled. She looked around wildly for a hiding place. Closet? Bathtub?

She heard low, tearful cursing, a few futile thuds, as if someone was swatting the door in a fit of frustrated pique. The muttering receded.

Guarded relief flooded through her. Of course. Diana's key card no longer worked since they had reprogrammed the lock for Becca. Thank God. Becca waited what she hoped was long enough for the woman to get down the hall, measuring time in galloping heartbeats.

She peered out the door and bolted like the hounds of hell were after her. The desk clerks had seen her and so had the security cameras. Chances were good that Diana would know in seconds that her privacy had been violated and would start making a big, fat fuss about it.

Becca really did not want to get into a catfight and exchange bitchslaps with Mathes's whining, weeping, urping mistress. Besides, if Diana wanted to call the cops on her, she would have the moral high ground. Becca would be printed and booked, have a record. Before Zhoglo subsequently slaughtered her, of course.

Once she got on the highway, she fought to keep under eighty miles per hour, she was so eager to put distance between herself and that woman. She was so rattled, she shrieked when her phone beeped to inform her that she had finally entered her cell phone's calling area.

It rang, seconds later. She checked the display. Mr. Big. Hah. Why was she not surprised?

Ringing, thank God. Three rings, and she finally picked up. "Hello? Nick?" She sounded wary.

"Becca. Where are you?" He tried to keep his voice expressionless.

All activity in the workroom abruptly froze. Davy swiveled his head from the computer screen. Seth, who was overhand chinning on the exercise bar, stopped in midpull and just hung there, muscles locked, eyes slitted. Alex Aaro, the ex-Ranger from Brighton Beach whom they had just briefed, crossed his thickly muscled arms over his broad chest and listened, his broad Slavic face impassive.

"Uh. Well, it's a long, complicated story," she began. "I—"

"Where the *fuck* are you?" This time, anger and fear punched through, undisguised.

Becca was unnerved by its force. "Calm down. I'm fine. And I—"

"You told me you were working at the club until midnight!"

"And what makes you think I wasn't?" Her voice was tart.

He was ready for that one. "Because your phone was out of area. I know Bothell's covered. We were messaging the entire goddamn day. So don't even try to jerk me around."

Desperate subtext. *Please do not lie to me. Do not lie. Do not.*

"Oh," she said, more subdued. "That's true. I'm sorry if I worried you. I haven't had a chance to stop and call from a land line—"

"Where are you?" he bellowed.

Becca made an irritated chuffing sound. "Don't yell, and stop interrupting me. My nerves are shot to hell already. I'm on the highway. I was in Kimble. I saw Mathes at the banquet, and got fired from my job—"

"Fired from your job? What the hell—You saw who? Who the fuck is this Mathes?" He felt like he was about to hyperventilate.

"Richard Mathes. The guy who came to see Zhoglo on the island. He's a famous surgeon, apparently, and he was there, at the banquet. That I organized. And I—"

"Holy Jesus. And you didn't call me?" His voice crackled with outrage. "Did he see you?"

"I don't think so. And I would have, except that I overheard this weird conversation he had with his mistress, and then I ended up following her car. It all happened really fast, and by the time I thought to call you, my cell was out of area, but I couldn't stop—"

"Wait a minute," he said. "Let me make sure I've got this straight. You saw Zhoglo's dinner guest at your banquet. You chose not to call me. Then, you spied on his conversation with his mistress. You chose not to call me once again. Then you followed her goddamn *car?*"

The other men in the room exchanged glances. Seth thudded to the ground and whistled.

"That's about the size of it," she said, sounding sheepish. "I lost her for a while when this black Mercedes SUV came to pick her up, and I couldn't get out of the parking lot fast enough to see where they—"

"Are you out of your fucking *mind?*" He was on his feet now, yelling into the phone. Seth grimaced, made a cut-it-out slicing gesture with his finger. Davy waved his arms, mouthing, *Cool it, cool it.*

She paused for a moment. "Not at all," she said, in her haughtiest voice. "I'm making an effort to help. That's quite a different thing."

"Like hell it is!" he shouted.

"I was heading for that hotel where I was supposed to meet you, but if you're just going to scream and carry on, I'll pass, and go home."

"No!" He sucked in a deep breath, exhaled it slowly, and struggled to get a grip on himself. It was like grappling with a gigantic, muscular, greased octopus. "It's not safe. Go to the hotel. I'll meet you there."

"What for? To scream at me some more?"

He spoke slowly and carefully through clenched teeth. "Please, go to the hotel," he said. "You scared the living shit out of me."

"Sorry," she murmured, finally sounding a little contrite. "OK, then. I'll tell you the whole story at the hotel. Till then. Bye."

The connection broke, and the force that had been holding the phone up to his ear deserted him. His arm flopped to his side and his knees gave way, dumping him into his chair.

So. She hadn't been abducted, tortured, murdered. And she was not running away from him. She was not lying to him, either. No, she was just off her rocker. Which was a whole different problem.

He breathed down the bizarre urge to burst into tears. Not in front of these guys, who were giving him assorted funny looks.

"Chick's got nerve," Davy observed, his voice dry.

"Bug-fuck crazy," was Aaro's comment.

"Those are the fun ones," Seth said with relish. "So she tailed this bad guy's mistress, huh? Hot damn. I can't wait to meet this girl. She sounds like a real firecracker. I'll tell Margot to put her at our table."

Nick barely heard them. "I've got to go," he said, distractedly.

"Yeah, you do," Seth said. "We've got things under control. We'll analyze the vid at Pavel's house and get something cobbled up tonight. Aaro's on the Ludmilla monitors. So go on, have some fun. Go get 'em, tiger. Show that chick who's boss."

Nick didn't have any extra mental energy to bother with Seth's bullshit. He turned to Davy. "Can you check out that guy she saw at the banquet? Richard Mathes is the name. Famous surgeon."

"Will do," Davy said. "Yo. Nick?"

He jerked around on his dash to the door. "What?" he snapped.

"Chill," Davy said quietly. "Step back. Watch yourself with her."

Like it was that easy. That was like telling a fire not to be hot. You could try all you wanted, but there wasn't a whole lot of point in it.

Chapter
21

Nick's giant black pickup loomed over the tame sedans lined up in the hotel lot like some big, sleek, crouching predator.

Becca pulled her suitcase out of the trunk of her own pussycat of a rented sedan. Tomorrow, she had to take it right back where she'd gotten it. Back to riding the bus. Rented cars were not in the budget of a recently fired person. Not that a recently fired person could really be said to have a budget at all. Such a person had, at best, an emergency fund. In her case, an almost nonexistent one.

Even with Carrie and Josh almost on their own, she barely scraped by from month to month. No margin for error now.

Stop it. She had bigger problems right now than her pathetic bank account.

Like her complicated, volatile new lover.

A part of her coolly observed the chattering voices in her mind, how they generated a cheerful fake buzz of white noise to hide from herself how incredibly nervous she was about seeing Nick.

But it wasn't working. She was on to the trick. What was the point of all this energy expended in self-deception if it didn't even work?

Habit, she supposed. She smiled at the desk clerk. A shivery sense of déjà vu went through her. "Hi. Has my husband, Rob Steiger, arrived yet?" The H-word gave her a shivery rush of emotion.

The chubby brunette behind the desk smiled and passed her a key card. "He sure has, Mrs. Steiger, just about ten minutes ago. He told us to be on the lookout for you. Have a good night!"

She took the elevator up and walked slowly down the hall. Knees wobbling, heart thudding, head dizzy, breath shallow, hands damp and cold—symptom for symptom, she was in more of a nervous tizzy now than she had been while breaking into Diana Evans's hotel room.

How ridiculous was that. She needed to grow a backbone. Right now. She took a deep breath, and stuck the key card in. The light flashed green, and she pushed the heavy door open.

Nick sat on the bed in the dim room, framed by the room's dark entryway. Facing the door, simply waiting.

He smoldered at her. There was simply no other word for it. The harsh lines of his handsome face were grimly expressionless, but his eyes burned. The power of his anger pulsed at her. The hairs on her neck tingled.

Something sinuous and powerful moved inside her. Behind the fear and the white noise. A hungry pull of hot desire, as she sensed that simmering power in him. Hers to use, if she could rise to the occasion. If she could handle him.

"Hello, Mr. Steiger," she said.

He waited a long time to answer, and finally inclined his head. "Mrs. Steiger," he said guardedly.

"How was your day?" she asked.

"It was shitty." His voice sliced through the silence. "Don't fuck with me, Becca. I'm not in the mood."

Tactical retreat. New strategy. Nix the playfulness.

She shrugged off her coat, hung it up, lifted her suitcase onto the rack. Caught a glimpse of herself in the mirror. She didn't recognize herself, with the teased, tangled cloud of hair, the shockingly red mouth. She shrugged off the blazer, and contemplated ways to stage this confrontation. His body language did not invite her to sit with him on the bed, but neither did she want to stand before him like an accused criminal before a judge.

She grabbed a chair, perched in it. Took a deep breath and tilted her rib cage so that the high-necked white knit tank pulled sexily over her boobs. Crossed her legs, to hike the straight skirt up. Let her crossed foot dangle, in the stiletto-heeled strappy sandal. She'd bought those shoes for her engagement party. This seemed like a much, much better use for them.

He stared at her, hot eyes moving up and down her body.

Ah. That was better. So she was not entirely without resources.

"What's with the slut-red lipstick?" he asked.

"Oh. That." She hesitated. "I, ah, stole it. From Diana."

"And Diana is . . . ?" His voice went soft, almost menacing.

"Mathes's mistress," she admitted. "The woman I've been tailing."

The quality of his silence deepened. It was like the moment of inevitability after a fuse is lit, but before the explosion.

Becca rushed on, trying to keep her shaking voice light. "I think the color is a little extreme, but it's growing on me. Do you like it?"

"Don't know," he said slowly. "It makes me want to fuck you hard, up against the wall. Was that your intention when you put it on?"

She blinked, nonplussed. "Ah . . . maybe we're getting a little ahead of ourselves in the agenda for the evening," she murmured. "Don't you want to be debriefed? Is that the right word?"

"Yeah. Debrief me." He jerked his chin. "Get the fuck on with it. I want to move right along to the other part of the evening's agenda. I've got big plans for you, babe. Big, big plans."

She shivered at the implied threat in his low voice. "Stop trying to intimidate me, Nick. I do not appreciate it."

"And I don't appreciate you skipping town, chasing around after dangerous criminals. You didn't call me! You could have gotten killed!"

"That's true, and I'll be the first to admit it, but why can't I make you understand that it was a onetime opportunity, goddamnit!" she yelled. "It was me or it was nobody, Nick! I knew she was going someplace significant, and there was just no time to—"

"How did you know where she was going?" he cut in.

"Do you want to hear this story told properly, from start to finish?" she shot back. "Or shall I just go?"

"Oh, you aren't going anywhere," he said softly. "No longer an option."

"You're doing it again." She waggled an admonishing finger at him. "Don't threaten me, you big rude lout. I saw an opportunity to find out something useful, and I took it before it slipped away forever. I think you could be a little more appreciative of my efforts!"

"Oh, I do appreciate you," he said. "I fully intend to appreciate the living hell out of you, all night long. What's with those new stockings? I like the seam up the back. Very hot. Did you steal those off this Diana chick, too? How'd you pull that off? Hit her over the head?"

"I bought these at the mall on my lunch break," she huffed. "To please you, though I'm starting to regret it. And I infuriated my now-ex-boss in the process."

"Oh. So this is the formerly frigid lingerie you told me about in the messages. Take your clothes off, Becca. Let me see it."

The blaze of sexual heat from him almost rocked her backwards. "Like hell." She got up, and turned her back on him, searching for her blazer. "I've had enough of your crap.

I just spent three very scary hours trying to help you out, and it took a lot out of me. Screw your stupid tantrums. If you're not interested in what I discovered tonight, then I'll just leave—owf!"

She hadn't even seen his shadow shift before she found her back pinned to his chest, legs flailing six inches above the ground. His hard arm clamped around her middle, under her rib cage.

The world flipped, she flew, and landed, bouncing on the bed. He was on top of her before she could gather her wits to scramble away.

He was all over her. His hands pinned hers on either side of her head, his elbows flanked her shoulders, his eyes bored into hers, inches away. His breath smelled of coffee. He shifted without breaking eye contact and reached down to shove her skirt up, her thighs open, and rolled between them, rocking her hips back so that she cradled him.

The penetrating heat of his bulging erection pressed against her most intimate parts, protected only by the sheer film of stretch chiffon of her new panties. Which was to say, not protected at all.

"I told you, Becca," he said. "You're not going anywhere."

She bucked and strained against his implacable weight. "This is juvenile," she snapped. "Get off me. Right now."

"No. Tell me your story. I like this position. This way, I don't have to worry about you storming out in a huff when I piss you off. Since I know for a fact that I'm going to piss you off. It's a given. Sad, but true."

"Oh, yeah. Like you're going to listen to me while you're—mmph!"

He cut off her words with a fierce, hungry kiss that took her completely by surprise. She got lost in it, done in by the hunger of his surprisingly tender mouth, his magic skill at melting her, softening her, getting her off balance.

He lifted his head, his pupils dilated. "So? Go for it, babe. You have my full attention. Body and soul. I promise."

"Can't . . . breathe," she said, wiggling.

He rolled smoothly onto his side, thrusting a leg through hers and yanking her very close.

That was much better. Sure, she was still being confined in the cage of his body, but this could almost be classified as a hug. He might be a mean, controlling bastard, but she needed the comfort of contact with his big, hot body. God knows she'd better take what comfort she could when she could. Since Nick did not excel in giving it.

She huddled gratefully inside the warm shelter of his body, and slowly, haltingly, told him the tale from the beginning: from seeing Mathes at the banquet, then overhearing him and Diana in the office, then following her to the hotel in Kimble. His face darkened when she got to the part about the parking lot of the Starlight Lounge. Breaking into the car, stealing the sunglasses, the lipstick, impersonating Diana to search the room, those details made him hiss in disapproval, his body going rigid.

"Jesus! You're out of your freaking skull!"

"Maybe, but is that relevant?" She hurried on before he could respond to that highly rhetorical question. "In any case, the only interesting thing I found was that box. It had seven vials of blood in it. And urine samples, and those big cotton swabs, like monster Q-tips, in plastic bags."

"Blood and urine?" He jerked up onto his elbows, frowning.

"Everything was labeled and numbered. I wrote down the numbers. Want to see?"

He nodded, and let go of her, sitting up on the bed. She was obscurely gratified that he was interested enough in her adventure to forget about his sexual power games. She fished through her purse for the scrap of paper, and handed it to him. "The first six digits looked like birthdates," she said. "That would make them all little kids."

He stared silently at the list. "Yeah," he said faintly.

The silence got longer, heavier. It started to make her nervous. "Um, Nick? What are you thinking? What could this mean?"

He shook the dark thoughts that had gripped him away with a violent shudder, like a dog shaking off water. "Was there paperwork?"

"I didn't find anything like that in the room. But in the seat of her car, there was a package for a digital voice recorder," Becca said. "Probably she dictated notes into it. And then stuck it in her pocket or her purse."

He nodded, pulled out his wallet and tucked the scrap of paper carefully inside. Then he pulled out his cell phone and dialed a number.

"I have another name," he said into it. "The mistress. Diana Evans. Some kind of health professional. Doctor, nurse, lab tech, something like that." He looked at Becca. "Got a plate number for her?"

"It was a black PT Cruiser, if that's relevant," she told him. She recited the plate number to him. He relayed it and hung up again.

Becca had to gather her nerve to ask the question, with the creeping dread she felt on her neck. "Nick? Do you have any idea why . . . or what? About these blood and urine samples?"

"No," he said flatly.

"Nothing good, though, right?" she whispered.

Nick shook his head. "No. Nothing good. You can count on that."

The unspoken possibilities hung between them in the dark. Becca's skin prickled and crawled. She wondered, wistfully, if she could ask him for another hug. Maybe her luck would be better if she just jumped on him, and took her hug from him by force.

If she did, she would probably find herself flat on her back with him about three miles inside her body before she knew what hit her. Which was fine. She was up for it.

He got up, moved towards her, eyes gleaming. Abruptly,

the energy shifted. Out of nowhere, she was on the defensive again.

"So," he said. "We're done with the debriefing? Anything to add?"

She shook her head. "That's it."

"Excellent. So we can move on to the next item on the agenda."

Her toes tightened, then her chest, then her thighs. "Which is?"

"Which is the burning-in-hell agony you put me through this evening. And exactly what you'll have to do to make it up to me."

"Fuck you," she said sharply. "Is this necessary? Do you have to put things in those terms? Do you really need the upper hand so badly?"

"Yes, I do." His voice was matter-of-fact.

She was mad. Her face got hot, and her breath got short. The manipulative bastard. "You can't have it," she snapped. "You've already pissed me off. Anyway, what exactly is it that you want from me?"

Nick seized the chair, and placed it facing the one spot of blank wall in the room. Then he took her wrist and placed her before him, back to the wall. He slowly sank into the chair, slouching luxuriously.

"You'll see," he said lazily. "First . . . strip."

It was a risk. He knew this kind of head game would piss her off, wound up as she was, but he couldn't stop himself. He was pissed off, too. They both needed this.

Besides, he knew, in a deep part of his brain, what got her off. She liked it when he came on strong, liked being overwhelmed. She liked extreme. Almost as much as he liked dishing it out to her. God, look at her. Following that bastard's mistress, stealing the woman's stuff out of her car, impersonating her to get into her room—Becca had nerves of steel. She was an adrenaline freak. Just like him.

He could see it, arousal at war with pride on her flushed face. His dick ached, as he looked at her. Time to nudge and push some more.

"Scared?" he taunted her.

Her chin went up, her eyes sparkled. "Hah. Not of you. Jerk."

"Then get your clothes off," he ordered. "Before I tear them off."

She tossed her hair with a sniff, and took off her glasses. Tossed them on the desk top, trying so hard to look nonchalant.

Her awkward, fumbling striptease was unselfconsciously erotic. He could feel his own thudding heartbeat in his engorged cock, pressing painfully against the crotch of his jeans.

She peeled off the tank, revealing a retro-looking bustier made out of skin-toned satin. Rocket-launcher-pointy bra cups that propped her tits up high and offered them to the observer's eye like the gift of God that they were. She shimmied and twisted to undo the hooks of the tight black skirt, and then wiggled out of it.

The rest of the formerly frigid lingerie made his mouth go dry. Sheer silky stockings, hooked up to a satin garter belt. French-cut satin panties with ribbon ties holding the front and back panels together over the smooth curve of her hip. A transparent chiffon garter belt stretched over her belly, trimmed with satin ribbon, accentuating the alluring curves of her thighs, how they hollowed into her groin. Sheer silk stretched over her plump mound, the dark swatch of hair showing through. A web of tangled satin ribbon strips, holding the whole thing onto her perfect, sexy, lickable, fuckable body.

He was speechless. She was so beautiful, it killed him.

And she'd gone out and bought all that stuff today. For him.

She stood before him, hands moving helplessly, like she wanted to cover herself but was too proud to admit to feeling vulnerable.

He seized her wrists, tugged until she swayed forward. "Turn around," he said. "Put your hands against the wall. Arch your back."

"Nick, I—"

"I want to see what that outfit does for your ass," he explained. "Don't argue." He hesitated. "Unless, of course . . . you're scared."

She made a derisive sound but did as he asked, looking back over her shoulder at him. "You," she said breathlessly, "are very bossy. And crude. And I should not encourage you."

"Probably not," he agreed, staring at her ass. The outfit exalted it, as it deserved to be exalted. The back of the panties nestled tenderly up into the shadowy cleft of her ass, letting the bottom half of her smooth, perfect butt cheeks emerge, to be admired and worshipped.

He leaned forward, and nuzzled the undercurve with his lips. Jerked her thighs wide and tugged on her hips so she bent at a sharper angle, making it possible to press his lips right against the warm, puffy cushion of her soft, silk-covered labia. She gasped, wiggled.

He was sweating, too damn hot for her, so he ripped off the pullover and flung it away, reaching for her again with hands that were hungry for her amazing softness. Soft as goosedown, soft as dandelion fluff, soft as newly unfurled leaves, things so fine and delicate, they were almost untouchable, but he couldn't stop, even though the rough spots on his hand snagged and caught on the fine fabric. They rasped over her fine-grained, perfect skin. Her breath was fast. Her legs shook. She liked it.

"So," she said, her voice full of fake bravado. "Does this getup fit your pornographic formerly frigid fantasy?"

He slid his hand between her legs, nudging it right up into that cloud of silky heat. She made an almost inaudible squeak, and her hot, soft thighs closed, trembling, around his hand.

"Actually, this is in a whole different league," he admitted. "This leaves my fantasies in the dust. You blow my mind, angel. I am humbled by your beauty."

"Humbled, hah. I hardly think so," she said, sighing as his hand was drawn in by the shadowy involuted glories of her cunt. "Ohh . . . if it works for you, it was money well spent."

"Oh, yeah. It works." He tugged on the ribbon ties of the panties, and pulled them off, letting them fall. He spun her around again.

Stared up at her glowing eyes, her parted red lips, the rise and fall of her chest, her naked, gorgeous muff.

Wow. He was wired to blow. His hands shook.

It scared him, how raw, how out of control he felt. He had to slow this down. Once he touched her with his tongue or his cock, that would be it. His technique would fly out the window.

He didn't want to feel out of control. He'd felt that way all evening, staring at that fucking icon moving across the screen. He wanted to be sure of making her come, screaming. Blow her mind with orgasm after orgasm. He had to time it right. Slow it down. Way, way down.

He wanted to howl with frustration, but he leaned back in the chair, gripping the pads of upholstery over the wooden chair arms. "Showtime," he said.

She looked wary. "What on earth does that mean?"

"Make yourself come," he suggested. "Right here. For me."

"You mean, standing up?" She sounded scandalized. "I don't even know if I can do that. Women are different, you know. It's not as easy as you might think. The conditions have to be right."

"What conditions? Check out this condition." He popped open the buttons of his jeans, jerked them down just far enough so that his cock could spring out heavily before him, purple and taut, full to bursting.

She stared at him, looking dazed and worried. "I don't know if I—"

"Not even with me sitting here, twenty inches away? Salivating?"

Her eyes narrowed. "Especially not with you there salivating," she said haughtily. "I have to be comfortable, to start with, and I—"

"Start somewhere. Do something," he said bluntly. "Get to it. Put your hand on yourself."

"But I—"

"It's OK if it takes a while," he assured her. "I'm patient."

Still, she stood there, frozen with shyness and indecision. He seized her hand, moved it to the dark satiny swath of her pubic hair. He loved the way it stayed flush and gleaming smooth to her skin until it got down to her slit, and then suddenly curled out every which way into a dark frill over the hood of her clit.

He pressed her fingertips to it. "Start there," he suggested.

She stared into his eyes, her gleaming red lower lip caught between her teeth like she'd forgotten it was there, and waited until he thought he was going to die of the suspense. . . .

And then she closed her eyes, lips curling up in a little smile . . . and did as he asked.

It wasn't what he expected. Not that he'd had the presence of mind to expect anything, but he didn't expect to stare at her with hot, burning eyes, humbled. Moved. Aching with lust.

There was something intensely intimate about the sight of her touching herself. It was nothing like porn masturbation scenes he'd watched, numbly, on late-night adult cable channels. With Becca there was nothing for show, nothing for the camera, nothing faked. She didn't undulate, flaunt herself, stroke her breasts. Her vulva was hidden by her fingers. Her energy was turned entirely inward. She squeezed her thighs around her hand, eyes shut, biting her lip. Lost in it.

He wanted in there with her, but he was the one who had pressured her into going there alone. Far from him. "Open your eyes," he said.

"Stop it. You're distracting me," she whispered. "This is hard enough as it is."

"Open them," he urged. "I want you to see me looking at you."

That smile again. "Don't worry. I don't have to see you to know you're there. You make your presence felt."

She was getting closer, working herself up to it with tight circles, panting breaths. He felt the power building.

And he was on his feet, in her face. "Open your eyes," he pleaded.

"Goddamn it, Nick," she gasped out. "I'm so close. . . ."

He forced his hand between her clamped thighs, into the moist heat behind her fingers. "Now." He made his voice sharp, a whip crack.

Her eyes popped open, startled, and he thrust two fingers into her slick depths just as the pleasure jolted through her. Her cunt clenched hard around his fingers, and he saw right into her unguarded eyes, right into that sweet, secret space inside her, where he wanted to be.

God. Where he wanted to *live*.

He held her up there against the wall until she could more or less stand again, and then gave in to the inevitable and sank to his knees, lifting up one of her legs and placing it on the seat of the chair.

"Hold open your pussy for me," he told her.

She fumbled to obey him, and just shook there, poised over him on wobbling legs, and holding her labia wide for him. He went at her with his hungry tongue, sliding it up and down the sopping length of her pink vulva with swirls around the taut, swollen clit at the top, deep darting thrusts into it, over and over until she came again with a low wail, jerking and shuddering against his face. Too soon. He could stay there, drinking from that sweet fountain of life. For hours.

He held her steady as he got to his feet and rolled the condom he had at the ready over himself, then shoved her back against the wall and nudged his cock head inside her, pushing until he felt that delicious resistance of that plushy glove of perfect woman flesh.

"I won't be able to stop once I start," he told her.

"I'd hit you in the face if you tried to stop," she shot back.

God, he loved it when she was feisty. "I can't go slow, either."

"I don't want you to." She dug her nails into his shoulders and hung on. "Stop being such a chatterbox. You're pissing me off again."

Her words became a low moan in chorus with his own as he nudged deeper, pushing and pushing, digging the slow, tight glide into her body. He eased back a little, surged in, and just went at her, wildly, desperate to lunge inside her before he was even done with the stroke he was on. He jolted her against the wall with a cry at every deep plunge.

A simultaneous orgasm was building up, her charge added to his own. They exploded, souls touching for a timeless instant. And he was there, in that magic place where he had longed to be. Part of her. Awed by her. So beautiful.

He locked his wobbling knees by sheer force of will, and let his weight prop their shaking, sweating bodies against the wall.

"So," he said, looking for words for the thought pervading his mind. "So it wasn't just those vid cams that did it for you, then."

It took her a second to register what he was referring to, but her eyes popped open, bright with righteous anger. "Hell, no! As if! What kind of pervert do you think I am, anyway? It was you!"

"Me," he repeated, in a shaky whisper. "Me." He took a deep breath, forcing enough strength into his limbs to lift her up and carry her over to the bed, still wrapped around him.

His cock still inside. He wasn't ready to let go of this contact yet. No fucking way.

He sat down on the bed, arranging her legs so that she was kneeling astride him, and flopped back onto the coverlet.

He stared up at her, still speechless. She stared down, petting his chest, her fingertips exploring him with tender, idle curiosity.

Her eyelashes swept down over her eyes, shadowing them from his gaze. "Well? So? Did that, um . . ." Her voice trailed off.

"What?" he demanded, impatient.

"Did that make it up to you? For the burning-in-hell agony?"

He refused to let the smile loose, even though his face desperately wanted to. "Nah," he said. "You've made a dent, maybe. No more."

She looked outraged. "You call that a *dent?*" Her mouth twitched. "You really do have to keep the upper hand, don't you? At all costs?"

"Absolutely," he agreed. He reached up, tangling his fingers into her hair. "To my last breath."

"Doesn't that make you tired? Always having to be in control?"

The question made him vaguely uncomfortable. "No," he said.

She picked at the buckles on her sexy spike-heeled sandals, pulled the sandals off and tossed them away, and she looked at him, her eyes big and thoughtful. "I scared you that badly?" Her voice was soft.

He hesitated for a moment. "I was beside myself," he said.

Her eyelashes swept down, and she spent a couple of minutes stroking his chest hair. Which made his dick twitch and thicken inside her.

She leaned down, and startled him by dropping a tender kiss right between his eyes. "I'm sorry I scared you," she said.

Sorry. Hah. Part of him wanted to hoot with laughter. Another part wanted to seize the advantage quick, roll her over and fuck her again.

Another part altogether took him entirely by surprise when it spoke up. "I thought you were running away from me," he blurted.

Her sexy mouth fell open. She stared down at him, eyes wide, startled. "From you? But why on earth would I . . . how could you think that, Nick?"

He'd gone red in the face, was already regretting the stupid confession. He shrugged, almost angrily. "How the fuck should I know how your mind works?" he muttered. "I haven't had much luck with women. I thought maybe it was too much. Maybe I was too much."

She shook her head, distressed. "That's nuts, Nick! After all we've—after all you did for me! I wouldn't run from you! I love . . ."

Her voice trailed off. Her eyes got huge, her white throat bobbing, as she realized that he knew exactly what she had almost said.

I love you. She had almost said it. And she had stopped herself.

The silence that thudded down around them had physical weight.

He broke eye contact. Whatever. Big fucking deal. So she didn't want to say the L-word to him. It was a lot to ask of the woman, all things considered. He couldn't blame her. Hell, he was glad she hadn't.

After all. What the fuck would he have done if she'd said it? If she'd meant it? Christ. What a freaking responsibility. Who needed it.

He rolled her over so they were on their sides, so he could

slide his cock out of her, look the other way, get rid of the condom. Think of something to say to break the tension of that awful silence, to make those goddamn unsaid words stop burning in the air between them in letters of fire. But he didn't trust his voice yet. He didn't trust his face.

There was a hollow feeling in his chest. It ached and burned.

She recovered first. "Nick, I didn't mean—"

"Don't worry about it." He cut her off, without looking up, and sat back down on the bed so he could start prying off his shoes. "It's OK. Take it easy. I wouldn't have held you to it."

He winced inwardly. Stupid thing to say. As if he could.

"No! That's not what I meant!" Her voice sounded anxious. "It's just that—"

"I understand." He kicked his jeans the rest of the way off so they'd stop hobbling his knees, dug the strip of condoms out of his pocket. "It's a weird time in your life. You've got a lot to deal with. So do I. So we keep it simple. Just sex. That's fine with me, OK? That's cool."

"But I didn't mean—"

"Becca, for Christ's sake," he cut in savagely. "Let it fucking *go.*"

He kept his back to her, ignoring the hurt silence as he ripped a condom open, pried it out of its envelope. She grabbed his arm.

He turned. "Nick, I . . . oh, for God's sake," she finished, staring down at his erection as he sheathed it, with a swift, one-handed swipe.

"Let's get back to that dent of yours," he said.

She rolled her eyes. "Oh, please. I thought we'd moved on."

Tell him about it. He'd thought so, too. He'd stopped himself just in time from embarrassing the hell out of her by throwing himself at her feet. Making a bunch of dramatic declarations. Jesus. Narrow escape.

But hey. That was no reason not to nail her another few

hundred times. She definitely seemed to like that aspect of their relationship, whatever else might be lacking. Might as well accentuate the positive.

As long as he had the breath to hang on to her and the mojo to seduce her, he would. To the fucking bitter end.

He reached around behind her, unhooked the bustier and lifted it reverently away from her gorgeous tits. The garter belt and stockings were welcome to stay, but he wanted to see those tits jiggle with each thrust. There were red marks in her soft, creamy flesh, from where the tight garment had pinched her. He stroked his fingertips over them.

"You're evading me," she accused him.

Evading himself was more like it. He grunted, shoved her legs open, folded them wide, and gazed down at the divine spectacle of her pussy. He loved the contrasts in color, the dark hair, the white skin, the slick pink and red of her inner folds.

She wiggled and made soft, breathless gasping sounds as he petted them, sliding his fingers inside to find the slick, hot fluid that he loved so much to lick, pulling the hood up off that tight, swollen pink clit with his fingers, to admire it. He rubbed his cock head against it, swirling it around and around her clit, and nudged inside the wet pink hole beneath it, shoving until her tender tissues were distended around his thick cock head, tenderly clasping him.

"Does this feel like evasion?" he asked.

Her amusement made her sheath contract rhythmically around his cock. "Hah. Smart-ass. Invasion is more like it."

He invaded her some more, squeezing deeper into that quivering sheath. The teeth-grinding, heart-pounding excitement almost canceled out the ache in his chest.

She put her hands against his chest, dug in her nails, and pushed. "I'm not letting this go," she said. "Sooner or later, we have to talk about it. Just keep that in mind."

He flexed his hips and drove the rest of the way inside. She let out a shocked gasp, her nails digging deep.

He froze. *Shit.* "Did I hurt you?" He braced himself.

She swallowed, bit her lip. "Little bit. You bumped some-thing. But I'm OK."

"Sorry," he said helplessly.

Becca wiggled and adjusted herself around the hard, un-yielding shaft of his cock. "That won't work," she said. "I don't want just sex. That's not what I meant at all. Not. At all."

He shut her up the only way he could think of. He kissed her.

A double invasion, with his cock embedded in her slick, squirming warmth of her pussy, his mouth moving hungrily over her soft lips. The taste of the paint on them was unfa-miliar, contrasting oddly with the sweet taste of her inner depths, her little tongue.

Again. He had no idea why he made this same goddamn mistake, over and over. This double contact did something to his chest, stretching him out between those two focus points of intense awareness and need. The aching, hollow place in his chest took over his whole body. He clutched her like she was life itself. He was kissing her like he'd die if he stopped. Fucking her with hard, frenzied lunges. Desperate to get in-side her, as deep as he could go. She struggled just as hard, straining towards what she needed. Her body clutching, de-manding, as her orgasm called forth his own.

He obeyed, rode the crest of that wave for as long as he could, feeling for her, waiting for her before he topped the rise and let himself be battered under the tons of pounding foam.

She was already asleep when he finally had the strength to lift his eyelids. He was grateful for that. Somehow sum-moned the strength to reach out, flip off the bedside light.

The light that leaked out of the bathroom loved up the graceful curves and lines and hollows of her body.

He tried not to think about it. Tried again. Christ. He fid-geted.

Hey, he would have stopped himself, too. No one knew

better than he what Becca had to deal with in Nick Ward. He was a rude, irritable, oversexed pain in the ass. Since he'd met her, their encounters all had more or less the same arc. First, he scolded and bullied her; then he subsequently tossed her on her back and fucked her brains out.

Not much of a base there for "I love you."

He'd never had the nerve in his life to say those words to anybody.

At least not in English. The thought came to him suddenly. He'd said them to his mother, in Ukrainian. And there he went, right off the cliff. Bad move. Thinking about his mother was all he needed right now.

No "I love you's." It was against his rules. It was like painting a big bull's-eye on your chest and saying, *Go on, shoot me. Shoot me, please.*

He was a fucking chump idiot to get his tender feelings hurt.

He dragged her closer, his arm jealously tight around her smooth body, and tried like hell to grow up, and get some goddamn sleep.

Chapter
22

"I can't do it, Richie," Diana said brokenly. "I thought I could, but I can't. I'm so sorry."

Dismayed, Richard Mathes stared at the woman swaying on his front porch. Diana looked awful. Eyes bloodshot, lids swollen and fiery red, ringed with tear-streaked makeup. Her mouth was marred with a bubbling mosaic of fever blisters; her hair was a rat's nest, squashed into a bizarre one-sided crest. Her clothes looked like she'd slept in them. She stank of old sweat—and of alcohol.

His shock lasted only a moment before his practical nature snapped into action, checking rapidly to see if any nosy neighbors were out pruning their flowers to witness this tableau.

"Richard? Who's at the door?" Helen's voice floated out the open door, growing nearer.

"Wait here," he hissed at her. "No one," he called, whipping the door shut just as Helen appeared at the top of the stairs, fastening an earring.

"Don't get absorbed in anything, please," she said, in a crisp, admonishing voice. "The Zimmer girl's birthday party starts in twenty minutes, and I can't take Chloe because I'm taking Libby to get her hair done at GianPiero's, so you have to give her a ride. Remember?"

Mathes gave her a placating smile, though his teeth clenched hard enough to send bursts of pain up into his skull. "Of course."

He waited until his wife disappeared back into the master bedroom before he permitted the smile to fade. He had no idea what the real expression beneath it might be, but it was better that the nagging, irritating bitch not see it. He had enough problems.

He slipped out the door, spun Diana around and frog-marched her over the vast expanse of the Mathes lawn and into the shade of the big maple that overhung the drive, and from there into the garage. "Where is your car?" he demanded.

"It's around the corner," she said faintly. "On the Avenue."

He abruptly ruled out the possibility of sending her packing back to her own vehicle. She was drunk, for one thing. Worse still, in this neighborhood, she would be remembered in this deplorable condition. Bad enough that she'd staggered this far.

Time for damage control. He jerked her into the garage, unlocked his BMW coupe and bundled her into the passenger's seat. Not gently, he shoved her down onto her side. "Keep your head down," he snarled.

He left her there weeping while he went in to deal with Helen.

He found her in the foyer, shrugging on the elegantly crumpled white linen jacket that matched her suit, tucking a nonexistent wisp up into her smoothly coiffed blond hair. She glimmered with accents of gold and diamonds. Who'd guess that a world-class bitch lurked behind that perfectly groomed, angelic façade?

He gathered his energy. "Something's come up," he said. "A medical emergency. I can't take Chloe to the party."

Helen's eyes went blank for a moment, and then the lower lids quivered and crept up, as they always did when she was angry with him. Which was to say, every instant of every goddamn day.

"You're lying. Of course." Her voice had that low tremor of martyrdom that made him want to wrap his fingers around that slender white throat and squeeze until her blue eyes popped. "You're going to play with one of your whores, I imagine."

He grabbed his briefcase, which was always at the ready near the door. "It's work, Helen," he said, with steely patience.

"Isn't it always?" She folded her arms across her chest. "Well then, why not take Chloe on your way? The Zimmers are en route to your office. Which I assume is the site of your, ah, 'medical emergency'?" Her voice rang with righteous challenge.

He thought of Diana, sweating and sobbing outside in his car, and silently cursed her for being so weak. Falling apart on him like a wet paper bag just when things got critical. "I do not have time to swing by the Zimmers'. Just as I do not have time for this conversation."

"Daddy?" Chloe appeared on the stairs. His daughter had inherited her mother's spectacularly bad timing. She gave him a dewy-lashed look of desperate entreaty. "If I have to wait for Mom to take Libby to GianPiero's, I'll miss the party! I swear, you just have to drop me off; it's not like you have to go in and chat, and I—"

"No!" he bellowed. "God, how many times do I have to say it?"

Chloe jerked back, mouth quivering, and ran up the stairs.

Mathes beat a hasty retreat, so he wouldn't have to look at Helen's thunderous face. God, a man got no peace in his own home.

All this family drama sweetened his mood nicely for when he slid into the driver's seat of the car. Diana was sitting up again, to his extreme irritation. He seized a handful of her hair and yanked it down. Her face whacked the plastic cupholder on the fold-down center console. That was going to leave a bruise, he thought. The next thought came quickly, resolute and cold.

It doesn't matter now.

He grimly wrapped his mind around the idea as he put some distance between them and his own neighborhood. If Diana was so far gone that she would accost him at his own home, she had become dangerously unpredictable. A security liability. He suppressed a pang of melancholy, let anger well up to replace it. This was going to be embarrassing and reflect very badly upon him with Zhoglo. And her whimpering was driving him crazy.

"Shut up," he said.

She did, touching her face with the tips of her fingers. "Can I sit up now?"

"Yes."

He saw a crimson flash of blood out of the corner of his eye, and slanted a look. He'd given her a split lip. Her face was distorted by the weeping.

"I am interested to know exactly what you think could justify a crazy stunt like this," he said. "Last night's spectacle was bad enough."

She put her hand over her mouth and made a visible effort to compose herself.

"Did you get the samples?" he demanded.

"I delivered them directly to the lab," she quavered. "I got there around three in the morning and left them with Jankins. And I specified that the older girl's samples were a rush job."

"Good. Then why are you falling apart?"

Her shoulders convulsed. He realized with a grinding sense of dismay that she was starting to cry again.

"Richie, it was horrible," she forced out. "They looked just terrible, for one thing—all of them are so thin and starved-looking, and they have so many bruises. Somebody should fire those horrible people who are watching them. And the little ones screamed and cried, and the oldest girl— oh, God, Richie, she kept trying and trying to talk to me, and then she . . . she *attacked* me!"

He waited, a measured pause. "It doesn't seem as if she injured you too badly. We discussed this, Diana. At length. You told me you could handle it. That you were good at compartmentalizing feelings."

"After all these years with you? Of course I'm good at it," she said, with a sudden flare of heat. "But I wasn't expecting . . . I didn't think they would be so—"

"Those children are refuse from the worst orphanages in the world," he lectured. "They were abandoned and raised in institutions that drastically inhibited their cognitive development. What they have lost can never be regained and they are irreparably damaged. They will never lead normal lives. Never have fulfilling relationships. Never be contributing members of society."

"But Richie—"

"And we have been through this! It's a difficult ethical decision, but we made it together! The time for philosophical debate is past!"

He abandoned his harangue. She was sobbing too hard to hear it.

He wondered why he bothered. Habit, maybe. He should have realized at the banquet that she was breaking down, but the time crunch had stressed him, Helen had been chewing his ass all evening, and he hadn't been able to think of an alternative plan on the spot. Besides, he shouldn't stop scolding too soon. Diana may be going to rack and ruin, but she was an intelligent ruin. When she cared to be.

"That girl . . . her eyes . . ." Diana faltered. "She looked so desperate. She tried to speak to me, Richie. She asked for help."

"And then she attacked you, remember?" He thought of Henry Metgers, who had already paid fifteen million dollars for his sixteen-year-old daughter's new heart, and decided it was time to try a new tack.

"The Metgers girl is an artistic genius," he said. "A budding concert pianist. With her rare blood type, it could be months before a match became available through normal channels. She doesn't have months, Diana. She will die in a matter of days without that heart."

"I know, I know," Diana whispered.

"And you would deny her that?" He pounded away at her, ruthlessly. "Edeline Metgers barely has the strength to speak. She's a lovely, gifted child. She deserves to live. Doesn't she?"

"Of course she does, but Richie, I—"

"Life is like that, Diana. I'm sorry, but it is. Either this brilliant child lives and shares her incredible talent with all humanity, or she goes out like a candle. And for what? For the continued existence of a stunted, mentally deficient girl, destined to huddle in a locked room for her entire meaningless existence?"

"Richie, it was her eyes," Diana wailed. "You don't understand!"

He cut off his tirade, which was wasted on her anyway, and pulled up to the curb, a block away from Diana's bungalow.

"Try not to think about it," he suggested, forcing a gentleness into his voice that he did not feel. "Go on home." He reached into the back seat for his briefcase, rummaged through the contents until he found the right bottle, and shook four pills out into his hand.

There was a small bottle of mineral water in the seat. He held them out to her. "Take these," he urged. "By the time you get to bed, you'll already be feeling calmer. You're exhausted. Get some rest."

She hesitated for a moment, but he held them out again, and she tossed them into her mouth and gulped them down. He began to relax.

She took a deep breath, let out a shuddering sigh. "Richie, there's something else."

He felt his skull throb again, from the teeth-gritting. "And that is?"

"I think someone was watching me last night," she whispered, after a nervous pause. "I think I was followed."

"Oh, for God's sake, Diana," he snapped. "That's ridiculous. Of all times to start having paranoid delusions—"

"Really! When I got back to the hotel, my key card didn't work. When I went down to get another, they told me I'd been there five minutes before to get a key redone! Someone who looked like me pretended to be me, and searched my room. I know it sounds crazy."

Mathes stared into her wide, wet, mascara-ringed eyes, wondering if this went deeper than a simple nervous breakdown. Perhaps Diana was having bona fide hallucinations.

It hardly mattered. The outcome for her was the same.

"Richie, I'm so sorry about all this," she said brokenly.

He found the pack of tissues in the center console, pulled one out with slow, deliberate care and forced himself to wipe away the blood drying on her chin. He tried to pat down that wayward crest of hair.

"Don't cry," he said. "You're more tenderhearted than you knew. But you're misplacing your compassion. Save it for those who deserve it. Those who can benefit from it. Otherwise, what's it worth? Who benefits?" He stroked her sticky cheek.

"Come up with me," she pleaded, her long red nails digging into his forearm. "I need you. Please, Richie."

Her bleating whine grated on his raw nerves. He clamped down on the urge to shake her off. Apart from the fact that she could never arouse him in this condition, he also thought it unwise to let himself be seen by her neighbors entering her house. Much less filling any of her orifices with his genetic material. Considering.

He touched her face with manufactured gentleness. "I can't. I'm overbooked already. Helen and the girls are furious with me. And besides, you never get any rest when I'm with you. You need your rest."

She blinked, and then her eyes narrowed as if she were squinting into bright sunshine. "Why are you being so nice?"

He was alarmed by the question. "Good God, Diana."

"It just seemed strange, that's all," she said softly. "You don't have a nice bone in your body."

He tried to smile. "I'm not comfortable with it, either. So hurry and get back in top form, so I can be my nasty familiar self again."

She tried to smile with her swollen mouth. The results were painful. She got out of the car, teetered her unsteady way up the street.

Hurry, hurry, he urged her mentally. He didn't want anyone to notice how she looked or ask her if she'd been mugged. If she needed help. Or God forbid, the police.

She went up her porch steps, and entered the house without encountering anyone. He pulled out into the street and dialed a number on the dedicated cell phone he had been given at the island.

Zhoglo answered. "Dr. Mathes? Is there a problem?"

He suppressed the unfamiliar nervousness the man's baritone voice provoked in him. It was unacceptable that this man should actually intimidate him. He was beyond all that.

"Ah, unfortunately yes," he admitted. "Diana Evans, the anesthesiologist whom I had chosen for my team. She, ah . . . she—"

"Has proven to be less than worthy?" Zhoglo finished smoothly.

"She's become erratic and unpredictable," Mathes said, reluctantly. "I think that she's close to a total breakdown."

"Ah. I see. Sad. She is pretty. I saw pictures. I could have told you not to go into partnership with a woman whom you are fucking, Doctor."

Mathes swallowed down his angry response before he realized that he had done it, and was left with nothing left to say. Jaw flapping.

Maybe it was the scene at the island that intimidated him. A man could hardly be blamed for being a tad unnerved by throat-slashed, bullet-ridden corpses strewn left and right. Even Dr. Richard Mathes.

"You will be able to manage without her, I presume?" Zhoglo asked. "The team I assembled for you is adequate, no?"

"Yes," he admitted. He had not yet met the members of the secret surgical teams, all of whom were from Eastern Europe, but he had studied their CV's. All of them were superbly qualified. It made one wonder how Zhoglo had managed to hire so many fine doctors.

He had a sudden flash of the two Parisian girls, tied to the bed, throats gaping red. Nigel Dobbs, smiling cordially in the foreground.

Perhaps it was not such a mystery. All those doctors had families.

"I've given her sedatives," he said. "She should sleep for several hours today."

"Meaning that you want me to hurry up and clean up your mess for you, Doctor? By rights, you should put her down yourself."

Mathes was utterly taken aback. "I—"

"Yes, I know." Zhoglo sounded bored. "You are not competent. Such things require a specialist. I will send someone to take care of it. Is there anything more?"

Diana's mysterious double flashed through Mathes's mind, and just as quickly he dismissed it. His situation was bad enough as it was. "No."

Zhoglo waited another moment and grunted. "Very well. I am not impressed, Doctor. Your Diana is not the security risk. You are."

Mathes hurried to excuse himself, flustered. "I am sorry—"

"Do better, from now on," Zhoglo said. "I do not tolerate

failure. The effect of further failure upon your family would be . . . unfortunate."

The connection broke. Mathes let the phone drop from a hand that was numb with an emotion he barely remembered. Fear.

He'd awakened a beast by poking a stick through the bars of its cage, just for fun—only to discover that the cage door hung wide open.

Becca woke up with an odd feeling of well-being. Her body felt boneless and warm, limp. She wiggled, felt the deep ache in her groin that was beginning to feel almost normal. The feeling she always had after a mad marathon of hot, crazy sex with Nick. Wow.

Not that the sensation was unpleasant. In fact, she squeezed, flexed, stretched, savored it. Her muff hurt quite a bit less than it had the previous mornings. It would seem that she was getting in shape, sex-wise. For the first time in her life.

She reached out across the bed, found it empty. Her eyes popped open, searching for him.

There he was. And how. He sat cross-legged on the rumpled sheets of the other bed, from which he'd stripped the covers. Not a stitch of clothing. He contemplated a large-screen laptop. The screen illuminated his somber face with an eerie glow. The room was dim, lit only by the sunlight that glowed around the borders of the blackout curtains.

In the gloom, Nick looked like a naked space-age monk deep in meditation, with that supernatural focus in his eyes. His concentration was laser sharp, slicing through whatever he saw. Including herself.

His pose was outwardly relaxed, but the profound stillness of his body gave her the sense that he could explode into movement in a fraction of an instant. Explosive, volcanic emotions, hidden behind his steely façade, under constant, relentless pressure.

He was so beautiful. It was outrageous. Every detail, those smoldering dark eyes beneath the thick, straight black brows that winged straight back, the hard, sealed mouth, the sharp cliff of his cheekbones. The bumpy terrain of his nose. And his body, all that hard, slabbed, ripped complexity of his heavy musculature. He was so lean, every muscle, every tendon visible, ready and willing to do its job. Not a speck of pinchable fat on him. Which was hardly surprising, since he forgot to eat for days at a time.

Speaking of which. She was startled to realize that she'd done the same thing. Her last chance to eat had been lunchtime the day before, and she'd sacrificed that opportunity to go to the mall and buy slut lingerie. Not that she regretted it, but still. She was ravenous.

And not just for food, either. She'd developed a host of other appetites. She wanted to grab and stroke and caress every inch of that man's succulent, sinewy body. But she'd probably have to tie him down with rope to get the chance, he was so sexually aggressive.

Tying him. Hmm. The idea had merit. She started to grin. Ten to one, he wouldn't go for it, control freak that he was, but the resulting argument would be, well, stimulating. And the final outcome would be a lot of fun. She squirmed, just imagining it.

Nick sensed the intensity of her gaze and glanced over, giving her a slow smile that made a string of inner firecrackers detonate inside her. Heat, sparks, colors. Excitement, confusion, fear.

And joy. Of all things to find, in the midst of this mess. Blooming out of the wreckage of her life, like a perfect tulip in a trash heap.

"Hi," she whispered, blushing. Remembering just how many times he'd wakened her in the night, to start again. And again.

He just nodded, studying her intently. She became suddenly aware of how she must look, with wild bed head, puffy morning face, smeared makeup. A Picasso woman, with nose and mouth and eyes all scrambled up. And even so, he had that look in his eyes about which there could be no mistake. She looked away, flustered, and her eyes fell on the digital clock on the bedstand. 12:24 P.M.

Panic jangled through her, and hard on its heels, disorientation. She sought to anchor herself in this new world.

Cool it. No reason to sweat. She'd been canned. No job to be late for, no responsibilities she was neglecting, no place to go, no one who was waiting for her angrily, tapping a foot, looking at a watch.

It made her feel so lost. Adrift in nowhere. She had Carrie and Josh, of course, but she was desperately hoping to keep them at arm's length until she managed to resolve this situation. God alone knew how.

Every other point of reference in her life was gone. Except for Nick. He was a big one. Right now, he was her only one.

A dangerous state of affairs, for both of them. She must not glom onto this guy, make him her reason to exist. The danger was there. As sexy and charismatic as he was, as scared and vulnerable as she felt.

As madly in love with him as she was.

She thought of that bad moment last night, when she'd practically blurted it out. And stopped herself, with the grace and subtlety of a stampeding elephant. It was just that she was so terrified of destroying this thing before it even unfolded, before she was even sure what it was. The way she'd somehow managed to destroy all her other relationships.

Nick was so much more important than any of the others. All the more reason not to trash it by opening her big mouth too soon. Scaring him off with inappropriate demands, inconvenient emotions.

She stared at his sexy dimples. "It's late," she offered.

"You were tired," he said. "Me too. I slept more than I have in the last two months combined. Hours on end." He sounded faintly amazed as he tapped a few keys, snapped the laptop shut and slid off the bed.

Stood there before her, showing off. Inviting her to gape at his gorgeous bod. "I'm glad you're awake," he said. "I missed you."

She smothered a giggle. "Don't even look at me that way until I've had a shower."

"I don't care," he said. His penis lengthened before her eyes.

"I do," she said, scrambling out of the far side of the bed. She backed up towards the bathroom, shimmying out of the garter belt. "Plus, I'm ravenous. Don't even think about it. You sex freak."

He stared at her body, looking wistful. "Get your shower," he said. "We've got to get moving if we want time to grab something to eat."

She teetered on one leg to peel a stocking off. "What? What's our hurry? Where are we going?"

He looked embarrassed, and uncomfortable. "You're not going to believe this," he said. "I don't believe it myself."

"Just tell me," she snapped.

He lifted his hands helplessly. "We're going to a wedding."

She was so startled, she thudded against the wall and almost slid down onto her butt. "You have got to be kidding."

"I wish I was," he said. "It's one of the guys I told you about, the guys who're helping me track down the big Z. They keep inviting me to their weddings and barbecues and christenings, and Christ knows what all, and it seems ruder than shit to blow them off, since I'm mooching favors right and left. Big, expensive favors. So fuck it. We're going."

"Uh-uh. Not me," she said. "I'm not going to any weddings."

"We can stop at a mall if you need a dress," he offered. "I can blow some bucks on a couple of my cards. Or not. That suit with the tank top that you wore yesterday looked really hot. You could wear that again."

"It's not the dress. I have a nice dress," she snapped. "The one I meant to seduce you in."

His eyes lit up. "Let's see it," he said.

"Don't get sidetracked," she said, scowling at him. "I'm not going to some strange couple's wedding, and that is final."

He shook his head. "It's a done deal. Davy's wife booked us a room. She ordered me a suit from Macy's when I told her I couldn't go back to my condo. They got a guy to man the surveillance set-up who speaks Ukrainian. I'm outmaneuvered. My ass is grass if I don't go."

"That's your problem, not mine." She marched into the bathroom. "Just go without me, if you must."

He followed her in, staring at her naked body in the mirror. "Not happening." His quiet voice had a tone of finality.

Becca started feeling trapped, almost panicked. "Nick. Be reasonable. I'm not prepared to go to a wedding." Her voice rose in pitch. "I don't know these people. I just got fired from my job, I'm on the run from a sadistic mafiya killer, and I don't even have a gift!"

"That's OK. They won't care. On the plus side, it'll be a great place for us to catch our breath," Nick coaxed. "The party will be swarming with cops, ex-cops, security professionals. It'll be the safest place to go dancing in the Pacific Northwest."

She waved all that away. "It's a really bad time, Nick. I'm not presentable right now."

"Bullshit," he said. "You're gorgeous. You make my eyes hurt."

"Oh, stop it," she muttered, charmed into smiling at him in spite of herself. He was giving her that unbelievable, radiant, devastating grin. It was a fucking lethal weapon. He should be charged with carrying concealed.

"I didn't want to go either," he admitted. "Then yesterday I started to imagine how it would be to go with you." He slid his arms around her waist, pulling her back against his scorching heat. The blunt end of his phallus prodded between her thighs. "I started to think jeez, this might even be kind of fun. I've forgotten what fun felt like, if I ever knew. But to have a beautiful date who makes me sweat every time I look at her lips, or her ass, or her toenails, mmm. Big fun. Hot fun."

"Stop it," she snapped.

"Nah." He kissed the sensitive spot where her throat and shoulder joined. His breath whispered across her skin like a silk scarf. "Picture it. Dancing to a hot band, eating a fine meal, getting buzzed on expensive booze while everybody kisses and hugs and loves it up. We let everybody check you out, and then it's off to our room with the private deck and the hot tub. Champagne chilling in the ice bucket. I'll dribble it down into the hollows of your body and then lap it up for hours on end." One of his hands covered her breast, hefting it.

It did sound nice. It sounded romantic, sensual. Lighthearted.

She tried again, with less conviction. "It's just the timing—"

"It's perfect." He slid his other hand into her muff, seizing her clitoris tenderly between his index and middle finger. Kneading it, slowly circling. He was so good. Practically better than she was herself. "So wet . . . and soft . . . and ready for me. Give me this, Becca. It's not much. Just one night when I don't have to worry. One night someplace safe, where I can just relax and enjoy you. Enjoy this. And then I swear I'll be good. I'll get right back down to business."

She got the feeling he was talking to himself, from the faraway look in his eye. He grabbed her hands, and placed them on the edge of the counter, then pulled her hips back to get the angle right before he prodded the blunt bulb of his penis into her opening. They stared at each other in the mirror. She was shocked by her own face. It was so different when he turned her on, as if she were lit from inside. Her eyes were wide, pupils huge, her mouth still had the remnants of Diana's lipstick, a matte red stain on her kiss-swollen lips.

She braced herself against the sink, and pressed back eagerly to take him inside. A long, slow, stretching glide that pressed all those intensely sensitive spots that pulsed and glowed and melted around his thick shaft. He had changed her, inside and out. Her body, her mind, she didn't know if there was any separation. She'd been rewired. Pleasure no longer had to be anxiously sought or chased, or pinned down by force. With Nick, it rose up to meet him, it enveloped him, it welcomed him in its melting, pulsing clasp, it celebrated him.

It could not be kept down, could not be denied. Or controlled.

A slow, slick, pulsing slide. In, out. Their eyes were locked in the mirror. "Nick." She licked her lips. "You're not wearing a condom."

"I won't come. Just . . . a few. I meant to do just one, but it feels . . . so fucking *good*." He drove in again with a ragged groan, the jolt making her gasp, pushing her closer. In and out, in and out, slow, twisting, pumping thrusts. She shook with desperate excitement. So close to that piercing rapture. She wanted it. Now.

He stopped, rested his hot face on her shoulder, panting. She looked around at him. "Well? Get a condom. Finish what you started."

He shook his head, without looking up. She was getting alarmed. "Now, Nick. Or I won't answer for the consequences," she warned.

He dragged his cock out with a ragged gasp of effort. "Sorry, babe. I'm all out of condoms. We'll have to save it for after the party. On the deck. With the champagne. And the hot tub. I'll make it up to you."

She gasped with outrage. Teasing cheat. "You bastard! You're kidding! You can't do this to me!"

He licked sweat off her shoulder. "I'll suffer right at your side," he offered. "And my suffering is visible to the naked eye." He gestured at his engorged penis. "Everybody will know how desperate I am."

"Are you trying to make me feel sorry for you? Get out!" She shoved him out the bathroom door. "You dog! Go!"

She finally managed to shove his big body out the door and shut it. She locked it, too, on principle. She was weak in the knees, wound up like a spring. That bastard. How could he. Whipping her up into a state . . . and just leaving her there. Shaking with lust. Argh.

She showered, shampooed, and stomped out to rummage for the jeans, T-shirt and sneakers she'd packed into her suitcase. She pulled them on, without looking at Nick. Evil.

"I assume you'll be getting dressed at the lodge." She knew him well enough now to hear the steel underlying his quiet tone. "Because that's where you're going. Are you ready?"

There was no point fighting it, she thought. It was silly, resisting for resistance's sake. God knows, she had nothing better to do. And she felt a hundred times safer with Nick. Even when he drove her crazy.

"As I'll ever be," Becca said, resigned.

A quick stop at a breakfast drive-thru, and they were on the road, speeding down the highway in Nick's big predator pickup, on the way to Three Creeks Lodge. Becca stared out the window at the highway speeding by as she nibbled her ham and egg bagel. She was dazed by the unexpected U-turn her life had taken. She fished her telephone out of her bag, thinking about Carrie and Josh with a stab of uneasy guilt.

But what could she say? That she'd been fired from her job? That she was running away with a tall, dark stranger? They would just panic and get on her case, the nosy little stinkers. She'd never had much luck at teaching the two of them manners or boundaries. She'd always been a cream puff when it came to discipline. Hell, no one was perfect.

She couldn't face them yet. She would call them both tonight.

Nick drove the truck the way he did everything, balls out. Which left her nothing to do except think about her problems. She had her choice of things to stress about. Being poor again? Career shot to hell? Carrie and Josh taking you-want-fries-with-that jobs? An ugly death at the hands of a mafiya thug?

And if that wasn't enough, there was always the niggling little matter of exactly how long it had been since her last period.

She needed a distraction, fast. She looked over at Nick. "Um, do you ever talk?" she asked him. "You know . . . converse?"

"I talk all the time with you," he said guardedly. "I don't think I've ever talked so much in my life. My throat hurts from talking so much."

"Oh, really? Then why is it that I know so little about you?"

He slanted her a narrow look. "I decline to answer that question."

"Oh, really? And why is that?"

"It's a trap," he said. "I know a trap when I see one. Ask me straight questions, if you're curious. I'll answer them. If I can, that is."

"Oh, of course," she muttered. "Mr. Control Freak has got to cover his ass, at all costs."

"Stop snarking, and ask your fucking questions, already."

Now that he was actually willing to answer her, she was caught unprepared.

"Um, where did you grow up?" she ventured. Lame, but it would do.

"Waylon, Wyoming. Otherwise known as the ass end of nowhere."

"Good start," she said, cautiously approving. "And your parents?"

"Dead," he said.

She waited. "Oh," she said delicately. "I don't suppose

you could elaborate on that? Do I get to know anything other than the fact that they're dead?"

His face in profile looked clouded and sulky. "Like what?"

Becca sighed. Maybe stressing about her problems would be more restful. "Your mother, for instance," she said patiently. "How old were you when she—"

"Twelve," he said. "Breast cancer."

Becca had to look away for a minute and wait for sudden tears to ease down. She swallowed, willing them away. "That's awful," she said, thinking of the hospital bed, the bedpan, the smell of disinfectant. The constant ache of grief. "We have something in common then."

He frowned out the windshield. "How's that?"

"I lost my dad when I was twelve, too. Pancreatic cancer."

He let out a long sigh. "Sucked, didn't it?"

"Oh, yeah," she said. "Big-time."

"How about your mom?" he asked abruptly.

She was unprepared for him to take the initiative, and had to gather her composure. "Suicide, five years later," she said. "She never got over Dad. She swallowed all of his leftover pain pills one night. I found her."

He drew in a breath. "Jesus. That's bad."

"Yes, it was. And? That still leaves your father unaccounted for."

"He died twelve years ago," Nick said. "Drank himself to death. Counts as suicide. Just slower. He was one tough bastard. He ran a business in Waylon. Sold farm equipment."

She waited to see if there was more and was on the verge of changing the subject when Nick blew out a sharp breath, shaking his head. "He was a violent, evil-tempered son of a bitch," he said, his voice harsh. "I was glad when he died."

Becca was daunted. It was hard to think of a response to that declaration that was not inane or incredibly invasive.

She opted for invasive. "Did he hit you?" she asked timidly.

He shook with bitter laughter. "Oh, hell, only when he was

drunk. He tossed me through a plate glass window when I was seventeen." He touched the scar that slashed crosswise through his thick eyebrow, rubbing it as if it ached. "That was when I decided it was time to beat hell out of there. Before he killed me."

She winced. "Oh, God. That's awful."

He shrugged. "I did OK, once I left his house. Joined the Army. Got sent to the Middle East in the first Gulf war. I made MP after a few years. Suited my personality. I got a degree in criminology and Eastern European studies when I got out of the service. Then I joined the Feds. That's it. My life."

"I'm sorry," she said softly. "About your dad."

He acknowledged her words with a curt nod. "As far as crappy childhoods go, I think we're pretty much neck and neck."

"I guess so." Becca gazed at his profile, moved by what he had revealed. It explained so much about who he was. How he was.

The silence between them now felt very different. It was no longer a barrier. They were together in it. Connected by it.

"It's better in a way," he went on awkwardly. "Don't get me wrong, I'm sorry you didn't have a perfect TV childhood, but at least that means I don't have to be so embarrassed about my own."

That held true for her as well. She patted his arm with her fingertips, following the smooth nap of silken dark body hair on his forearm all the way down to his hand.

"Actually, my childhood was pretty good, until Dad got sick," she said. "And at least I have Carrie and Josh to show for it all."

"Meaning what?" he demanded. "That I win the crappy childhood contest after all?"

"Yes, but just by a nose," she told him. "I'm the runner-up."

"Great. Lucky me," he said sourly.

It seemed inappropriate to laugh even a little in the face of past tragedy, but she couldn't stop herself.

"So? Does this meet your high conversational standards?" he asked.

"Actually, it's more than I bargained for," she admitted.

He let out a harsh bark of laughter. "Tell me about it. That's how most women feel after spending time with me."

That stung her. She glared at him. "Do not lump me in with 'most women.' I am not 'most women,' thank you very much."

"You sure aren't," he said, after a thoughtful pause. "I've never talked about all this stuff with a woman before. Come to think of it, I've never talked about it to anyone. At all."

She was startled at the depth of silence and solitude that admission revealed. "Um, wow. I guess . . . I should be honored."

He shrugged. "If you like. I guess it never felt to me like date-type chitchat material. Such a downer. Big conversation stopper."

"We've never had a date, Nick."

He looked at her sidelong. "We're having one now, aren't we?"

"No," she said loftily. "Going to a wedding is not a date. Going to a wedding is much more demanding, much more public, much more committed. It's a much, *much* bigger deal than a date."

He nodded. "Yeah, well. That makes sense. You're a much bigger deal than my other women. Maybe that's why I can't pull off the charming conversation routine with you."

"Oh, really?" She squinted at him. "And what routine is that?"

His grin came and went quickly. "Oh, the usual bullshit men say. I was slick, funny, witty, suave. I would compliment them, on their perfume, their earrings, the way their asses looked in their jeans—"

"Oh, shut up, you dog." She flapped her hands at him.

"I would ask them how they felt," he went on. "I even pretended to listen to their answers."

"Calculating bastard," she muttered, punching his shoulder.

"I controlled my foul language. I was good at that gentlemanly stuff when I wanted to get laid. Before my life went down the toilet."

She frowned. "Huh. I certainly haven't seen any gentlemanly moments. I think you're a big, grumpy bear. With a potty mouth."

"I can't do the charming and suave routine with you," he said, in a wondering voice. "I just can't do it."

"Hmph," she sniffed. "I'm not sure how I feel about that. Should I take it as a compliment or an insult?"

She was joking, but he took her question at face value. "I think it's a compliment," he said. "I can't be anything but flat out real with you. Even if what's real is rude and ugly."

She opened her mouth, but nothing came out. She stared at him.

"And it's weird, because I never wanted to nail any woman the way I want to nail you," he went on. "You'd think I could control myself a little better, considering how motivated I am."

"Oh. Gee. How very romantic." She started turning pink.

He grabbed her hand, and placed it on the thick, long bulge of his erection. "Don't be sarcastic," he said. "I'm baring my soul here. Just look what happens to me when I do that."

"Your soul or your dick?" She stared down at her hand, rubbing up and down over that hard, hot bulge. Her toes curled up in her sneakers. "This is your natural state. You're always at the ready."

He closed her fingers within the hot cage of his fist, rubbing it harder over his unyielding flesh. "No, actually, this is new. I've only had this problem since I met you. You're under my skin. You drive me nuts."

"Wow. Lovely," she muttered. "I sound like a bad rash. Here comes Becca. Grab the cortisone cream."

He let out a crack of laughter. "You do inflame me, that's for sure. There's a raging fire in my loins, babe. Only you can put it out."

She hooted. "Put it out, hah! That's a joke. It never gets put out. You're like those trick birthday candles. You blow and blow and . . ." Her voice trailed off as his grin widened.

"Oh, yeah." He waggled his eyebrows with cheerful lewdness.

She blushed. "Oh, stop it. That's not what I meant."

He looked comically downcast. "It's not? Aw. Too bad."

It took a minute to gather her nerve. "Do you like, um, that?"

"Do I like what? Blow jobs?" He snorted. "I have a dick, don't I? Of course I like blow jobs. What a weird question."

"Was it?" She tried to pull her hand back, but he trapped it, lazily continuing to massage his cock with it.

"I figured you didn't like them," he said, his tone measured. "Giving them, I mean. You never suggested it. So I didn't want to push my luck. I drive it into the ground with you anyway."

"It's not that I don't like them," she confessed. "It's just that I'm not—I'm not—"

"Not what?" he snapped.

"Not very good at them." The words came out in a rush.

There was a shocked silence in the truck.

"Bullshit," he said finally. "I don't believe that for a second. You're white-hot in bed. Who told you that? The dickless wonder?"

She giggled. "Ah . . . well . . ."

"And you believed him? You would trust the judgment of a guy who would put his dick into the mouth of a carnivorous bimbo like Kaia? When he had *you*?"

"Well, uh . . ." She struggled to control her quivering voice. "I'm sure she didn't mean to—"

"But she did," he said emphatically. "You've never put a guy in the hospital by blowing him, babe, which means that pointwise, you're way ahead of Jaws."

She exploded with laughter. "Stop it," she said, waving her hand at him. "Stop being ridiculous."

"Not as long as it makes you laugh," he said. "I get off on that."

He lifted her hand off his erection and tugged it up to drop a kiss on her knuckles. Then he threaded his fingers through hers.

The simple gesture felt wonderful. She wanted to jump on him and kiss him all over, for making her feel like this. So pretty, so sexy. Desirable. Even . . . well, powerful.

It actually made her want to try that all-too-emotionally-charged sexual technique with Nick. Just to see if it would be different. Not so stiff, awkward, uncomfortable, embarrassing. He had turned the rest of her life upside down. "Do you, um, want one?" she asked, on impulse.

"A blow job? From you? Fuck, yeah," he said promptly. "How many times do I have to say it?"

She gulped. "No, I mean, ah . . . now." She blushed, furiously.

He swiveled his head, wide-eyed. "Right now? You mean literally right now? In the truck? On the road? At seventy-five an hour?"

She nodded a nervous yes. "I would. If you wanted me to."

"Are you nuts?" He looked like he was trying not to laugh. "After what happened to the dickless wonder?"

Her face went from hot pink to tomato red. "Oh, God. Sorry, then. Forget I said it."

"Like hell." The turn signal started clicking. Becca squeaked in alarm as they swerved, and juddered over the rumble strip onto an exit ramp at the last second.

He pulled off the main strip at the first hotel he came to, a long, dilapidated, one-story clapboard building. "The place is a dump," he said, yanking up the hand brake. "But I, for one, am not going to notice."

"Nick. Please. It was a dumb suggestion," she pleaded. "You don't have to be macho about this. Just ignore it and we'll—"

"No fucking way. You think I'm passing up a chance like this?"

"But—"

"It's not a dumb suggestion," he said. "It's just the setting that's wrong. I don't want to be a menace to public safety while you have my cock in your mouth. To say nothing of your safety. And my cock's safety. Call me a pussy if you want, but I just don't have that kind of nerve."

"Uh, believe me. I'm not going to call you that. Ever. But I think you're overestimating my abilities," she said. "I'm not, you know, Mata Hari, or anything."

"And you're underestimating your power to turn me on," he said. "It's hard enough to keep my eyes on the road when you're just sitting next to me, giving me a hard time. Imagine if you were sucking my cock. I'd go straight into a lane of oncoming traffic."

"Uh—"

"You wait here. I'll get us a room. This place probably rents by the hour, for cash." He jumped out of the truck and loped into the office.

She buried her face in her hands, shaking with laughter and nerves. That clown. He was doing it again, laying on his own special brand of rough, in-your-face charm that she found utterly irresistible.

He was out again in no time at all, yanking open her door. The urgency in his grip, the anticipation in his eyes, sent her into a tizzy of performance anxiety. Why did she do this to herself? She should have just gone for him some night when they were fooling around, and experimented with oral sex, spontaneously, lightheartedly. Without all the build-up and the fanfare and hoo hah.

Too late now. Her feet barely hit the ground, he was dragging her down the cracked, buckled concrete walkway so fast.

"Nick, please. Just keep in mind, it's not like I'm this big expert," she babbled. "The truth is, I've hardly ever—"

He swung her around, and she bumped up against the door. He shoved the key into the knob lock, and leaned down to kiss her, a long, clinging, sweet kiss that left her dazzled.

He lifted his head, gazed into her eyes. "A few pointers," he said.

She blinked at him, bit her lip. "I'm listening," she whispered.

"Simple." He held up a finger. "One. Enthusiasm. Two. Be gentle, but not too gentle. Three. Use your hands. Four, the more spit, the better. Five, no moving motor vehicles. Last, but not least—no teeth. Other than that, anything goes."

He turned the key in the lock and pushed her inside.

Chapter
23

Nick had a bad moment when he looked around the hotel room. Cramped, stale-smoke-smelling, funky carpet, fake, peeling wood paneling, water-stained ceiling. Squalid.

But they wouldn't be there long enough for it to matter. They weren't even going to use that sagging, sad-looking bed.

"Talk about atmosphere," he said. "This place is steeped in the vibe of illicit sex. We might be the first licit sex this room has ever seen."

Her eyes did that sparkling thing they did when she smiled. "What's licit sex?"

He thought about it for a second. "Nobody paid, nobody betrayed."

She nodded, and they stared at each other for an awkward moment. Becca's face turned pink.

"Um, so, where does one begin?" she asked. "I mean, shall we just get right to it? Or would you like, you know, a lead in? What do guys prefer, anyhow? I've never actually asked one."

His grin spread helplessly over his face. This was going to be fun, watching her flail around, clueless. She was so fucking cute.

"I mean, how would you like me to . . . should I undress?" she demanded. "Damn it, Nick, stop smirking at me like that!"

"I'm sorry," he said. "I can't help it. I love to watch you stammer and get all flustered. The clueless virgin act really turns me on."

"What a surprise," she snapped. "Like, what doesn't turn you on, Nick? It's a simple yes or no question. Dressed or undressed?"

"Think about it. Maybe you can figure it out for yourself. A guy's cock is harder than a railroad spike. What's better? Getting it sucked by a gorgeous chick who's wearing jeans and a T-shirt? Or getting it sucked by a gorgeous chick who's bare-ass naked? Huh. Tough call."

"I see," she murmured. "You don't have to be sarcastic—"

"Round ass cheeks," he went on dreamily. "Silky white thighs. Big, soft, jiggling tits with tight nipples just begging to be licked and sucked. And that hot pussy is the best part—"

"OK! I get the picture! You've made your point! Stop grinning at me like that. If you piss me off, I'll change my mind."

He felt the grin on his face go hard and predatory. "Uh-uh," he said softly. "You're not leaving this room until I get what I want."

She rolled her eyes. "Here we go again with the sexual power-tripping, hmm? Nick, the master of all that he surveys."

"Hell, yeah. I do my best. I have to overcompensate like hell, since most of it rolls right off your back. Otherwise you'd steamroll over me."

"Oh, yeah. Right," she snapped. She yanked off her glasses, and started taking off her clothes without ceremony, but her matter-of-fact striptease had its usual effect. It made him sweaty-palmed, breathless, to watch her kick off the sneakers, shimmy out of her jeans, peel off the T-shirt, unhook the bra, pull down the panties. He unbuckled his jeans and shoved them down far enough to free his cock, which sprang up to bounce and sway like it was spring-loaded. He stroked it idly in his hands and waited for her to make another move. Her show, her call.

"Aren't you going to take off your clothes?" she asked.

He shook his head. "No," he said softly. "Me clothed, you naked. Me on my feet, you kneeling."

She harrumphed, crossing her arms over her lush tits. "What is this, some male domination fantasy of yours?"

"What if it is?" he asked. "Anything wrong with that?"

She didn't have a ready answer for that one and he pressed his advantage. "You'll get your turn," he assured her. "I'll kneel before you naked and put my tongue up the imperial pussy for as long as you want. Hours, days. You'll have to kick me away to make me stop."

"That's not the same thing," she said primly.

"Why not?" he snapped.

"Because you're a man," she said as if it were obvious.

He snorted. "So I should hope. Stop your stalling." He yanked the coverlet and the puffy synthetic blanket off the bed, folded them and tossed them onto the floor. "For your knees," he explained.

"Ah," she murmured. "How thoughtful of you." She reached out, curling her smooth, cool fingers around his cock. "You're burning hot."

"Oh, yeah. One more thing," he said. "That lipstick. The stuff you lifted off the mafiya mistress. The slut red. You got that stuff with you?"

Her gorgeous lips twitched. "In my purse," she said demurely.

"Put some on," he said.

"Of course. I'm ashamed I didn't think of it myself." She grabbed her purse from the bed, rummaging through it till she found the silver tube. Then she turned to the stained, dim-looking mirror, and peeked at him mischievously as she put the stuff on.

He wished he was a photographer who could catch that moment forever. Her gorgeous ass stuck out, legs parted for his viewing pleasure so that he could see just a shadowy glimpse of her cunt. Her front reflected in the mirror, tits swaying, dawning wonder in her eyes. Mouth pursed up as she painted herself with painstaking slowness. Dragging it out.

And him, in the background, clutching his dick in his hand. His eyes looked like staring holes in his stark face. He looked desperate.

Power tripping, hell. He was helpless, pleading, at her mercy. In the palm of her slender hand. The only place on earth he wanted to be.

He had to toughen up. Keep up his macho dominator schtick, if he could swing it. Melting down into molten slop for her was not a turn-on. Not a confidence builder. Not if he wanted to keep things light.

No "I love you's." He'd learned his lesson the night before.

She looked back over her shoulder and gave him a hot red smile. "You like this color?"

"Yeah," he rasped. "I think that color would look really great around the base of my dick."

It was a risk, but he knew it had paid off when her nose wrinkled up and he heard the telltale snuffle of suppressed giggles. "Pig," she muttered, tossing the lipstick in the general direction of her purse.

She grabbed his cock as she sank to her knees, and oh, man. He was a goner. As usual, everything was different with Becca.

Including himself. He liked it. The fun, the teasing, the arguing. His face felt strange these days. It actually ached from smiling so much.

She rubbed the head of his cock against her hot, cloud-soft cheek, and flashed him a teasing look. "Does this remind you of something?"

She puntuated her question with a swipe of her pink tongue along the slit on his cock head that oozed clear, slippery drops of precome. She licked it up, swirling her tongue round his glans.

He struggled to remember what the hell she'd said. "Huh? Remind me of what? I can't think straight when you're doing that."

"The night we met. Remember? Me naked, you clothed?"

He grinned. "You bet I remember. Me on my feet, you on your knees." His breath hissing through his teeth in a shocked gasp of pleasure as she lapped up one side of his shaft, twisted around the glans again and swiped down the other side.

"So strange," she murmured, between voluptuous strokes of her tongue. "It was like I was split in two. One part thinking, God, he is the most gorgeous thing I've ever seen . . ." She took time out to flutter her tongue flirtatiously against the taut pucker of flesh on the underside of his cock head. "The other part thinking, this guy is going to kill me."

He shook with a burst of silent laughter. "Same here."

She rolled her eyes. "Oh, yeah, I'm so sure," she scoffed. "As if I could be so scary, buck naked and dripping wet."

His laughter shocked off as she did something totally amazing with her tongue, fluttering it underneath and around while she worked the base of his cock with her hands. "Oh, you were plenty scary," he told her. "I thought I was meat. I thought Zhoglo'd sent you."

That jolted her so much, she took her mouth away from that excellent thing she'd been doing with her tongue against his cock head.

Not a desirable outcome. He should have kept his goddamn mouth shut. But it was his own fault. Served him right, for falling ass over head for a talkative woman.

"No way!" she breathed. "Zhoglo? *Me?*"

"I thought, oh, shit, they're onto me," he confessed. "I thought, either you were a black widow assassin sent to fuck me and kill me, or else you were a call girl sent to fuck me and distract me so that somebody else could kill me. Either way, I was dead meat. I was consoled only by the fact that either way I also got to fuck you. Split-second response. Couldn't call it thinking."

"Oh, my God," she whispered.

"Then I looked at your bare-ass naked perfect dripping body, and all I could think was, wow. What a way to go," he concluded.

"You thought that I could be a call girl? Or an *assassin?*" Her voice squeaked till it broke. "A milquetoast wuss like me? Puh-leeze."

"Yeah, well," he said, "I know exactly what to do with an assassin or a call girl. I had no fucking clue what to do with you."

She snickered. "Oh, you improvised well enough, as I recall."

He ignored her, cupped her jaw and stared intently down into her beautiful upturned face as he struggled to frame the thought in words.

"You are so much more than I bargained for," he said slowly. "You are like, the secret weapon, sweetheart. You take me to pieces."

Her giggles stopped, the smile faded to a somber gaze, and she covered his hands with her own. She kissed both his palms, grabbed his cock and brought it to her mouth. And oh, sweet Jesus.

He would never survive pleasure of this intensity.

He'd had lots of blow jobs in his life. He'd started young, and never lacked for opportunities. He loved the lazy luxury of them, the feeling of godlike power, the wallowing in carnal bliss. Throwing his head back and just enjoying the sensation of a woman's hot mouth sucking on his swollen cock until he exploded. It was one of those perennially dependable things like pizza. Even when it was bad, it was good.

True to form, with Becca, it was different. New world,

new rules. She was honey sweet, red hot, a wildcat. He'd been with women with lots more experience and sheer technical expertise, but he'd never felt a woman go down on him as if she—

Loved him.

Whoa. No. Don't go there. Not even in the privacy of his own mind. Shudders racked him, pleasure and terror in equal measure. He forgot all about godlike power, about power-tripping sex games. He just struggled to stay on his feet before this onslaught of selfless, ardent generosity. It humbled him, made him want to fall to his knees.

Her lush mouth moved over him, her strong hands twisted sensuously around the root while she laved the crown and sucked him in, deeper and deeper. So deep, for a clueless novice. And that agonizing . . . slow . . . swirl on every in-stroke, the deep hungry pull of suction, friction on every out-stroke, and again, and again, and *again. Yes.*

He couldn't hold back, couldn't slow down. With the volcanic force gathering, it was too damn soon, but that was just too damn bad—

He wound his fingers through her hair and shouted, hoarsely. Spasms of violent pleasure wrenched through him.

He was kind of surprised, some time later, to find that he was sitting on the bed. Good thing it had been right behind his knees, or he'd be flat on his ass. He was hobbled by the jeans that Becca at some point had jerked halfway down his thighs. His torso was collapsed over her body. Her head was cradled on his lap, her warm lips kissing his thigh. His cock, still long but finally softened, was nestled tenderly in her damp hand. Spent, home safe and happy. He couldn't stop making that sobbing sound with every breath he sucked into his lungs.

He didn't dare even look at her until it eased down, and that took what felt like forever. A dark, hot forever of nuzzling, of cuddling, wordless closeness, skin on skin. He never wanted it to end.

But everything had to end. Everything had to be let go.

He forced himself to sit upright. Every muscle in his body shook. He was soft and limp. Weak with pleasure, wet with sweat. Speechless.

Becca smiled at him as she raised her head. She wiped her mouth, and stroked her fingers through the wiry tuft of dark hair that curled around the base of his cock. "You know what? You were right," she said, in a tone of discovery.

He cleared his throat. "About what?" he asked cautiously.

"This color," she said, lifting his cock to the side to show him the smears of lipstick she'd left on it. "Slut red. It does look good on you."

He started to laugh, helplessly. The laughter dissolved almost instantly into something else. Something that he was afraid to face.

All he could do was just grab her again, hide his face in her hair.

Her slender arms slid around his ribs and gripped him. Holding him as tightly as he needed to be held. They strained, fighting to pull the other closer, hold the other tighter.

Muscles shaking with the effort of becoming a single being.

The Vor was intensely irritated.

He jerked his chin in the direction of his coffee cup, but it took Kristoff ten seconds to catch on, and then the man fumbled, slopping coffee dangerously close to Zhoglo's snowy cuff. If the coffee had spattered one centimeter closer, Kristoff would be dead.

Or perhaps not. His ranks of useful and experienced men had been decimated by Solokov's bloody spree on Frakes Island. He could not afford to kill any more out of pique. Too much work to be done, now that the thrill junkie surgeon was creating extra work.

Idiot, to involve his half-witted mistress in his business schemes.

He stared at the weekly schedule laid out on his laptop. The secret clinic was now fully operational, the doctors comfortably settled into their new homes, ready and waiting for the call. Each one of them was firmly in his grip, pinned by a complicated web of threats and promises. Fear and greed, the great motivators of humankind.

He should have brought more men, he fretted. Perhaps he should contract out the anesthesiologist's demise. They were being watched from God knew which angles and directions. Anyone who left the house would be seen, and followed.

Then again, it would be a very easy hit. The woman lived alone, in a single home surrounded by foliage. If Mathes was correct, she should be in a drugged sleep. No intelligence was required for this.

He cast an appraising eye on Pavel, and dismissed him out of hand. Pavel would have to be put down soon. Until that moment, he required close watching. But it seemed a shame not to delay the mercy blow until Pavel's punishment reached its grand climax. Zhoglo was always curious to see how people came apart in extremis. It was like watching a scientific experiment. This chemical, plus that, created such and such a reaction. Add heat, add pressure . . . ah, fascinating.

It had destroyed Pavel. His haggard face was dull, vacant.

Zhoglo stirred more cream into his freshened coffee, and toyed for a moment with the thought of lifting the sword that hung over the man's neck. Letting little Sasha live. He could be merciful. Theoretically.

Then he thought of the bodies Solokov had left behind on the island, and hardened his resolve. Going back on his word would undermine his authority with the other men. Besides, Mathes had found profitable homes for everything Sasha's scrawny little body had to offer, right down to the boy's corneas. It satisfied Zhoglo's penchant for thriftiness. And the fees added up to a handsome total.

He could hardly wait to observe the debut harvest, scheduled for tomorrow night. Sergei's girl. Finally. It would be fascinating to watch.

But back to business. Kristoff, no. Too stupid. Perhaps he should kill the man after all, just so he wouldn't have to look at him. Mikhail, perhaps. Zhoglo observed the new man, Mikhail, who had done the hacking for him. He had a scholarly look, but beneath it, an air of chill competence. "Mikhail, have you been observing the activity outside?"

"A worker from a utility company up the telephone pole at five A.M.," Mikhail said promptly. "And two new vehicles are parked on the block, none of the license plates corresponding to residences on this street. I assume cameras are trained on the house, but unless I approach them to sweep for radio signals, I cannot confirm—"

"And have them know we know?" Zhoglo snapped. "Don't be thick."

Mikhail subsided, mouth tightening.

"We have that meeting with Dahler on Monday," Pavel said dully. "We cannot go forward with that meeting with this security breach."

Zhoglo turned unbelieving eyes on the man. After all this, the fool dared to critizice his Vor's judgment. The look pierced even Pavel's apathy. His eyes dropped to the carpet.

"Ironic, to hear you voice concern about security, Pavel, since your incompetence was what caused this necessity. We will relocate soon. When the trap is baited."

"Vor, it is dangerous to—"

"I must have Solokov." Zhoglo's voice smashed down on the other man's words like a club. "I want to crush his beating heart in my hand."

Pavel shut up, and turned to stare out the window.

Zhoglo clicked on his mouse, and activated the monitor mounted on the wall. Several windows were open, each showing a different location. One showed a flicker of movement.

He clicked to enlarge it, until the image filled the entire screen. The garden apartment downstairs, where Rebecca Cattrell's lusty young brother Joshua was fornicating enthusiastically, dog style, with the beautiful prostitute, Nadia. It had been so easy, reeling him in. Though not, perhaps, for Nadia. The boy's stamina was incredible. Well into day number two, and they had barely stopped to sleep. Ah, youth.

The men in the room all watched with rapt attention. Nadia swayed back to meet the boy's vigorous thrusts, hair and breasts swinging, mouth open with gasping wails of simulated pleasure.

"You are recording this, are you not?" he asked Mikhail.

"Certainly, Vor," Mikhail assured him.

Nadia looked over her shoulder, said something to the boy. He pulled out, and sprawled on the bed with an obliging grin. Nadia gripped his stiff penis, swung her leg over him, and inserted him into her perfectly shaven, delicate pink genitalia with practiced skill.

She flung her head back, tossed her hair and smiled for the camera as her hips pulsed rhythmically over the boy's long, lanky body.

Watching the girl perform soothed Zhoglo's ruffled temper. Perhaps he would sample her charms himself. The subtleties of her art were wasted on that gangling boy. But Joshua would serve his purpose, before he was broken down for parts.

Bait. When Zhoglo wished, Rebecca would come running.

And her lover would follow her.

Nick was a good dancer. Becca wasn't sure why she found that so surprising. Ballroom dancing seemed so lighthearted a skill for a basically grim guy, but sheesh, he was smiling today and that affected her even more than the admittedly excellent champagne. It was dizzy, madcap fun, being swirled and dipped, spun and yanked smoothly back into the confident grip of his hands. He led with such graceful self-confidence, she'd even managed to relax and follow him without stumbling too often. Which said a great deal for his ability, since she'd certainly never had the leisure to acquire a nonessential skill like dancing. She just faked it and hoped for the best.

And Nick, coincidentally, was the best.

"Where did you learn to dance?" she asked him, when a slow dance had them swaying in a breathlessly tight clinch.

He grinned. "The military. Lost a bet once. Had to take a ballroom dancing course as a penalty. Found out I liked it. Or maybe it was the teacher I liked. She was this cute little blonde who explained to me that dancing was just like sex. That made a big impression on me."

"I can well imagine," she said sourly. "And did she do a demonstration, for comparison purposes?"

His grin widened. "Do you really want an honest answer to that question?"

She opened her mouth to reply, and he cut her off with a slow kiss that turned her knees to pudding, right out in front of that crowd.

Weddings were dangerous. Becca had realized that as soon as she saw the look on the groom's face as his bride came up the aisle on her father's arm. Sean McCloud's face literally shone with happiness.

It made her eyes fog up and her throat turn hot and tight, and her chest ache with longing she was afraid to define. All the stuff that seemed so far beyond her reach. Love. Rootedness. A real home. Babies. Weddings brought all those sad, silly dreams up to the surface.

The service had been brief and beautiful. While the bride and groom exchanged rings, Nick's hand slid beneath her own, and his fingers threaded through hers. It made her heart thud, and her face flame hot with emotion. How did she dare interpret that gesture?

No. Don't even. She couldn't afford to make silly assumptions. Life was too uncertain. He probably just didn't like to hear her crying.

She'd sniffed the tears back, gritted her teeth and clutched Nick's strong hand, hard, so he couldn't change his mind and pull it back.

The bride and groom's passionate kiss released the tension. The room exploded in a storm of hoots, whistles and wild applause. Nick turned to her and gave her a hungry, possessive kiss, like he was staking his claim, in front of everyone.

God, it was enough to make a girl dizzy. Confused. Dangerously hopeful. The handholding, the jealous grip around her waist, the way he introduced her to everybody as his girlfriend . . . wow. To think that she, Busy Becca with the glasses and the to-do lists, was this hot, sexy, mysterious guy's girlfriend. It seemed so wonderfully improbable.

The party had been great, just as Nick had said. The food was great, the wine was wonderful, the music was blazing hot, and his friends were all so nice to her. Everybody had made such a big fuss.

The band ended their set, and the DJ put on some interim music as the catering staff began distributing the plates of wedding cake. Nick escorted her back to their table and pulled out her chair.

"Gotta go check the surveillance set-up," he murmured into her ear. "Save me a piece of cake, babe." And off he went. Becca ran her eye hastily over the other occupants of the table, trying to remember their names. The black-haired guy with the wicked grin was Seth, the willowy silver blond with him was his wife Raine. Margot was collapsed in her chair looking exhausted, and no wonder, with that enormous pregnant belly of hers. The hunky blond guy hovering anxiously over her was Davy, one of the brothers of the equally hunky blond groom.

In fact, she'd never seen such a high concentration of good-looking people in one room in her entire life. Eye candy everywhere.

Then there was the pretty brunette, Erin, who had an adorable baby she was discreetly preparing to nurse under her midnight blue shawl, while her husband Connor looked on adoringly.

She met Margot's eyes. The woman was smiling at her, like a soft-eyed madonna. "You're really good for him," she said quietly. "I've never seen Nick smile like that. He was even laughing. It's incredible."

Becca blushed. "Oh, yeah. If there's one thing I'm good for, it's comic relief."

"Uh-uh," the silver blonde named Raine said. "He's head over heels. And about time. We were all starting to worry. We've been trying to fix him up with our single girlfriends for years, but nothing stuck."

Becca felt vaguely panicked, as if their easy assumptions about a happy ending could somehow jinx her dawning hopes. "Oh, no, we just met," she said. "It's not—I mean, we haven't—we're definitely not, um, stuck. Yet."

"Oh, no," Seth said, chortling. "Not stuck. Just locking lips every ten seconds. And for what? To confuse us? For the record, it's working."

"Margot. I'm hurt. Why didn't you seat me at the love-birds' table? The one with Nikolai's new little friend?"

Becca turned at the sound of that husky, sensual alto voice. It was a woman she'd noticed in the bridal party. A spectacular beauty with a corona of braided dark hair and tilted golden eyes, resplendent in a bronze taffeta evening dress trimmed with dangling jet beads.

"Because I didn't want you to scare her to death and put her off us all forever," Margot said, in a warning tone. "Be nice, Tam."

"Bullshit. If she can handle that foul-mouthed lout Nikolai, she can handle me." The woman named Tam pulled out Nick's chair and sank down next to Becca, with a whispering rustle of full skirts. She gave Becca a slow and not particularly friendly once-over.

Becca shrank back. Her simple bias-cut dress in dusty pink was very pretty, particularly with the aggressive way that her new bustier propped up her boobs, but the outfit was no match for the other woman's Marie Antoinette splendor.

Tam reached out, and plucked the spaghetti strap of Becca's gown. "Nice dress," she said. "Good color for you and it showcases your breasts. But those glasses are harsh for a pretty pink flower like you. And someone has to break it to you, honey. When you're wearing cool-toned pink, don't go for hot-red lipstick. It hurts the eyes."

Becca's hairs prickled. She resisted the impulse to cover her slut-red mouth with her hand. "I'm not a flower," she said in a very clear voice. "And what a lucky thing it is for us both that I don't need your approval."

Tam froze for a moment. She blinked. A slow smile curved her perfect mocha-painted mouth. "I was hoping you'd have backbone, just to make things more interesting," she said. "You'll need all of it to wrangle that man into shape. No woman's ever succeeded so far."

"Good. That's just as well," Becca said loftily. "I actually prefer to be the first. That way I can break him in properly."

Seth, Davy and Connor all coughed and sputtered into their coffee. Tam applauded slowly. "Ah. That's the spirit. I'm starting to see why Nikolai lost his head. The dewy green eyes that go blink blink, the big bouncing tits, the alabaster skin. Laid out naked on Zhoglo's altar."

Blood drained from Becca's face, and the warmth from her body disappeared into an invisible sinkhole, leaving her ice cold and shivering with fear, to hear that name invoked here.

"What do you know about that?" she whispered.

Tam smiled, and chucked Becca under the chin. "Ah, sweetheart," she murmured. "I know everything."

An uncomfortable silence followed, and after a few teeth-grinding seconds of it, Seth clapped his hands together heartily. "Uh, well, then. Moving right along. Raine made me promise not to ask any questions about that crazy shit, but since Tam's already broken the ice—"

"Seth!" Raine said, in a warning tone. "I meant what I said."

"But I want more details!" Seth complained. "Nick just gave us bare bones, and I mean, white, bleached, dry as dust bones. Tight-lipped son of a bitch. Mr. Monosyllable. It breaks my balls."

Becca floundered for a moment. "Ah, well, maybe after some more time has gone by," she hedged. "It's not something I want to dwell on."

Not while she was on the man's hit list, that was for sure.

"What did I tell you?" Raine tapped her husband's chest with an admonishing finger. "Jerk. Now you pay the penalty."

"Oh, no!" Seth turned a comically sad face Becca's way. "She's boycotting my second favorite sexual activity for a week!"

Becca held back giggles. "Oh, dear. That's terrible. What will you do?"

"Oh, I'll live," he assured her. "There's always my first favorite activity to fall back on, and there's nothing I love more than—ow!" He turned to Raine, looking hurt. "Hey! Those stiletto heels are sharp!"

Raine shot Becca a sidelong, embarrassed smile. "Sorry about that," she said. "He's a wild animal. I told him not to bug you about it. I can well imagine why you wouldn't want to talk about Zhoglo."

"Don't." Nick's adamant voice cut across Raine's and silenced everyone at the table. "Don't mention his name. He might hear you."

Everyone turned to look at Nick, who was staring down at Tam, slit-eyed.

"So what's Milla up to?" Davy asked quietly.

Nick shrugged. Tam smiled coolly back at him. "Plying her trade," he said. "Nothing out of the ordinary. Hey, Tam."

"Nikolai," she cooed. "At last we meet. You've been avoiding me like a pro all day. And here I was, dying to meet the virgin sacrifice."

"Yeah? Were you?" His jaw was taut. "And?"

"She's absolutely succulent," Tam said. "I congratulate you on your lovely acquisition. So my confidence was not betrayed in vain, hm? And my contact was not put in mortal danger for nothing. At least you're finally getting properly laid. There's an up side to everything, eh?"

Becca leaped to her feet. "It wasn't his fault that I showed up and ruined everything! So you can just back off, lady!"

Her voice rang loud enough so that people from the other tables started to look around, intrigued. Nick gave her a startled look.

"Lay off, Tam," Erin said, her face somber as she cuddled her suckling baby. "Don't be a horrible bitch."

"Sorry, Erin. Face reality. Unfortunately, I *am* a horrible bitch," was Tam's crisp rejoinder. "Let him defend himself. Our Nikolai, the constant fuck-up. You'll see what I mean, honey, when that inevitable day comes that you're on the receiving end of one of his big, fat, mortal errors. If you live long enough to realize what happened, that is."

Becca bristled. "He is not a fuck-up!"

"No?" Tam's crack of laughter had a brittle edge to it, like broken glass. "Ask him to tell you about Novak sometime."

Davy's chair scraped as he rose to his feet and glowered down at her. "Goddamnit, Tam. Leave, if you can't bring yourself to be civil."

"Civil?" Tam snorted. "Civility is just the denial of reality. I'm very bad at denying reality. I suppose that's why I tend to be unpopular."

Becca grabbed Nick's hand. It was stiff and unresponsive.

The look on his face made her stomach clench. The man she'd been kissing and laughing with and dancing with was gone. His face was pale and his eyes had that dead flatness they'd had during the very worst moments of their deadly adventure this weekend.

She hated to see him like that. All the life drained out of his beautiful face, grim, iron-jawed endurance in its place.

"I think it's time for us to take a break," she said, to the table at large. "It was a fabulous party. Thank you for being so welcoming and sweet to me. It was great to meet you all." She shot a cold glance at Tam. "Except for you." She grabbed Nick's hand. "Come on, Nick."

He followed her like an automaton.

Chapter
24

Nick allowed himself to be towed along. His limbs felt stiff.

He was a fool for giving in to it. Letting himself go, getting mushy and mellow. After a lifetime of training, he oughta know better.

Well, hell. He was used to being a disappointment, after seeing that look on his father's face for years.

There was a trick to surviving it. You just had to not give a shit.

He'd mastered that trick with his father, though it had taken years of practice to get it right. But it was entirely a different proposition to do it with Becca.

They'd reached the room. He stood, passively, while Becca dug for her key in her tiny pink purse. He felt her soft hands at the small of his back, herding him into the big, comfortable room. It was still in wild disarray from the frantic speed with which they'd dressed when they arrived. They'd run late, on account of that transcendental blow job.

He sank down on to the bed, which was covered with discarded clothes. His back to her. His eyes fell on the ice bucket, the champagne.

God. He covered his eyes, gut churning. So much for that.

Becca waited a couple of minutes and then started in on him, an edge of frustration in her voice. "Nick? Do you want to tell me what the hell that was all about?"

"No," he said.

She let out a sharp, angry sigh, and came around the bed, facing him. One high-heeled foot tapped with nervous energy, her hands were on hips, legs apart. Ready to give him hell. He braced himself.

"All right. I guess I phrased that wrong," she said, her voice sharp with anger. "Let me try it again. Nick, what the *hell* was that all about?"

He tried to shrug, but his shoulders felt too heavy to lift. "It's about facing reality."

She stomped her foot. "Don't you dare get cryptic and inscrutable on me, mister, or I'll kick your ass."

That jolted an unwilling smile out of him. "Get in line," he said. "Take a number. The whole world wants to kick my ass. Why should you be any different?"

"Stop it," she snapped. She gave his chest an angry shove. "Feeling sorry for yourself will not help. Now tell me what she was referring to, because I will not be left hanging while you glower and sulk. Out with it. Who's this . . . what's the name? Novak?"

He let out a careful, measured breath, and tightened all his muscles against the ache of impending loss. "Kurt Novak. He was a Zhoglo clone," he said dully. "Hungarian mob family."

He took a deep breath, sucked it up, and told her the whole sorry, miserable tale of how he'd fucked Connor over left, right, and sideways in the Novak debacle.

He kept his head down for a while after. Unwilling to meet her eyes and face what he was sure would be there. She didn't say a word.

Finally he couldn't stand the suspense any longer. He looked up.

Becca's angry, belligerent pose was gone. She gazed at him, her head cocked at a thoughtful angle. Faintly puzzled.

"Is that all?" she asked.

An ugly laugh ripped through his throat. "All? Fuck, isn't that enough for you?"

"Not really," she said. "I mean, yes, it's a terrible story, and I'm so glad it turned out well, but I don't see where your great sin was."

"He was my friend," he snarled.

"Well, of course," she said. "So you made a mistake. It must have hurt you terribly, and I'm very sorry for that, but it turned out well in the end, so what's the big—"

"People are dead and rotting in the ground because of my mistakes!"

She flinched at the violence in his tone. "Are you talking about that other thing now?" she asked, her voice cautious. "That cop in the Ukraine who died because of the security leak? The one whose daughter disappeared? Um . . . Nick? You were not the security leak."

He shot to his feet, and headed towards the door. "Fuck," he hissed. "There's a reason why I don't have conversations like this—"

"Oh, no. No way." She darted between him and the door. "Don't you dare storm off in a huff before I've made my point. In the Novak thing, you were deceived. In the Ukraine thing, you were betrayed. Deceiving, betraying, those things are sins, and they are hateful and evil, yes, no question about it. Being deceived, being betrayed, these are mistakes, Nick. These are bad breaks. Big, big difference!"

"No, there isn't!" he yelled. "I should have known better! I should have figured it out, and—"

"Well, you're not God! Too bad!" she yelled back. "And neither are any of the rest of us! Get the hell over it! I'm sick of your histrionics!"

"Don't try to put a sparkly positive spin on this, babe." His voice was low and vicious. "What counts are results.

You have to draw your ultimate conclusions from results. That's called facing reality."

She stubbornly shook her head. "Strike out 'sparkly positive spin,' and replace it with 'the voice of sweet reason.' Besides, nobody around here seems to hold it against you, except for that bitch Tam. And you yourself, of course."

He made a derisive sound. "Oh, yeah. You can bet they haven't forgotten it for one instant, sweetheart."

"Nick. News flash." Her tone was sarcastic. "They invite you to their weddings. Hello? People do not invite people they don't like to their weddings, unless you're talking about rich uncles with oil wells. Weddings are expensive, they're personal, they're important. So face reality, OK? Your friends care about you. Deal with it!"

He shook his head, and sank down onto the bed again, resting his aching head in his hands. "I don't know," he said dully. "I just don't fucking know. I'm always waiting for the other shoe to drop. Always."

"The other shoe? What are you talking about?"

"My next mistake. The ultimate fuckup. When they finally get a clue. It always happens, sooner or later. When they're disappointed."

He forced himself to look up minutes later, tormented by the silence. And he wished he hadn't.

Becca's eyes swam with tears. She wiped them away, and flung her head back, sniffing aggressively. "You think I'm going to be disappointed, too. Don't you?"

She was demanding the truth and he didn't dare respond.

Christ, he had to get real. Every woman he'd ever been remotely involved with had been ultimately disappointed by him. There was no reason to think that this time would be any different. How could it be?

But neither did he want to cut it short by saying as much. He would take what he could get for as long as he could get it.

A yes would be a pathetic, doglike whine for reassurance.

A no was a lie that would jinx his sorry ass for sure. There was no good answer for her.

"Just forget I said it," he muttered. "Please."

"No," she said. She wiped her eyes with her fingers, sniffing hard. "I will not forget it. Don't ask me to. It doesn't work that way."

"Let's just drop it, OK? I can't deal with—"

"I am *alive* because of you, Nick!" Her voice came through the gurgle of tears with startling force. "You saved me! You were doing a brave, heroic thing in the first place, and you put it aside when I showed up and did another brave, heroic thing, for me! How's that for results, buddy? You're the reason I'm not dead!"

"Yet," he cut in harshly. "The vote's not in on that."

"Well, my vote is already cast, no matter how this turns out!" she snapped. "And my vote counts, goddamnit! Is that clear?"

The blaze of righteous fury from her cowed him as much as it dazzled him. God, she was pretty. "Uh, yeah," he muttered. "Whatever."

She harrumphed. "Good," she said, after a moment, mollified.

He sat there, stupefied to realize that he actually did feel a little bit better. It probably didn't run too deep, and it probably wouldn't last too long, but hey. He would take what he could get and be grateful.

Besides. Getting bitched out by a girl in a low-cut dress whose tits bounced seductively every time her chest heaved had its positive side.

Then she kicked off her shoes, sat down on the chair, and hiked her skirt up so he could see the strip of pale skin above her stockings. She unhooked her garter, and started slowly, sensuously pulling her stockings off. His heart rate kicked up.

So did another part of his anatomy.

* * *

Becca's hands shook with the effort to maintain the appearance of cool nonchalance. She wasn't sure exactly what she was getting into, coming on to him when his mood was so unstable.

But if sweet reason wouldn't do the job, hot pounding sex might.

"What's with the striptease, Becca?" he asked, his voice hard. "Do you want to have sex?"

She shrugged with feigned indifference, moved on to the other stocking. "I don't know. Have you finished sulking yet?"

"I could maybe put it aside for long enough to fuck you," he said.

"Hmmph," she sniffed. She twitched down first one spaghetti strap, and then the other, and reached back, struggling for the zipper. "Does this mean your grumpy mood is going to crash right back down on me right after you come? Because you know damn well I hate that."

"Anybody's guess," was his bland rejoinder. "No guarantees."

"I will, of course, stick pins under your fingernails if you do that to me again," she informed him.

His mouth twitched. "Yeah? You got pins in your bag?"

"Oh, yes. My handy-dandy portable torture kit is always at the ready," she assured him. He looked like he was trying not to smile, which was already a victory, so she swiftly followed up her advantage with a slow, hip-swaying walk towards him. She turned her back.

"Unzip me," she ordered.

He did, and his hands fastened over her, so hot and buzzing with delicious energy that sent shivers racing through her, his fingers closely following the slow slide of the fabric down over her hips, bringing every tiny hair on her body to attention. His lips pressed against her back, moved against her spine. A slow, hot lick of his tongue. Ooh. Nice.

She turned around, spinning inside the strong circle of his

arms, and wound her own arms around his neck. Burying her nose in his hair, inhaling his warm scent. "Aren't you going to undress?"

He nuzzled her cleavage with a sigh, squeezing her bottom. "I have to go down to the men's room in the lobby, and buy some condoms from the machine," he said, sounding chagrined. "I meant to stop someplace on the way up here, but we got sidetracked by the blow job."

OK. Here it was, the moment to make the big announcement. Or offer. Or mistake. Or whatever it was. Only time would tell.

"Um, Nick?" she asked, her voice small. "About the condoms . . ."

"Yeah? What about them?"

"I, ah . . . I brought an alternative, if you want to use it," she burst out. "I have a diaphragm. It's just been sitting around in a drawer for ages, and I would love to . . . well, only if you want to."

She waited expectantly for a response, but he didn't move a muscle. His face didn't change. He just stared up at her.

She was nonplussed and started to falter. "Um, of course, I can only use this assuming that you're not planning on, um . . . this is kind of awkward, because we've never discussed the simple ground rules for our relationship, what with all the life-and-death drama—"

"You mean, I can't fuck anybody else," he finished.

She didn't have the nerve to speak after that blunt rejoinder. She could only wait. And wait and wait.

"I'm not," he finally said, his voice flat.

Something relaxed inside her. She'd been lecturing herself, reminding herself that she had no objective reason to demand exclusivity from him. She'd been bracing herself for being brought up short and sharp.

But he hadn't. He *hadn't*. She swallowed over a joyful lump. "And you, um, won't?" she asked delicately. "For the duration?"

His hands tightened on her hips. "Duration of what? Of our affair, you mean? You see an end point to it? Nice of you to tell me."

His harsh tone made her panic, like things were slipping in a direction she'd never intended. "No! That's not what I meant at all! It's just, you know, a thing I said. It doesn't mean anything."

"Then don't say it." He got up, breaking the circle of her arms, and walked away, staring out the big picture window, his broad back radiating intense emotion as only his could.

He shrugged off his jacket. "It goes both ways, you know."

"What do you mean?" Becca finally succeeded in getting her bustier unhooked. "What are you talking about?"

"About you not fucking other guys." He shoved his shirt off.

"Oh. That. That goes without saying."

"I want to hear it said," he said. "Out loud. Just like I did."

It was hard not to laugh at his intensity, when she considered her spotty track record with men. Hah. As if she would when she had him.

"I will not have sex with anyone but you," she said quietly.

He undid his belt, shoved down the pants. His broad, thick erection sprang out, stiff and swaying. At the ready. He gripped it, fixing a steely gaze on her. "Don't even look at other guys," he said softly.

"I'm not," she said simply. "I can't. All I can think about is you."

Her face went beet red at that admission. She looked down quickly, pulling off the garter belt and untangling the ribbon ties of the panties. When she finally got it sorted out, he was right in front of her. Vibing his hot energy at her, scorching her with his hungry gaze.

"Good," he said thickly. "That's how I like it."

He reached for her, but she stumbled back, arms out to hold him at bay. "Wait, wait. I haven't put the thing in, so please don't melt my brain yet. Let me pop into the bathroom and see if I can get it in."

"I'll help. I've got long, strong fingers. And there's no place on earth I'd rather put them than up your tight, juicy—"

"Thanks, but no thanks," she cut him off crisply. "I'll muddle through it alone. If you'll excuse me."

"Fine. I'll wait for you out on the deck, in the tub. Hurry up."

She fled to the bathroom with her cosmetic bag and collapsed on the edge of the clawfoot tub, doubling over the shaky knot of emotions. Laughter, tears, fear, amazed disbelief, that she'd come so far, so fast. Like a snowball rolling downhill, gaining crazy momentum.

She pulled herself together, squeezed some jelly into the latex device, and started. It took a lot of false starts and struggling and cursing. She'd never used the damn thing enough to develop any skill at inserting it. She finally got it lodged in what she sincerely hoped was the correct position.

She walked slowly onto the little wooden deck. In front, it looked out over a densely wooded slope that fell away before them, offering a spectacular view of Mt. Rainier in the daytime. On the sides of the deck, high cedar-slat walls ensured their privacy.

Nick was already in the tub. Foam swirled and bubbled around him. His arms were stretched out on the tub's rim, his head flung back. The cold patter of rain dotted his face, and made his black hair shiny and spiky with water, gleaming like an otter's pelt.

He watched her approach out of lazy, half-lidded eyes.

She sank down into the delicious warmth and floated, drifting through the water towards him as if they were magnetized. Suspended in liquid heat, inches from his wet, gorgeous body. She swirled her hand through the water. Found his cock on the first pass, though admittedly it was kind of hard to miss a thick, rock-hard pole like that.

She drifted closer, laid her head on his shoulder and relaxed against him while she caressed him with her hands under the water. Listening to him groan and hiss, racked with shudders of pleasure.

Finally, he grabbed her hands, pulled them away. "Stop," he muttered thickly. "Cool it. Not yet. I have big plans for this hard-on."

He put her to the side and burst out of the water with a heave and a surge and a violent back slosh, and shook himself as he climbed out. "I'm overheating," he said abruptly, by way of explanation.

He sat down on the end of a wooden bench and turned his face up to catch the cool rain that pelted down on his body, eyes shut.

Becca got up, and followed him. The rain didn't feel cold at all. It was deliciously soothing against her feverish body.

No desperate rush, now. All her doubts were gone. She came on, inexorable as the tide. He had no place to hide from her. Not anymore.

She sank down in front of him onto her knees on the wet wooden boards, her hands on his knees, and stared into the inscrutable mask of his face as her hands stroked slowly up his wet thighs, against the grain of his gleaming hair. Her fingers tangled in the wet, wiry curls at his groin. Fastened around the thick, taut root of his penis.

She could read the language of his face. The tension in his jaw, the tremor in his eyelids, the flare of his nostrils. Cords standing out on his neck. And that hot, urgent heartbeat, pulsing in her hands.

She put her mouth to him and began to hone her newly acquired oral skills. The dim blue glow was the only light, the only sound was the hum of the churning tub and the rushing whisper of rain hitting the deck, and pattering against their skin. The pine, cedar and spruce released an intoxicating perfume. She felt so hot. Rain should sizzle right off her body into steam. She felt so excited. So vibrant and alive.

She laved and licked, swirled and massaged, loved him

with her tongue, her lips, her hands, until he hung over her, gasping for breath.

She dragged it out until her own need ached and throbbed, too sharp to ignore. Then she rose to her feet, and straddled him.

He held his cock up for her, as she lowered herself. She swirled the blunt bulb of his phallus inside her cleft to make him slicker, and then sank down, letting her own weight do the work. Tears welled into her eyes at the mingled pain and perfection of that slow, huge penetration. She moved, squeezed, writhed around that thick pole. Pleasure licked and throbbed. Pressure mounted.

He pulled her face around, cupped her jaw to stare into her eyes with his wet hand. Rain dropped down his face in rivulets.

"I love you," he blurted, his voice raw.

She stared at him, her mouth shaking for a few dumbfounded moments. "I love you, too," she whispered back. "I wanted to say it yesterday. I almost did, but I was so afraid you wouldn't want—"

"I do," he broke in roughly. "I want you. I want it all."

She gulped back the tears and tried to smile, wiping away the rain that was running into her eyes. "That's good," she quavered.

He kissed her again. They held each other, and every subtle sway, every sigh, every clasp and pulse and squeeze was a sultry bloom of pleasure, bursting open to astonish them. Revelation after revelation.

He pulled his lips away. "Don't leave me," he said.

"I won't," she promised. "Not ever."

Rain pounded down, a shower of sweet sensation, an outburst of pure emotion straight from the sky to cool their molten bodies.

"I mean it," he said, emphasizing each hoarse word as if she might not have understood. "I mean for keeps. For life. Marry me."

"Yes. All yours," She was laughing, weeping for joy. "Everything."

He clutched her. She wrapped her legs around him. They were a single entity, poised on the edge of the world.

In a state of utter grace.

Chapter
25

Becca spooned up the last bit of hollandaise sauce from her eggs Benedict and tried both numbers again, for the tenth time. Carrie, then Josh. Both numbers, still turned off. Very unlike them. All three of the Cattrell siblings had strong feelings about the importance of being connected. The niggling pinch of fear in her belly eroded even her sweet glow of euphoria from that amazing night with Nick.

And guilt, too. That she hadn't tried harder the day before.

"What's wrong, babe?"

Nick had paused in shoveling the last scraps of what was left of his enormous ham, cheese and vegetable omelette. He was frowning.

"My brother and sister," she said. "I can't reach them."

He swallowed a big bite of toast, and glanced at his watch. "It's 10:40 on a Sunday morning," he offered. "I'd have my phone turned off too, if I were them. Try them when we're back in town."

She nodded and sipped coffee, trying to dismiss this full-blown case of the heebie-jeebies. It was probably just a function of the extreme stress she was under. Not some psychic premonition of disaster.

Of course not. Nothing so woo woo. She wasn't that kind of girl.

She'd already tried Carrie's dorm, but no one had seen her in days. Same with Josh. None of the guys at his bachelor pad, known affectionately as the HellHole, remembered seeing him that weekend. Damn, she was going to be glad when she spoke to them, and could feel embarrassed about these creepy crawlies. In fact, she could hardly wait for the crushing embarrassment to descend. Bring it on. Anytime.

"What's on your agenda for today?" she asked him.

"I've got Alex Aaro to cover for me for another few hours," Nick said. "I'm going to go see Diana Evans." He tapped his finger on a manila file folder that lay next to his plate. "Davy found her for me. Mathes, too, but I don't think it's a good idea to interview him."

She blinked at him. "Wow. Can I . . . maybe not. She'd probably recognize me. I passed her in the hotel and the parking lot both."

"Yeah. That's exactly why you should hang out in the hotel. Better yet, I'll leave you at the SafeGuard headquarters. That's the best place."

She sighed and shook her head. She and Nick had already had this argument this morning, more than once. Heartfelt declarations of love and marriage proposals were great and romantic, but they did not soften the guy up, or make him any more manageable. On the contrary, he seemed more protective and prickly about her safety than ever.

But since she had no idea how long this stressful state of alarm was going to continue, she was reluctant to give in to his bossing and set a dangerous precedent. She had no intention of living her life in an airless box, Zhoglo or no Zhoglo. She would grit her teeth, lift her chin, stick her tits out and go about her business like normal.

At least until she had clear and obvious reason to hide.

"I have my own errands to run," she told him. "I need to

take back my rental car, I need to get money from my account, I need some fresh clothes from my apartment—"

"So I'll take you to do all that stuff when I get back," he said. "And then we can go out and shop for the ring."

His eagerness gave her a warm, fuzzy glow. She reached up and touched his cheek, smoothing his spiky brush of hair. "We can wait on the ring," she told him. "There's no rush. If you're low on money—"

"I want to see it on you," he said. "I can't wait."

They grinned at each other. A couple of giddy fools in love.

The groom, Sean McCloud, sauntered by, looking tousled, sleepy and very pleased with himself. He winked at Becca, and slapped Nick on the back. "Marriage is excellent," he informed them. "You're next, man."

"Damn straight," Nick said. "Get ready."

Sean's eyes widened. So did Nick's grin. "Whoa," Sean breathed. "Uh, you mean, like, you two—you've already, uh—"

"Yeah. Done deal," Nick said. "Go ahead. Congratulate me."

Sean blinked and ran his hands through his blond hair, making it stick straight up into the air. "Wait, wait. Didn't you just pull this chick out of a swimming pool, what, just a couple of days ago?"

"Like Venus rising from the foam," Seth said with a snicker, as he passed by, bearing a tray heaped with food. "Dripping wet, and a gun to her head. I'm telling you, gets 'em every time."

"Hot damn!" Sean's grin was incandescent. "That's great news!" He leaned over Becca and gave her a kiss on the cheek. "And she's so cute, too. She adds to the scenery, bigtime. I gotta tell Liv."

He bounded off to the table where his bride was still eating breakfast, and within seconds, smiles and thumbs-up and sentimental glances were flashing their way from every side.

Becca clutched her coffee, and tried to breathe. Whew. She hadn't been quite ready for a big announcement. It was so new, and she'd have preferred to treasure the secret for a while, but it wasn't as if she'd communicated that preference to Nick. She hadn't had time.

It occurred to her that Nick's restless drive to get on with it, the way he was so hot to buy a ring even when his funds were tapped out, the way he was so eager to tell everyone . . . it was sort of like the way she'd been when she got engaged to Justin. It hadn't felt real to her, so she'd carried on and told the whole world to make it feel more real.

So he was still feeling insecure. And after what they'd gotten up to all night, too. Wow. She had her work cut out for her to soothe this guy.

A rush of tenderness came over her for Nick, and for the lonely, vulnerable boy he had once been. She was going to make him realize that this thing was for real. That she was for real. Starting right now.

She got up, circled the table, and sat down on Nick's lap. She cupped his face in her hands, and slowly, tenderly, publicly kissed him.

There were wolf whistles, cheers, even some scattered applause. She ignored it all. She could hardly help doing so, especially when he dug his fingers into her hair and returned her kiss as only he could.

When she finally came up for air, his eyes were closed with bliss, his face had hot streaks of red along his cheekbones, and his erection prodded her bottom. "When was check-out time, anyhow?" he muttered.

"Eleven," Becca informed him.

He glanced at his watch. "Great. Let's go back on upstairs."

She started to laugh. "Oh, come on! We've already brought down our bags, and it's only twelve minutes, so—"

"Who needs bags? Twelve minutes is enough. You done with breakfast?"

"Yes, but I—" She squeaked as he stood up, dumping her

off his lap and dragging her up the big staircase that curved up right outside the entrance to the grand dining room.

They got on the road considerably later than they'd planned. Twelve minutes stretched to thirty-five, and he'd even tried to follow her when she retreated into the shower. She'd had to shove her lust-crazed Romeo bodily out the bathroom door, and lock it, just to get a few minutes' peace to put herself back together.

She sat in the truck, on her tingling, tenderized bottom and sneaked amazed peeks at him as he drove. God, he was handsome.

And he was her fiancé. He loved her. Wanted to be with her forever. It was like a dizzy dream, and she never wanted to wake up.

Nick was not happy with the situation as it stood.

Another fierce, heated argument in the hotel parking lot had gone nowhere. Becca was in danger and she clearly did not yet know what the fuck she was dealing with, despite a good, long look on that goddamn island. But he was hog-tied, for the first time in his life, by the effort to meet her halfway. To act like a fucking team player.

To act like a fiancé. A husband, even.

He couldn't throw his weight around now. He wanted to marry her, for fuck's sake. She had the upper hand. It was making him nuts.

He'd had a really bad moment when she'd driven off in her rental car, waving at him. A stab of panic, like he might never see her again.

Ease down, bozo. He had to stay mellow. No panic, no freak-outs. Things were relatively mellow right now, and he had to be too, or risk scaring her off. He would not fuck this up. Not now that he was almost convinced that something so good might actually be in his grasp. That he might have more going for him than he'd ever dreamed possible.

That amazing, sweet woman. With him. Every day. Wow.

Engaged. His heart practically jumped out of his chest whenever he thought about it, which was every other second, if not more. It was like the positive equivalent of pressing down on a bruise. Instead of pain, he got a rush of pleasure, a tangle of random erotic images, a tingle in his balls. He wanted a ring on her finger. To marry her quick, before she had a chance to come to her senses and change her mind.

Love. He'd thought it was something that happened when a guy's glands went nuts. When hormones tragically overtook him. A dangerous chemical imbalance that led a man into life-destroying choices.

Well, his glands were nuts. He was overtaken by hormones, and he wanted to stay surrendered to them for all time, flat on his back, crying uncle, with Becca on top of him, riding him like a cowgirl. With that smile on her face that made him laugh and cry like a fucking idiot.

A fucking *happy* idiot.

He wondered what kind of ring she would choose. That thought was quickly followed by wondering how he was going to pay for it. Maybe he could sell one of his motorcycles. Or a couple of guns.

He put all that mental noise gently aside as he approached Diana Evans's block. He circled the big, comfortable 1930s bungalow-style house, surrounded by trees, rhododendrons and hydrangea bushes. A deep-set porch girdled the entire house.

Nick parked on the next block and assessed the other houses as he walked by. Not much activity. No kids playing, no one washing cars or trimming hedges. The approach to her house was screened by foliage.

He had a bunch of possible cover stories ready on the tip of his tongue as he climbed the stairs to the front porch. But when he knocked on the door, it gave way, swinging inward at the pressure, and he had a sudden, cold premonition that he wasn't going to need them.

One last glance over his shoulder to make sure that no one was watching, and he pushed the door open with his knuckles and went in.

The place had been tossed. Completely trashed. He walked slowly through the wreckage, careful not to touch or disarrange anything.

Room after room, the same thing. The silence was absolute.

He climbed the stairs, his neck crawling and his stomach rolling.

He found her in the master bedroom, sprawled half-in, half-out of the adjoining bath. He stared down at her slender, twisted white form.

She was naked. The length of her hair, her coloring—she did look like Becca, superficially. Apart from the fact that she was very dead.

Her face was grotesquely distorted. She had been strangled. Her face was livid, her eyes bugged out, her tongue protruding. There were marks on her throat.

He kneeled down, for a better look, although the gesture was more ceremonial than anything else. She was stone cold, her skin already taking on a greenish tinge. He found a washcloth, not wanting to leave any accidental trace of himself and lifted her wrist. Stiff as a board.

So they had come for her yesterday sometime. He thought of the conversation with Mathes that Becca had recounted, how the man had bullied Diana into doing something that scared her to death. Of her distress later in the evening. The drinking, the vomiting, the weeping.

So the woman hadn't been mean and cold enough to suit them. This was to her credit, but he would withhold his sympathy for now.

Greed had gotten her into this, after all. It was always greed.

He had absolutely no desire to involve the cops in his problems, but he didn't have it in him to just leave Diana

Evans's body there, without announcing her death to anyone. She'd paid the ultimate price for whatever hellacious shit she'd gotten herself mixed up in. She deserved for her mortal remains to be treated with respect. At least.

He finished his sweep of all the rooms, just to be thorough, and ran down the stairs again. He picked up the phone using his own sleeve to cover his hand, and dialed 911.

The dispatcher answered the emergency line. "I'm at Number 5958 Whittaker Street," he said. "A woman has been murdered here."

He laid the phone down, leaving the line open, the dispatcher's voice still squawking out high-pitched questions, demanding more info.

He walked out the door. Still no one around. He went swiftly to his truck and got the hell away from the place. He was feeling woozy, queasy and emotional. Him, Nick Ward, the so-called ice man. Christ, what was his problem? He fell in love, and turned suddenly to slop.

He wanted to hear Becca's voice. He wanted comfort. He yanked out his cell, pulled her up.

Damn. Her fucking phone was busy. He wanted to throw the worthless piece of junk right out the window.

Becca smiled as she drove off in her rental, thinking of Nick. She was a big girl. She had to learn to act like an alpha female, or he would stomp all over her.

The first stop after the bank machine was her apartment. It felt odd, as if she were visiting a place she remembered from when she was very small. The sights and smells were familiar, but it had shrunk. She was a bigger person now. The ceiling felt lower, the furniture cramped.

She poured some water on her plants, tossed her dirty clothes into the hamper, pulled out fresh clothing, as much as would fit in the suitcase. She tried to think of anything she might conceivably need in the next couple of weeks, and tossed it higgledy-piggledy into the bag.

She hauled it out into the front room, feeling vaguely anxious and twitchy. Goaded by some inner urge to move, move, *move.*

She stopped in the living room and tried to breathe the jittery feeling down, but as she looked around, her back prickled coldly.

She looked around again. What was it? Something wasn't the way she'd left it. She never pushed the phone to the exact middle of the table. She never propped the pillows in that particular way.

Someone had been here. Someone had touched her stuff. She felt an ice-cold churning, wonky and unstable in her lower body. She stared around, wondering if this was just stress, psyching her out. Making her nuts. And then her eyes focused on the stuffed animals on the shelf.

Bingo.

She always had Carrie's threadbare pink bunny with the long arms embracing Josh's tortoise on one side, and Carrie's Goldilocks bear on the other. But the bunny was flopped forward, one long pink ear draped across the bear's lap. Arms out, in dangling supplication.

She reached up, pulled the animals down. Her blood ran cold.

A small, squat black video camera sat there, its gleaming round eye regarding her coldly.

Her mind whirled. Stomach, too. The Spider had found her. He knew where she was, and who. Which meant that he knew about Josh and Carrie, too. She wanted to throw up. She didn't have time. She was being watched. Right now, as she stared up with horrified eyes.

She swallowed hard. Lifted her hand. Gave the camera the finger.

And with that act of empty defiance, she pulled the camera down and shoved it into the kitchen garbage, with the tinfoil and the coffee grounds. The garbage was ripe and nasty after three days of neglect.

And now? She stepped out onto the porch with her suit-case and ran her eye up and down the street. Would she be shot or abducted? Or simply followed? She tried to memo-rize every make and color of car in sight as she hauled her suitcase down the stairs. Her legs shook beneath her.

No one appeared to follow once she turned onto the big street, but that didn't mean they weren't there. It meant she'd been fooled. She'd been fooled before. She tried Josh again, then Carrie. Still nothing.

She was unnerved, shaking, on the verge of tears as she drove. She wanted to call Nick, but he would just go bananas on her, and at this point, there was nothing he could do. She might as well proceed with her day's agenda. Ditch that damned rental before it bled her dry.

She called a cab as soon as she started in on the paper-work at the rental place, and told it to meet her at a nearby intersection that was a couple of blocks the wrong way down a one-way street. She hoped that was a crafty enough evasion technique to fool seasoned mobsters, as she puffed down the sidewalk, dragging her suitcase behind her.

She finally managed to breathe once she'd slid into the back of the cab and slumped down out of sight in the seat. She dragged out her phone again and pulled up Josh's num-ber.

Wonder of wonders. It was ringing. "Hello? Becca?"

"Josh! You scared me to death! Where the hell have you been?"

"Oh, well . . ." His voice trailed off. "I, um, I met some-one."

His evasiveness in the face of her own stark fear made her furious. "Do you have any idea how worried I've been? Where the hell are you?"

"I'm at my new apartment," Josh said cheerfully. "I'm moving in with Nadia."

"Nadia? Who the hell is Nadia?" Her voice cracked.

"Calm down, Becca. Nadia's wonderful. I met her a couple days ago, and we've been together twenty-four-seven ever since, and now she's invited me to move in with her. Todd can have my room in the HellHole, since he's been sleeping on the downstairs couch for three months anyhow, and I'll move in here and help Nadia with the rent on this place. I can work extra shifts at the Electronics Barn to cover—"

"Moving in with her? You just met this girl *when?*"

She was being a hysterical harpy, which never worked with Josh, but she couldn't stop herself. She was too freaked out, too scared.

"Night before yesterday. But you've got to understand, Becca. She's amazing. She's sweet, and smart, and she's so amazingly beautiful, I just can't believe that she—hey! Stop that, Nadia. No, it is true! No, really, stop . . . that tickles . . . oh, shit . . ."

The voices on the other end of the line degenerated into a goofy, giggling scuffle, and Becca waited, teeth clenched, for them to sort it out and get themselves under control. "Becca?" Josh's voice came back, raw with laughter. "You still there?"

"Yes. I am," she said grimly.

"It's weird. I just turned on my phone for one second to call the pastry place to send us some cupcakes, and the same second, boom, you call me. You must be, like, psychic."

"No, just desperate," she snapped. "Look, Josh, I've been calling all morning. I've been out of my mind, because Carrie—"

"Don't worry," Josh wheedled. "Everything's great. I've never been so great in my life. Oh, hey. That's a great idea—hold on a sec—" There was a murmur and Josh came back on. "Nadia says, why don't you just come over? Come have brunch with us or lunch or whatever! See for yourself how special she is. She really wants to meet you. I told her how you basically raised me and Carrie, and she said that when her mom died, she and her little sister in Moldova were just like—"

"Joshie, I can't," she said. "I'm in trouble, and I need to—"

"Sure you can! Tell me all about it here. I'll text you the address. Come over. I'm turning off my phone. I really want you to come. OK?"

"Josh, please, I—"

Click. The connection broke. Becca stared at the phone in dismay. She tried the number again. Sure enough, he really had turned off his phone. She could have shrieked in frustration.

She already disliked this seductress Nadia. Whoever the hell she was, she had to come out of the woodwork right now, at the worst possible time, and turn Josh's brain to mush.

Which was kind of unfair, considering her own whirlwind romance, and the distinctly mushlike state of her own silly brain.

Still. God help them all. She tried Carrie's number. Still off. She wished she'd mentioned that to Josh before he turned his phone off.

Her phone chirped. Message. She checked it.

855 Gavin St. Garden Apt. C u there!

Argh. The only thing to do was just go there and jerk on the lovesick little punk's ear in person. If she could get him alone without Nadia, the perfect shining angel, in attendance, she'd just lay out the whole damn story for him. The real deal. Uncensored.

Maybe it would scare some sense into him. She could only hope.

She leaned forward to get the cabbie's attention. "Excuse me. You have to take me to another address. Do you know Gavin Street?"

* * *

Nick wasn't sure why he was driving by Richard Mathes's house. It didn't make sense to tip the guy off to being observed, wiping out any chance of following him. But planting a beacon on Mathes's car without being seen, now that was a risk that could yield big benefits.

He was startled by how rattled he'd been from finding Diana Evans's body, although stuff like that tended to take him by surprise long after the fact. He'd be thinking he was fine, as cool as a popsicle, and then he'd find out he couldn't sleep for a month.

Evans's murder was definitely Zhoglo's work, but he was sure this prick Mathes had something to do with it.

He drove by the house. Hell of a place. He guessed that famous heart surgeons had to make a pretty decent buck, but this place looked like more than a pretty-decent-buck house.

This place looked like a bottomless-bank-account house.

It was a sprawling white mansion. A three-story, turn-of-the-century Victorian, with lace and frills, a widow's walk, pointy towers, turrets and beveled bay windows. More like a cake than a house. A big, perfectly landscaped flowering garden. A huge lawn, dotted with majestic, century-old trees.

He circled around the big loop and took another look. The black BMW with the plates that Davy had detailed for him was parked in the driveway, not inside the enclosed garage. Nick took that as a written invitation from fate to go plant a discreet slap-on beacon bug. Five days of battery juice to monitor the good doctor with X-Ray Specs. Yeah.

Anybody stopped him—well, he didn't think he could pass for a Jehovah's Witness or a vacuum cleaner salesman, but fuck it. He'd improvise. He was good at it. In fact, a lot of the time, his seat-of-the-pants solutions to problems were ultimately better than when he slapped his brains around for an advance plan.

He parked his truck a discreet distance away and strolled

through the pricey neighborhood. Dappled sun filtered through the moving leaves, making a constant green shadow-show on the ground. The ground was still fragrant and humid from the rainstorm the night before. It was beautiful . . . birds twittering, wind rustling.

And all he could see was that naked woman on the floor, eyes bugged out, the marks of hands clutching her throat. The image was burned into his retinas.

The long driveway stretched and curved before him. Here went nothing. He peeled the protective film off the powerful rubber cement that backed the beacon as he walked by the car, and bent as if checking his shoe. Slipped that sucker right under the bumper.

He straightened up, hands in pockets, and looked at the house.

Mathes was home. He should beat hell out of here. It made no sense to get closer now that he'd tagged the car. He risked tipping the guy off, losing his link to whatever project Zhoglo had planned.

And yet, he kept drifting closer, as if the place pulled him. He gazed up at the big, ornate porch, Diana's pale, twisted body still superimposed in his mind over the image of the handsome old house.

He was gathering the presence of mind to turn away and leave when the door opened. Adrenaline jolted through him.

An elegant, slender blond woman in her forties stepped out onto the porch. "Hello?" she asked suspiciously. "Can I help you?"

He did what he always did in these seat-of-the-pants situations. He opened his big mouth and let 'er rip.

"I'd like to speak to Dr. Mathes," he said. "I'm a colleague of his."

The woman's eyes narrowed. She was very beautiful, in a chilly, stretched sort of way. She might have had help from the knife to keep the line of her jaw so sharp, and her eyes and brow so unlined. Hard to tell.

"He's asleep," she said. "He was at the hospital all night, doing an emergency transplant. I'm afraid I can't wake him for you."

"Too bad, then," he said. "Another time. You're Mrs. Mathes?"

"I am." She took a step forward, gripping one of the porch columns. "May I tell him your name, Dr . . . ?"

"Warbitsky," he said. His birth name was buried in obscurity, not on any of his records, so it was fine as a throwaway alias.

Her eyes narrowed to pale blue slits. "I don't believe I've ever seen you before. What's your specialty, Doctor?"

"Pathology," he said. Close enough as far as it went.

But Mathes's wife wasn't buying it. She came down the stairs towards him, a strange, almost avid look on her face. She stopped about two yards away from him. "You're no doctor." Her voice quivered with strain. "You're lying."

He kept silent. Quietly waited to see where she was going with it.

"What are you here for?" she demanded, voice rising. "What is my husband mixed up in?"

Now that she was closer, he saw the lines of strain on her face. The shadows under her eyes, cleverly concealed with makeup. Her excessive thinness. She wasn't a stupid woman. She was catching a strong whiff of rot, and she didn't like it.

Well, she shouldn't. He slowly shook his head.

"Tell me." She was almost yelling at him. "What is he involved in?"

He blew out a breath to buy him a second to decide whether or not this was a mistake. Too late now. He saw Diana's bugged-out eyes.

"Nothing good, ma'am," he said quietly.

She crossed the distance between them with a lunge and grabbed his arm. "I have two children," she said sharply. "Two young girls."

He looked down at the manicured white and pink claw

that shook with strain as it dug into his arm. "I've got a piece of advice for you, then," he said. "Take your girls, put them on a plane, and get them the hell away from here."

She stumbled back, and put her hand to her throat.

"I say this as a friend," he added.

"You're not his friend," she hissed. "Don't bullshit me."

"Not his," he admitted. "But I've got nothing against your girls."

Her throat worked. She looked older when her mouth was pursed up. "I am not involved with it, whatever it is," she said stiffly.

He looked around and a mean laugh jerked his chest. "Get real, lady," he said. "You're living in it. You're driving it." He gestured at the double-strand pearl necklace held together with diamond baguettes that gleamed in the vee of her silk blouse. "You're wearing it."

She jerked back as if she'd been burned. "Get out," she said. "Get off my property, before I call the police."

Typical. Concerned for her girls' safety, sure, but don't fuck with the diamonds. He turned, and got the hell out of there. He could feel the unfriendly pressure of that woman's eyes against his back.

Well, shit. Chances were good that she would tell her husband what she had seen, and the guy would make whatever he liked of it. But even so, Richard Mathes didn't seem to care about letting the women who were close to him die at Zhoglo's hands.

He guessed that was the real reason he'd come here. Fuckup or no fuckup, after seeing Diana Evans's body lying on the floor, he was glad he'd given that woman a heads-up. He hoped she was smart enough to take it and run with it. Before Zhoglo ate her kids for lunch.

He got into his truck and took off with a roar of the engine, but when he turned the first corner, he had a weird, déjà vu zing to his brain. He'd noticed it before when driving around that particular block.

He swung around the loop again to see if he could pin it down.

This time he saw it with his conscious mind. That car. He'd noticed it out of the corner of his eye before, but he hadn't put it together. A shiny black PT Cruiser. Becca said that Diana drove one of those. He pulled in ahead of it, and checked the plates, just in case.

Holy shit. It really was the woman's car. Parked right there.

He got out and went to take a look. It was a mess inside. A long beige raincoat was crumpled in the back seat, as though she'd slept on it. The passenger seat was littered with junk. Too many people driving by on the busy avenue for him to be comfortable with jimmying the lock, but he remembered Becca's experience, and tried the door handle. Just for the hell of it.

It opened. He got into the driver's side, and was hit with the heady stench of whiskey. A short search revealed an uncapped flask of what smelled like scotch. The liquor had drained out onto the floor.

The glove box had nothing but the registration and a fistful of maps. He went through all the garbage on the seats; crumpled tissues stained with makeup, receipts, paper coffee cups with bright red lipstick marks, medical journals, a silk scarf, breath mints and chewing gum to hide her alcohol breath, not that it ever worked. The package for the digital voice recorder Becca had noticed. A couple of mismatched earrings. They looked expensive.

The center console yielded a handful of CD's, more garbage, more mints, and a stash of quarters for tolls.

He checked out the back seat and hit pay dirt with the beige raincoat. There was a small, hard object in the depths of one of her coat pockets. Just what he'd been hoping for, ever since Becca's tale of blood and urine samples.

He fished out the voice recorder rod and stared at it, then pushed its on button. Nothing happened. Nothing lit up.

The phone rang. He pulled it out, hoping it was Becca,

but the display informed him that it was Davy. He pocketed the recorder, let out a flat sigh of disappointment, and hit talk. "Yeah?"

"Nick. Get your ass over here right now." Davy's voice was hard and clipped. As grim as death.

His gut clenched. "What happened? Did Zhoglo—"

"I don't want to talk about it on the phone. Hang up, and *move.*"

Chapter 26

"Aw, Becca, come on," Josh wheedled, scratching tufts of hair on his naked chest. "I wish you'd get this bug out of your ass and chill."

"Joshie, you had an appointment with Carrie on Friday night!" Becca's voice was getting shriller. "You blew her off, and then you were incommunicado all weekend! And now we can't get in touch with her at all! Don't you think she would have at least left us a text message?"

"I'm sure there's an explanation," Josh grumbled. He leaned over the big dining room table, which was covered with the remains of a bacchanalian breakfast: a bowl of fruit, a towering heap of breakfast pastries, ziplock plastic bags of sliced deli meats and cheeses. He snagged a glazed lemon cupcake. "Have a muffin and relax. What's the big deal? So we'll drive down to the college today and roust her out. Give her a hard time for scaring us."

"You don't look overly scared," Becca observed sourly.

In fact, Josh looked like he was having the time of his life. He looked like a prince wallowing in the lap of sensual luxury, naked but for baggy silk paisley boxer shorts. He pinched a slice of honey-roasted ham out of one of the bags, and dangled it over his mouth.

"I will go with you," Nadia volunteered. "I wish to meet this little sister." Her cool glance in Becca's direction clearly implied that she hoped that the little sister would be an improvement on the big one.

Becca clenched her teeth, and reminded herself to be polite. Something about this over-the-top sexpot blonde put her teeth on edge. She had already told herself that maybe it was just Kaia fallout, and the girl could hardly be blamed for that—but even so.

Becca would never have chosen to meet her new boyfriend's sister in a pink ostrich-feather-trimmed silk robe that gaped over her breasts and barely covered her butt cheeks.

Besides. There was something strange about the whole thing. That girl was too perfect to be real. Granted, Joshie was a cute guy in his own right, with a nice body, if a bit skinny, and bright green eyes that made lots of girls swoon. But there was something so polished and gleaming and smooth about Nadia. She would look more believable on the arm of a much older man. Or, rather, a much richer one.

Or maybe Becca was just feeling jealous and insecure about a beautiful younger girl, in which case, she should be smacked. Becca sipped her coffee and fought for a more adult perspective.

It was hard to come by. Now Nadia was amusing herself by squirting whipped cream out of a tube can onto a ripe, red strawberry, thoroughly licking it all off, and then slowly inserting the pointed red end of the strawberry between her shiny lips.

Josh watched, rapt, and grabbed a berry. "Can I have one?"

Nadia licked bits of berry juice off her lips. "Of course, Josh," she cooed. "You can have anything you wish of me."

He held out his berry. Nadia anointed it, both of them giggling.

Oh, for the love of God. Becca couldn't take any more of this crap.

"Nadia," she said. "Please don't be offended, but would

you mind letting me speak to my brother in private for just a few minutes?"

Nadia froze, her pink mouth dangling open, her blue eyes wide. She stuck Josh's berry into his open mouth, and wiped her fingers daintily with a deli napkin, looking hurt. She got up with a fluttery swirl of pink silk and feathers that revealed a whole lot more than Becca had ever wanted to see of her anatomy. She was clearly not a believer in underwear. Or even pubic hair, for that matter.

"Very well," she said. "I go to the bedroom now. Please let me know when I am welcome again to come into my own kitchen, no?"

"Nadia!" Josh leaped up, alarmed. "Wait! She didn't mean—"

Slam. The door to the living room rattled in its frame.

"Nice going, Becca. That was just swell," Josh said stonily.

"Joshie, please. I need you to listen to me. You don't have time to be fooling around like an idiot while Carrie—"

"You've been fooling around like an idiot with your boy toy thug, right?" Josh shot back. "Works for you, so why not me?"

That barb hit the mark. Becca tried to rally and think of some way to express her misgivings about Nadia in a way that would not alienate him.

It was a useless exercise. "Joshie, something's off about this—"

"Don't start with me," he snarled. "Just shut up, OK?"

"No, really. Look at this place." She indicated the huge, beautiful kitchen. "Tuscan tile? Marble countertops? State-of-the-art appliances? This furniture?" She swept her hand at the antique dining table, the mellow blond parquet, the restored molding of the townhouse. "This isn't housing for a foreign student, Joshie. This kitchen alone is bigger than my entire apartment. You can't pay rent on this place with extra shifts at Eric's Electronics Barn. There's something else going on here. Can't you feel it?"

"What I feel is that you're doing your best to fuck this up for me," Josh snarled. "And I'm not going to let you do it."

"No. Joshie, I swear—"

"Life will kick you in the teeth every fucking chance it gets. You know that. So when something great comes along, you should grab it! Appreciate it! Not just spit on it because it's too good to be true!"

Josh's impassioned words did have a ring of truth to them, even if they were inspired by horndog lust. But he had to listen. "That's not what I'm asking you to do," she said quietly. "I'm sorry. Look, Joshie. Never mind this thing with Nadia. I've got big problems. I've got to tell you why I'm so scared. For my life."

That got his attention. "Huh? What do you mean, your life?"

"Sit down," Becca said wearily. "I'll be quick. For Nadia's sake."

Zhoglo was enjoying the spectacle of Rebecca pouring out her woes to her brother, with no idea that they were all in the jaws of the tiger. Her reaction to Nadia had been wonderfully amusing.

The door opened and Nadia entered. Zhoglo shot her a critical look. He was unimpressed with the floating pink confection she wore. She was impersonating a poor student. It should be obvious to the humblest intelligence that she should avoid dressing like a costly whore.

Deliberate stupidity annoyed him terribly.

"Did you bring her purse?" he snapped.

Nadia held up the new-looking black bag, worth fifteen dollars at most, along with Rebecca's cotton jacket. "I had her leave them in the foyer."

"I did not ask you for tedious details." He glanced at Mikhail, jerked his chin at the items Nadia held. "Well? Get to it."

Mikhail got to work, slicing open the lining of Rebecca's purse for the first GPS locator, hiding the second more carefully by unstitching the cloth strap. Another was tucked into the hem of Rebecca's jacket. Hopefully, Arkady Solokov would find one, but not the others. Of course, if he had a bug detector, he would eventually find them all, but no matter.

Zhoglo was not concerned about controlling Rebecca. Everything she cared about was in his grasp. She would fall right into line.

He rummaged through the woman's purse in a desultory way, but found nothing of interest. He tucked the envelope he'd prepared for Solokov to find into the inside pocket. He held it out to Nadia. "Well?" he prompted. "Take all this back down to the foyer. And come right back here. Immediately."

Nadia was back in the room in less than a minute. Zhoglo was deeply involved in Becca's fascinating if somewhat disjointed account of what had really happened on Frakes Island, when that idiot prostitute had the unbelievable insolence to interrupt him.

"Are you . . . going to hurt him?" Her voice was very small.

Zhoglo turned his head and gave her a look calculated to stop her heart. "You are not being paid to concern yourself with that, whore."

She was actually opening her mouth to speak to him again.

"Have you grown fond of the boy?" he asked, cutting her off. "A whore should know better. But I will promise you this much. When the time comes for his mercy blow—and it will be a long, long time in coming—I will tell him that it is from you. From the lovely Nadia. He will die screaming your name. Does that satisfy you?"

Color drained from Nadia's face. For a moment, she was not remotely beautiful. She was a death's head, hollow-eyed beneath her blush pink paint. The depth of the fear in her eyes stirred him.

The girl needed to be reminded of her place. A creature as excessively beautiful as she sometimes ran the risk of thinking her beauty gave her a special power. That it made her immune to discipline.

A dangerous state of affairs. He had to nip it in the bud.

He rubbed his hands together, considering possibilities. Mikhail had done well yesterday. He had succeeded in leaving without being followed, and had dispatched the Evans woman in a brisk and professional manner. He was due a reward. Kristoff and Pavel, both out of favor, could look on and salivate.

"Nadia, my dear," he said. "I would like a more intimate demonstration of your oral skills. Upon him." He indicated Mikhail.

It took Nadia a moment to break her paralysis, but her faltering smile came back, and she sank down in front of the flushed, grinning Mikhail, the very image of charming submission, and got right to it.

Zhoglo immediately regretted the impulse. Mikhail was noisy. His gasps and groans were extremely annoying. In fact, it was almost impossible to hear what Rebecca and Joshua were saying to each other.

"Be quiet, man," he snapped. "I wish to hear this conversation."

Mikhail sucked in a breath and got his response down to a high-pitched keening sound, like a dog's whine.

Kristoff and Pavel watched, enthralled, as Mikhail's penis slid in and out of the girl's pink mouth, but Zhoglo soon grew bored. Rebecca and her brother were now arguing heatedly about whether or not Nadia should accompany them on their trip to look for their sister Carrie. Which was, of course, a non-issue.

He got up, leaving the grunting, wheezing Mikhail and his captive audience behind, and walked down to the end of the hall, to the smallest bedroom, more a cell than anything else. He walked in, with a friendly smile for the wretched creature tied to the bed.

Ah, how he loved the sight of a lovely girl, tied and gagged.

Her pale green eyes were wide with terror. Remarkably similar to Rebecca, although her hair was straighter, and her face more narrow. Her slender body strained against her bonds, bucking and heaving. She wore only the gray string tank top and underwear she'd been wearing when his men collected her from her dorm room bed.

He put his hand on her cool, silken thigh, just for the pleasure of feeling her muscles jerk and recoil. "I imagine you are wondering why you are here," he said. "It's your sister, you see. She's been playing dangerous games. She cost me money and time. She must be punished." He shrugged almost apologetically. "Your family is small, so my choices were limited. But watching you and your brother die should be enough."

Her body seized up in a shuddering paroxysm. He stroked her rigid body and realized that he had an erection. He massaged it idly.

"You may be interested to know that your brother and sister are in this very house right now," he informed her. "Last I heard, they were arguing about going to look for you. They are so worried that you have not called. How good of them to care, no?"

Another jerk. She mewled desperately behind her gag, her horrified eyes dropping to where he massaged his crotch.

The impulse was strong, but the girl lay on her back, strapped to the bed. Faceup, feet fastened together with tight, complicated knots. He was irritated at the thought of picking them apart, or fetching a knife to sever them. He was even more irritated with the idiot who had tied her. A little foresight from this pack of fools who served him—was it too much to ask? Then he heard water running in the bathroom on the other side of the wall. He left the room just in time to intercept Nadia, who was patting her face dry, presumably after rinsing out her mouth.

Nadia would do to soothe his itch. Her fear was just as powerful.

"I hoped to catch you before you went downstairs," he purred.

Nadia pulled back before she could stop herself. She tried to smile to cover the gaffe, but her lips trembled.

He took her by the arm, and guided her to the door of his own master bedroom. He pushed open the door and gestured with a smiling flourish for her to precede him inside.

She stared at him, frozen in place. "I . . . I . . . but he will be expecting me downstairs . . ." Her voice trailed off into a trembling thread. She sucked in air, tried again. "And I must be, ah . . ."

"Fresh?" His smile widened. Her fear honed his desire to razor-sharp intensity, and this was only the beginning. "Not a problem, my dear. There is a bathroom. Wash afterwards. Make yourself as clean and sweet as a new-blown rose." He shoved her before him, making her stumble, and followed her in. "Your little friend will never know."

"Run it back. Play it again."

"Nick." Davy's voice was heavy. "You've seen it ten times since I unscrambled it."

"Run the fucking thing back and play it again," Nick snarled.

Davy sighed, and obliged him. The recorded digital image of the woman on the monitor went back out the door of Zhoglo's house, put her suitcase back into the trunk of the yellow cab, was sucked backwards into the rear seat. The cab began to move.

Freeze frame. Davy hit play. And Nick watched it again.

He guessed he kept hoping it would be different, that it

would be some other woman who would get out, collect her suitcase, pay the driver, shoulder her purse—and walk right into Zhoglo's lair.

As if it were no big deal. Something she did all the time.

But no. It was Becca who disappeared into the maw of that door. The door shut. The house seemed to stare at him with blank insolence.

His whole self was screaming and struggling against the blunt, inescapable conclusion. He didn't want to give in to it, but it was winning. Full realization was dawning, without his help, without his consent. The taste in his mouth was as bitter as gall.

He'd been had.

His brain stretched like a tortured body on the rack around this new piece of information. Joints wrenching loose, muscles and tendons tearing as he tried to accommodate it. His breakfast had turned into a lump of jagged ice. The coffee sloshing around was corrosive acid.

Seth sat in the swivel chair on the other side of Nick, his face a mask. Connor was there, too, his arms folded tightly across his chest. All three men looked grim. And embarrassed as hell.

No one would look him in the face. Just as well. Nick didn't want to look into anybody's face, for the rest of what passed for his life.

"Play it again," he said hoarsely.

Davy gave a muttered curse. "Look, man. Please. Stop torturing yourself," he pleaded. "Don't make us watch this."

"Look sharp. She's coming out again, in real time," Connor said.

They all lunged to the trio of real-time monitors that covered the three angles of the Gavin Street house. Sure enough, there was Becca. Dragging her suitcase back out to the curb. Another cab idled there. The driver got out, and put the suitcase in the trunk for her. She slid into the seat, and the car pulled away. So flat, so anticlimactic.

"How long was she in there?" Connor asked.

"Thirty-eight minutes, seventeen seconds," Seth said promptly.

The fact that Becca had left the Vor's hideout had broken the bubble of false hope in his mind. Nick no longer wanted Davy to play that footage back. He was going to be looking at that footage in his head for a long, long time to come.

Unless he got himself offed. The odds of which were looking pretty good, considering how things were shaping up.

Hey. He might even get lucky and buy the big one this very day. Then he wouldn't have to feel this way anymore. A guy could hope.

The silence was deafening. He was tempted to throw a computer, just to break that wall of silent pity and judgment.

But these guys had enough to put up with from him as it was.

Seth cleared his throat with a cough. "Weird," he said cautiously. "That she would go there, if she knew that we were watching—"

"She didn't know," Nick cut in. "I never discussed too many details with her. She knew Zhoglo's name, yeah. And she knew I was watching someone, but not who or where."

"Well. Thank God for that, at least," Connor said.

Yeah. Thank God. If she'd known they were surveilling Zhoglo's digs, she would never have exposed herself. And he'd still be racking his brains trying to figure out what the fuck he could sell to pay for the rock he wanted to buy her. He still would not know that the woman he had begged to marry him was a treacherous, two-faced whore, hired by that scum-sucking vermin to seduce him, enthrall him, monitor him. Control him.

She'd been doing an amazing job of it. She was *good*. She must have been pleased with herself. Zhoglo must have been fucking thrilled. She'd probably be able to set herself up for life for what he'd paid her for this stunt. He wondered where the hell Zhoglo had found her.

He racked his brains, in a last-ditch desperate effort to think of any reason, any explanation at all for why Becca might saunter into a mobster's house, hang out for the better part of an hour, and then trot out again, all with that calm, businesslike air.

He wondered if she'd ever serviced The Vor. Maybe she had today. Thirty-eight minutes and seventeen seconds was more than enough time for that, even with lead-in and cleanup, if they were brisk.

What burned in his chest now like a red-hot coal was the thought that he had let go of his search for Sveti for the sake of this lying bitch.

Davy let out a slow sigh. "Nick. I'm sorry that your—"

"Don't," he said. "Please. Just don't."

"You've got to look ahead, man," Davy went on, his voice flat and implacable. "You need a plan, and you need it now."

"Fuck it," Nick said savagely. "Fuck you. Fuck this. All of it—"

"Shut up." Connor's voice slashed down, making him jerk. "You do not have the luxury of freaking out. You got used. You got fucked over. It's bad, it hurts, we've all been there, we all survived—"

"Leave me alone, Con—"

"Hear me out," Connor pressed grimly on. "The only useful thing you can do with this now is to turn it to your own advantage."

"Advantage?" He started to laugh, incredulous. "Yeah. Right."

"Yes. Advantage. You cannot confront her about this, Nick."

Three sets of eyes bored into him as that sank in. "Holy fuck," he muttered, helplessly. "You mean I—"

"Yeah," Davy said heavily. "You have to keep on just as you are. Like nothing ever happened. Play it cool. Go and buy the fucking ring."

That crack stung like the lash of a whip. He recoiled from it, and covered his eyes with his hands. "Oh, Christ."

The silence stretched out again, as cold and silent as doom.

"Can you do it?" Seth asked quietly.

"Do what?" he snarled. "You mean, can I fuck her?" He imagined it. Imagined putting it to her, looking into those luminous green eyes. Their bodies joined, juicily rocking together.

Knowing what he knew.

His gut rebelled, and it took all his willpower to keep breakfast down. No fucking way was he giving in. He'd yarked a few times in his life from stomach viruses and hangovers. Never from hurt feelings.

Fuck that shit. He wasn't so far gone as that. He swallowed, shut his eyes, tried to breathe. *Control.*

He knew how to play this game. He'd worked undercover his whole adult life. He knew how to play a part. How to make it convincing.

Nick opened his eyes, and found the three men still staring at him, a question in their eyes.

"I can do whatever has to be done." His voice sounded, to his own ears, like a dead man talking.

Chapter
27

Becca paced the cramped hotel room. She tried Carrie's cell again. Then Nick. She'd been calling them an average of three times a minute, but it was always the same. Nick, for some strange reason, was not answering and Carrie's phone was still turned off.

The memory of that squat, malevolent-looking vid cam behind the pink bunny on the shelf haunted her. Her stomach cramped with fear.

She tried to push away nightmare images of Carrie and Nick, in the trunk of a car, speeding off to some horrible fate. Leaving her hanging, obsessively punching the buttons on her phone.

Oh, stop. Nick could look out for himself. He'd probably just left his phone in the car. She hoped he either came back soon or got in touch soon, because she had a date with Josh in less than an hour to drive down to Olympia to look for Carrie. Nick would be extremely unhappy with her if she went off on a road trip without telling him.

She tried to stretch out on the bed, watch cable TV, but she was too jittery, too restless. She kept bounding up again.

The door lock clicked. She sprang a foot into the air, and

lunged towards Nick as he walked in, throwing her arms around him.

"Oh, thank God," she said. "You weren't answering your phone!"

He felt oddly stiff in her arms for a second, but then his arms circled her. His nose nuzzled the top of her head. "Sorry," he said. His voice sounded exhausted. "Got sidetracked. Left the thing in the truck."

"Don't do that to me," she scolded, squeezing him again.

He sat down heavily onto the bed. She sat down next to him, and twined her arm through his. "So?" she prompted. "What happened? Did you see Diana Evans?"

"Yes," he said dully, rubbing his face. "Sort of. She was dead. Someone strangled her. Yesterday, from the looks of it."

A chilling wave of cold pumped through Becca's body. "Oh, my God," she whispered. "That's horrible. That poor woman."

He shrugged. "Her own goddamn fault. Getting herself mixed up with that kind of people. She probably deserved it."

"Maybe so," Becca faltered. "But she was definitely regretting it."

"She was a day late and a dollar short."

She was taken aback by the stony, cold tone of his voice. Her stomach fluttered uneasily at the look on his face. Maybe she was reading too much into it, but his face reminded her of that awful expression he'd had when they were on the island.

And when Tam had tormented him with the ghosts of his past.

She lifted his hand to her lips and kissed it. Nick was a great deal more sensitive than he let on. Probably a lot more sensitive than he even knew himself. It was probably seeing Diana Evans's body that had disturbed him so deeply. It would have done the same for her.

"Did you learn anything else?" she asked.

"The house was tossed," he said. "It looked like a standard B&E gone bad. Someone looking for quick drug money, and she was unlucky enough to be home. An unfortunate urban statistic."

"I see," she murmured. "You didn't, um, contact Mathes, then?"

He looked directly into her eyes. "Seeing the dead lady was the sum total of my investigative accomplishments for the day, sweetheart."

She leaned forward, pulled his head down to hers and kissed him. "I'm sorry," she said softly. "That must have been hard."

"I'm handling it," he said. "Enough about me. Let's talk about you. Tell me about your day, babe."

Mr. Super Cool to the last. She rubbed his hand against her cheek. "Well, one good thing is that I finally got in touch with Josh."

"That's good news. Where was he?"

"Shacked up," she said ruefully. "With this beautiful girl named Nadia. He wants to move in with her. I have my doubts, but whatever. He'll have to figure it out the hard way. That's why he didn't call. He's been rolling around in bed for the past thirty-six hours."

"Lucky boy," he said. "Anything from your sister?"

"Not yet," she said glumly. "In fact, Joshie and I are driving down to Olympia this afternoon to look for her."

"Are you now." His voice was cool, strangely distant.

It made her feel flustered. "Um, you could come with us, if you like," she said. "But I assumed . . . you would probably want to concentrate on whatever's happening up here. Your investigation and all. Since I'll be with my brother, of course. I won't be all alone."

"Is that what you assumed?" He stroked the palm of her hand with his forefinger, without meeting her eyes. "So you talked to your brother on the phone. What else did you do? Give me a blow by blow."

"Well, I went to my apartment. Oh, yes, and I wanted to tell you about this—I guess they, uh . . . they've found me."

"What?" His eyes fastened onto hers, suddenly intent. "What do you mean, found you?"

"I found a video camera," she confessed. "On the shelf. Behind the stuffed animals." She braced herself for an explosion.

It didn't come. He just stared at her, his eyes thoughtful and shuttered. "No shit," he said softly. "A vid cam. How about that."

"I was really careful afterwards to make sure I wasn't being followed," she offered. "And when I was at the rental place, I think I lost anyone who might have been tailing me when I got the cab."

"Good thinking," he said. "You're getting slick at this stuff, Becca."

God, his voice was so bland. So unemotional. It was unnerving.

She struggled to gather her thoughts. They were getting scrambled by a strange, staticky buzz of interference from him.

"That's why I've been so freaked out about Carrie," she confessed. "If they know where I live, then Zhoglo knows about Carrie too."

"Don't panic about Carrie yet," he said. "What else did you do?"

She'd been internally debating the wisdom of confessing to her Gavin Street detour, since it hadn't been on the trajectory she'd originally laid out to him. In his current mood, she was less and less inclined to do so. She was jittery, nervous, tearful. She did not want to be yelled at or harangued. And what did it matter, if that conversation with Josh took place on the phone in the cab, or in person?

"I think I've covered it all," she said. "Bank machine, apartment, rental car place. Then I came back here."

"That's it?" He stared straight ahead.

"Uh, yeah," she said.

He looked away from her, as if the blackout curtains over

the window had suddenly taken on some deep significance. "I see."

She felt so alone all of a sudden. Bereft. Which was silly. He was just depressed and stressed-out, and no wonder, for God's sake. She should try not to be clingy and demanding. It was the kiss of death.

Still. It made her ache.

But she knew a quick, surefire way to find him again, and she had the time, before Joshie picked her up. She got off the bed, and slid her arms around his head. "Nick?" she asked gently. "Where are you?"

He looked up at her. "Nowhere," he said.

She stripped off her clingy blue microfiber tee in one sinuous move, and cradled his face against her cleavage. "I know of a nicer place that you could be," she murmured.

"Oh, yeah? Do you?" His voice was faintly challenging. "Show me."

She smiled at him and unhooked her bra. She was getting more sexually confident every day that passed, and that big bulge in his jeans encouraged her. She unbuttoned her jeans, kicked them away.

Nick put his hands on her hips, and stripped the panties down, with a hard, impatient jerk. She heard a rip, felt a seam give way.

Whatever. Ripped underwear was a small price to pay for what he was always willing to deliver. She let the savaged garment fall, and lifted her ankles out of it delicately. Stood before him naked.

He nuzzled her breasts, eyes shut tight, mouthing her nipples, suckling her. Using his swirling, rasping tongue to make her shiver with anticipation. Then he got up and yanked off the fleece polo he wore. He opened his pants, and let his erect cock spring free.

He looked at her expectantly, dragging his hand slowly up and down the veined shaft. Gave her a what-are-you-waiting-for jerk of his stubbly chin. Uppity bastard. She was spoiling him rotten, if he was starting to take this sex slave business for granted.

It pissed her off, but as always, her emotions for him were a volatile, dangerous mix. Everything about him stirred and heightened her, even when he was arrogant.

But now was definitely not the time to scold him for it.

She sank to her knees and took him into her mouth, using all of her newfound skill on him. He went rigid, his fingers digging painfully into her hair. She could hear his rough, ragged breathing.

All the other times she had gone down on him, he'd melted for her, shivering and pleading. Vulnerable. This time he didn't. He turned his face up, eyes closed, gripping her hair, guiding her head to show her how he wanted her to take him. How deep, how fast. It was much harder this way, to breathe, not to gag on his thick, broad member, not to get tired. He didn't make a sound, didn't look at her.

What was with him? She pulled away from his hands, alarmed as well as angry, and struggled to her feet. "Nick, I'm not—"

"Shhh." He spun her around, and pushed her down onto the bed, hard. She tumbled onto her hands and knees. He gripped her hips. "Let's try something different," he said, nudging himself into her hot cleft. "Let's try it with no talk. No sound track, for once. Let's just fuck."

She gasped, at his first hard, penetrating shove. She wasn't wet enough yet. "I like the way we do it," she said shakily. "I like the talk."

"I don't, right now. I'm not in the mood."

"But I—"

"Shhh." He actually had the nerve to put his hand over her mouth, the bastard, but when she reached up to paw it away, that left only one arm holding her up, and she sprawled onto her chest, bed bouncing, his hot, smothering weight on top of her, his thick phallus prodding deeper. He slid his hand around her hip, threaded his fingers down into the curls that covered her labia. Caught her clit tenderly in the vee of his index and middle finger.

She struggled against his muffling hands, fighting against the confinement as well as the pleasure that he drew from her unwilling body. His skill was unerring: that urgent pump and squeeze in perfect time with the deep plunge and glide of his rigid shaft.

The climax wrenched through her, long and jolting and almost painful. She flushed for shame in the glowing aftermath. What kind of head case was she, to get off like this on his freaky games?

Her body was in thrall to him. It was unbearable.

He took his hand from her mouth to jerk her hips higher, and she twisted to look at him. "Stop this," she said. "Get off me."

"I want to make you come with my cock first," was his flat reply, and she started to say something sharp, but her words snarled up into a shocked, whimpering gasp as he abruptly deepened his strokes.

The orgasm had made her slicker and softer, and his sensual, rocking thrust-and-swirl technique whipped up the hot, frothy sweetness inside her till it rose up, cresting.

She couldn't handle it. She couldn't be catapulted all alone over the edge of the world. She needed him to go with her. Be one with her.

"Let me turn around," she pleaded. "Hold me. Please, Nick."

"No. Come for me," he demanded. "Right now. Show me what you can do, Becca. Display your very special talents for me. Right . . . *now.*"

That final jarring thrust and stroke carried her away. Throbbing heat rolled over her. Oblivion. She pitched, all alone, in the blackness.

When her eyes fluttered open, her face was shoved into the

pillow. She was weeping. Nick was poised over her, utterly motionless, his cock still throbbing against the mouth of her womb.

"You are amazing," he whispered. "How the fuck do you do that?"

"It's you who does it to me," she forced out, through trembling lips and chattering teeth. "You know that."

"Oh, no, babe," he said. "I think you can take credit for this all by yourself." He gripped her hips, to hold her in place. "I need to finish."

She braced herself as his deep thrusts met her most sensitive flesh. He went rigid when he finally came, hips pumping against her painfully hard, in absolute silence.

He rolled off her, got to his feet, and fastened his jeans. No lingering, no cuddling. Not that she was surprised. She rolled onto her side, feeling bruised and used in every way. She curled into a ball and covered her face, trying at least to keep the tears silent.

The sadness was huge. She'd felt it before. Something was slipping away from her, something beautiful and ineffable. No clinging or pleading could hold it. The way Mom had slipped away.

There was a hole that could not be patched, and all the joy was draining away into it. All wasted, all lost, all gone.

It broke her heart. Made her so goddamn furious. So desperate.

"What the fuck is wrong with you?" Nick demanded gruffly.

"Shut up," she whispered. "You don't want to know."

He grunted expressively. "Probably not."

She dragged herself up till she sat on the edge of the bed with her back to him. She felt heavy, exhausted. Stupid, too, for bringing this down on herself. She knew exactly how unpredictable he could be.

This was the last time she would ever try using sex to

sweeten him up. It had blown up in her face like a grenade. She had no way to distance herself from him, and she could not bear his dark moods when they were channeled into the intense, driving intimacy of sex.

Her cell phone began to ring. She turned her head, tried to get up, but she felt too lethargic to move fast. Nick fished it out of the outer pocket of her purse, and wordlessly handed it to her.

She leaped to her feet, mood soaring skyward when she saw the display. *Carrie.* Oh, thank God, thank God. She hit talk.

"Carrie, am I ever glad you finally—"

"No, my dear. No, it is not Carrie."

That oozing, faintly accented voice made her sink right back down onto the bed, suddenly boneless and cold. "Who is this?" she whispered.

"You know very well who this is." The caller chuckled, pleased with himself.

"Zhoglo?" she whispered.

Nick went motionless, eyes wide.

"No names, for now, my dear. Are you alone?"

"What does that matter?" she asked, inanely.

"Because my message is for you alone. Not for your lover."

"Why do you have Carrie's phone?" she demanded.

"Why do you think?" His voice sounded almost pitying. "One moment. I will remove the gag just long enough for you to speak with your little sister. Excuse me . . . just a moment . . ." The phone was quiet for a second, and Becca heard a muffled, dry cough and a choking sound. A small voice said, "Becky?"

Cold faintness threatened her. The icy pit yawned inside her. Carrie had not called her older sister Becky since she was a tiny girl, four years old maybe. Tears sprang to her eyes, spilled out. She wasn't big enough to contain this fear. It would shake her to pieces.

"Carrie? Baby? Are you OK?" she quavered.

"Becky?" the little voice croaked. "Becky? Please, I want to go home—"

The voice went away. Zhoglo returned. "That will do for now. Lovely creature, your sister. She's been my guest for two days now. I confess, I'm getting fond of her. Your brother, too. Fine young man."

"Josh? How . . . but he was just . . . I just—"

"Don't waste time trying to find them in the house you visited today," he told her. "They have already been moved to another location."

She had to concentrate to get the words out of her shaking mouth. "What d-d-do you want?"

"I want Solokov," Zhoglo said. "Your lover. Whatever his real name is. You need not say anything right now, of course. I know he must be with you. Just listen. If you wish to have your brother and sister back, you must think of a way to bring Solokov to a certain location, which I will communicate to you in our next conversation. When I have him, I will give you your family back, and you will all be free to go, back to your normal lives."

"But I—"

"But if you do not succeed in bringing Solokov to me at the appointed place and time, you will receive a DVD in the mail, the contents of which will be most upsetting to you. I will use just one of them, for now. I will flip a coin to choose either your brother or your sister to star in it. I need not elaborate, no?"

"N-n-no," she croaked. "Please, don't."

"Then, after you see this DVD, we will renegotiate," Zhoglo said complacently. "Do we understand each other, my dear?"

It took several tries to get the word out. "Yes," she said.

"Very well. I look forward to speaking with you again. Until then, my lovely Rebecca."

Click. The line went dead.

The phone dropped from her numb hand, bounced on the carpet. Becca slid off the bed, down onto her knees, and curled around that awful hole of pure terror. Her entire body stuttered with fear.

She felt Nick's big warm hands gripping her shoulders. "Becca?" he asked cautiously. "What's up? Talk to me, babe."

"He has Carrie and Josh," she blurted out.

"Yeah?" He slid his hands under her armpits and lifted her up, setting her gently on the edge of the bed. She doubled over again, unable to bear the sucker-punch agony in her middle. "What does he want?"

Becca's eyes overflowed with tears as she looked at him. It was the moment of truth. She could not betray him and deliver him up to Zhoglo. That was simply not an option. She didn't have it in her.

The instant she told him, the instant she made that move and put Nick on his guard, Carrie and Josh would be lost forever.

So was she. Worse than lost. She was damned to hell for all time.

Nick shook her shoulders. "What does he want, Becca?"

Her lips formed the word, but could get only the faintest puff of air behind it to turn it into a tiny whisper. *"You."*

Chapter
28

Wow. Amazing performance. He watched her weep and carry on with all his senses wide open, feeling for the vibe behind the vibe behind the vibe, and it rang perfectly true. She was a world-class actress.

Or maybe she was just nuts. Maybe she'd psyched herself into believing the tales she told. That was how it worked under deep cover. Who knew better than him? You pumped the false persona full of life and juice and detail and emotion. Until it lived and breathed. It made you half-crazy, yes, but he'd been more than half-crazy to begin with.

There might even be a part of Becca's splintered brain that sincerely believed that she loved him. Every instinct told him she was for real. That her evident distress for this sister and brother was real.

If only he hadn't seen that footage.

Christ, he wished he could throw it in her face and examine how she reacted, but Davy and the rest were right. He'd lose every possible advantage the situation might give him, for the sake of a stupid, desperate hope. He would not permit himself to do that. *No.*

"He wants me?" he asked quietly. "Tell me."

She mopped her face with a trembling hand. "I'm supposed to lure you into a trap, for him. When they have you, he says he'll—he'll give Carrie and Josh back to me. And if not . . ." She was gasping for air.

"Don't tell me what happens if not," he said. "I've seen it."

Strange twist. He pondered it. Why alert him to the trap? She might have sensed that he smelled a rat. Maybe this was a salvage job. She was smart enough, intuitive enough. Games within games within games. It tied his brain in knots. This chick was seriously complicated.

"Where's the trap?" he asked. "When's the meeting?"

She shook her head "He'll call with that info later," she whispered.

He hesitated for a moment. "Why'd you tell me, babe?"

She looked up at him, wet-eyed, utterly bewildered. "Come again?"

"Why tell me about the trap?" he repeated. "Why not just do the trade?"

Her back straightened. She wiped her eyes. "You son of a bitch. How dare you say that. If you have to ask me that question, then you don't deserve a goddamn answer!"

He shrugged. "Don't take it personally. I just figured, hey, your first responsibility is to Carrie and Josh, right? Goes without saying."

"And you think I'd be capable of doing that? Of turning you over to that monster after what you did for me? I love you, you stupid jackass!"

He thought about how he'd felt, staring at the blank façade of that town house today. "And what about Carrie and Josh?"

Her face crumpled. She sagged into herself.

Huh. He was not sure what, if anything, he'd learned from this touching melodrama, other than the fact that her performance remained watertight. The backstory was so believable. The dinky apartment, authentic-looking photos of the little brother and sister. That fucking phone call from Josh, at just the right moment—how the hell had she organized that? She must have had visual monitoring already in place. She must have been so sure Nick'd crawl back, begging for more, after the island. He didn't blame her. He'd have been sure too, if he were her.

The heart-wrenching tale that they'd bonded over: dear old Dad, Mom eating the pills, Becca raising little bro and sis all alone. That vibe of stoic endurance, tinged with stubborn good humor. Such a likable, masterful touch. He'd eaten it up with a spoon.

But why had she waited so long to turn him in? She could have delivered him at any point in the last few days. He'd been utterly off his guard. His head between her legs, his brain melted down.

Maybe she was going for a bigger prize. After all, Daddy Novak would pay big money for Tamara. And he'd enjoy cutting the McClouds into bloody pieces, too, for what they'd done to his son.

With his usual legendary bad judgment, Nick had exposed and endangered every last friend he had. "Get dressed, babe," he said.

She looked like she was going to be sick. "Where are we going?"

"I don't know," he told her honestly. "Anywhere. I don't give a fuck. I'd rather be a moving target. And I think better when I'm moving."

She plugged her cell phone charger into the wall, attached the phone, stumbled into the bathroom. The shower began to hiss.

Nick sat down heavily on the bed, and stared at her purse. He wasn't sure where the impulse came from, to unsnap the clasp and look through it. Self-torture, maybe. Punishment for his own stupidity.

The envelope in the inside pocket made his jaw twitch. It was a European envelope, the dimensions different from American stationery. The paper was thinner, shinier, yellower. The flaps folded differently. It was unsealed, and barely big enough to contain the wad of cash it held.

He flipped through it. Fifteen thousand, in crisp new hundreds. The bills stuck to the cold sweat on his clammy hands.

He shoved them back into the envelope, stuck it into the purse, and looked again, more carefully. Found a slit in the lining of her purse. He groped in, pulled out a GPS locating device. A commercial brand. Not professional level, but it did the job. The shower shut off. He shoved the locater back into the lining, tossed the purse where it had been.

So, then. That solved that mystery. She'd gone to Gavin Street to make her report, pick up cash for miscellaneous expenses, obtain a monitoring device. Maybe she'd been ordered to plant it on him.

Which meant he couldn't lose it without her copping to him.

He groaned, dropped his face into his hands. His head throbbed. Complicated, hell. Complicated didn't even begin to describe it.

She burst out of the bathroom, damp and naked and beautiful in a billowing cloud of back-lit steam. "Did my phone ring?"

He shook his head, watched her dress with frantic speed. Her hands shook. She kept dropping things. Shirt on inside out. Tripping when she put her legs into her pants. When she got to the laces of her shoes, he couldn't bear to watch it anymore, act or no act.

He kneeled and pulled the laces of her sneakers tight, tied them for her. Mr. Solicitous. She reached out to touch his face with her fingertips, a butterfly caress. Her eyes were glowing with tears.

Whoo-hah. Brace yourself for the tender moment, chump. *Jesus.* He had his limits. He flinched away. "You ready to go?" he asked.

She grabbed her purse, checked her cell phone, tossed the

charger into it and the phone into the outside pocket. "Ready," she said.

His mind spun in circles as they got into the truck, considering all his options. All of them ugly. He could ask Tam for some girl assassin trick, something like a nerve gas capsule he could tape to the roof of his mouth. Crush it with his teeth and spit death into Zhoglo's face while the prick was gloating over his broken body. That would be satisfying, for the brief seconds he would have to enjoy it before his own lung tissue melted. Tam always had a stash of wicked shit like that on hand for her wearable weaponry biz, but her studio was pretty far away.

He'd improvise with what she had on hand. Assuming that she was in town, and that she would speak to him. She just might be willing to provide him with the means of his own death, she was that pissed at him. That would be better than asking for help, organizing an ambush. He didn't want to put his friends into more danger than they were in already. They were family men, all in some stage of procreation. Except for Sean, who was on a plane to Italy with his bride for his honeymoon.

The other happy bonus that the Lone Ranger suicide plan had to offer was that he would no longer have to wonder what the fuck to do with his own inconvenient self for the rest of his useless life.

His life for Zhoglo's. A fair trade. Hell, it would be a blessed relief.

He just had to figure out what to do with Becca first. He had to plan for this, to prepare, and he couldn't let her witness it. Nor could he take his eyes off her at this point. And he couldn't bring her with him on a suicide mission. The chances of her getting killed were too great, even if she was on Zhoglo's team. It was her job to keep him under control. If she failed to do that, she was dead meat.

He didn't want that to happen. Whether she deserved it or not.

Besides. There was always the possibility that he was wrong. He'd been wrong before. He would never again trust his own reading of events the way he had before the Novak disaster. But he didn't dare examine that possibility too closely. His judgment was whacked already. There was a crushing load of evidence massed against her. Fifteen K in a European envelope, for fuck's sake. What more did he need?

Weird, that she'd given him Mathes and Evans, though. That wasn't in Zhoglo's best interests. Maybe she figured they were harmless bits of meat to throw to the panting, whining dog under the table. After all, Diana Evans was already dead.

What the fuck. He didn't care. Lying, two-faced whore or not, Becca was in deep. He would protect her if he could, from Zhoglo, from herself. Let the lawyers and judges thrash it out afterwards. He wasn't going to have to watch.

He would be long gone.

They were both silent, each lost in a private hell of dark thoughts as he drove aimlessly around the city, formulating the key elements of a plan for dealing with her. It began to come together in his mind, painful and flawed and ugly as hell, but so was everything else.

He pulled into a strip mall that boasted both a supermarket and a Staples store. Becca gave him a questioning look as he parked.

"Got to pick up some supplies," he said. "Come in with me?"

"I'll wait for you here, if you don't mind. If he calls, I don't want to take the call in public. I might cry, throw up. Faint. Who knows."

He grunted. Fair enough. But he didn't like leaving her unsupervised. She could plant that locator somewhere on his vehicle. Or make phone calls to her boss. Still, he'd rather get provisions unobserved. And once he got her settled, he could always make sure the locator was still in her purse and behave accordingly. So whatever.

He was brisk and focused in the supermarket, now that

he'd decided what to do. Some bottles of water, some meal replacement protein bars, some snak-pak cheese and cracker combos. A heavy-duty dog chain, like one you'd buy for a Doberman or pit bull. Done.

He loped across the parking lot, ducked into the Staples. Grabbed the first clerk he found, a pimply blond youth, and yanked the digital voice recorder out of his pocket. "Got the right battery for this?"

The kid examined it, frowning. "Aisle five, on your right, at the end."

Found them. Bought five. The fucking things were tiny.

There was a FedEx machine in the store. One more detail. He scrounged a piece of paper off a clerk, and scribbled a terse message to his ex-boss at the Cave. He filled out forms, swiped his credit card, watched to make sure that sucker wasn't maxed out. It took. He dumped it into the deposit slot.

It wasn't going to go out until Monday morning, but that was OK. He'd chosen the quickest, most expensive option. It should be on her desk by Monday afternoon, max. And his name on the sender's line should serve as a red flag that would get it to the top of the in-box.

He climbed into the truck just in time to hear Becca's phone ring.

One. The playful twittering, chirping sound that distinguished a call from Carrie was bizarre in this context. Becca was paralyzed. She could not move her hand. Two twittery chirps. Three. Her body vibrated.

Nick plucked the cell phone out of the pocket on her purse, glanced at the display, held it out. Four twitter chirps. "Pull yourself together, babe," he said. "Showtime."

Five twittery chirps. She hit talk. "Yes?" she croaked.

"Rebecca. How rude. I was beginning to think you didn't care. Or that you were angry at me." Zhoglo's voice was full of mock hurt.

She could think of nothing to say to his taunting. She waited.

He grunted, and got on with it. "Telling you the location of the meeting so far ahead of time is risky for me, but I am aware that you will need lead time. You must fabricate a convincing story to lead your lover in, no? I am not an unreasonable man, you see."

"Um," she said. "Ah, no."

"There is a house, outside of Cedar Mills. Number 6 Wrigley Lane. Any GPS navigational system will have no trouble finding it. A humble place, on high ground, with a clear visual for three hundred and sixty degrees. You will bring Solokov to this house at ten o'clock this evening. I personally will not be there, so please, no clever tricks, no heroics, no police. Or Carrie and Josh . . . need I go on?"

"No," she whispered.

"My men will be waiting for you there. You will be covered by hidden gunmen. All must be exactly as I dictate. Or both your siblings will die tonight. Along with you and Solokov. Very, very slowly."

"I understand," she said.

"Till later, then." The line went dead. Becca's hand dropped, limp.

"And?" Nick prompted. "Ten o'clock, in Cedar Mills," she said dully. "Number 6 Wrigley Lane. A house, I suppose, in a rural area. He says he won't be there. No police, no heroics, or he'll kill everybody."

"Hmm. OK."

Nick's voice sounded so detached. She glared at him, incredulous. "Huh? Hmm, OK?" Her voice vibrated with strain. "What are we going to do, Nick? What the hell *can* we do?"

"Calm down, and let me think it through," Nick said in that weirdly cool, distant voice. "We've got time."

"Time?" Her voice rose to a shriek. "What do you mean, time? My brother and sister have a knife to their throats! Three hours until—Jesus, Nick! There's no thinking through this! There is no way through this!"

"Panicking won't help. Shut up and breathe," was Nick's pitiless rejoinder.

Becca covered her face in her hands and tried to do exactly that. Breathe. Oxygenate her body. She had to stay functional. It was hard. She'd never tried breathing with a thousand-pound weight of pure terror weighing her lungs down. Her rib cage would not budge.

The miles flew beneath their wheels. The sun was down. It was getting dark. She saw signs for SeaTac, and for Southcenter. Nick was driving with more purpose than before. They had entered an industrial area. Warehouses, towers of giant, multicolored shipping containers. Chain-link fences, semi trucks. Nick pulled up outside a big steel gate and got out, leaving the truck idling. He picked at a combination lock that closed it. Pushed the gate wide, with a rusty, protesting screech of metal.

Becca stared at him as he got back into the truck. "What is this place? Where are we?"

He accelerated into a big, dim complex of deserted buildings. "You'll see," he said.

"Hey, Nick. Now's not the time for you to get cryptic on me. What the hell is—"

"Shut up and let me think. You think you're the only person who's stressed out? Do not fucking scold me, Becca."

She flinched at the brutal edge in his voice, and shut her mouth.

Nick braked in front of a blank-looking building with huge, sliding metal doors. The place had an air of decay and abandonment. Some of the windows were broken. There was a chain held by another heavy-duty combination padlock. Remnants of faded yellow crime scene tape tangled on the ground and stuck to the door. What on earth?

Nick picked that lock too and wrenched the thing loose. He reached into the back seat of the truck, grabbed a couple plastic bags that were stowed there, yanked the passenger side door open, and grabbed Becca's arm. "Out you get."

She slid out of the truck. "But where are we—"

"Later. Move." His tone was like the flick of a whip. The jolt to her tortured nerves got her going.

He shoved her before him in a stumbling trot, into the big, empty building. Dim light filtered in from the high, filthy windows. There was a little more light from the open door. The ceiling was vast, many stories high. There was a huge metal scaffolding system, designed to hold industrial quantities of who knew what. The scaffolds were empty now.

Startled bats fluttered and swooped. An owl hooted, whooshed down over their heads and soared, flapping, out the open door. Becca smelled the reek of animal shit, mold, dust, rot. The place was cold, damp. Incredibly desolate.

"What is this?" she whispered.

"A few years ago, there was a big drug raid here," Nick said. "This was a storage point for heroin coming out of the southern ex-Soviet republics. The owners are rotting in jail."

"But why are we here?" she asked.

He crouched, did something with his hands inside the plastic bag that she could not see. She heard the clink and rattle of metal, like the links of a chain. He grabbed her hands, yanked them unexpectedly downward.

Snick. Snick. "Because this is the only place I know of where no one will find you, and no one will hear you scream," he replied.

She stared at her hands, fastened with handcuffs. One was attached directly to the heavy metal scaffolding, the other was cuffed to a long, heavy chain which Nick then buckled to the next metal pillar.

She gaped at him in terrified astonishment.

Chapter
29

Something cool and wet kept stroking his face, but Josh didn't want to drag himself up to consciousness. Something bad waited for him there. But that wet thing petting his face was making him curious. Groggily, he let his eyelids flutter open. Regretted it as light sliced into his brain like a hot knife.

Oh, God. All pain. He was nothing but pain, his head a throbbing, sickening knot of it. Every heartbeat a hammer blow.

Josh tried to reach up to feel his head and discovered another source of pain. His shoulders were wrenched behind his back. Wrists on fire from tourniquet-tight bonds, his fingers numb and cold. His face felt crusty. His back hurt, his balls hurt, his stomach rolled. He tasted blood. Felt loose teeth. He knotted his gut to rock-hardness, and tried peering out one slitted eye.

Eyes. That was all he saw. Big, hazel eyes. Long-lashed, shadowy eyes, gazing at him thoughtfully. It seemed to hurt a fraction less, so he opened his one eye a little more to take in the whole face.

A girl's face. Heart-shaped, hollow-cheeked. Delicate and beautiful. He would have taken her for an angel coming to carry him away if she hadn't looked so damn sad.

There was an old bruise under one of her eyes. She was scary thin. Someone said something, in a questioning tone. A small child's voice. He couldn't make out the muffled, garbled words. The girl looked down, and replied gently in a language he could not place.

He opened both eyes. Curiosity was getting the better of him, but he had to close them and wait through several violent explosions of pain before he could gather the courage to do it again, and take in the entire scene.

Holy shit. It took a while for it all to sink in. So many kids. This raggedy girl, dressed in a shrunken T-shirt and baggy sweatpants, was in front. The shirt didn't hide her shape. Pretty. No, beautiful, despite her thinness.

He averted his eyes and was punished by a searing bolt of pain from his optic nerve. Served him right, though. This chick was way too young for him to be noticing anything below the collarbone.

She was surrounded by other children. Lots of children. Skinny, dirty looking. Most of them were sucking on their thumbs.

They were in a white room, flooded with light. Big, nasty, buzzing fluorescent bar lamps hung over them, blazing cold, head-splitting light that washed out all the details like an overexposed photo. He was reminded of a pop psych quiz someone had given him once. *So, like, you wake up in this completely white room. How do you feel?*

His answer was supposed to have revealed his true feelings about death. That kind of drivel annoyed the shit out of him. He didn't need a quiz to know how he felt about death. Death sucked. He wasn't looking forward to it, not for himself or anyone he cared about. End of story.

But no one had ever asked him how he would feel if he woke up in a white room with a bunch of starved-looking kids in rags. He wondered what deep psychological truths that question would reveal about a person.

The kids huddled around him in a semicircle, staring as if

he were an alien fallen from space. Like they might start worshipping him as a god. The girl leaned forward with her bloody rag and dabbed his forehead again. She said something. Said it again, louder. It wasn't until the third repetition that he realized she was trying to say something in English. "Hurts?" she said again. It had sounded more like "huts."

"Yeah," he croaked. Speaking made him cough, which provoked instant, skull-crushing agony with every jolt of his chest. Once he started, he couldn't stop. Bam, crash, pound, *fuck*.

It was starting to come back, in broken, jagged pieces. He remembered feelings—horror, betrayal, fear, shame—but the memories and sequences that had provoked them were broken to shards.

Image by image, he fit them together. Nadia, in the bedroom, naked. Hands clamped over her mouth, eyes streaming tears, watching silently as three big guys tied him up and kicked the shit out of him.

And the fat guy. He remembered him, too. Looming over him at some bizarre sideways angle, smiling. The bags of his puffy, bloated face swelling as he gloated. Crazy, blank gray eyes. He'd nudged Josh's face with the toe of his expensive loafers, and taunted him about something . . . something that scared him out of his mind, even before the memory slid back into place. *Carrie. Becca.*

"Carrie?" he said loudly. He looked around at the other kids. "Becca? Are my sisters here? Have you seen my sisters?"

The oldest girl frowned. "Sister?" she repeated slowly.

"My sisters! Have you seen them?"

The girl looked around at the others. The kids shuffled back. His vista opened up. Cinder-block walls, painted white. Concrete floor. Very cold. He was lying on it. There was a series of small mattresses. Each had a dirty blanket.

Holy shit. These kids lived here, in this freaky white limbo.

Carrie lay on the mattress nearest him. Her eyes were closed. She wore only underwear. Her hair was draped over her face.

Josh jerked up, tried to move, but he was trussed like a bird for the oven. "Carrie!" he yelled. "Carrie? You OK?"

The girl tapped him on the cheek, a brisk pat-pat. Then she held up a white plastic knife, leaned behind him, and began to saw.

It took a long time, but finally his hands came loose. They burned as blood flowed back into them. He reached up, prodded his head. Found a big, blood-encrusted lump on his temple. Then the rag, knotted around his neck. The corners of his mouth were chafed and sore.

He twisted round to look at the dark-haired girl, who was now working on his ankles. She mimed a gag in his mouth and nodded.

"You took it out," he said. "Thanks."

She gave him a cautious, fleeting smile. His legs came free, and he pulled himself up to his knees, wobbling like a baby who had never walked. Still wearing nothing but those stupid silk boxers.

He crawled to Carrie, brushed her hair away. Her face was white, with dark smudges under purplish eyelids. She didn't respond when he shook her. Her pulse was faint and rapid. She felt clammy. She made a raspy sound with each shallow breath. He couldn't stop shaking her, begging her to wake up. He realized after a while that he was sobbing.

He felt that pat-pat on his shoulder again, so he wiped his face and turned to look into the girl's big somber eyes. She mimed the injection of a hypodermic in her arm, and gestured towards Carrie.

Drugged, then. Those pricks had drugged his little sister. He tried to comfort himself with the fact that she was breathing.

He snorted back the tears, wiped his nose. "What's your name?"

She looked confused, so he pointed to himself. "I'm Josh." He stroked Carrie's hair. "This is my sister. Carrie."

She gave him that fleeting, beautiful smile again. "Sveti." She started in on the others, rattling off a list of foreign names, too fast for his battered brain to take in. She finished with the littlest one, a toddler who was clinging to her arm, ruffling the child's snarled black curls tenderly. "Rachel," she said.

Rachel held up her arms to be picked up. Two years old, maybe less. Scratchy little voice. The kid's face was so thin, she looked like a wizened little monkey. Sveti picked her up and settled the child on her slender hip. Skinny arms wound around the girl's neck; dirty little legs with black-soled feet wrapped around her waist like a strangling vine. The toddler wore a tunic made from an adult's white T-shirt, artfully knotted so that it would stay on her tiny body.

Sveti cuddled Rachel and gazed at Josh. Her calm, steady regard made him feel nervous. He was scared shitless, but she looked like she'd been afraid and miserable for so long, she'd made some strange peace with it. Her eyes looked old. A hundred-year-old woman, in the body of a thirteen-year-old. Twelve, maybe. Hard to tell.

He looked around. A tide of dread rose inside him as the children stared at him hungrily. Jesus, how could people do this to little kids? No tables, chairs, books, toys, music, pictures. No windows, even. The place smelled of piss, dirty diapers, rotted food. Big, overflowing plastic bags of garbage bulged along the wall. This place was like a holding pen for animals, doomed to be put down whenever someone got around to it. "Where are you from?" he asked Sveti.

She considered the question carefully. "Ukraina," she replied.

The Ukraine. It was coming together. Becca's mobster was Ukrainian. Nadia had been Moldovan, or so she said. But what the fuck was a mobster doing with a cage full of sad, dirty little kids?

Christ. That was a question he was afraid to consider. Especially since being penned in with them might mean that he and Carrie were now slated to share their fate. And looking around himself, he couldn't imagine it was anything but bad.

His own fault. Falling for a lying whore. Reeled in like a fish on a hook, and the hook was his own stupid dick.

It made him cringe. He'd been such a butthead. Becca had tried so hard to warn him, and he'd given her nothing but attitude.

"What are you doing here?" he asked.

Sveti bit her lip, looked doubtful, and shook her head.

"Why? What the fuck is this place? What are they going to do to you?" He was shouting now, even though he knew it wasn't fair.

She didn't look offended. "First, Ukraina," she said, in a low, halting voice. "Apartment. Many month. Then truck, boat, many days." She made a face, a gagging gesture with her finger. "Bad, truck, bad, boat. Then, here." She held up the hand that wasn't supporting Rachel. Five fingers, a closed fist, four more fingers. "Days. Many days."

"Nine days?" he said.

"Many," she repeated. She sounded exhausted.

Josh pointed at the bruises on her face. "Who hit you?" God, how could anybody hit a face that looked that fragile?

Her face went blank and she turned away, putting the baby down. The kid started to whimper. He knew just how she felt. But it was time for him to man up. Do something. Anything.

He staggered towards the door, supporting himself against the wall. Seemed less energy consuming than asking complicated questions. The littler kids all followed him, in a straggling file. He was probably the first new thing they'd had to look at in months. He must be a hell of a spectacle, beat all to shit and streaked with blood. He tried the door. Locked, bolted. The one other door proved to be a bathroom. One filthy toilet, no toilet seat. A dirty sink. A cracked bar of yellow soap. An industrial-sized toilet paper dispenser. The stench of piss. That was all.

He crept slowly back, along the wall, to the spot next to Carrie, and sank down next to her. He felt queasy and terrified. He covered his eyes to block out the light and the penetrating gaze of all those thumb-sucking kids who were hunkered down to watch him.

A few moments later, he felt a tap on his knee. Sveti was holding out a little plastic tray, sort of like the meal you got on a plane. A shred of dry-looking meat, a dried, cracked glop of gluey mashed potatoes smeared with congealed gravy, gray vegetables, a half-pint container of milk. A small bottle of filtered water.

It looked and smelled like a frozen meal that had been thawed and refrozen several times before the final insult of being microwaved.

She patted her own belly. "Me, no eat. No hungry. You eat?"

That was it. His stomach was already roiling from the concussion, and the sight of that disgusting little meal slammed into him like a fist right into his gut.

He twisted to the side and vomited everything inside him, then hung over the foul mess he'd made, weeping for shame at his own weakness and for the pounding, crashing pain in his head.

Pat-pat, this time on his shoulder. Sveti shoved a handful of wet paper napkins into his hand and the bottle of filtered water into the other. She pushed at him, nudging until he understood that he was supposed to scoot closer to Carrie. Then she started cleaning up the vomit, like she was used to it.

He wiped his eyes, his mouth with the napkin. "Please don't," he forced out, through shaking lips. "I'll . . . I'll do it."

She shot him a sidelong look. He could read it. *You can't even walk without falling on your face, and if I don't, who will?*

So you wake up in a completely white room. How do you feel?

He almost laughed at the random thought, but he stopped himself. It would hurt too much. How did he feel? He felt like he was already dead. So was Carrie, and Sveti, and the rest of these poor kids. All that was left was the actual, bloody separation from his body.

He let her clean up his stinking mess, trying hard not to cry.

This was not possible. It had to be some kind of bizarre joke.

But Nick didn't joke at the best of times. He could not possibly be joking now. Becca's mouth worked, stuttering out words that made no sense. "But I—but you—Nick, what on earth? T-t-take these off me, for God's sake! We don't have time for this!"

"You have time for it now." He had that hateful cool tone that had been bothering her since he'd gotten back to the hotel that day. "You've got all the time in the world for the next couple of days."

"But why are you doing this? Carrie and Josh are—"

"Figments of your imagination," he said. "And as such, I'm not inclined to worry about them."

She gaped at him until she found her voice again. "But that's nuts! You know they exist! You talked to my brother on the phone!"

"Yeah, that call from Josh really had me going. For a long time. But we've reached the end of the line."

"Why?" she demanded, frantically. "When? What happened?"

"It happened today," he said. "At 1:16, when you got out of a taxi and went into Zhoglo's town house."

She floundered for a moment, bewildered. "Zhoglo's—

what? But I didn't . . . oh, Nick. My God." She clutched his arm with her free hand. "You mean, the Gavin Street house? That's where I went to see Josh! Now it makes sense! Josh said Nadia was here on a student visa, but that place was way too nice to be foreign student housing. I *knew* there was something off. That's how Zhoglo entrapped Josh! With Nadia! And Carrie was in that house the whole time!"

She could no longer make out his eyes, it was so dark, but she could actually feel the cold emanating from him. "Nice recovery," he said. "But you really think I'm that stupid? Why should I believe you now when you lied to me before? You didn't say anything about visiting a Gavin Street town house to see your brother. You lied, Becca. Why?"

"No." She squeezed her eyes shut and whispered, "I, ah, I thought that stop to see Josh was no big deal—"

"No big deal? Really. Your thought processes fascinate me."

His grating, ironic tone was chilling. "OK, I thought you would be angry," she blurted. "It just came up. He called me, and you'd been so intense about safety, and so I just—"

"I am angry," he said. "You cannot imagine how angry I am."

She rattled her cuffed hand against the scaffolding. "This is a pretty emphatic message," she said tartly. "Nick, get real. Wake up. You can't leave me here. You are wrong about me. I'm not with Zhoglo."

"What's this, then?" He retrieved her purse, which had fallen to the floor, and rummaged inside, pulling out an envelope. "Explain this to me, sweetheart."

She stared at it, utterly perplexed. "My new purse—I bought a replacement. But that? Never seen that before in my life. What is it?"

He pulled out a fantastically thick wad of bills. "Fifteen thousand bucks," he said. "For services rendered."

She stared at it, shaking her head. She felt hemmed in, on

every side, like the walls of a box were closing in on her. "No," she whispered.

"You must have shown Zhoglo one hell of a good time for that kind of money. Were you as passionate with him as you are with me?"

"No. Never. They must have planted it while I was talking to Josh," she said, but she could feel the wall that blocked her words from him. They bounced back, sounding even to her own ears like the meaningless babble of a liar, caught out.

"Or was that money you took for fucking me?" Nick went on. "When I see the guy tonight, I'll thank him. I have never been worked over like you worked me over. I'm not even the same man."

That was literally true. He was transformed, and she hated the transformation. "No, you're not," she said. "And I would never do what you are accusing me of, Nick. Never in a million years."

He groped around inside her purse again, took out a small, flat black device. "And this, too. I'll get rid of it when I leave."

"What is that?" She peered at it, trying to make it out in the dimness, but he'd already slipped it into his pocket.

"Don't play dumb. It's boring." He took out her cell phone, pocketed that. "Here. You take this." He reached inside her jacket, feeling for the inside pocket, and slipped the thick wad of cash carefully inside. She could feel its weight tugging on her shoulder like a brick. "Keep it safe, beautiful. God knows, you've earned it."

She shrank away from his touch. "Don't touch me."

"No?" His hands slid down and fastened around her waist. "Aw, come on. It's how you've been managing me all along, babe. Don't you want to give your sexual wiles one more try? I'm up for it." He grabbed her free hand and pressed it against his erection. "Amazing, isn't it? How the body and the mind just don't connect. My dick doesn't care about this convoluted bullshit. It just wants to have at that pussy one last time—"

"Nick, stop it. I can't stand this."

"Besides, you know how you go wild for extreme." His voice was a deep, ticklish growl against her ear that made shivers of conflicting emotions race down her spine. "Remember how turned on you got for Zhoglo's live sex show? What could be more extreme than being handcuffed and fucked in an abandoned warehouse? Talk about illicit sex. You've been paid, and I've been betrayed . . . and fifteen K should be good for one last whack, right?"

She shrank away. "I would rather die!"

He stepped away from her. "Not an option. That's what this whole thing is about, Becca. You, not dying."

She squinted at him. "Oh, come on. You're protecting me, by chaining me up in a warehouse?"

"Yeah," he said. "I'm doing the meeting, Becca. I'm going to let them take me to him. And I'm going to kill that fucker while he's gloating. That's my plan. You wait here. Out of harm's way. You can't harm me. He can't harm you. It's the best I can do for you."

"But . . . but you can't go to him," she faltered. "He'll—"

"Kill me? Cut me up? Oh, yeah. That goes without saying."

She stiffened, lurching towards him, and was brought up sharp by the painful tug of the metal cuffs. "Oh, God, Nick. You can't."

"Please don't pretend you care," he said. "It makes it that much worse. Now listen closely. I don't have much time. Truth is, I'm genuinely sorry to leave you here. This place gives me the creeps too. I would rather have used my own house, but it's too far to drive there and back. There are six big bottles of water. Some food, enough to keep you going for a couple days. But I doubt that you'll have to wait that long."

"Nick, don't. Don't do this. I can't let you—"

"You can't do shit about it. I've placed the cuffs low

enough so you can sit on the floor. You won't be comfortable, but you'll survive. I've FedExed your whereabouts to
my ex-boss. Should be on her desk tomorrow. You won't wait
more than two days, max. They'll come for you, and you can
do your explaining to them, not to me. Because I don't want
to hear it."

She turned her back. His footsteps receded. There was
nothing more to say.

She looked at the two sets of handcuffs. The one cuffed
directly to the scaffolding was placed at a height that en-
abled her to sit, with her arm fully extended upwards. If she
sat, the other cuff that was attached to the long chain had just
enough play so she could reach for the water and the bags of
food, but not enough play so she could touch her other hand.
Well planned, on the fly. But that was Nick for you.

Ironic, that her affair with him should both begin and end
with handcuffs. One would think that detail might have
given her an inkling of coming disaster, but no. Becca and
her problematic taste in men.

She started shaking with something like laughter, but it
died away abruptly at the sound of that door, scraping in its
rusty gooves with a ponderous groan. The reverberating boom
jolted her jittery bones as it slammed shut. The door blocked
what light remained.

So the agonized wondering about Carrie and Josh and
Nick was going to go on and on. Until someone opened a
FedEx package, and took the trouble to come for her. She
was all alone in the dark.

Or maybe not completely alone. She heard rustling, skittering, in the darkness. Her flesh crept. The other inhabitants of
the warehouse were wondering who'd come to visit.

Chapter
30

Nick leaned on the truck, fighting the clammy faintness that threatened him. His heart thudded. Get out the fucking smelling salts.

He was in his usual place, squarely between a rock and a hard place, and getting whacked. But it had never made him woozy before. He was on the verge of a full-blown anxiety attack.

He tried to do the right thing, but there was no right thing. He'd never had enough information to know what was the right thing.

One thing was for sure, though. This did not feel right. At all.

So fuck it. When he got close to Cedar Mills, he'd call the McClouds. Tell one of them to go collect Becca, and deliver her to the authorities. Fail-safe. You never knew with the FBI. She'd last until then. She was tough. She could deal.

That way he could make his appointment with death with a clear conscience. Which reminded him. He had to get in touch with Tam. He needed all the tricks he could fit up his sleeve, and she was the trickiest chick he knew. Aside from Becca, of course. Becca took the prize.

Not here, though. He got into the truck, put it in gear. He

had to get some distance between himself and her. He could feel her despair, waves of it spreading out of that place, slopping over him, making him sick and shaky. He relocked the gate and took off with a squeal of tires. He hit the interstate, pulled off at the first rest stop.

First errand, lose the tag. He strolled by an eighteen-wheeler that was hauling livestock, and slid the GPS locator into one of the slots on the container. Let it get eaten by a pig or a sheep. That would lead those fuckers on a fun chase. Second errand. He went back to the truck, put a small battery into the digital voice recorder, and pushed play as he pulled back out onto the highway.

". . . *subject number 100023, BD 021697,"* said a low female voice, presumably Diana Evans's. *"The subject is an eleven-year-old male, poorly nourished. Pulse rate 81, blood pressure 115 over 65, temperature 98.2. Listless and vacant in appearance . . ."*

The recorded voice droned, recording vital signs, noting bruises that suggested abuse and/or vitamin deficiency. An untreated rash, a slightly enlarged liver. She spoke of tissue typing, a buccal swab. She recommended blood screening to rule out viral infections, a urine culture to rule out bladder and kidney infections. In a detached way, she noted the subject's hygiene and state of emaciation. She recommended reevaluation before harvest of this subject was considered.

Harvest? What the fuck? She wanted to fatten this kid up for—

Oh, sweet holy Jesus. Realization clicked, like a round being chambered. Mathes was a cardiologist. Thoracic surgeon. Transplants.

Harvest. Organs. Lab tests, blood and urine samples. They were killing kids for their organs. Those filthy, ice-hearted sons of bitches.

Evans's voice went on. Another numbered subject, ten years old. Same shit. Vital signs, dispassionate, doctorly observations about how scrawny and miserable he looked, but this kid had more spunk than the other, and didn't like being poked and prodded and stuck with needles. He started to cry for his mama. In Ukrainian.

Evans persevered stubbornly, but her voice took on an edge, and finally, she said, *"shit,"* fiercely. *Click.* The recording resumed, presumably some time later. The kid was whimpering more quietly now.

"Shut up and stop bothering the doctor, you piece of dogshit, or I'll make you squeal like a stuck pig," snarled an evil male voice. Ukrainian, also. The kid choked off his sniffles, and Evans's voice continued with her report. But her voice had now begun to shake.

On and on. Child after child, number after number. The kids kept getting younger. All protested the needle. Some wept, some whimpered, some shrieked. Evans was breaking down. Her voice trembled, she stuttered, repeated herself, transposed words, got confused, had to run the tape back and start again. And if there was any ruckus, that voice was ready to intervene with its evil threats. It would have made Nick slit-his-wrists miserable even if he had not already been so.

Every last trace of sympathy he might have had for Diana Evans drained away. If she hadn't been evil and cold enough to suit those murdering pricks, it sure as shit wasn't from lack of trying.

For some reason, the fact that she'd tried made it worse. A psychopath couldn't help what he was. But why would a person who actually possessed a functioning conscience deliberately try to deactivate it? It made him so angry, so bewildered. He blew out air, tried to breathe. For money? Meaningless, stupid money? How could they value it so highly? He just didn't get it. He never had.

But fortunately, puzzling that mystery out was not his job.

"Subject 100089, BD 121396. Well-developed, poorly nourished adolescent female . . ."

He snapped to attention, pulled off at the exit and pulled over to listen more closely.

"*. . . pulse rate 79, blood pressure 120 over 70, temperature 97.9. What appeared to be a severe skin eruption on her neck now appears to be a port-wine birthmark. . . .*"

He sucked in air, electrified. *Sveti.* Oh, God. Alive. Holy fucking shit. Alive. As of forty-eight hours ago, she was *alive.*

And in the hands of organ pirates.

"*. . . priority rush on these lab tests, as Subject 100089 is scheduled for harvest on Sunday the twenty-seventh . . .*"

That was today. That was fucking *today.*

His lungs were locked and his throat burned. Christ, he couldn't stop breathing now. He might still have a chance to save her.

Sveti was speaking on the recorder. He recognized her soft voice, pleading for help from that worthless Evans bitch in the pidgin English that Nick had taught her. Being completely ignored.

She abandoned the English in favor of a babbling flood of high-pitched Ukrainian, but he couldn't make out most of it because Evans was screaming. *Damn it—shut up, you stupid cow, let me hear her—*

The recording cut off abruptly. His body shook. He wiped his eyes and nose on his sleeve. No time for feelings. No time for tears.

He wished he could call the Cave for back-up, but he didn't dare. He had no idea who in that crowd had sold Sergei out.

He put down the digital recorder, dragged out his phone and pulled up Tam's number.

"Nikolai. I'm surprised to hear from you," she cooed. "I heard the angel betrayed you. I thought you'd be licking your mortal wounds under a bush someplace. To think I got into it with one of Zhoglo's lackeys, and at Sean's wedding, too."

"Shut up, Tam." His voice cracked with emotion. "Remember Sergei's daughter? The one you said was dead, or worse?"

"Yes. Calm down. You sound like you're about to have a stroke."

"She's alive, Tam! As of two days ago, she was alive! But she's on the slab. They're going to break her down for parts. Today!"

"Break her down for parts? What the hell are you—"

"Organs!" he yelled. "They're fucking organ thieves!"

Tam was startled into total silence.

He waited, till he couldn't stand it anymore. "So?" he prompted. "Will you help me? She's alone in the dark. Gonna help me save her?"

Tam blew out a breath. "Oh, fuck, yes." Her voice was low and savage. "Where do you want me?"

"Stand ready. I'll call Davy. I'll call you back in a few, and we'll come up with a plan." He hit end and dialed Davy's number.

Davy answered on the first ring.

"Got some bad news for you," Davy said. "We lost Zhoglo."

That threw him for a second. "Huh?"

"They shook us. They loaded some shit into a couple of SUVs, and the whole pack piled in and took off. Marcus followed them to a parking garage, but a car stalled out at the entrance. By the time he got inside, they'd switched vehicles and were out of there. Which means they made us, probably a while ago. So consider that when you calculate your—"

"Never mind that," Nick cut in impatiently. "Fuck Zhoglo. Where's Mathes?"

Davy hesitated for a second, nonplussed. "Uh . . ."

"Hey. Where the fuck is Mathes's icon?" Nick demanded. "And where the fuck is Mathes?" he roared.

"All over the place," Davy said. "Left his house at three, went to his office suite, then a stop at a private medical lab in Bellevue, and then he got on the highway and went to a place called Kimble—"

"Kimble?" Alarm jangled every nerve. "Fuck! That's where they've got the kids! Why didn't you tell me he was moving? How long has he been there?"

"About an hour and a half," Davy said, his voice guarded. "What kids? You didn't tell us to tell you whenever Mathes moved. Granted, you were pretty distracted the last time you were here—"

"Never mind that. That filthy shithead Mathes is killing kids and harvesting their organs. You guys want to help me stop him?"

There were about two seconds of shocked silence. "I'm with you," Davy said. "I'll tell the others."

"Get all the firepower you can carry. Whatever you've got. Get on the road for Kimble. You got someone to spot us on the Specs monitor, in case the fucker moves?"

"Raine can—"

"Good. Call the FBI. Get their rapid response team moving. I'd be glad for the help. I'll tell Tamara to meet us in Kimble. Move. Go. *Now.*"

The boy named Josh was so beautiful. Even with blood streaking his face from that lump on his forehead, even vomiting his guts out, he was the most beautiful thing Sveti had ever seen. Those green eyes, like leaves, like grass, like life. All things she hadn't seen in so long.

She couldn't stop staring at him. She knew it was rude, but her eyes stayed on him. The other children sat around him and stared too, silent and owl-eyed.

And when he smiled at her, oh. Her heart bumped. No one had smiled at her in months, unless she counted Yuri's yellow-toothed leer.

She wondered if the girl on the bed was his girlfriend. She thought she'd understood the word "sister," but she couldn't be sure.

She was going to get a beating from Yuri for untying the boy. He'd told her not to touch those two or she would regret it. But it was worth it, just to talk to someone with a kind face.

She sat cross-legged on the mattress, rocking Rachel and crooning a lullaby. Peeking from behind her hair, like a lovesick cow. If the girl was his sister, she wondered if he had a girlfriend. Probably all the girls wanted him. Not that it mattered. She was thirteen, and he had to be at least eighteen. She was a plucked crow of a girl, skinny as a skeleton. Her hair was snarled, and she probably stank, though she was too used to bad smells to notice now. He had a nice body, too. Long and graceful, like a runner, with muscular legs. She liked nice legs.

Josh. What a beautiful name. It felt exotic. So nice, the way he was petting Carrie's hair. She was so thirsty to see any expression of kindness, even if it wasn't directed at herself. Her eyes just drank it in.

The rattle at the door made her belly sink. The door opened.

Yuri marched in, followed by Marina. He saw Josh sitting up, then turned his evil glare on Sveti. She put Rachel down hastily. Stumbled back, putting a safe distance between herself and the toddler.

"You stupid brat. I told you not to touch them." His hand flashed out with blinding quickness, a backhand slap that spun Sveti around in midair before the floor swooped up to deal her another huge smack.

Voices, yelling. Yuri, and another voice. Marina, too. Stephan and Mikhail joined the chorus, and Rachel shrieked.

She rolled over, her nose streaming blood. Josh was shouting at Yuri, words she didn't understand. His fist flashed up, a swift uppercut. Yuri stumbled backwards with a grunt. Josh dove for him again.

Ka-chunk. Marina leveled a black, squared-off gun at him.

"Back, pig," she spat out in English.

Josh stopped himself in mid-lunge, reeling for balance. He held up his hands, eyes wide. "Don't shoot," he said. "I'll stop."

Yuri yanked his own gun out of his pants, and pointed it at Josh with a shaking hand as he came on, swearing viciously.

"Don't," Marina snapped. "The boss wants to play with this one. Do not touch him. We've already had trouble for your stupid stunts."

Yuri spat a big, yellow glob on the floor, and smashed the big pistol into Josh's face. It made a bone-breaking sound.

Josh toppled like a tree falling, and lay horribly still. Sveti could see wet, bright red blood on his face, from where she lay. A sound came out of her, the despairing cry of a tormented animal.

Yuri heard it and spun around, the bloodshot whites of his eyes showing clear around the muddy dots of his irises. He seized her by the upper arm, and wrenched her to her feet. "You little bitch," he raged. "You come here. Your time has come."

He dragged her towards the door. She kicked and scrabbled, bruising her feet against the concrete floor. Sobbing helplessly over what Josh had just done for her, that sweet, kind, brave, *stupid* thing—

"Careful with her, dickhead." Marina's voice was as flat as a robot's. "They won't be happy with us if you damage her. How many times do I have to tell you?"

The little ones were all crying. Rachel wailed the loudest. Even after the door slammed shut and was triple locked and bolted, the baby's piercing screeches followed her down the corridor.

Sveti didn't stop fighting. A desperate jabber of thoughts buzzed through her mind; what would Rachel do without her? Would she sleep, or would she just cry? Would Sasha remember not to give her that nasty fruit slop with canned apricots that gave her hives? Had Yuri's blow split Josh's skull? What were they going to do to her? And was it going to hurt?

And oh, God, oh, Mother. *Mother. Please.*

They shoved her into a big room she'd never seen before.

A shower, surprisingly clean and antiseptic-smelling. Marina turned the water on, and wrenched the shirt off Sveti's head, shoving it against her bleeding nose. "Press that there until you stop leaking. And you," she directed the words at Yuri. "Outside. I don't trust you."

"Don't be a cunt." Yuri leered at Sveti's chest, which she covered with shaking, crisscrossed arms. "I want to see her clean and pretty, at least once. Before . . . you know." He smirked.

"Out." Marina's voice was adamant. "You bloodied her nose, asshole. They won't like that. It doesn't look good."

"I never hit the parts they care about," Yuri said, his voice sulky. "Just arms and legs."

"And faces? Jerkoff. Out." Marina gestured with her big, protruding chin towards the door. Yuri stomped out, muttering.

The shower was ice cold. The liquid disinfectant soap stank, burned her eyes, stung in all her scrapes and sores. She was shaking too hard when it was done to towel herself off. Marina had to dry her, while Sveti shuddered, teeth chattering, struggling to stay on her feet.

The older woman ripped a lightweight cotton thing out of a plastic package. Baggy green pants, the creases from the fold still sharp. A matching shirt, huge and floppy, that reached halfway to her knees. Her hair dripped down her back. Marina wrung it out, and wrenched a comb through it, dragging it straight back off her face.

Sveti found herself, barefoot and naked beneath the green thing, still shivering, her raked scalp stinging, the cold cotton fabric clinging to her wet back. She shuffled down the corridor, through the locked door at the end, out into another corridor. One she'd never seen.

It was wider, brighter. Much cleaner than the one she knew.

Marina dragged her down the cold gray concrete floor, and elbowed her into a metal elevator. She was horrified at her own reflection. She was so white, so skinny, so small. Those big eyes, that tiny face. She barely existed, next to Marina's imposing blond bulk. They ground slowly up. The moving chamber shuddered to a stop.

The doors sighed open into a new world. The walls were soft green. Everything glittered. It dazzled her. Lights flashed and twinkled on walls full of gleaming equipment.

Marina shoved her between the shoulder blades, sending her stumbling into the room. It was filled with people dressed in green, like herself. Their heads were capped, their mouths masked. Only eyes showed. So many eyes, looking at her. She shrank from their regard, retreating towards the elevator. Marina pushed her forward again.

A very tall masked ghost stepped forward, his cold gaze boring into her face. "Get her prepped," he said. "Fast. We're already late."

Becca counted her breaths. Tried to keep them slow, deep and steady. One. Two. Three. Four. All the way up to ten.

Then she slowly counted back down again. If she kept doing this, the night would end. It was finite. The world was turning, hurtling her through space into an unknown future. Day would come. Someone would come. And they would tell her what had happened out there.

She was not going nuts. She would not break down. She wasn't afraid of the dark, or of whatever creatures were rustling and skittering over the concrete floor around her. Rats, bats, roaches, no big deal. She was a grown-up. She could handle it. Not afraid. No, and no, and no.

She wondered if three hours had passed yet. Could have been six hours, it could have been ten minutes. Maybe Nick had already gone to meet Zhoglo. Maybe it was all over. Maybe Carrie and Josh . . . no.

Stop. She couldn't think about it. She'd start screaming.

One. Two. Three. Four . . .

The sound of a vehicle outside made her heart practically stop in her chest. Nick? It had to be Nick. He was the only one on earth who knew where she was, at least until tomorrow when the FedEx package was delivered. Maybe he'd had a change of heart. Maybe he'd realized that she couldn't have done what he thought she'd done.

Yeah. Hah. The cynical, grown-up realist deep inside her laughed.

She had to toughen up. She knew life was dangerous. Caring about people was the most dangerous thing of all. She'd known that brutal fact since she was twelve and nothing she'd learned since then had convinced her any different. But she'd never let herself think about how bottomless that dark pit truly was. She kept herself too busy.

The only real bottom was death. Death would stop the suffering. Death would break her fall.

She'd never understood the reasoning her mother must have gone through as she sat on her bed staring at that pill bottle. Falling, constantly, endlessly through inner space, into the dark.

Becca understood it now. And for the first time, she could almost forgive Mom for leaving them alone. Almost.

There was a rattling groan as the heavy door slid open on the rusty runners. Light flooded in, from the headlights of the vehicle rumbling outside. Fresh air moved her hair, chilled the sheen of cold sweat on her face.

Footsteps. *Thud, thud, thud.* She strained to see who it was, but the complex bulk of scaffolding was in the way, blocking her line of vision. She couldn't see the whole silhouette. Just disconnected slices, and a halo of blinding, blurring headlights behind it.

Thud, thud. Closer.

She sucked in air, forced herself to call out, in a thin, quavering voice. "Nick? Is that you?"

A flashlight flicked on, moved over her body, and settled

directly in her face. Blinding her even more than the head-lights had done.

Thud, thud. Not Nick. Nick would never do something like that. Even angry, he would not deliberately terrify her.

The holder of the flashlight shone it up under his own chin, grotesquely illuminating his fat, wild-eyed, grinning mask of horror.

"Charming," came that oily, complacent voice that froze her heart. "Tethered like a goat, ey? So convenient."

Becca hung onto consciousness. She was falling, through inner space. And all she dared to hope for now was that the death that broke her fall was a quick one.

Chapter
31

Davy flinched as Tam whipped off her microfiber tank. The woman's tits were just too much to take in the cramped back of the surveillance van. "Jesus, Tam," he snapped. "Could you warn us when you're going to pull a stunt like that?"

"Grow up. You're a married man. Haven't you seen tits before?"

"You use your tits the way a ninja assassin uses nunchaku," Davy complained. "I don't like to take a direct hit with no warning."

"Bullshit," she said. "Typical, projecting your lust onto an objectified woman."

"Not any objectified woman," Davy growled. "Just you, Tam."

"Could we skip the feminist crap?" Nick asked tersely.

"Could you gentlemen give me some space?" Tam fussed. "I have to make myself look good, and your combined bulk is getting in my way."

The five men crowded back against the walls as Tam rummaged through her bag of tricks. They were packed into the van, what with Tam, Davy, Connor, Seth, Nick and Alex Aaro.

Once Aaro had heard the words "kids" and "organ pirates" mentioned in the same sentence, he'd insisted on coming along for the ride. They had a plan. Full of holes, risky by its very improvised nature, but it was a plan.

Mathes's car was blipping away in a parking lot outside a large, nondescript complex of new brick buildings surrounded by a chain-link fence topped with razor wire and with God knew what kind of alarm system. Covert recon in Seth and Davy's thermal camo cloaks had revealed a prefab hut twenty meters from the big automatic gate, manned by four guys, according to Davy and Seth's thermal imaging goggles. There had to be more in the main building complex, and probably still more on patrol.

Tam yanked out a tangle of silvery latex straps, and proceeded to stuff her breasts into them. She rummaged again, pulled out two crescents that looked like bags of silicon gel, and wadded them into the base of the tit-web-slings, transforming her perfect C-cup tits into larger but equally perfect D-cups.

"So that's how girls do it," Seth said. "I've always wondered."

Tam yanked a silver latex skirt out of the bag, and a thong. "Gentlemen, fair warning," she said. "Anyone who does not want to see my cunt"—she shot a glance at Davy—"close your eyes now. Anyone who does want to see my cunt, be aware that you will pay dearly for the privilege at some later date. When you least expect it."

"With what?" Alex Aaro sounded fascinated.

"I like to leave it a mystery," she said. "Your life? Your firstborn? Your immortal soul? It depends on my mood."

"Your balls for a necklace," Nick told Aaro.

"I am always looking for new materials for my wearable weaponry lines," Tam said. "But shriveled testicles aren't that pretty." She punctuated her statement by yanking off her black briefs.

The men turned their heads so fast they risked whiplash.

They waited. "Is it safe?" Nick asked. "Can we open our eyes?"

"Safety is an illusion," Tam said. "Is any man ever safe with me?"

Nick opened one slitted eye. She was more or less decent, if you could call a skirt that short decent. It stretched over her perfect ass like plastic wrap as she bent over, adjusting a blond wig. She flung the hair back, slicked crimson paint over her lips, yanked on silver boots with four-inch heels. She grabbed an aerosol tube and sprayed herself with a choking cloud of glitter that made them all cough. When the sparkling fog cleared, she gave them a dazzling smile. "How do I look?"

No one dared to answer. She looked like a Vegas showgirl about to take the stage. She looked like a million bucks. She looked like trouble incarnate. Nick shook his head. "I don't like this," he muttered.

"Too fucking bad," Tam replied. "It's the best chance we have. The one weapon no man is ever completely defended against is femininity." She slanted a peek at Nick. "As our friend Nikolai can attest, hmm?"

The other guys winced. Nick clenched his jaw and let it pass.

Tam pulled out gem-studded clip-on earrings with a tiny receiver attached to one, which she tucked into her ear. A matching wrist unit was incorporated in a bracelet made of white gold and semiprecious stones. But she didn't stop there. Nick watched her don a chain with a mother of pearl egg-shaped thing studded with jewels and swirls of gold. A small, pearl-tipped round pin stuck out of the top of it that looked like a—

"Holy shit," he said. "Is that thing a grenade?"

"Hooray! He can be taught!" Tam said. "I'm sorry your women aren't here, boys. They're the ones who really appreciate my genius."

"We're appreciating it, but could you hurry the fuck up, Tam?"

Tam wrinkled her nose. "Never rush a woman." She draped herself with several more pieces of jewelry, the practical defense applications of which were anybody's guess, yanked the skirt up, and strapped on two custom-designed nylon net thigh holsters, one for a Walther PPK, and the other for Davy's mini dart gun.

"There," she said. "Now I'm done."

Nick ground his teeth as he looked at the shimmering expanse of bare chest, thigh, belly. The rest of them had bulletproof vests, gas masks, goggles, comm equipment, thermal cloaks, kick-ass firepower.

Tam was waltzing into the jaws of death practically naked. It wasn't right. It made him twitch. But he couldn't think of a better plan.

Tam slid out of the van, fluttering her fingers. "Good luck, boys."

The men were all silent for the drive to the gate. When the van came to a stop, they gathered around the monitor to watch her mince, slowly and sexily, over to the heavy gate. Nick braced himself for the crack of gunfire. And another friend's death on his conscience.

A floodlight flicked on, illuminating Tam's fluffy mane of blond hair from above, lighting up her whorish outfit as if she were clothed in scanty strips of molten metal. "Yoohoo!" She jumped, making her tits bounce. "Anybody there? Hellooo! I'm lost! Anybody there? Anybody?"

The door opened. A large man was silhouetted against the yellow light inside. He moved slowly towards the gate, an automatic rifle cradled in his hands. His thick, squarish face resembled that of a bulldog. "Who are you?" he called out.

"Oh, thank God! Am I glad to see you! I'm looking for Sumner Road," Tam said. "I've been going totally nuts. My name's Brandi."

It was always jarring to hear Tam cast off her usual crisp pan-European accent and do a flat, nasal American caricature.

"I don't know any Sumner Road. You should go back to Kimble and get directions there," Bulldog advised.

"Oh, God, that's going to take me forever," Tam moaned. "I was supposed to dance at this bachelor party, and now there's probably not even any point in going. And it's cold, too! Would you believe, I forgot my sweater? And dressed like this too! Just look at me!" She spun around for his benefit. "I am, like, freezing in this teensy little thing! I don't suppose you have any nice hot coffee in there, do you?"

Bulldog looked her over. "What are you, some kind of stripper?"

"Actually, my act is a little more complicated," Tam confided. "I use butterscotch syrup, you see. And the groom licks it off."

Bulldog stared at her for ten full seconds. "What part of you does he lick it off from?" he asked hoarsely.

Tam let out a throaty giggle. "Depends on how much I've been paid, big boy. The best man for this party only wanted to spring for lips and nipples. But if the groom is up for it, and the party wants to tip me enough, he can just paint me up with syrup and . . . move south."

"How far south?" Bulldog's voice sounded strangled.

Tam giggled again. "Oh, all the way," she whispered. "If he wants."

Davy's shoulders shook. He had both hands clamped over his mouth. Aaro and Seth and Connor were grinning like fools. Fucking pack of clowns, Nick thought, irritated. This was not a goddamn game.

"You mean, for a big enough tip, he can lick your—"

"I just love having it licked and licked and licked," Tam cooed. "And if he makes me come while he's at it, he gets a big discount."

Long silence. "Uh . . . on what?" Bulldog couldn't help but ask.

"On the next part of the evening's entertainment. Where I paint butterscotch over a body part of his choosing and lick it off of him."

They held their breaths for Bulldog's response.

"Uh, want to come in and have that cup of coffee?" the guy asked. "I want to introduce you to the guys. They have got to hear this."

"Oh, thanks! I would just love to!" Tam burbled.

The gate churned open. Tam slid her arm chummily through Bulldog's elbow and minced along with him towards the guardhouse. It was harder to follow the sound once she disappeared inside. A guy inside was scolding Bulldog, calling him an asshole.

"Lighten up, Roger," they heard Bulldog scoff. "It's just a cup of coffee. Here you go, gorgeous. Cream and sugar are right here."

"Oh, thanks! Oh, wow, that's cool equipment! What's that splotchy thing on the screen? Is that, like, infrared, or something?"

"Thermal imaging," Bulldog explained. "Hey, toots. Tell 'em about the butterscotch syrup."

They slid out of the van. The vehicle had a thermal barrier, so they'd been invisible inside it, and the thermal cloaks covered them once they were outside of it.

The five men crept slowly, flat to the ground. There wasn't much time before the ice-celled cloaks warmed up and their own body heat started to show.

Come on, Tam. Stop dicking around. Get on with it. Now. Please.

The guys in the guardhouse were loving it. Bulldog was now warmed up and jovial, trying to persuade Tam to go to a hotel with them when their shift was over and give them a private performance.

Tam balked, coyly. "It's tempting, but it would be so un-professional. I should find the Sumner Road guys. I mean, the guy's getting married tomorrow, so this is, like, his last chance, right?"

Bulldog chortled. "Last chance, my ass. I'm married too, gorgeous, but a guy's gotta do what a guy's gotta do. I like butterscotch."

"Oh, my. You great big bad boy, you," Tam purred.

Davy's voice cut into her performance. "Everybody in position."

A commotion in the guardhouse. A clatter, a gasp, heavy thuds. "Oh, my God! What's wrong with him? He, like, just keeled over on me!"

Thud, smack, a shout of alarm, several more thuds. "What the fuck are you—nngh!" A man began to scream. The sound was cut off.

Nothing. Nick held his breath. One second, two, three, four, five, oh no, six, oh *fuck*—

"All four down," came Tam's husky voice. Cool as a cucumber. The chick wasn't even breathing hard. "Stand ready for the gate, boys."

The thing began to grind. They slipped through and sprinted, to the guard hut. Tam was poised in the doorway. One guard was slumped in a chair on the far side of the room, a dart protruding from the back of his neck, the rest sprawled on the floor in the center of the room.

"Dead?" Nick asked.

Tam snorted. "Just tranked. Better than they deserve, the gutter dogs. They'll all have different recovery times, but we're good for a half hour. Unless you want to just kill them, Nikolai."

"Nah." He fished plasti-cuffs out of his pouch. "Bind them."

Davy was checking out the security. "Infrared and thermal imaging around the perimeter," Davy said. "Sentries every hundred yards. No motion detectors that I can see. The guards' uniforms transmit an identifying signal that shows up on both systems."

"Good. So Tam can spot us on the monitor from the guard-house and send alerts."

"Hell. I have to miss the big party?" Tam pouted as she collected the guns that the guards were carrying.

"You've partied enough," Connor said. "Butterscotch. Jesus."

"A hundred bucks says you try it with Erin, first chance you get."

Con clapped a gas mask over his face by way of reply, and ducked out the door.

What followed was a race against time at a slow crawl. The ice cells in the thermal cloaks were already warming, so they still had to ooze over the ground like slugs to avoid being spotted on the infrared.

"Monitor just lit up. Sentry coming around the building on the right," came Tam's low voice. "He's moving towards . . . ah. He's not moving anymore. Davy, you sneaky bastard, was that you?"

"Dart," was Davy's terse reply.

"Cover him quick with the cold cloth. He looks bad lying on his face," Tam warned. "And deactivate that transmitter on his shoulder. Two more coming from the other side . . . ah, nice work. Who was that?"

"Spray gas," Aaro's laconic voice said over the comm. "Never saw it coming. Fuckin' amateurs. I'll use one cold cloth to cover them both."

"Would you fuckers cut out the mutual congratulation and concentrate?" Nick snapped.

"Chill, Nikolai," Tam said. "Don't spoil our fun."

He ignored her, peering through the transparent window of the hood towards the building entrance. The door opened. Nick sagged into a pool of shadow. "Everybody stay put," he murmured, as some guy peered through binocs towards the guardhouse, put a comm device to his mouth, spoke into it.

Spoke again. Tapped it, irritated, when he got no response. He shut the door and set out towards the guardhouse.

His trajectory was taking him right over Nick. He slid his hand through the slit, gas at the ready . . . and reared up at the last minute.

Pffsssss. Down he went on top of Nick like a half ton of gravel.

"Good job, was that Nikolai?" Tam asked.

"Yeah." Nick struggled out from under the man's three-hundred-pound bulk, and jerked out a pouch with a camo thermal blanket. He ripped the transmitter pin off, and tossed the cloth over the guy's sprawled form, which would make him invisible until the ice cells melted.

He placed the transmitter on a rock and smashed it.

"Heads up. The rest of you reptilian sons of bitches are still invisible, but our hot-headed Nikolai is starting to show," Tam said. "Pick up the pace, gentlemen. Your window is closing."

Nick cursed. His goddamn elevated core body temperature could blow it for all of them. "I'm going for the door," he said.

He crawled forward, icy-cold condensation drizzling down from the inside over his face. He peered at the door through his binocs . . . shit.

A red light was glowing on top of a large black palm lock device.

"We need one of the guards," he hissed into the comm. "Palm lock."

"I'll bring mine," Davy said. "He's scrawnier than yours."

An irregular camo'ed lump glided towards him along the building. It was Davy, with the guard slung over his shoulder under the cloak.

"Davy, you're heating up too," Tam said. "And Nick looks like a neon sign."

"Almost there," Davy said calmly.

Nick and Davy converged on the door. Nick groped for the guy's limp hand, and splayed it against the pad. The light clicked green. The door sighed open. Another guy was on the other side, eyes bugged out.

Pffffssssss—another squirt of gas. The guy went down. They leaped over him. *Bam.* Connor stumbled back. Davy's arm swung up.

Thhtp. A dart spat into the shooter's throat. A guy peered around the doorway of the control room, took aim—

Thhtp. Nick nailed him in the shoulder with another drugged dart.

Nick rolled over to Connor, who had dropped to the floor. "You OK, man?" he demanded. "Tell me you're not shot."

"Nah," Connor gasped out. "Took it in the vest. Knocked out my wind, though. Broke some ribs."

Alex Aaro and Seth, on the far ends of the fan of cloaked creepers, slithered in like a couple of camo'ed ghosts. They shoved off their hoods. "Did we miss the fun? Aw, shit." Seth sounded miffed.

Davy came out of the glassed-in control room, wiping his brow with his forearms. "The room's secured," he said. "Tam can tell us who's coming from the outside."

Nick peered out the door into a long, empty corridor.

He turned to the others. "You guys stand guard. I'm going in."

"You don't need us all to hold the guardroom," Aaro said. "We're with you."

"Whatever," Nick muttered. "Just let's *move.*"

They took off down the corridor at a dead run, boots thudding.

The smell of Zhoglo's cigarettes made Becca nauseous. Though it could be argued that she would be nauseous any-way. Considering.

At first glance, the scene looked almost convivial. A man and a woman, on lounge chairs on a huge deck perched over a cliff. The view was a vast, spectacular panorama of Seattle cityscape, moonlit water and jagged mountain ranges, still topped with snow. A fragrant breeze swept over the deck, a chorus of crickets chirped. Owls hooted.

A bottle of wine sat on the table between their chairs. The ruby liquid rolled around in the goblet of the man as he savored the aroma.

Then, an observer might notice bizarre discrepancies. For instance, the semi-automatic rifle in the hands of the man behind them. The tape over the woman's mouth. The cuffs on her wrists, attached to a dog chain, which was wrapped around one of the four-by-fours that supported the huge deck. More duct tape was wrapped around her chest, binding her to the chair. Zhoglo had been amused by the chain, and had elected to leave it attached to her wrist.

Zhoglo ground out the butt of his cigarette. "To be honest, I was hoping he would kill you," he said, in a chatty tone. "For betraying him. My idea was that once he knew his error, his punishment would be his own guilt. Very dramatic." He sipped the wine, swishing it in his mouth with pursed lips. "But this scenario has its charm. I understand Solokov's specialty is quick death. So quick the victim does not even know that he is going to die. Pah. Anticlimactic." He leaned forward and flicked her cheek with his finger, chuckling when she flinched. "And that, my dear, is not what I have in mind for you."

Becca was almost grateful for the duct tape, since it canceled out any necessity for a reply.

"Would you like some wine? It's quite good. Kristoff, remove my guest's gag. I grow weary of talking to myself."

Kristoff picked at the tape and ripped it off. The pain jerked a squeak out of her throat. She coughed as she dragged in air.

Zhoglo leaned forward, and placed a glass of wine into her shaking hands. "Steady, my dear. Can you lift it to your mouth?"

Her hands were blocked by the length of the chain, fixed in place against her chest by the heavy tape wound around her body.

Zhoglo clucked in dismay. "Let me help." He lifted the glass to her lips. Wine sloshed over her chin, her chest. She choked, coughing.

Zhoglo waited until the spasms died down. "Would you care to know the fate of your brother and sister?"

Becca stared at him, lungs hitching, eyes streaming. He spoke in the tone she would use to offer someone a napkin.

"My plans have readjusted," he confided. "My natural instinct for thrift has prevailed. That disaster on the island cost me, and these funds have to be replenished. But now that I have you to play with, I can use your brother and sister to cover costs."

"Cover . . . what costs? What do you mean?"

Zhoglo settled himself more comfortably in his chair, and held up a cigarette. Kristoff hustled forward to light it. He crossed his legs and began himself to sip the glass of wine he had poured for Becca. "Mathes is a transplant surgeon. The very one who gave me this heart some years ago. Would you like to see the scar?" He groped at his shirt.

Becca shook her head. "No," she said faintly. "Please, it's fine."

He shrugged and rebuttoned his shirt. "That experience gave me the initial idea. Punishment is necessary in this wretched world, but waste is not. This surgeon has joined forces with me on . . . well, in this eco-mad world, one might even characterize it as a recycling operation."

"What on earth are you talking about?"

"Your brother and sister, for instance," he went on. "If they prove to be healthy, their combined donated organs, at the prices set by the doctor, will be worth upwards of fifty million dollars. Minus expenses, of course, which are considerable, but still. Consider the possibilities."

"Organs?" Her heart began to race. She felt sicker. "Oh, my God."

"In fact, the very first harvest has been scheduled for tonight," he said cheerfully. "I am looking forward to it."

"The little kids," she whispered. "You're killing those little kids."

"Oh?" His eyebrows shot up. "So you did make progress on your investigation." He slapped his knee. "Clever girl. You were busy, ey?"

Busy wasn't the word for it. Busy Becca. "I tried," she whispered.

"I put Josh and Carrie in with the rest of our repository of spare parts for now, pending tests to check their organ viability. They both certainly look healthy, but one never knows. I did watch your brother fornicate with a prostitute for thirty-six straight hours. I confess, I got exhausted just from watching. So naturally, we must test for HIV and so forth."

"Oh, no," she forced out. "Not Joshie. You can't do that."

"I can, and have. Actually, it's the oldest girl who's scheduled for harvest today," he went on. "Twelve? Thirteen? I don't remember. Hardly a child at all. Her father offended me some months ago, you see. I put her aside to settle his debt when this plan ripened. A debt that will be paid in full tonight."

She shook her head helplessly. "No," she whispered. "No."

"Three surgical teams stand ready to utilize everything she has to give," Zhoglo went on. "Heart, liver, kidneys, lungs, eyes, nothing wasted."

Tears flashed down Becca's face. "Sveti?"

Zhoglo's eyes widened. "Oh, so you know about her? Was that why he was infiltrating?" He began to laugh. "How excellent that I am having the event taped. He can watch her being butchered."

He leaned forward, patted her knee. "I will tell you a guilty secret." His hand lingered there, horribly moist. "My original fantasy was to punish the fools who opposed me by immobilizing them with drugs, and conducting their harvest while they were fully conscious. Feeling every slash, every tug. It is a traditional technique that I often employ. But the doctor explained to me that organs obtained in this way would not be viable for transplant. They would be polluted with the hormones provoked by pain and terror. I was forced to abandon my fantasy in favor of practical reality."

His hand began to move up, over her thigh. "Therefore, you will be happy to know that Joshua and Carrie's deaths will be pain free. Conducted under general anesthesia." He looked expectant, as if he was actually waiting for her to express her gratitude for his mercy.

He grunted with irritation when she failed to do so, and continued. "But not with you, Rebecca. I intend to enjoy every minute of yours, from your first scream to your last dying rasp. While Solokov watches, helpless. You, my dear, are pure, sinful indulgence. My little treat."

She tried to jerk her leg away, but his hand tightened. "And speaking of watching." He glanced at his watch. "Mikhail? Would you set up the large monitor out here for myself and my guest? I have arranged for direct video feed of the operating theater." He slapped her thigh. "We will watch the harvest together, my dear. In real time."

"No," she kept whispering. It was useless, but she couldn't stop.

"Oh, yes. Pavel, bring some snacks for myself and my guest. What would you like, my dear? Cheese? Crackers? Sliced meats? Perhaps some fresh fruit? There are apples and some grapes, I believe."

Her eyes were streaming. "Please. Don't do this. Don't."

He patted her knee again, and his fingers slid up between her thighs. Big mistake to weep and plead. It excited him.

A picture flickered onto the large screen. An overhead view, of a slender, dark-haired, incredibly pale girl who lay still on the table. Her eyelashes were so dark, brushstrokes against her white, sunken cheeks.

Falling deeper—and deeper still. Becca closed her eyes, and wished she could will her heart to stop beating.

But it would not obey her. It just kept thumping, painfully, stubbornly, stupidly on.

Chapter
32

The corridors were endless and they echoed. Doors opened onto empty rooms that weren't even finished—no floors, walls, no wiring, just the smell of paint and plasterboard and cement dust.

They got lucky at the fourth stairwell. Nick strained with all his senses as he leaned down to listen, and heard the vibration of voices, like someone had opened the door to a room where people were talking and then promptly closed it again.

They crept noiselessly one flight down, peered out. No guards, no guns. No apparent obstacles. Nick darted down the corridor, tried all the doors. Empty. No sound, no movement.

The next floor down, he heard that muffled hum of voices again. He waved Seth and Aaro behind him, and edged along the wall. Ahead was one of those big automatic doors, with a huge metal wall button. Right before it was the room from which the voices were coming.

He burst in. Seth and Aaro came behind him. Gasps, shrieks, shouts, terrified babbling in several languages. People scrambled for cover as three cloaked apparitions exploded into the room, bristling with guns. They scurried under tables, crouched behind couches.

It was a doctor's waiting room. Windowless, but luxurious and comfortable. Full of couches, walls painted in mellow tones of peach and beige, forgettable art, muted table lamps. There were even individual TVs, mounted on the end of each couch, with earphones provided. A large bookcase. A serve-yourself snack bar. A coffee maker.

One couple remained seated, squarely in the middle of one of the couches. Hands entwined. A tall, balding man with an anxious face, and a younger, ash blond woman, thin and pale. Expensively dressed.

"Henry?" whispered the woman. "What's going on?"

The man stood up, frowning. "Who are you people? What are you doing here? This is a private clinic!"

"Where is Dr. Richard Mathes?" Nick demanded.

The woman's eyes got huge with alarm. "Oh, God. Henry, no. I will not allow it." Her voice rose. "This is not happening! We're so close!"

"Where is Mathes?" Nick repeated, louder.

The woman leaped up and ran at him, shoving at his chest with her hands. "Get out of here!" she shrieked. "We've paid a fortune for that heart! You are not going to stop us! Get the hell out! *Out!*"

Nick pushed her back towards her husband. He had no time to deal with a hysterical woman.

Out in the corridor, he slapped the door button and the huge doors folded inward. The skinny blonde ran after them, shrieking, "No! You can't! You can't! You'll bring your germs into the operating—no! Stop! You'll kill her! You sons of bitches! She's fragile!"

Nick sprinted on. The woman's voice degenerated into a despairing wail. Another automatic door, punch, and on they ran. There were voices behind the door in this corridor.

He burst through. Into an operating theater. His heart thudded. Green, white, silver, glowing lights blazing down on a table, people in surgical scrubs bending over . . . oh, Christ, had they already—?

"Get away from her!" he bellowed. "Get the fuck *back!*"

The doctors scrambled away from the table with their hands in the air, eyes wide and fixed on the gun in his hand. He lunged over to the table, his heart thudding—

Not Sveti. It hit him in the chest like a pickaxe. Big, shadowy blue, white-lashed eyes looked up at him. So pale. Grayish skin, violet shadows around her eyes, every bone in her skull showing. An anesthesia mask over her mouth and nose. IVs and tubes and sensors everywhere. Not quite under. And not Sveti. This was the girl who was supposed to get Sveti's heart.

She was dying before his eyes.

The sight of her knocked all the air out of his lungs. Her eyes locked with his, full of terrible knowledge. The look of one who had crossed an invisible line and was moving swiftly onward.

Like the look on his mother's face when she had embraced death.

For this girl, he was the grim reaper, the killer of all hope, but she just gazed at him, trying to breathe. She hadn't really expected a reprieve.

She was ready to go. He could see it.

They understood each other perfectly, but words blurted out of him anyway. "I'm sorry," he said hoarsely. "It's not going to happen, kid. Game over."

A tiny nod, a weak flutter of her fingers. An almost smile.

"You're ruining everything! She was so close! So goddamn close!" the blond woman screeched, chasing him in. Alex Aaro followed close on her heels and grabbed her, pinning her against his massive chest.

The girl's mother. Nick stared at her and repeated the words mechanically. "I'm sorry. It's not going to happen."

Aaro locked the flailing, sobbing woman behind his arm, and yelled over her. "Go on! I'll secure this room." The doctors were starting to slink towards the door. Aaro leveled his H&K at them. "Everybody stop right where you are," he barked. "Sit down against the wall with your hands on your heads. *Now.*"

"Sorry," Nick whispered again to the girl on the table, and then he grabbed the elbow of the woman who was nearest the door and hauled her along with him into the corridor. She screamed and struggled, but he shoved her on ahead of himself. "Where's Mathes?" he asked.

"I'm just the perfusionist. I just run the bypass machine! I never hurt anybody! I swear it!" The woman had an Eastern European accent.

"Shut up and take me to Mathes," he snarled.

She started babbling, in . . . Estonian? Yeah, it was Estonian. Hard to tell, she was talking so fast, voice garbled with tears. She was nattering about her boy, what Zhoglo had threatened to do to him if she didn't comply. He had no time for this shit, no matter how pathetic.

Estonian wasn't his best language, but he could threaten in it.

He slammed her up to the wall, pointed the gun at her leg. "Take me to Mathes," he said, in her own language. "Or I start with the knee."

She wailed and sobbed, but when he took his hand away, she set out at an unsteady, shambling run, with Seth and him right behind.

They didn't have far to go. There was another operating theater, full of doctors. He veered towards it. The woman shook her head wildly, grabbed his arm and dragged him onward. "No, no. This is another recipient. All recipients. Mathes is not there, he is . . . he is *here.*"

More double doors. Slap. Another operating theater. The woman stumbled to her knees and pointed to the glass doors. "There," she sobbed. "He is there. Please, don't hurt me."

Nick left her and crashed through the door. Another table, another cluster of green masked ghosts, bending down over a table flooded with light. The light gleamed off a scalpel, and oh sweet bleeding Christ, one of them held a surgical saw—

"Get the fuck away from that table!" he yelled.

A clatter of equipment, shouts and shrieks, as the doctors leaped back from the table. Nick advanced, holding the gun on them.

Sveti. Unconscious, her thin white chest bared to the knife under the bright lights. Every rib showing. The guy standing over her with the scalpel had not moved. He stared at Nick, his eyes wide in disbelief.

"I said to get *back*, asshole!" he snarled.

The room was silent, but for the blip and whirr of machines, and the steady beep of Sveti's heart on the monitor. Still beating. Still inside her. Seth came up behind him, cool and grim.

"Which of you pieces of shit is Richard Mathes?" he asked.

The others shrank away from the table, leaving the one who held the scalpel standing all alone. The one who had not scurried at his first two warnings. The one who had held his ground.

The arrogant prick yanked his mask away, cursing. His handsome face was full of righteous indignation. "Who the hell are you? And how dare you burst in on us in this way. We are performing an extremely delicate life-saving surgery, and you have just—"

"Shut up, you lying butcher," Nick said. "I know exactly what you're doing. Step back. Right now. Or I will blow your head off."

Light flashed on the scalpel as Mathes's hands went slowly up, his mouth twisting in impotent rage. The urge to jump on the guy and kill him with his bare hands almost overwhelmed Nick.

He blinked back angry tears. Sveti's face was so white, so hollow. There was a fresh bruise under one eye, an old greenish-yellow one under the other. What had they done to her?

"Which of you dirtbags is the anesthesiologist?" he demanded.

The shrinking, not-me demeanor of the others singled out by elimination a pudgy woman with close-set eyes. He pointed. "You?"

She shrugged. Her eyes were sullen and dead above her mask.

"How long will she be out?" he demanded.

"Ten minutes. Unless I give her more." Her voice was flat.

There was a flurry of movement behind him, a terrified gabble. A shriek. Nick jerked around. Mathes was holding a pistol on him.

Bam. Mathes shrieked at the gunshot. His pistol flew in a lazy arc over the operating table. It crashed, slid into the corner.

Mathes fell to his knees, cradling his right hand. If you could still call it a hand. It was now a mangled mass of blood, splintered bone and tendons.

None of the crowd of doctors made any move to help him.

Seth gave Nick an apologetic shrug. "I probably should have just wasted him, but I wanted to zap the hand that did the dirty work. And besides, I liked the idea of the fun he'll have in prison, once the inmates find out that he gets off on gutting little kids."

"Fair enough," Nick said. "Thanks." He turned back to the anesthesiologist. "Where are the rest of the kids?"

"What kids?" The sulky bitch was holding out on him.

He gestured with his gun at the moaning Mathes, blood dripping down onto the floor. "Do you see that fuckhead? Do you see his hand?"

"Yes," she said reluctantly.

"Do you want to be next?" he asked. She shook her head.

"Good," he said. "Then let's try this question again. The kids?"

She blinked, staring at the gun. "Downstairs somewhere. Never been down there. None of us have. They brought her up in the elevator."

"They? Who's they?"

"The ones who take care of the kids," she snapped.

Take care, his ass. He thought of how thin Sveti was, of the bruises on her face. "How many of them are there?"

"Two that I've seen," she said. "A man and a woman."

Nick glanced at Seth. "I'm going on down."

Seth looked troubled. "Alone?"

"You stay with Sveti," Nick said. No way was he leaving her alone with a roomful of people who'd been about to cut out her heart.

"Problem solved," Tam said coolly from the doorway.

All eyes cut to her. They could hardly help it. She strutted into the room on four-inch silver heels, shimmering, gleaming, violently blond, an elegant silver Walther PPK in her hand.

"I'll go with you," she said. "The cops are on their way to pick up the rest of this garbage." Her narrowed eyes swept the huddled doctors.

"Good," Seth said. "Go on down, then. I'll just make sure none of these guys decides to leave before that."

The elevator functioned without a key. Evidently, once you got this deep in the guts of this killing factory, they were no longer worried about security. Five levels of sub-basements. He glanced at Tam, who gave him a your-call shrug.

He hit the bottom floor. It seemed symbolically appropriate.

The door ground open onto another corridor, but this one was less finished, with snakelike tubes running along the ceiling and a gray concrete floor. On the left, the corridor dead-ended after twenty yards. On the right, there was an L-turn after fifty.

They turned right.

The sound of frantically slapping feet froze them in their tracks. Rasping, panicked breaths. A man careened around the L-turn, wild-eyed, knees pumping high, gun in hand. A maniacal goblin of a man with greasy blond locks straggling from his oily pate.

He screamed shrilly at the sight of them, reeled back, and jackrabbited off the way he came.

Nick and Tam gave chase. A door slammed. They peered around the corner. They were blocked by heavy-duty doors, with a small window of wire-reinforced glass. They sprinted for it. Locked and barred.

Beyond the window there appeared to be nothing other than still more of that endless fucking corridor. Nick smashed the glass with the butt of his gun. There were kids wailing, far away down the corridor.

Nick slammed the door with his fists. "We've got to get in there! He'll kill them so that they can't testify!"

Tam yanked his elbow. "Get back around the corner." She lifted the gem-studded grenade necklace off her neck. "It will blow the door, but that's all. The kids are far enough away to risk using this."

She pulled out the jeweled pin as they turned the corner, and bowled it on the fly with graceful skill. It slid to the end of the corridor and came to rest against the door.

Tam sank down next to him. "Five . . . four . . . three . . . *ears,* Nikolai!" He stuck his fingers in his ears as she mouthed, *One.*

Just in time. The sound slammed every molecule of his body against every other molecule. They looked around the corner. There was a jagged, twisted hole where the door had been. Cinder-block rubble, a cloud of choking dust. They sprinted through it. The yellow-haired man lay on his face about thirty feet from the door, screaming hoarsely in Ukrainian.

"My ears! My ears!" he howled.

Blood ran out of both his ears and down his neck. He pawed at the air like a maddened animal and stared at his bloody hands, tried to grab them as they passed. "My ears!"

"Where are the children?" Nick yelled in Ukrainian.

The guy just reared up onto his knees, howling and gabbling and sobbing. Tam made a disgusted sound, plucked out one of her earrings, gave it a brisk twist. She stabbed it into his shoulder.

He groaned, toppled slowly to the ground and lay still.

They ran on, slowing to listen as a new sound became audible. A baby, wailing behind a door. More than one. The closer they came, the stronger it got.

The door with the screaming behind it was locked and bolted. They threw the bolt, but the lock was a good one that would take an expert hours to pick. He couldn't shoot it out with kids behind it.

Movement, flashing in the corner of his eye. He and Tam turned, and took off after a big, bulky blond woman who was sneaking out a door and sprinting towards the hole they'd blasted.

Panic made the woman fast, but she was heavy and stubby-legged, no match for the infuriated Nick and a thoroughbred racehorse like Tam, even when the chick was sporting four-inch silver heels.

They caught up with her at the stairwell. Nick took her down with a flying tackle. She grunted as he landed on top of her. She was soaked with sweat. "Not so fast, lady. I want the key to that door," he told her.

"No understand," she said. "No speak English."

A garnet-handled knife suddenly appeared in Tam's fist. She grabbed the woman's coarse blond hair and wrenched her head back, and screamed in Ukrainian, "The key, bitch!"

"I don't know what you're talking about—"

The tip dug in. Blood welled up, trickled down the woman's neck. "I suggest you figure it out, before I cut off your ear," Tam hissed.

"No! No cut. I give you keys," the woman gasped out in English. She struggled under Nick's weight to get her hand into one of her pockets, dragged out a small bunch of keys. "Here. Keys. Take. Take."

Nick and Tam glanced at each other.

"We'll let you open the door, you donkey-faced hell-witch," Tam said. "If you gave us the wrong key, we can renegotiate, no? Maybe I'll go for an eye. God knows you can't get any uglier."

They hauled the woman to her feet and frog-marched her back to the door with the screaming kids behind it.

"I did nothing wrong," the woman protested, sounding put upon. "I take care of children, I feed, I wipe bottoms, I no hurt!"

"Shut up," Nick snarled.

They shoved her up to the door. As soon as the locks gave way and the door handle turned, Tam pulled out her hair clip, twisted a small nozzle, and squirted the woman's face.

She fell sideways against the wall, eyes rolled to the whites, and slid down. Good. Two down, ready for custody.

Nick blew out a sharp breath, and pushed the door open.

The first impression he got was that there was a single malformed organism, with multiple staring eyes, multiple clutching limbs. Then the mutant being resolved into a tight knot of dirty, terrified-looking kids.

They were scared into silence except for the smallest one, who squalled lustily in the arms of a tall young man. The guy was naked but for boxer shorts, his face battered and bloody.

The heavy fog of piss, vomit, unwashed bodies and rotten food made it hard to breathe. Nick let his gun hand drop to his side.

"We're not going to hurt you," he said quietly in Ukrainian.

A scrawny little kid who looked about ten tried to speak,

and coughed. He tried again. His voice was hoarse and scratchy. "Where are Marina and Yuri?" he replied, in the same language.

"Outside," Tam said from behind him. "The police will take them away and punish them. They can't hurt you anymore."

They stared at each other, at a loss. The children were paralyzed with shock. Nick was struck dumb by the squalor of the room.

The toddler wiggled in the guy's arms. He put her gently down, and she toddled forward on dirty little legs, huge eyes locked onto Tam, who glittered under the fluorescent lights with supernatural brightness.

"Pretty," the toddler lisped in Ukrainian. "Mama."

Tam shrank back. "Oh, no. Not me," she told the kid. "I'm not your mama, little one."

The kid lifted up her thin arms. "Mama? Mama?"

Tam backed up. Nick had never seen Tam intimidated, or even at a disadvantage since he'd known her, but this two-year-old seemed to terrify her. "No," she said, shaking her finger. "Not me. Not your mama."

The tiny girl's face crumpled with woe. She started to wail.

Tam began to swear viciously, in some thick, obscure language that Nick could not immediately place. "Hell," she muttered. "Come here, then." She picked the kid up.

Nick went in and looked them all over. Half-starved and pale but they were all on their feet. Except for one older girl slumped against the wall dressed in her underwear, who looked very weak and ill. The rest of the lot were smaller than the ten-year-old.

"Is Sveti all right?" asked the kid who'd spoken before.

"We got to her just in time," Nick told him. "She'll be fine."

The kid put his hands over his eyes. His shoulders began

to shake. From behind, he heard snippets of Tam's conversation with the kid. "Stop that! Oh, God, don't touch that, it's filled with sulfuric acid!"

"Pretty," the little girl gurgled. "Pretty."

He looked at the stained mattresses, the wall lined with plastic bags stuffed with rotting trash that no one had bothered to haul out. "Holy shit," he murmured softly. "Those filthy assholes."

A tall young guy stepped forward. "Hey! You speak English, mister?"

Nick swung around, startled. "You're an American?"

"Hell, yeah! Me and my sister Carrie. The rest of these kids are Ukrainian, I think. They dumped us in this room today. And there was this other girl, too, Sveti. They took her away a couple hours ago. Look, man, have you seen my sister Becca around here?"

Nick's chest flash-froze. The world fell away, whirling and shifting, everything changing around that phrase. "Who are you?" he asked.

"I'm Josh Cattrell," the guy said. "That fat guy, the mobster dude, I think he's got my big sister Becca locked up someplace too. Maybe she's here. You haven't seen her around, have you?"

Nick stared at the kid's wide-set green eyes. Just like Becca's. So were the reddened eyes of the girl hugging her knees on the floor. Josh and Carrie. Holy fucking shit. What had he done?

He swallowed hard. "She's not here." His throat closed tight around the words, strangling them so they were barely audible.

"How do you know, if you don't—hey." The kid's eyes narrowed to wary slits. "Wait a sec. You know Becca. Don't you?"

"You could say that," Nick said, his voice raw. "I thought I did."

Suspicion dawned on the kid's battered face. "Wait a

freakin' minute. You must be the thug," he said. "Becca's boy toy. The one Becca was having the hot affair with. You're that guy I talked to on the phone, right?"

"Yeah. Did she meet you today? At a house on Gavin Street?"

"Yeah, that's where Nadia took me," Josh said. "She said it was her place, but I guess it was this mobster guy's house all along—hey, man, are you OK? You look like you're going to be sick, or something."

Nick was so fucked. More than fucked. He was doomed.

"So where the hell is my sister?" Josh demanded.

He tried to suck in enough air to answer. "Somewhere she shouldn't be," he said. "I've got to haul ass to go fix it." He turned to Tam, who was trying to throw her deadly pendants over her shoulder.

The baby was grabbing for them, chortling with glee.

"Becca was telling the truth," he said. "I have to go get her. Zhoglo had her tagged. He could trace her to the place where I left her."

"Ay. That's bad. Go, then." Tam's eyes went bleak. "We'll finish here without you. Run like the devil is after you, Nikolai. Because he is."

He did, spurred on by bone-chilling fear, and wild, crazy hope.

Chapter 33

There was screaming in the room behind the picture window. Something shattered against the wall. Zhoglo was in a bloody rage.

Eventually he would take it out on her. That was going to be bad.

But it hadn't happened yet. One thing at a time. Becca still had a few moments to smell the pines, throw her head back, look up at the moon lighting the holes in the clouds, and weep for joy.

Josh and Carrie were safe. She'd seen it with her own eyes on the monitor. Seen Nick, bursting in at the last moment and stopping those monsters cutting that poor girl. And if Sveti was saved, then Josh and Carrie were, too. And all the rest of them, too. Free and clear. *Saved.*

Zhoglo's henchmen had forgotten the monitor, which kept on transmitting the live video feed. Sveti still lay on the table, with a woman in scrubs bending over her, checking her pulse. Seth stood next to her, half visible on the screen, grimly holding a gun on someone or many someones, all of whom were off camera. Someone was moaning and babbling in pain. Not Sveti. Seth didn't appear at all concerned about it.

Becca was crying, but she didn't care. She flung her head back, sniffling, listening to the trees rustle above her head. Dragging in lungfuls of the sweet breeze. A big circle opened in the clouds, lined with light. Stars, clouds, moon, trees. Beautiful.

Carrie and Josh would have to live it for her. Love it for her.

She ached with sorrow for her own loss, but Josh and Carrie would go on. They would grow up, choose mates, make families. Ripen into strong, happy people. Live long, full lives. She hoped for it desperately. Wished it for them, with all her strength, all her love.

And when it came to living fully, well. She may have skimped on life experience up to a week ago, but her affair with Nick had been so intense, it was like years of living crammed into a few short days.

She'd loved him. Fully. Not wisely, but well. That was a blessing. More than a lot of women had to look back on at the end of their lives.

She would cling to that as best she could, when the time came.

Nick had never driven so fast in his life. He floored it through the interior of the warehouse complex, his flesh creeping at the thought of Becca, staked out in the dark. The virgin sacrifice. *Innocent.*

He fished in the glove box for the flashlight. He should've left it with her in the first place. Hell, he shouldn't have left her at all.

Moonlight came and went as clouds scudded by. Inside, that place would be as dark as the pits of hell.

And he was the one who had chained her there.

Stop. Focus. No point in flogging himself for fucking up again. He had the rest of his life for that. Becca herself could do the honors. For now, he was focused on making it right. As right as it could ever be.

This kind of wound was the kind that never healed. He knew about wounds like that. He'd watched them inflicted, seen them fester, for his entire childhood. Until love was just a distant, bitter memory.

She would never want to see him again. He knew that. But it would be enough to know that the Becca he loved still existed on earth, exactly who he had believed her to be the first time around. Even if he wasn't worthy of her himself, cold, suspicious, screwed-up, brain-dead bastard that he was.

But even all alone, the idea of her existence would comfort him.

He heaved the doors open, with a rattling roar. The beam of his flashlight sliced through the cavernous dark, and caught a small, furry body that scurried for cover. *Rats.* Oh, Jesus. Another nail for his coffin.

"Becca?" he called out. "Hey!"

No answer. That chilled him. No way could she be asleep. Maybe she just didn't feel like speaking to him. He could hardly blame her.

"Becca!" He sprinted down the center aisle towards the fifth bank of scaffolding where he had chained her. "I know you're pissed, but—"

He rounded the corner and skidded to a stop, his heart squeezed tight to bursting in a claw of icy terror and dismay. Rats scattered.

Not there. The bags were there, the water bottles, the scattered protein bars, but Becca, the handcuffs and the chain were gone.

He wanted to vomit. Oh, fuck. He had no idea where to start, where to turn. What cliff to jump off of.

He wanted to howl like a mad dog.

There was no sound, but the air behind him shifted and moved, alerting him just in time to spin around—and take the length of metal pipe on the front of his skull, rather than the back.

A burst of blinding, white-red light, and he slid right down a long, agonizingly painful slope, into an oily black nowhere.

Becca had thought that what had happened in the warehouse would burn away the tender feelings she had for Nick. That she could fall no further. She was dead wrong.

Kristoff and the man that Zhoglo called Mikhail had hauled Nick in, unconscious, trussed up and bleeding. Zhoglo began taking out his rage by kicking him—back, legs, belly, groin, face. Every awful thud of contact against Nick's limp body was like a blow to her own flesh.

There were depths left to come. That was Zhoglo's specialty, after all. Untold depths of pain, of shame, of despair.

Nick's hands and feet were bound before him with a ratcheted plastic cuff. Another tie fastened hands and feet together, folding him in half.

Zhoglo kicked over the table that held the snack foods that Pavel had brought out to them. Crystal goblets smashed, food scattered and flew, wine glugged from the bottle, dark and heavy as blood.

Becca flinched as Zhoglo hauled off for another violent kick to Nick's ribs, which drew the man's attention to her own unlucky self.

He swung around and hung over her, panting. "Hundreds of millions of dollars!" Spittle from his wet red mouth hit Becca's face, making her flinch again. "Do you have any idea how much money you and this bleeding piece of shit have cost me? Can you even conceive of the magnitude of waste?"

"The important things were saved," Becca said softly. "Money is nothing." Her sane side cringed at her own brash idiocy. Where had that come from? A fatalistic desire to speed up her own death? God.

"Nothing?" Zhoglo shrieked. "Nothing?" He slapped her hard across the face. "Arrogant bitch! Who are you to say that money is nothing? Have you ever survived without it?"

Yes, she wanted to say, but she didn't have the nerve to speak when she looked into that maddened face, livid with rage, those staring white eyes, pupils contracted to pin-points.

He whacked her again, backhand. Her eyes teared. "Have you ever had to steal it?" he bellowed. "Have you killed for it? Felt hot blood well over your hands for it? How hungry have you ever been, you goddamn American rich bitch?" *Whack.* "Have you fought rats to eat rotten meat from a garbage dump? Have you bent over in an alley and let yourself be buggered by swine for a crust of bread?" *Whack.* "Have you?"

His voice rose to a grinding scream of fury. He grabbed thick handfuls of her hair, and flung her, chair and all, onto the deck. Right next to Nick's booted feet. She could almost touch them.

Food lay all around her. Smashed grapes, apple peels. Crumbled water crackers, little triangles of cheese. A slice of ham lay next to her face, spread out like a panting dog's long, pink tongue. The fatty, meaty smell of it made her stomach heave in protest.

And the fruit knife. It gleamed and flashed before her eyes, catching the light. The little paring knife that Zhoglo had used to peel his apples and his grapes. Right beyond reach of her fingertips.

Zhoglo turned away from her, kicking at the metal stand that held the computer monitor, knocking it to the ground. She lunged for the tiny knife while he occupied himself with kicking the portable computer into ruins. His henchmen were watching him, beady eyed and cautious not to pull any more rage down on themselves than they had to. No one watched her as she strained her body, pulling against the tape until it cut against her skin, reaching—

Got it. She palmed it. Nick's boots were right in her face. If she tried again, she could just about reach . . . *yes.*

She kept the blade hidden in her hands, let her hair flop over her face and tried to look limp and defeated while she picked at the thick plastic tie that held his hands and feet together.

It took forever. No way could she get through it before they saw her. But she had to try. She had an atom of a chance to actually do something. She'd be damned if she'd waste it.

The tie popped loose. Zhoglo was still bellowing in Ukrainian, flinging the detached monitor screen at the plate glass window—

Crash, the window shattered. Shards peppered her arms, her back. Becca dug around until she found the tie that bound his legs together, and sawed desperately while the rest of them scrambled out of range, pulling slivers of glass out of their flesh.

The tie popped loose. She tried to reach the one that fastened Nick's hands together, but she came up about two inches short. She willed him to shift, to wake, to help her out. Please, Nick. *Please.*

He just lay there. Like a dead man.

"Cut her out of that chair," Zhoglo ordered shrilly in Ukrainian. "Get that tape off of her. Get everything off her. I want to get started."

Nick held the hurting at bay, with all the mental muscle he possessed. He had to be ready to use what Becca had given him. Courageous goddess that she was. Chained to a chair and mouthing off to that maniac while he was in one of his rages—the chick had suicidal nerve. But then again, who knew that better than him?

Hold the position, damn it. Cuffed hands tethered to cuffed ankles, while looking limp, unconscious. His hands were still bound, but they were in front of him. And feet were a hell of a lot better than nothing.

It hurt like fire to breathe. His ribs were cracked, maybe broken. Everything hurt. *Push it back.* He remembered a taunt his father used to throw at him when he was young, when he blubbered after beatings.

Pain can't hurt you, kid, so shut up.

He repeated it to himself now. Broken bones, ruptured organs, ripped tendons, who gave a fuck. He wasn't going to be needing his body again after this move, so he did not need any of this sensory information from his peripheral nervous system. Thanks, but no thanks.

The data was irrelevant. Pain can't hurt you. *Push it back.*

Through swollen, slitted eyes, he could see that ogre Kristoff, yanking Becca by her dog chain off the chair and slicing off her snug shirt with his knife. Then, the knife snapped beneath her bra cups. The evil bastard licked his lips, chuckling.

"Mikhail. Wake that stinking turd up," Zhoglo ordered. "I want him to watch. Everything we do to her. Every last instant of it."

Mikhail stood at his head and bent over him, then flopped him onto his back so he could start slapping Nick's face. *Smack, whack.*

Right . . . *now.*

He whipped his legs up, clamping the guy's head between his thighs. A violent twist and jerk, and he scooped his bound hands around the guy's off-balance body. Flip-twist again, and he yanked with desperate strength. Pure instinct, blind technique, no fucking clue if it would work—then *pop,* a wet crunching sound.

A choked shriek from Mikhail, and the sudden smell of shit as the man's bowels loosened. His spine had been snapped.

Nick panted as he rolled away from the limp body and rolled up onto his feet. Kristoff dove for him, roaring like a bull, and somehow Nick figured out, on the fly, how to counter-

balance the frontal kicks with his hands bound, n̶
Kristoff's slashing blows to the head. He dance
swung a swift roundhouse kick that connected with Krist
face, and sent that fuckhead gorilla reeling back, blood spur
ing from his nose. He hauled off to follow it up with a—

Bam. The gunshot rocked him. Zhoglo was brandishing a
pistol.

A sensation of fire-edged cold spread in his chest, high
on the right. Nick tried to breathe as he staggered back.
Blood welled hot from the hole. Air, bubbling, sucking. Shit.
The lung. He was gone. Oh, Becca. *Becca.*

The trees twirled crazily, and then the deck twisted and
whirled up, and slammed right into him like a speeding
truck.

Becca jerked back as Kristoff practically landed in her
lap. Nick took forever to fall. He tipped and teetered, turning, and then crashed to the deck with a slow inevitability.
Drops of blood flew off his chest, illuminated by the big
light from the house as he hit, bounced and lay still.

Blood began to pool next to his chest. So much blood.

She was pushed beyond herself now. Beyond pain, beyond fear, beyond everything she'd ever believed or known
about herself. She was conscious only of a huge, hurricane-
force rage at those men for hurting him. For their monstrous,
unspeakable cruelty.

She looked at the dog chain in her shaking hands. The
rage threw a switch, clicked her brain out of victim mode and
into terrible focus. She finally saw the thing for the deadly
weapon that it actually was.

Her hands tingled.

Kristoff was taunting Nick in Ukrainian. She couldn't
make out the words, but the tone was unmistakable. Blood
bubbled out of Kristoff's nose as he pulled himself up into a
crouch. He didn't consider her.

She leaped. Her arms shot out, looping the length of chain across the guy's thick neck.

She jerked him backwards, almost toppling under his weight, but the strength of desperation kept her on her feet. He grunted, gasped, clutching his throat, but he was still scrambling, crablike, trying to get his feet under himself when her back hit the railing. She hooked a foot on the bottom slat, heaved herself up, perched her butt on the rail—

And flung herself over backwards.

Free fall. Into the dark. Until she was brought up short by the chain. She shrieked. Her entire weight hung on her cuffed hands, and the thick lengths of chain she'd wrapped around her hands and wrists. The cuffs cut into her skin, the chain pulled brutally tight, crushing her wrists and fingers like a vise. Oh, God, that hurt, hurt, *hurt*.

She peered up, blinked the tears out of her eyes, tried to stop making that panicked sobbing sound. She'd had the vague notion of dragging Kristoff with her, making him fall to his death, but the outcome was different. He'd fetched up against the post, throttled.

He made no sound. There was no sound but the rustling trees. She swayed back and forth in the dark like a crazy pendulum, in a haze of pain and dread. Soft pine needles tickled her arms, her legs. Blood trickled down her forearms.

A hideous laugh sounded from high above her.

She looked up. Zhoglo's face hung over the railing, like a full moon. His mouth was stretched wide in a parody of mirth.

He clapped, slowly. "Bravo, Rebecca," he said. "You have done me a favor. I was bored at the prospect of killing that blockhead. You spared me that, and in such an entertaining way too. Grisly. Would you like to see? Here, Pavel, help me pull her up. I want to show her the rewards of defiance."

Pavel appeared beside the other man, his cadaverous face

expressionless. Becca could not hold back a keening moan as he pulled her up, a slicing, fiery agony burning her hands as the distance between herself and that smirking nightmare shortened. Finally Pavel grabbed her under the armpits and heaved her over the rail. He set her on her feet.

Blood slicked the chain, the cuffs, her hands. Her fingers were crushed, throbbing with pain. Zhoglo seized the chain and yanked on it. She fell forward, shrieking.

"I love a defiant woman," he said. "It makes her cringing and begging all the sweeter in the end." He gestured at Kristoff. "Look at what you did," he said. "And you are so sylphlike. So delicate."

Kristoff's head was flung back, a dark, bloody mark across his crushed larynx. Her fall, her chain, had caught him across the throat and killed him. His face was purplish, his eyes wide. Becca's gaze darted away, and she suddenly saw the widening pool of blood beside Nick's limp body. As she watched, Nick started to move.

She let her eyes slide off him as if she hadn't noticed him. Saw him drag himself to his feet out of the corner of her eye.

Zhoglo clutched her blood-streaked breast in his hands. He lifted bloody fingers to his lips. Slowly sucked them clean, one after the other, smiling. She was about to faint.

Nick took a shuffling step forward. Another.

The noise that had been brushing against the back of her mind finally identified itself. Police sirens screaming. Getting louder.

"The cops are on their way," Nick said. "Hear them?"

Pavel and Zhoglo jerked around at the sound of his deep voice, and pointed their guns at him. Nick's hands were pressed to his chest. Blood trickled through them. His eyes were terribly calm.

Zhoglo's insane laugh shook his big belly. He looked at Becca. "You see, my dear? How it is with me, every time? Always, I must abandon my juicy treats right before I sink my teeth into them. Such a shame to kill you this way, when you deserve to die slowly, screaming. But as I told you before . . . I can be flexible."

He shoved her away and trained the gun on her, lips twisting into a hideous leer. Nick launched into the air and slammed into her.

Bam, a gun went off. They hit the ground with all the rib-crunching force of their combined weights, knocking out her wind.

Over Nick's shoulder, Zhoglo stared down at her for a moment, a look of pure hate in his eyes. Slowly, he toppled forward.

He landed on top of Nick, eyes frozen wide. Blood seeped through his buzzcut silver hair, trickling into his staring eyes and around the thick, swollen lumps of his fleshy face.

What? How . . . ?

Becca was close to smothering under the combined weight of the two men, her lungs hitching in and out. Pavel was the only one still standing. He held a pistol in one limp hand as if he'd forgotten it was there. His eyes were empty in his haggard face.

Lack of oxygen was pulling a veil over her eyes. Blood from two different death wounds pooled around her, hot and thickening.

Pavel nudged Zhoglo's body with his foot. He flipped it off Becca and Nick, and onto its back. He crouched down, said a few quiet words that Becca could not understand, and spat into the dead man's face.

Then he rolled Nick's body off her, on to the other side. Nick flopped onto his back. Air rushed painfully back into Becca's lungs.

Pavel knelt beside her and pulled her up till she was sitting. He fished something small and bright out of his pocket. A key. He inserted it into the bloody handcuffs and unlocked them.

She stared into his face, utterly confounded.

"Why?" she whispered as soon as she had the breath to speak.

"For my son." Pavel's voice was somber. He did not meet her eyes.

She shook her head, uncomprehending, but he said nothing more. He retreated, boots crunching over broken glass into the dark house.

Becca stared after him. The heat of the pooling blood reached her thigh, startling her out of her shocked stupor. Nick. Oh, God, Nick.

She bent over him, peering at the wound in the dim light from the room behind them. It looked awful. Blood was everywhere. His face was ashy pale and his breath bubbled in his lungs.

But he'd picked himself up and tried to take a bullet for her.

The sirens were deafening now. Lights swirled through the trees, blue and red. They were coming. Good. No time to lose. God knows, she was no medic. She tried to remember her high school first aid course.

Apply direct pressure. She stripped off the scrap of T-shirt still clinging to her shoulders, wadded it into a ball and pressed it against the wound. The best she could do, other than praying, desperately.

She sagged over him, resting her forehead against his. Waited, eyes shut tight to block out the unseeing gaze of the corpses.

Presently, people and loud noises boiled out onto the deck, hustling and bustling, asking her loud, urgent questions that she could not bring herself to comprehend, let alone answer. She had nothing left for them, whoever they were. She was used up. All done.

Finally someone had the kindness to sting her in the arm with a needle and lay her gently down on something flat.

That was the last she knew.

Chapter
34

Six weeks later . . .

Nick fidgeted behind the wheel of his truck, staring at the carved wooden sign on the storefront that read "The Wandering Gourmet—Fine Catering." He'd been there for an hour. This was stupid.

He slid out of the truck, fed the meter for the third time, and pressed his hand against the dull ache in his chest. It took a while for a hole through the lung to heal. They'd thought he was going to bite the big one, he'd been told. He'd also been told that Becca had stayed at his side the whole time he'd been in intensive care and various other wards, all the way till they downgraded his condition to conscious-but-miserable-piece-of-shit-in-fiery-pain.

At which point, she'd made herself scarce. She'd left him there, all alone, to stare at the IV bag dripping into his arm and ponder what he'd done, and what it had cost him. She'd changed her phone numbers.

He knew a "fuck off" when he heard one and yet here he was. She had to tell him to fuck off in person, to his face. Maybe it would sink in.

He couldn't take any more of this. Stumbling through his

days like the walking dead. Dreaming of her every night, waking up in tears with his dick stone hard.

He walked towards the catering place. His legs felt like they might just give way at the knees at the prospect of the ultimate Fuck Off.

He walked into the reception area. A fresh-faced blond girl manned the front counter. "Hello, can I help you?" she chirped.

"I want to talk to your boss," he said.

"Just a sec. I'll go get her."

She scampered through the swinging doors. He glimpsed a high-tech kitchen, lots of gleaming equipment.

Becca burst through. She stopped, so abruptly the blonde bumped into her. Her professional smile switched off like a light.

They stared at each other. She looked sharper, her chin and jaw more defined. Her hair was longer, the ringlets lengthening into waves. She was so beautiful, it made his eyes ache. "Hey," he forced out.

She put her hand to her throat. "I see you're all healed up."

"More or less," he said.

"That's great news." She folded her arms under her breasts. The blond girl cut her gaze back and forth between them, at a loss.

"I see you've, uh, gone into business for yourself." He gestured around at the place. "Good for you. Looks great."

She shrugged. "I decided it was time to get out of the kiddie pool," she said coolly. "Besides, not much scares me these days. I had to take out a huge loan, but it's a good location. And my ex-boss from the country club is passing me a lot of great referrals. Out of pure guilt, I think, but that's fine with me. I'll use guilt, if it works."

"Oh, it works," he told her. "Believe me. It definitely works."

That clammed her right up. There was a long, tense silence, and he hardened his belly and gathered the nerve to break it.

"Is there someplace private we could go to talk?" he asked.

"No need," she said. "We don't have anything to talk about that can't be said right out in public."

He tried to breathe out the pain. He'd known this would be bad.

"How did you find this place?" Her tone was faintly accusatory.

"Margot told me," he admitted.

"Oh. Yes, I catered Jeannie's christening party last week," she said. "Such a cute baby. Margot brought her in when she came in to choose the menu. Adorable, with all that fuzzy red hair."

"Yeah, she's real cute," he said mechanically. "Margot told me she'd seen you. But you weren't at the party."

"Oh, no. I had to work another event that night. We're super busy on weekends," she said crisply. "Carrie did the McCloud job. She's working for me this summer, you know?"

"You were avoiding me," he said baldly.

Becca stared at him, and did not respond. He sighed and dug into his pocket. He pulled out a battered envelope, handed it to her.

She took it gingerly. "What's this?"

"For Josh," he said. "From Sveti. She has a huge crush on him. Six pages, thanking him for what he did. Jumping Yuri, and all that. She made me translate it for her." He rolled his eyes. "Very fervent."

"Oh," she murmured. "I see. I'll give it to him."

"He's a good guy," he offered. "Brave. It was the first nice thing anybody had done for her in months. It made a big impression on her. I think she's hoping he'll keep himself pure for her until she grows up."

"Hmm," Becca murmured noncommittally. "I wouldn't hold my breath, if I were her, knowing Joshie. Is she, um, OK?"

"She's fine now," he said. "The McClouds flew her mom over from Kiev right away, while I was still in the hospital. She and Sveti went back home to Ukraina last week."

"And the others? What about Pavel's son?"

"Back with his mother and brother. The kid's marked for life, but he might pull through. The rest of them are still stateside, in protective custody. When this thing hit the news, there were thousands of offers to adopt them, so we'll see. All except for Rachel, that is."

"What about Rachel?"

He rolled his eyes. "Tam," he said. "Rachel's with Tam."

Becca's eyes got huge. "No way!"

He couldn't help but grin. "Way," he said. "They hit it off. Now they're inseparable. Who'd have thought, huh?"

"Oh, God. That poor little girl!" Becca said, dismayed.

"It's OK. Tam's good to her, in her own weird way. Rachel worships her. And there's something to be said for a mom who could take out a squadron of Delta Force soldiers using nothing but her tits and her earrings. The McCloud crowd thinks it's a great joke. I saw them at the party. They look good together. Surreal, but good."

His hands darted out and grabbed her wrists before she could jerk out of range. He pulled them forward to examine. The scars from the cuffs were still angry red. In time, they would fade.

But she would always bear the marks.

"Do they hurt?" he asked softly.

She yanked them back. "They're fine. Please, Nick. I've got a garden party this afternoon, and I've got to finish my prep, so—"

"I've had enough chitchat too. I've figured out that catching a bullet for you hasn't earned me enough points for you to take me back. But it sure as hell ought to earn me a fucking private conversation."

Becca's eyes fell. She bit her lip. The blond girl's eyes got big.

"I'll say what I need to say in front of an audience if I have to," he went on grimly. "But you're the one who'll be embarrassed. Not me."

"Manipulative bastard," she whispered.

"Um, Becca? Should I, like, go?" the girl faltered.

"No, Cheryl Ann. Mind the desk," Becca said. "You," she jerked her chin at Nick. "Come on in here. If you must."

She would be calm. She was strong now, she told herself. She'd been through the fire, and she'd emerged hardened, tempered. Tough.

For awhile, after that awful night, she thought she might never feel again. Anything, good or bad. She'd been relieved at the time. She hadn't cried since then. Hadn't crumbled once. She'd kept it together.

She was glad he was behind her on the stairs so he couldn't see her face. Glad, too, that she was wearing this gauzy blue sundress. Not that she wanted to attract him. But looking nice gave a woman a slight advantage, and she needed every advantage she could get.

He was so . . . oh, there was no word for how he was. No defense against it. It wasn't fair, for him to come here and flaunt his mojo at her. Throbbing all those intense male vibes at her on purpose to muddle her and scramble her. Looking at her with his trademark gaze of smoldering volcanic desire. Making her weak with longing.

She couldn't give in. He was too hard for her. He was a rock that she would break herself on, and she was shipwrecked already. Still in salvage mode, trying to find all the chunks of herself.

She led him into the shabby accounting office above the kitchen space. It was sparsely furnished, just a desk heaped with paperwork and a folding chair. She shut the door.

Nick opened his mouth. She held up her hand to forestall

him. "Before we say anything, let's just get one thing straight. Thank you."

He frowned. "Huh?"

"Thank you," she repeated, her voice stiff and mechanical. "I have a lot to be thankful for. What you did on the island, to begin with. Saving Josh and Carrie, and those others. Coming back for me, getting shot for me. It was very brave and noble. Very heroic."

He waited. "And?"

She threw up her hands. "Isn't that enough for you?"

"I sense there's more," he said. "Let me have it."

"No," she said. "There isn't. That's the point, Nick. It ends right there. Thank you. Period. Stop."

He shook his head. "Oh, no," he said. "It can't end there."

"Oh, yes it can," she said. "I will be the first to admit that you deserve a medal for what you did—"

"But I don't deserve you?"

Doubt gripped her, anxious, sucking, awful. Oh, God, why did it hurt so much? How could it be so painful just to do the right thing?

She forced herself to remember the dense darkness of the warehouse. The pit of despair she was still trying to climb out of.

Some things could not be forgiven. Ever.

She would always have that darkness in the back of her mind now. She would always be hearing the rustling of the rats, feeling that shrinking helplessness, the rage, the hurt, the horrible fear.

She shook her head. "No, Nick. I can't do it," she whispered. "I cannot risk you. You are too dangerous for me."

"No, I'm not," he said. "I would die for you. I tried to."

Her belly contracted in pain. "Oh, God. Stop. Don't do this to me."

"I know you're angry." His voice was low, careful. "Try to see it from my point of view."

"No." She took her hands away from her wet eyes and glared at him. "I've given that up. This isn't about me being angry. This is about me surviving. I have to put my own damn point of view first for that. My point of view wasn't pretty. I still feel the rats nibbling my shoes."

A muscle pulsed in his tight jaw. "Jesus, Becca. I'm sorry."

"You should be." She turned her back on him.

She didn't hear him move, but she felt that hot force field buzzing around her, making her hyperaware of his nearness.

"A very wise, kind person gave me a lecture once," he said quietly. "She told me that deceiving and betraying are sins, but that being deceived and being betrayed were mistakes. Bad breaks."

"Maybe. I was the one who was betrayed, though," she said.

"Not by me," he said. "I did the best I could with the information I had. But like you said yourself. I'm not God. And I'm so sorry."

"I'm sure you did do the best you could, Nick," she said stiffly. "It's not your fault your best just wasn't good enough."

She could feel the silent hurt she'd caused radiating off him.

He stepped back. The silence yawned, creating a distance that widened, deepened, making her heart burn, ache. Break.

"OK," he said flatly. "I hear you. I won't bother you again."

The warped door scraped open, and clicked shut after him. She heard his boots descending on the creaking stairs.

Grief roared up, and morphed unexpectedly into fury. Why her? Why should she suffer like this? What had she done to deserve it?

Ping, something pulled too tight and snapped inside her like piano wire. She lunged for the door and yanked it open.

"Goddamn you, Nick Ward!" she yelled.

He turned at the foot of the stairs, and stared up, startled. "Huh?"

"Do I mean so little to you? Is it that easy to walk away?"

she raged. "Say 'I'm sorry' and slink off, telling me you won't bother me again. Hah! Bother me? To hell with you! Sniveling goddamn *coward!*"

"Uh, whoa." He looked nervous, but intrigued. "I thought you wanted me to . . . well, shit, Becca. What do you want me to do?"

"Use your tiny, shriveled pea brain, and figure it out!" she yelled. "Can you handle how pissed off I am at you, Nick? Because I am so pissed. I am royally, severely pissed, and that won't just go away just because you say you're sorry! So forget it!"

His lips twitched, but he wisely suppressed the smile. "I'm one tough son of a bitch," he said. He took a step up the stairs. "I can take a whole lot of abuse."

"Oh yeah? But can you take me, Nick?" Her voice shook with emotion. "Do you have the guts for that?"

He climbed the stairs, staring intently into her face. "I can take you," he said. "Hell yes. It's giving you up that I can't take."

"Oh, yeah? Well, let's just see." She gestured imperiously for him to get back into the office. She slammed the door shut, crossed her arms over her chest and barred the exit with her body. No way was he getting away from her before she got her ya-yas out.

"What's with the screaming harpy act?" His eyes were wary.

"News flash, Nick," she said. "It's not an act. I *am* a screaming harpy. What you see is what you get. So cope."

An appreciative grin spread over his face. "You're hot when you're feisty," he said. "I fucking love that."

She shoved at his hard midriff, but did not succeed in budging him. "Only an idiot would say that to a woman as pissed as me."

"I never claimed to be a rocket scientist," Nick admitted. "You know me. Mouth opens, truth falls out. Plop. Whether it's in my best interests or not."

"Then I suggest you keep your big mouth shut," she snapped. "Let me see your scar."

He looked startled, but pulled up his navy T-shirt over his lean torso obligingly enough. She kept her face impassive as she looked at the long, jagged, angry weal, the marks of the clamps and the stitches. It made her heart hurt. She wanted to press her lips against it.

But he wasn't getting off that easy. She brushed her fingertips over it. He sucked in a harsh breath.

She whipped her hand back, alarmed. "Did I hurt you?"

He shook his head. That hot glow in his eyes was all too familiar. She let her eyes roam over his body, lingering on the thick bulge in his jeans. His eyes followed her gaze. With one swift gesture, he peeled the T-shirt right off, letting it drop from his wrist to the scarred linoleum.

Showoff. Doing a double whammy on her, flaunting his gorgeous bod and his heroic bullet wound at the same time.

It shamed her to her bones that it was working so well.

"Put that back on," she said breathlessly. "Exhibitionist jerk."

He shook his head, grabbed her hand and placed it on his scar again, trapping it under his own. "Do that again," he said. "I liked it."

She tugged, in vain, on her hand. "You think I give a damn what you like, Nick Ward?"

"I know that you do," he said.

She wrenched her hand away with a growl of rage, and hauled off, as if she were going to hit him. She stopped herself, muscles locked.

"Go ahead," he said. "Hit me. Whale on me, if you want."

"I can't," she said crabbily. "You're wounded, goddamnit."

"That's OK. I'm tough. I can take it."

Oh, God. Something about the stoic acceptance in his voice just broke her heart all over again. That was the heart of the problem with Nick. He was always expecting a blow. Always braced for it. Never surprised when it landed.

She wouldn't be the one to deal him that blow.

Tears were sliding down her face, her throat melting into a shimmering hot coal. "I don't care if you can take it or not," she said shakily. "You've taken enough, goddamnit."

Of all times for the big thaw to come crashing down on her. Damn, damn, damn. This was so undignified. She grabbed tissues from the desk and hid her face in the fluffy wad of paper.

Nick pulled her against his hard, naked chest, wrapping her in the steely strength of his arms. His skin was feverishly hot.

It took a while for the backed-up tears to move through her. There was a lot to cry about: that awful night, that day that she'd steeled herself to leave him at the hospital. All the times she hadn't let herself call to see how he was. The sleepless nights, staring at the ceiling.

She'd tried so hard to let him go. But she couldn't.

And she wouldn't. The relief of giving in was so sweet, such a liberating rush of emotion, she thought for a moment that she might swoon, like a Victorian maiden. But Nick held her up. He didn't get bored with her protracted crying jag, either. He seemed glad for the excuse to touch her. He buried his face in her hair. Rubbed her back as if trying to memorize every bump of her spine, every muscle, every rib.

The tears moved through her and trailed away, leaving her limp and soft. Very light, as if she might float up and away if he didn't keep a tight grip. Never one to waste an advantage, Nick tilted her head back and started kissing her wet, closed eyelids, her flushed red cheeks.

"Stop that," she whispered. "We haven't made it that far yet."

"No? How about this, then?" He sank to his knees, staring up at her body. "I love this view. Your gorgeous tits, from below." His hands swept up the outside of her thighs under her skirt. He hooked her panties with his thumbs and yanked them down around her ankles.

She sucked in a breath. Oh, whoa. No way. Not a chance.

She stumbled back, her bottom fetching up against the desk as he tossed up her skirt and pressed his hot face to her muff. He parted her labia gently with his fingers and his eager tongue licked and probed.

Her knees almost gave way and dumped her on the floor as the sensations swirled in her lower body, a liquid shimmer of heat, of light.

She panicked. She couldn't bear it, as raw and emotional as she felt. She pushed his face away. "No. Please. Don't, Nick."

"No?" He wiped his mouth, looked up at her. "Pretty please?"

"Can't take it," she said, unevenly. "It's too much. I'll come apart."

He stood up, standing between her parted legs so the length of their bodies was flush, touching at every point. "Sorry," he said. "Oh, wait. It pisses you off when I say I'm sorry. Everything pisses you off."

"Don't you dare get mouthy on me."

He shrugged, and stared into her eyes, waiting patiently for her to tell him what he could do. Vibrating sexual eagerness at her.

And now she wanted it, too. The bastard had gotten her whipped up into a state. Restless and anxious and hungry for him.

Well, and why not? She lifted her chin, and pointed to the bulge at his crotch. "Stop talking, Nick. And whip that thing out. Right now."

He hesitated, looking alarmed. "What do you intend to do to it?"

"That's for me to know and for you to worry about," she said.

He unbuckled his belt. "You're making me nervous, babe," he complained.

"Oh, yeah? Well, guess what, buddy? You've made me

nervous from the moment I met you. It's about time you knew how it felt!"

Nick shrugged, fatalistically, and jerked the jeans down. His cock sprang up to attention.

She petted it, testing its hardness, the ropy thickness. This was improvised madness. She had no idea what she was doing. Only that it was a really bad idea. And that she couldn't stop herself to save her life.

The words leaped out, rash and crazy. "Make love to me."

His eyes flashed. "Hell yes, babe. I live to serve. Just let me go down on you first, so you can—"

"No." She shook her head frantically. "I want you inside me. Now."

His brows knitted. "You're not ready. I'll hurt you."

"I don't care," she said wildly. "Just do it."

He shoved papers off the desk to make space, sending stuff tumbling and fluttering to the floor, and set her bottom on the desk, lifting her skirt. "*I* care," he said, his tone steely. "I know you're in a crazy mood, but you'll wait till you're ready, and that is fucking final."

"Damn it, Nick—" She shut up with a gasp as he slid his hand between her thighs and thrust his finger inside her.

She was already slick and hot, writhing around his hand, but he persisted, caressing her and spreading her slick hot juice where it was needed most. "I don't have a condom," he told her.

"Oh, what a shame." Her voice shook. "Then I guess you just can't come. Too bad for you. But that's your problem, not mine."

His grin flashed as he pressed her legs wide. "Cruel Becca."

She clutched his shoulders, panting. They pressed their damp foreheads together for that magic moment of connection, when he eased his thick, blunt bulb inside her and slowly, slowly started to push.

Every tiny delicious stroke, every rocking movement made her want to writhe and moan, but for some reason she fought it, biting her lip. Still afraid to give in to pleasure, to him. Walls within walls.

He stopped. "What's this all about, Becca? What does it mean?"

"Nothing," she said, defiantly. "It means nothing. Just that I want this, and you're handy, so I'm taking it. No promises. No strings."

He narrowed his eyes and slowly withdrew, leaving only the tip of himself inside her, caressing her. "So this is part of my punishment?"

She reached down to grip his butt, pulling on him. "Just get to it, damn it!"

Her ferocity made him grin. "I'm just your boy toy thug, then? Your tattooed lowlife? Use me for sex, and then kick me to the curb?"

"You talk too much," she snapped, breathless. "Just . . . fuck me."

"You're so tough," he whispered. He thrust deep, staring into her eyes. "But you will melt for me," he said, his voice caressing, as if he were putting a spell on her. "And you will come for me, too. You love me."

"Arrogant bastard," she gasped, staring at the sight of his thick shaft disappearing inside her, pulling out again, shiny with her juice.

"If I'm going to be your boy toy, I ought to live with you full time," he said. "So that I'm available to service you night and day."

She couldn't think of a comeback to that, not while he was rotating his thumb around her clit as he pumped and thrust.

"And if I'm fucking you night and day, you might as well just marry me," he pointed out. "So the children we have will be legitimate."

She choked back the urge to laugh. "Watch out, buddy. You're getting all masterful again."

His grin was wicked. "That's how you like me," he said.

"I know what you like. I'm going to give it to you hard. So brace yourself."

He settled into a sensual rhythm that made her whimper and gasp. She wrapped her arms around his neck and yielded to it, her body softening, blooming brighter and hotter as their bodies merged.

She felt his orgasm gathering, felt him clench, and start to pull away from her—

No. She gripped his butt, sank her nails in, trapping him inside her. Letting his scalding heat pump through her, fill her, like healing balm. Melting that stiff, frozen place inside her, melting her anger and doubt. Opening her up to hope again.

To everything. Life, the future, her dreams and longings. Love.

After, her head rested against his damp chest. She lifted it, and kissed his scar, as she'd been longing to do. Tender, smooching kisses.

They swayed together, damp and clinging, for a timeless interval.

Nick tilted her chin up. "So this is the deal, babe," he said. "You could punish me by keeping me in suspense if you want, but it's a big waste of time. I love you. And I'm never going to let you go."

She sought words, but the emotions pressed too hard against her throat to permit her to speak. She gazed into his earnest, worried eyes.

"I'm not perfect," he said roughly. "I know I fucked up. But I will never let you down again. I swear it. I will treat you like a goddess."

Her eyes overflowed. She mopped the tears, sniffling. He waited.

"I want those strings, Becca," he prompted. "I want the promises. Done deal. Signed and sealed. Till death do us part."

She laughed, limply. "One hot lay, and you think it's all better?"

He grinned. "You want more? I'll give you more. Watch me."

She grabbed him. "Just hold me," she said, exhausted. "For now."

"As long as you want," he said promptly.

She kissed his scar again. "Forever?"

He made a rough sound and hid his face against her hair. "To the end of time, sweetheart," he muttered. "And beyond."

If you enjoyed EXTREME DANGER,
you won't want to miss Shannon McKenna's
next thrilling romantic suspense novel,
and her return to the supersexy, intense, and rugged
McCloud brothers!

Turn the page for a special excerpt of

FADE TO MIDNIGHT,

a Brava hardcover on sale in June 2010.

Prologue

*T*ony Ranieri sucked in smoke and fingered the tarnished dog tag in his hand. He had no patience for mysteries. Not in books, not on TV. Mind-squeezing, time-wasting bullshit. But there he was. In Tony's face.

He stared at the kid, watching him squirt disinfectant into the bucket and start in on the floor. Tony stared at the ponytail of streaky, dirty blond hair. The thick muscles of the kid's shoulders, emerging from the sprung-out tank top of Tony's that was fully two sizes too big for him. The flesh-creeping pattern of scars that snaked and spiraled over the kid's skin. Those wounds had still been oozing the night he found the unlucky son of a bitch. Almost two years ago, now. He hadn't dared take the kid to a hospital. The guys who'd done him would be watching.

Tony had braced himself to see those wounds go bad. There was internal bleeding, broken bones. And the kid's face. Mother of God.

He'd steeled himself to have to hide the body, pretend

he'd never found the kid. Like he didn't have enough shit on his conscience.

But he hadn't died. Tony sucked his cigarette, in defiance of the no-smoking rule in the diner kitchen. His sister Rosa, colossal ballbreaker, was home, asleep. His young nephew Bruno had crashed out hours ago upstairs. And the kid wasn't going to rat him out. The kid couldn't talk for shit. He could wash dishes, chop onions, scrape plates, and fight like a fucking demon from hell. But he couldn't say a damn word.

He wasn't a kid, really, either. He'd been twentyish when Tony found him, but Tony hadn't gotten a good handle on him yet, so he'd just stuck with "the kid." Since he offered no other satisfying defining characteristic, besides his silence, and his scars. Too bad, about those scars. The kid would be movie-star good-looking, if not for that. He was lucky they hadn't taken his eyes. But Tony'd bet his left nut that the tor-turer had been working up to the eyes, the balls.

Tony knew what got that kind of guy off. He knew it all too well.

Something had interrupted the torturefest, though. The bastard had decided to finish the kid off. Just beat him to death and dump the body. Who knew why. Mysteries. Fuck 'em.

The kid paused in his mopping, looked over his shoulder. He wanted to say something, wanted it bad. His green eyes burned with urgency. But nothing came out. The wires were cut. He was all fucked up. It hurt to look at him.

The kid's shoulders slumped. He got back to work. Slop, dip, swab.

Tony's fingers closed around the dog tags. He stubbed out the cigarette. He was a straight-shooting guy. Kill or be killed, that was the kind of motto he could get behind. Ambi-guity fucked with his digestion.

Tony wound the chain around his hand til it burned his fingers. He'd found the tags in the kid's jeans, the night he'd chased off the killer. Not the kid's own, though that was Tony's first assumption.

These tags were of an older soldier. Tony's generation. Tony's war.

Tony had nosed around, asked his Marine buddies, and heard stories to curdle a guy's blood. The name on that tag struck fear into the hearts of battle-hardened men. Sniper, killer, monster. Accused of unspeakable atrocities. Disappeared after 'Nam, before they could court-martial him. Probably slitting throats for the criminal underworld.

He'd be Tony's age, by now, with a team under him. Guys as badass as him, or worse. There was always worse.

Tony stared at that lost, fucked-up kid, bent over his bucket, and renewed the decision he made every night. The kid was in no shape to deal with the people who had reduced him to this. They would squish him like a cockroach. He was better off scraping plates, swabbing floors. Tony stared at him, hating the sick feeling of doubt in his guts.

Eamon McCloud. What was he, to this kid? He cursed under his breath, in thick Calabrese dialect. The name on that dog tag could put the kid's broken life together.

Or it could get him killed, once and for all.

Chapter 1

I am fucked.
The thought flicked through Kev's head, calm and detached, as the roar of the icy water filled his ears. The current
would pull him loose in counted seconds, measured by the
pounding pulse of blood through his brain. Each throb hurt
like a raving motherlover, but there was nothing like immi-
nent death to take a guy's mind off a headache.

His little angel's face flashed through his mind. His dream
companion, his spirit guide through the labyrinth of his mind.
She looked worried for him. Her big eyes looked sad, and
scared.

He'd known since he got out of bed that it was going to be
a dangerous day. He'd had that fuzzy, electrical prickling on
his skin, as if someone was looking intensely at the back of
his neck. Not surprising, since he'd set the day aside for high-
adrenaline death-defying sports activities. His chief joy in
what passed for his life.

One would think that having gotten a loud clue from the
great beyond that death lurked nearby like a crazed stalker,
a reasonable, sane person would spend the day on the couch,
watching reruns. Not him. He'd left the reasonable, sane parts
of himself out in space. Along with his memory, his man-

ners, and his normal and natural fear of death. Danger?
Bring it on. Bring it the fuck *on*.

He should have been dead long ago. Look at his face. Little
kids ran screaming to mommy when they saw his bad side.

The cold had numbed the pain. He could no longer feel
his hand, clamped around the boughs of the dead tree. He
did not feel the compound fracture in his other arm. His injured limb flopped uselessly in the water, sucked by the current, just a few yards from the head of the falls. His broken
bone tented out the nylon of his jacket, pinkish with blood. But
the arm was not relevant. He doubted he'd be using it again,
once the water dragged him loose and flung him over the brink.

Whatever. He'd been smash totaled years ago anyhow, living on borrowed time. Half a brain, half a life. And no clue at
all.

Don't start with that. Just shut the fuck up, he told himself. He did crazy shit like this for the express purpose of keeping himself too busy for self pity. That was why he jumped
out of planes, hung off the edge of cliffs, hang-glided treacherous air currents, rafted bad-ass rapids.

Close to death, he felt almost alive. Since Tony found him
half dead, he'd had some internal protective mechanism
functioning that damped down his emotional volume. Probably caused by whatever trauma to his brain that had caused
the amnesia. Whatever had rendered him speechless and lost
inside his head, for all those years.

Whatever it was, he was bored with it. If he could, he'd
join the military, to fly their fighter jets. Playing with toys
like that, velocities like that, oh shit, yeah. Talk about a coping mechanism. But the military wouldn't want a guy with
crossed wires, a questionable identity, and a big black hole
in his mind to fly their hundred-million-dollar toys. They'd
put him to work cleaning engines. If they took him at all.

No, he had to make do with high-risk sports. He liked the
color, the noise. The buzz of being awake to it, aware of it.
Giving a shit.

He'd gotten what he wanted. But he was going to pay for it, and pay big. He stared at the top of the falls, water shooting off. Clouds of vapor rose from the thundering weight of tons of water crashing down, hundreds of feet below. How many hundreds? He tried to remember. Several, he thought. More than three. Whoo hah.

Not that he was afraid of dying. At most, he was curious. Sorry he would never unravel the great questions of his existence, at least not as a living man, and who knew what happened after death? He didn't have the energy to speculate.

At least the boy was going to make it. Kev was immobilized by tons of rushing icewater, but out of the corner of his eye, he saw activity in the trees that choked the cliffside shore. Rescue proceedings were underway. Others had seen the kids sweep by on the rapids, from the place where Kev had put ashore, spinning out of control towards the falls. Only a guy with a black hole in his brain would be suicidal enough to jump in after them, but he'd taken no time to ponder that implacable truth. He just went for it. A long, hopeless, mindless wrestle with nature while the water got wilder, the roar of the falls louder.

While death approached, smiling. Happy to see him. His old pal.

The kids had capsized when he caught up. Kev had seen a bobbing head and scooped one of the children out of the water. Then they plunged into a trough, the raft flipped, and he was tossed like a twig, the boy flailing, choking. He clamped the kid against him, struggled, kicked. He'd wanted to save that damn kid. Wanted it ferociously. He was played out, now, though. In fact, he felt strangely relaxed. Serene.

The other boy was long gone, over the falls. That was fucked, and he was sorry. Rescue was on the way for the boy he'd grabbed, but the greedy way the water sucked at the tree told him the hard truth.

He himself was going down. Any time now. So he'd better get ready.

He forced his head to turn a fraction. Checked on the kid. Sixteen or so. A drowned rat, clinging to the lucky side of the rock that split the top of the falls into two long, thin tails. The weight of rushing water pinned him against the rock. Couldn't move. But he'd live.

It wasn't strength or skill that had smacked them up against that jutting rock. Just chance. And just as fast, *bam*. That bastard had come up so fast, he barely had time to shove the kid out of the way. The tree trunk snapped his arm, smashed God knew what else in his thorax, knocked him loose—but the trunk spun out perpendicular to the falls, caught on a rock across the torrent, and formed a barrier, leaving him trapped against a temporary dam. But not for long.

Smashing him. Then saving him. When it worked loose, it would fuck him again, definitively. He'd ride that bastard out over the cliff.

The story of his life. Something deep inside him laughed, with stony irony. Wasn't that always the way. Like Tony, who'd dragged Kev out of his own rapids years ago, and kept him there, brain damaged, shambling and speechless. Washing dishes, mopping floors for no pay at the diner. Lying on a sagging cot, watching paint peel on the walls of the window-less mildewed room behind the diner. For fucking *years*.

The rope thrown out to save him. The same rope that he strangled himself on. It was almost funny. Except that it wasn't.

The tree was about to go. The branches stuck on the rocks on the other side were wavering, wild water bending the flexible limbs, teasing them loose. The tree shuddered, rolled. The water sucked and insisted.

Any time now. He composed himself, tried to pay attention, to be present for it, to breathe. Difficult. So cold. So much water.

The kid's mouth was wide open, begging Kev to do something.

A final swell shook the tree loose. Agonizing, ponderous

slow motion made those last moments of clinging stretch out, infinitely long.

He struggled to stay conscious. This was the last wild ride, so he'd better enjoy it. He wondered if he'd know, once he was dead, who he'd been before. What he'd done, who he'd known. Who he'd loved.

Probably not. This was all he got. It would just have to do.

Whoosh, the river rolled him under the tree and spat him far out into vastness, into endless space above, below. Turning head over ass.

The angel flashed across his mind. Those big eyes, so sweet. A sting of regret that he didn't understand. And another face, too, which scowled his disapproval as the immutable laws of physics had their stern way with him. A face he saw in his dreams, every night. A young guy. His face was maddeningly familiar. Kev had been having a dream argument with that guy, that very morning. The man had been scolding him. "*Dying is easy. You told me that yourself,*" the guy said. "*It's living that's hard. Meathead hypocrite. You piss me off.*"

So that was how he'd known today would be dangerous.

Part of him hooted and shrieked with wild, unreasoning joy at the icy rush of air and water, on his face as he fell. *Whoa. This shit is fun.*

He fell, spinning. A part of his mind pondered the acceleration rates of falling objects, wind shear. The probable force of impending impact on the rocks below. He calculated it down to ten digits after the decimal in that last endless, eternal instant—

And hurtled into a blank, white nothing.

Goddamnit to hell. Thick, stupid, useless cow.

Ava Cheung refocused her mind to a laser point. So much information streamed through the human nervous system to make a body move smoothly through space. So much of it was automatic. One couldn't fathom it until one tried to provide the impulses for someone else's body, while simultaneously suppressing theirs.

Mandy was responding poorly. Ava could not get the girl to shut her mouth and keep it closed. The drooling was driving her crazy.

Ava had often fancied that X-Cog master-crowning required a skill level comparable to what it must take to play an instrument at a professional level. It required constant practice to make the interface smooth, to make the crowned person move and speak naturally. Unless you upped the doses, of course, which lowered resistance, but melted the subjects' brains. Which was simply not cost efficient.

Ava was committed to finding a way to make X-Cog accessible to anyone, and infinitely more profitable thereby. But a virtuoso needed a decent instrument. Not a dull, unresponsive piece of stinking *shit*.

Ava yanked off the master crown and flung it onto the table. Her brilliance was wasted on Mandy. Mandy whimpered as Ava wrenched the slave glasses off the girl's head, yanking out strands of blond hair in the process. Stupid cow. Crowning her was like trying to send nervous impulses through a lump of clay.

Mandy swayed on her feet. She was dressed in the silver spandex jog bra and shorts that Ava had mandated as a uniform for X-Cog test subjects. She liked her girls to look sexy and sharp. But Mandy looked anything but sharp, with that thread of drool trailing off her chin.

The look on the girl's face disgusted her. She slapped Mandy, hard. The girl stumbled against the table, vaguely confused.

Ava slapped her again, harder. Again. *Smack. Smack.* Blood trickled from Mandy's nose, from her split lip. The girl's hands crept up, tried to cover her face. Ava struck Mandy's ears, whapped the back of her head, knocking her forward. Mandy thudded to her knees, moaning.

"Back off, Av. That's millions of dollars you're kicking around."

Ava shot a poisonous look at the man who had just walked in. "Mind your own fucking business, Des."

"Don't take your frustration out on her." Desmond's know-it-all tone made her want to put out his bright blue eyes. "It was your idea to alter her surgically. You were wrong. Too bad. It was an honest mistake, and we won't make it again. Grow up, Ava. Move on."

"But the idea is sound! Next time, I'll recalibrate the—"

"No," Desmond said. "We reached the point of diminishing returns weeks ago. We're not cutting or burning any more of them."

"But if I don't make the interface more direct, we'll never—"

"No more cutting, no more burning. That's final."

There was no arguing with Des when he got that tone in his voice. Stupid, shortsighted dickhead. Bumping up against the limits of her power over him made her bad-tempered. She kicked Mandy's backside with her pointy-toed pump, and the girl tumbled forward with a grunt.

"Don't lecture me, Des," she said, sulkily. "I'm the one who's clubbing every night with the stinking masses to troll for test subjects! Wasting time I should be spending on research, bumping and grinding with cheap Ecstasy whores like her!" She pointed at Mandy. "I need to delegate this tedious shit! I cannot do it all myself!"

"I'm trying, babe. I don't understand why you're so set on wiping them. I enjoy crowning the ones who aren't burned or cut much better. It's that inner resistance that makes it exciting, you know?"

Ava snorted, derisively. "It's not about excitement. You've never tried to crown a subject into doing anything more complex than sucking on your dick. Try making one of them type a string of code onto a keyboard, and see how far you get. You can compel a girl to blow you by putting a twenty-dollar gun to her head, if that's what gets you off. You don't need a ten-million-dollar X-Cog crown for that. I want to market X-Cog to defense contractors. Understand? Are you with me here?"

"Fellatio is actually a pretty complex motor process," Desmond protested, sounding faintly hurt. "Particularly when you're hung."

Ava rolled her eyes. "Leave the neuroscience to me, Des."

Des waved that away. "Whatever. I've got bad news."

"I don't want to hear it," she said pettishly.

"Too bad. I was at a Parrish Foundation Board meeting today. Parrish is up to his old tricks. He's proposed a panel of financial forensics experts to examine every penny of research money that's been spent in the past three years. And to vet all future projects."

"Oh, God," Ava moaned. "Not now."

"Yeah. He's as much of a pit bull as his ballbusting wife, may she burn in hell. The Morality Police don't want anything naughty going on after the Dr. O. scandal, don't cha know."

"Fucking hypocrites. 'Helix was a victim, too,'" Ava mimicked.

Des looked down at the moaning girl at his feet. "We have to clean up our act, Av. This shit does not look good. You should save it until after we get control of the Foundation Board."

"It can't wait! Besides, no one will miss her. I scraped her off the bathroom floor of a dance club. No wonder she's a dud." She kicked Mandy in the buttock. "Charles Parrish has been raking in hundreds of millions in medical patents for years. Like he ever cared where the smell came from before his nose got rubbed in shit."

"Thank God he's retiring," Des said. "I'm supposed to give the fawning speech for that pompous tightass at the retirement banquet."

"Retiring? That's good."

"Not really. It leaves him more time to be possessive and controlling about Parrish Foundation research money."

Ava smiled. "So let's kill him."

Des looked startled, but not unduly so. "That wouldn't solve our problem."

"No? You handpicked the last two Board members. If Parrish disappeared, the rest of them will do anything you want. 400K salaries, the Skybox, the company Lear jet. The paid luxury vacations. It's easy."

Des grunted. "Don't oversimplify, Av."

"But it is simple," Ava said. "We create the perfect Board. We eliminate the watchdogs. We create a perfect screen of bland, squeaky-clean product development projects that they can all feel virtuous about. We siphon a percentage of the money back to the real stuff, like Dr. O did. Except that we won't fuck up and let it explode in our faces."

Des looked dubious, but he wasn't rejecting it out of hand.

"Who inherits Parrish's fortune when he dies?" Ava asked.

Des ruminated. "His daughters, Edie and Ronnie. Ronnie's twelve. Edie's your age. She was at the Haven, remember? Glasses, braces. The cog enhancement program bombed on her. She never got into Club O."

Ava nodded. She remembered the tongue-tied Edie. One of the priveleged ones, like Des himself. Rich, coddled kids who did the soft-core version of Dr. O's dirty mind games, because Mommy and Daddy wanted better grades. Ava hated the pampered little cunt for that.

"Who inherits if she and her sister die?" Her voice hardened.

"Av. Please," Des complained. "We can't kill everyone in sight."

"Who?" she persisted.

He shrugged. "The Foundation, I guess. Edie's out of the will. I overheard Dad and Charles talking about Edie once, over

Scotch. He was arranging to disinherit her. That was a few years ago."

"Why? What did she do? Drugs? Fucking the wrong men?"

Des shook his head. "I think she's just weird. She had some, ah, problems. You know . . . these kind of problems." He twirled his index finger in a circle at his temple, crossing his eyes.

Ava tapped her lip. "Dr. O wanted to do an interface with Edie Parrish so bad, he was practically pissing himself," she said. "She had perfect MRI's, perfect test results. But she was Charles Parrish's little girl. He had to keep her in bubble-wrap. It drove him crazy."

Des looked baffled. "What was it that he liked about her? What can you see from test results and MRI's?"

Ava's smile was bitter. Des was such an ignorant dickface sometimes. "They were exactly like mine."

Des's face was still blank. "Meaning?"

Ava sighed. "I was his best X-Cog interface, Dessie. Besides Kev McCloud, of course. We were the only ones who didn't burn out and die of brain bleed. Some lasted a few days, but only McCloud and I were genuinely re-usable. That's why I survived, Des. That's why I wasn't flushed down the john with the rest of them." She brushed her hair back with a swipe of her hand, preening. "And being pretty helped, too. So Dr. O was always looking for test results like his, and like mine. And Edie Parrish had them."

Des let out a dubious grunt. "Kev McCloud managed to escape and practically fuck the whole project. Looks like that interface had some pretty big fucking holes in it. And his twin, Sean, forced Dr. O to slit his own throat, remember? That should give you pause, Av."

Pause, hah. That had given her sleepless nights. Wondering how Sean McCloud had managed it, when she had not. How the *fuck* had he done that? All those years of being Dr. O's slave-crowned dollbaby. No choice, no chance. Used like a puppet, all the while dreaming of crushing hammers, knives gouging, axe blades hacking. Gouts of arterial blood. Her hands began to shake, just thinking about it.

She pushed those feelings away, locked them down so that she could function. "The McClouds are freaks," she said. "Edie will be different. She's female, she's artistic and creative. Shy, introverted personality. Probably she's been crushed by her dickhead father, which is great for our purposes. She'll be a good girl. She won't slit my throat."

Des's blue eyes narrowed. "What is this? First you want to kill her. Then you want to crown her."

"Crown first, kill later," she said airily. "Waste not, want not. So what are we going to do about Parrish?"

Des looked irritated. "Shit," he muttered. "I don't know."

Ava sighed. Des was so fucking slow sometimes. "Des. Honey. Brainstorm with me. He's about to retire, right? It's a dangerous age for a man. Health problems, sleep disturbances, chronic pain? And he was bereaved last year. He must be feeling fragile. Depressed. And his daughter, with her mental problems? Plus, he disinherited her. She must be so furious with him, Des. Maybe even . . ." Her voice sank to a whisper. "Murderous?"

Des's face wore an expression of dawning discovery. "She might," he agreed. "It wouldn't surprise anyone. He's such a self-righteous, pompous tight-ass. I'm surprised someone hasn't beaten her to it."

"So sad," Ava said solemnly. "All those years of staunch service to the community, and it has to end like this, at the hand of his own flesh and blood. That poor man. It's practically Shakespearean in scope."

"But there's Ronnie to consider, if you're talking about the money," Des said. "Ronnie would inherit the—"

"Edie must be so jealous of her little sister," Ava whispered dreamily. "Daddo's little favorite, right? I bet Edie lies awake nights, contemplating how that complacent, self-satisfied little piece of shit deserves to die. She offs the sister—and then she kills herself. Awful."

Des chuckled. "I love the way your mind works," he said, with frank admiration. "Your twisted genius knows no bounds."

"Except for your pussy squeamishness." Ava kicked the girl curled on the floor. "Get rid of this trash. I'm sick of looking at her."

Desmond's smile vanished. "It's not that easy. Dr. O had Gordon to do his dirty work. We don't have a Gordon."

"Do it yourself," Ava suggested. "If you're man enough."

Desmond's mouth tightened. "I don't do wet work, Av. Even though I know it would turn you on."

"So get us more money. That would turn me on, too. Think outside the box. Isn't that what Dr. O trained us for?" She licked her red lips, and strolled to the chaise. "Break the chains that bind your brains, hmm? Like Dr. O said. Think about it, Dessie. Complete control of the Parrish Foundation. Parrish's personal fortune, too. All his billions, invested in X-Cog, and giving us a thousand percent return."

His smile showed off perfect teeth. Desmond Marr, her slave and personal toy. Future president of Helix. Harvard man. Pampered prince.

Des had been one of Dr. O's pets, too, but The Haven had been a very different place for the son of Helix president Raymond Marr, who had founded Helix with Charles Parrish. Des had been a rich pet. He had never experienced a slave crown interface in his life. Ava had been in the other category. The parentless, penniless kind. Ava worked for her keep, like the rest of the runaways, prostitutes, junkies, and punks. The ones Dr. O could fuck with and get measurable results. Helix was built upon their backs. Or their bones, rather. They were all dead. All but her. And maybe Kev Mc-Cloud. Somewhere.

Des had been her lover for years, ever since they'd met at Dr. O's oasis of depravity, the Haven. But certain things Dessie could never understand. If you'd never been a slave, how could you know what it meant to dominate? A privileged boy with billions behind him could never get that essential thing. It was a gulf between them. Sad.

But look at her now. She hadn't croaked from brain bleed, like the rest of the lab rats. She was special, and Dr. O had realized it. From slave crowned zombie, she'd become Dr. O's crowning achievement. She'd undergone the most intense and rigorous of Dr. O's cognitive enhancement techniques. He'd arranged for her studies, her multiple degrees in neuroscience and bioengineering. He'd used her hard, but he had groomed her into something extraordinary.

Sometimes, she even missed that depraved, sadistic psychopathic prick. It was nice, to have someone be proud of you. To own you.

Even when it broke your bones, and hacked off your limbs and sucked your blood. Crushed you to dust. Burned you to fucking ashes.

Des reached down, caressing his erection, staring at her curvy body, her tight blouse, her short skirt. His throat bobbed. He cast an uncertain glance at the girl, moaning and whimpering on the floor.

"Ignore her," Ava commanded. "I'll give her an injection after, and put her in the cooler, since you can't soil your lily-white hands."

His face reddened. Scolding him sharpened his lust, but going too far made the situation unmanageable. He liked to punish. She had to be very, very careful with him.

"No more cracks about the wet work," he growled.

"Oh, Dessie." Her voice was throaty. "I love it when you're stern."

"Do you? Turn around. I'll show you stern."

She hesitated, to feel the pressure, the pull. The heat, the heaviness, pulsing in the air between them. The timing had to be right.

She turned, with sensual, deliberate slowness, positioning

herself carefully on the chaise, presenting herself. Ass out, thighs spread. Her miniskirt shadowed the private parts she kept shaved, perfumed, and pantiless. Ready for immediate use, on demand. Old training died hard.

She swayed, watching herself reflected in the shiny surface of the silver file cabinets opposite her. Checking out the effect of her gleaming, loose blue-black hair, artfully mussed, swirling and swinging over her hands. Her red lips, panting, parted. She looked good, she concluded, pleased. Dangerous, unstable. Hot. Ready for action.

Des undid his belt as he approached, jerked open his pants. Yanked out that horselike member of which he was so proud.

He wrenched up her skirt, and startled to handle her, parting her buttocks, fingering her pussy. She writhed and gasped with theatrical enthusiasm in response to his delving fingers. His ego was so big, he always bought her act, no matter how extravagantly she overplayed it. Men.

He thrust his hand deeper, growling. "You're sopping wet."

Actually, it was hitting Mandy that had excited her, but Ava saw no reason to deny him the credit for her arousal. Besides, she could lube on command. She knew what nasty, secret things to think about to get that hot rush. "It's you who does it to me." She injected a quaver into her voice, hinting at hidden vulnerability. Calculated to puff him up. Big man. King of her world. Thinking he ruled her with his throbbing scepter. He grasped her ass cheeks, and drove inside.

Ava whimpered as he started pumping. This was the tedious part. All the bucking and moaning. Des was relatively skilled, too, so the thrusting went on for a tiresomely long time before he allowed himself to squirt. Ironic. Personal politics dictated that she praise him for that quality when she would infinitely prefer it to be quick.

But she managed. She just defaulted to her habitual state

of floating detachment, where she always went to endure sex. Leaving just enough of herself to keep the show convincing. The rest of her highly functioning mind worked on her strategy for preparing the next X-Cog subject. Too bad that subject couldn't be Edie Parrish herself.

The thought triggered a rush of genuine sexual heat that took her completely by surprise. Wow. This was a way to get Des on her side, by using his weakest point, and it turned her on, too. Big bonus points.

"Is she cute?" she demanded.

"Who?" Des grunted as his body thudded against hers. "What the fuck are you talking about?"

"Edie Parrish. I haven't seen her in years. Is she cute?"

His thrusting slowed. "I don't know. All right, I guess. Tall, long hair, bad glasses. She hides. Nice tits, though. Why do you care?"

Ava twisted her head around, to fix him with a hot, wild stare. "When we take her, I want to crown you. And fuck you. Through her."

He was so taken aback, he stopped moving. "Huh?"

"Don't worry," she soothed, rocking back to envelop his cock once again. "I'm good with the crown. She'll be the best interface ever. It'll blow your mind. I'll make her into a red-hot nymphet. I'll make her do things that you've never imagined."

"I can imagine a whole hell of a lot," he warned.

She smiled at him sweetly. "Things I'd never do myself," she explained. "With my own body. Wild, nasty, dirty things."

Desmond rammed his hips against hers, making her grunt and brace herself. "You are one depraved bitch, Ava."

"Why, thank you." She fluttered her eyelashes at him, and turned back, bracing herself against each hard jolt.

She'd gotten him. He'd do anything to make it happen now.

But she realized, as the pounding ride thundered to its inevitable finish, that this fantasy of their X-Cog threesome compelling Edie Parrish was . . . oh, God . . . it was actually making her come.

Explosively.

Romantic Suspense from
Lisa Jackson

See How She Dies	0-8217-7605-3	$6.99US/$9.99CAN
Final Scream	0-8217-7712-2	$7.99US/$10.99CAN
Wishes	0-8217-6309-1	$5.99US/$7.99CAN
Whispers	0-8217-7603-7	$6.99US/$9.99CAN
Twice Kissed	0-8217-6038-6	$5.99US/$7.99CAN
Unspoken	0-8217-6402-0	$6.50US/$8.50CAN
If She Only Knew	0-8217-6708-9	$6.50US/$8.50CAN
Hot Blooded	0-8217-6841-7	$6.99US/$9.99CAN
Cold Blooded	0-8217-6934-0	$6.99US/$9.99CAN
The Night Before	0-8217-6936-7	$6.99US/$9.99CAN
The Morning After	0-8217-7295-3	$6.99US/$9.99CAN
Deep Freeze	0-8217-7296-1	$7.99US/$10.99CAN
Fatal Burn	0-8217-7577-4	$7.99US/$10.99CAN
Shiver	0-8217-7578-2	$7.99US/$10.99CAN
Most Likely to Die	0-8217-7576-6	$7.99US/$10.99CAN
Absolute Fear	0-8217-7936-2	$7.99US/$9.49CAN
Almost Dead	0-8217-7579-0	$7.99US/$10.99CAN
Lost Souls	0-8217-7938-9	$7.99US/$10.99CAN
Left to Die	1-4201-0276-1	$7.99US/$10.99CAN
Wicked Game	1-4201-0338-5	$7.99US/$9.99CAN
Malice	0-8217-7940-0	$7.99US/$9.49CAN

Available Wherever Books Are Sold!
Visit our website at **www.kensingtonbooks.com**